Armada

Penguin Books

M. J. Rodríguez-Salgado and the staff of the National Maritime Museum

ARMADA

1588–1988

Penguin Books
in association with the National Maritime Museum

Penguin Books Ltd, 27 Wrights Lane, London W8 5TZ (Publishing and Editorial)
and Harmondsworth, Middlesex, England (Distribution and Warehouse)
Viking Penguin Inc., 40 West 23rd Street, New York, New York 10010, USA
Penguin Books Australia Ltd, Ringwood, Victoria, Australia
Penguin Books Canada Ltd, 2801 John Street, Markham, Ontario, Canada L3R 1B4
Penguin Books (NZ) Ltd, 182–190 Wairau Road, Auckland 10, New Zealand

Published in Penguin Books 1988

Catalogue designed by Paul McAlinden
Maps researched by Ian Friel
and drawn by Chapman Bounford & Associates

Filmset in Linotron Plantin by Wyvern Typesetting Ltd, Bristol
Made and printed in Great Britain by William Clowes Ltd, Beccles

Exhibition designed by Martyn Bainbridge.
Production management by James H. Duff.
Contractors: Ralnic Ltd, Michael Whiteley Associates, Ricron Metal Fabrications
Ltd, L.W.C. Metal Fabrications Ltd, Solarglass, One Stop Photographics Ltd,
Serge Savard, Photobition, Andy Murray, James Butler Ltd, Waveney Apple
Growers, Kinnasand UK Ltd, Ploeg Ltd, Kelvin Thatcher, John Copper, Radcliffe
Transport Services, Bridon Fibres Ltd, Peter Crombie, Pinnerwood, Merlin
Aluminium.

ARMADA
1588~1988

Exhibition dates

National Maritime Museum
Greenwich London
20 April – 4 September 1988

Ulster Museum
Botanic Gardens Belfast
12 October 1988 – 8 January 1989

·PEARSON·   Sponsored by Pearson plc

Contents

Maps

Tables

The National Maritime Museum is very proud that its largest ever exhibition is commemorating one of the great naval events in British history. When the planning for *Armada* first began more than five years ago, the museum realized it would have to mount something spectacular. However, no one at that early stage realized just how superb and varied the materials of the exhibition would prove to be. As the themes of the exhibition began to take shape, early research revealed the wealth of objects, documents and pictures that survived to illustrate them. This was an exhibition that was rich in visual images and human association; that brought the event and the chief players in it to life; and at the same time demonstrated the achievements of late-sixteenth-century art, culture and technology. We decided early on to take a wide compass for *Armada*: to explore the political context in which hostilities broke out; to look at the personalities and courts of the two leading protagonists, Philip II and Elizabeth I; to illustrate the immediate events that led to the launching of the Armada, to review the respective capabilities of the two fleets; to speculate on the military confrontation that never took place, to tell the story of the battle as it actually happened; to describe the horrors of shipwreck and massacre endured by the Spanish; to analyse the political significance of the event in broader European terms.

Throughout the preparations for the exhibition we have had tremendous support from a wide range of organizations and individuals, none more so than from our sponsor, Pearson plc. Without its contribution, we could never have contemplated an exhibition of this scale and importance. From the moment that the company funded our first tentative research efforts, it has remained a committed ally and friend, providing resources on a generous scale but never attempting to interfere in the plans for the exhibition. I would like especially to thank the chairman, Lord Blakenham, the finance director, James Joll, who has taken a close personal interest in all matters *Armada*, and the head of PR, John Tustin, who has provided valuable liaison services.

Though the exhibition is Greenwich-inspired we have been very fortunate in our choice of partner. The Ulster Museum has backed the idea of the exhibition from the start, and its support has been an important factor in all subsequent negotiations. It owns much of the original shipwreck material, which forms such a gripping and central part of the exhibition. We are grateful to the museum's trustees and to the acting director, Sean Nolan, for all the help and advice we have received. Our collaboration with the staff of the Antiquities and Conservation Departments there has been both productive and pleasurable.

Sponsor, partner and now lenders. Without the response of all those who own Armada treasures, the exhibition would never have materialized in such spectacular fashion. And the response has been quite overwhelming. Her Majesty the Queen heads a distinguished list of lenders in this country, who have risen to the importance of the occasion in their willingness to part with incredibly rare and valuable artefacts. The Heneage jewel from the Victoria and Albert Museum, the Armada portrait of Elizabeth from the Tyrwhitt–Drake Collection, the Earl of Leicester's armour from the Tower of London. These are only a few random examples of British contributions. From abroad, the response has been equally heartening, a recognition that *Armada* is an event of European significance that deserves full support. Without the high level of Spanish loans, the exhibition would have been very one-sided, and we are immensely grateful to the authorities of the Patrimonio Nacional, to the Archives of Simancas, where so many key documents are housed, and to museums in Madrid and Barcelona, for some truly sensational contributions. From Vienna comes the helmet and shield of a parade armour given by Philip II to the Duke of Parma, from the Vatican, the only extant portrait of Sixtus V, from the Netherlands, the San Mateo pennant, from Texas, Spanish gold and silver. In all, we are receiving some 400 loans from a dozen countries. To all of them we extend very warm thanks.

The prestige of the exhibition has been greatly enhanced by the presence of so many distinguished members on the Committee of Honour. We are especially grateful to Sir Geoffrey Howe, the Foreign Secretary, for his interest in the exhibition, and to His Excellency Don José J. Puig de la Bellacasa, the Spanish Ambassador to the Court of St James's, who has shown a personal commitment to *Armada* far beyond the call of public duty; he has proved a tower of strength and a fund of good advice in matters too numerous to list. The part played in early negotiations by the former chairman of the museum's Board of Trustees, the Hon. Anthony Cayzer, is also recorded with gratitude.

I inherited responsibility for the exhibition from Ann Shirley when I became Head of the Pictures Department in 1983. I passed on that responsibility to Dr Stephen Deuchar, Curator of Oil Paintings, in 1985, and it is to his energy and flair that the realization of the exhibition is very largely due. He has masterminded the project in all its many facets – loans, design, research, catalogue, transport and finance – and for one so relatively new to museums he has revealed exceptional capabilities. Dr Deuchar has been ably supported by a small *Armada* team. Mr Ian Friel, the research coordinator, has not only undertaken a great deal of work on the catalogue, but he has been responsible for editing much of the text. With thirty-two authors, this has been no light or easy task. Hélène Mitchell has helped to coordinate the detailed and complex negotiations of individual loans, and acted as an invaluable assistant in many other areas.

8

The other key performers deserve to be acknowledged here. Dr Mía Rodríguez-Salgado, Lecturer in International History at the London School of Economics, has acted as research consultant and historian to the exhibition for the past four years. She has shared her deep knowledge of the period with us, and it is she who has done most to shape the form of the exhibition and to define its main themes. It is appropriate that she is also the author of the keynote essay in this catalogue, a synopsis of the ideas the exhibition enshrines and an original contribution to the subject in its own right.

I had known and admired Martyn Bainbridge's work as a designer for some time prior to *Armada*, and when the exhibition was first mooted he seemed the obvious man to design it. He combines a keen nose for historical detail and atmosphere with imaginative gifts of a high order. The settings are full of surprises, a sumptuous background to pictures and jewels one minute, a dramatic presentation of actual events the next. Theatre and sober display are counterpointed to create a vivid experience of what the Armada and its contextual events were like. Without his gifts the exhibition would have been a much duller and more conventional affair.

Richard Ormond
Director

Patron: Her Majesty The Queen

Committee of Honour

His Excellency Don Jose J. Puig de la Bellacasa GCVO
Viscount Blakenham
Professor John Elliott FBA
Professor Sir Geoffrey Elton LittD, PhD, FBA
Roger de Grey RA Esq
The Right Hon. Sir Geoffrey Howe QC, MP
Viscount de l'Isle VC, KG
Lord Nicholas Gordon Lennox KCMG, LVO
Sir Ronald Lindsay of Dowhill, Bt.
The Right Hon. Richard Luce MP
Admiral Sir William Staveley GCB, ADC
The Right Hon. Lord St John-Stevas PC
The Duke of Wellington LVO, OBE, MC DL

It is Pearson's policy on arts sponsorship to support one major event in London every year. When we first heard about the Armada Exhibition we felt sure that it had all the ingredients of success. It presents with dramatic effect a major turning point of the first Elizabethan era and brings to life the military, political and social history of the time. The skills and effort of the National Maritime Museum in assembling so many splendid artefacts and displaying them so imaginatively will give pleasure and instruction to all who visit the exhibition. For any who cannot, we hope that this Penguin catalogue will give an enjoyable flavour of what they have missed

Michael Blakenham
Chairman, Pearson plc

Acknowledgements

A substantial portion of this book has been written and co-edited by Mía Rodríguez-Salgado, and we are very grateful for the considerable work she has undertaken on the National Maritime Museum's behalf. Most of the catalogue entries are by staff members of the museum, but other outside contributors, led by Laurence Flanagan, have kindly provided additional text. We are pleased to thank: Michael Barkham (postgraduate student in the Department of Geography, University of Cambridge), Dr Colin Martin (Lecturer in Maritime Archaeology, Scottish Institute of Maritime Studies, University of St Andrews), David Gaimster of the British Museum, Thomas Richardson of the Royal Armouries, Dr Margarita Russell (Adjunct Professor, Department of Art, University of Miami) and Surgeon Vice-Admiral Sir James Watt RN (Retd). Joan Dormer gave invaluable help with collating and editing the text; Marilla Fletcher typed the final manuscript with great care; and James Stevenson undertook a considerable photographic programme with his customary efficiency.

In mounting the exhibition itself, we have also relied on the skills and commitment of museum staff and outside professionals. Martyn Bainbridge's inspired exhibition design was brought to realization by James Duff, production manager, who oversaw the work of the exhibition's various contractors and worked closely with the National Maritime Museum's Works Officer, Gary Stewart. The task of preparing exhibits and ensuring their safe display was supervised in Greenwich by Gillian Lewis with the assistance of Peter van Geersdaele, and in Belfast by Brian Scott. Transport of loans was undertaken by MoMart Ltd, a complex operation that was greatly eased by the exceptional efficiency of the National Maritime Museum's Loans Officer, Claire Venner. Amongst those responsible for installing the exhibits at the two venues we are especially grateful to David Taylor, George Spalding, Bernard Radford and Roy Service.

It is a pleasure to acknowledge in addition the kind cooperation of Charles Alabaster, María Teresa Ruíz Alcón, Kenneth Andrews, Malcolm Baker, Christian Beaufort, Sarah Bevan, David Blackmore, J. Braat, Xanthe Brooke, John Brooke-Little, Ruth Brown, Louise Campbell, Frances Carey, Angels Casanovas, Rosemary Clarey, Bryan Clarke, Richard Clarke, David Cordingly, Rodney Dennys, Ian Eaves, Felipe Fernández-Armesto, Nicholas Forbes, Hazel Forsyth, Arthur Fowler, David Gaimster, Gary Gardner, Eduardo Garrigues, Cynthia Gaskell-Brown, Philippa Glanville, Philip Gray, Chris Gregson, the Conde de Güemes, Vivien Hamilton, Elizabeth Hamilton-Eddy, Caroline Hampton, Robin Harcourt Williams, C. P. Hartley, William Hauptman, Peter Ince, Angus Konstam, C. Laken, Ann de Lara, Nicholas Lawson, Ann Leane, David Legg-Willis, María José Lorente, Lindsey Macfarlane, Fernando Alberto Martín, Jane Matthews, Charles Mould, A. V. B. Norman, Hugo O'Donnell, Roger Paine, Brenda Pittman, Pamela Porter, Mac Pritchard, David Quinn, Denis Rider, Stephen Riley, Graham Rimer, Phillis Rogers, Terry Sandell, Ascensión de la Plaza Santiago, María del Carmen Mañueco Santurtan, Fredericka Smith, Polly Smith, Stewart Smith, Peter Spurrier, Kay Staniland, Kelvin Thatcher, Marjorie Trusted, Gervaise Vaz, Sally Wakelin, Susan Wallace-Shaddad, Rosemary Weinstein, Chris Wheatley, David White, Andrew Williamson, Timothy Wilson and Sarah Wimbush.

Finally I would like to thank Dr Alan McGowan, the museum's Chief Curator and chairman of the exhibition steering committee, for his important contribution to the final stages of the project.

Stephen Deuchar
Exhibition organizer

9

List of Contributors to the Catalogue

numbers refer to catalogue entries

Robert Baldwin: 5.1; 6.15; 7.9; 7.70; 8.39; 8.42; 12.4–7; 12.14; 12.23–5; 15.1; 15.3; 16.20
Patricia Blackett Barber: 2.4; 7.7; 7.17–18; 7.36; 7.39–40; 7.47–9
Michael Barkham: 8.2; 8.6–9
Jane Dacey: 1.18; 2.3; 2.10–12; 2.46; 2.54; 5.17–18; 6.2; 6.10; 7.43; 7.60
Erica Davies: 7.13; 16.35
Stephen Deuchar: 1.1; 1.3; 2.1; 2.6; 2.24–6; 2.29–30; 2.38; 2.44; 3.2; 3.4; 3.21–2; 4.1–4; 4.6; 4.13–14; 4.17; 6.2–3; 6.6; 6.11; 7.3; 7.58; 7.59; 10.1; 13.19; 13.21; 13.26; 14.1; 14.27; 14.53; 16.1; 16.30–31; 16.36
Joan Dormer: 4.12; 5.2; 5.15; 5.20; 8.31; 8.35; 13.3; 16.22
Laurence Flanagan: 2.18–23; 2.49–52; 5.10–12; 7.2; 7.41; 8.19–22; 8.24; 8.26–7; 10.6–52; 12.13; 12.16; 12.19; 12.21; 13.6–17; 14.43
Ian Friel: 1.6–11; 1.14; 2.5; 2.7–9; 2.27–8; 2.37; 2.41–3; 2.47; 2.53; 2.55; 3.8; 3.12; 3.15–16; 4.7; 4.18; 5.19; 6.4–5; 6.9; 6.14; 6.20; 7.4–6; 7.8; 7.11; 7.16; 7.28; 7.31–3; 7.35; 7.50; 7.57; 7.63–9; 7.71; 8.1; 8.3–5; 8.10–12; 8.30; 8.36; 8.40; 9.31; 10.1–3; 11.1–10; 12.22; 13.2; 13.4; 14.2–21; 14.33; 14.35; 14.40–42; 14.46; 14.48–9; 14.52; 15.7–9; 15.15; 16.2; 16.6–11; 16.24; 16.36
David Gaimster: 3.18
Roger Knight: 13.25; 16.30; 16.34
David Lyon: 7.22–3; 9.1–2; 9.28–30; 14.37
Alan McGowan: 2.36; 8.29; 13.24
Colin Martin: 1.2; 7.1; 9.3–26; 14.36; 14.39
Pieter van der Merwe: 2.31–3; 2.35; 14.29–31; 16.29
Richard Ormond: 3.3
Christine Parkes: 5.3–8; 7.62; 13.20
Mary Patrick: 2.13–14; 2.16–17; 3.17
Daphne Pipe: 1.4–5; 13.23; 16.18; 16.32
Rina Prentice: 3.6–7; 3.20; 6.16–18; 7.24–7; 7.45–6; 15.16; 16.27
Roger Quarm: 3.5; 3.9–11; 3.13; 4.11; 6.7; 6.19; 7.61; 13.22; 13.29; 14.22–6; 16.26
Thomas Richardson: 7.14; 7.15; 13.1
Caroline Roberts: 1.15–16; 3.18–19; 7.34; 7.51–3
Margarita Russell: 6.1; 6.8; 14.28; 16.23; 16.25
Mía Rodríguez-Salgado: 1.13; 1.17; 2.2; 2.15; 2.39–40; 4.5; 4.15–16; 4.19; 6.12–13; 6.21–4; 7.12; 8.37–8; 8.41; 9.27; 10.4–5; 10.53; 11.11; 13.5; 14.2–21; 14.44–5; 14.47; 14.50–51; 15.2; 15.5; 15.10–14; 16.19; 16.21
Ann Savours: 5.16; 8.13–18; 12.18; 12.20; 13.27
Carole Stott: 12.9–12
Christopher Terrell: 12.1–3; 12.8; 12.15; 12.17

Barbara Tomlinson: 1.12; 2.34; 7.42; 10.54; 13.18; 16.12–17; 16.28
Liza Verity: 4.8–10; 5.13; 7.19–21; 7.29; 7.37–8; 7.44; 14.38
Michael Webb: 2.45; 2.48; 3.14; 5.14; 8.25; 8.28; 14.34; 16.3; 16.33
Elizabeth Wiggans: 7.10; 7.30; 7.54–6; 13.28; 14.32; 15.4; 15.6; 16.4–5

10

Lenders to the Exhibition

Archivo General de Simancas, Valladolid
Duke of Atholl, Blair Castle
Trustee of the Will of the 8th Earl of Berkeley
Bibliothèque Nationale, Paris
The Curators of the Bodleian Library, Oxford
British Library, London
Trustees of the British Museum, London
College of Arms, London
Viscount De L'Isle, Penshurst Place, Kent
East Sussex Record Office
French Protestant Church of London
The Mayor and Aldermen, Gemeente Arnemuiden
Hon. Clive and Mrs Gibson
Glasgow Museums and Art Galleries
Glasgow University Library
Trustees of the Goodwood Collections, Goodwood
    House
Kunsthistorisches Museum, Vienna
Royal Cabinet of Paintings, Mauritshuis, The
    Hague
Musée Cantonal des Beaux-Arts, Lausanne
Musée Carnavalet, Paris
Musée National du Château de Pau
Musée National du Château de Versailles
Musées Royaux des Beaux-Arts de Belgique,
    Brussels
Museo Arqueológico Nacional, Madrid
Museo del Ejército, Madrid
Museo Naval, Madrid
Museo del Prado, Madrid
Museu Marítim de Barcelona
The Museum, Charterhouse
Museum of London
National Museum, Poznań
National Museums and Galleries on Merseyside
National Portrait Gallery
The National Trust
Nederlands Scheepvaart Museum, Amsterdam
The Collection at Parham Park, West Sussex
Patrimonio Nacional. Monasterio de las Descalzas
    Reales
Patrimonio Nacional. Monasterio de El Escorial
Patrimonio Nacional. Real Armería de Madrid
Pinacoteca Nazionale, Siena
City of Plymouth Museums and Art Gallery
Public Record Office, London
Her Majesty the Queen
Rijksmuseum, Amsterdam
Trustees of the Royal Armouries, London
Royal Artillery Institution, Woolwich
Lord Sackville, Knole
The Marquess of Salisbury, Hatfield House

La Marquesa de Santa Cruz
Earl of Scarbrough, Leeds Castle
Parish Church of St Faith, Gaywood
Parish Church of St Mary the Virgin, Mendlesham
Science Museum, London
Scottish National Portrait Gallery
Shetland Museum, Lerwick
Staatliche Kunstsammlungen, Kassel
Staffordshire Record Office
Stedelijk Museum De Lakenhal, Leiden
Stedelijk Museum Het Prinsenhof, Delft
Stedelijk Museum, Oudenaarde
Trustees of the Sudeley Collection, Sudeley Castle
Texas Antiquities Committee
Tiroler Landesmuseum Ferdinandeum, Innsbruck
William Tyrwhitt-Drake, Esq.
Ulster Museum, Belfast
Vatican Museums
Board of Trustees of the Victoria and Albert
    Museum, London
Wellcome Institute for the History of Medicine,
    London
Duke of Westminster
N. C. Worms, Esq.
Master and Wardens of the Worshipful Company of
    Barbers, London
Worshipful Society of Apothecaries, London

and several lenders who prefer to remain anonymous

11

Philip II and the 'Great Armada' of 1588[1]

On 18 August 1588, in the palace-monastery at San Lorenzo de El Escorial, the ten-year-old Spanish prince, Philip, heir to the largest Christian state in the world, added another page to his ink-stained exercise book. He was learning how to write both Castilian and Latin by copying from works designed to teach the principles of Christian government. In a clear but at times unsteady hand, he noted his duty to go to mass frequently, to keep good company, to distribute justice fairly and to help the poor. On matters of war, he learned above all to do God's bidding and always to act in conjunction with the papacy. Close by his son, King Philip II attended to matters of government. The atmosphere was tense as he awaited news of his forces in the English Channel. After several years of preparation and endless delays, the Great Armada or 'most happy fleet' had at last sailed in July, and the army in the Netherlands was ready to embark and invade England. This enterprise was considered by Philip and his advisers as a fine example of the ideal war the young prince was learning about. It was a holy war, blessed by the pope and destined to strengthen the Roman Catholic faith. That same day the first trustworthy news of the fighting arrived at the palace: the English admiral and redoubtable corsair, Sir Francis Drake, had at last been defeated and fifteen enemy ships had been sunk.[2] Yet there was barely a hint of joy in the brief note the king wrote immediately to the Duke of Medina Sidonia, Captain-General of the Fleet. Philip was a cautious man who had learned not to believe news until it was confirmed. Moreover, his aim was to do more than sink a few ships: for that purpose a small fleet would have sufficed. This large fleet and army were intended to achieve far greater goals – the reconversion of England to Catholicism, and the reconquest of the Netherlands. He expressed his hope that the Armada had followed up the victory wisely, and prevented the enemy from regrouping its forces. Now the Spanish commanders could proceed to the heart of the enterprise – rendezvous with the army of the Netherlands and attack England.[3]

Philip, who had a mind for detail, may have recalled that 18 August was also the anniversary of his formal entry into London as king-consort of Queen Mary I in 1554. Then the English had cheered him and acknowledged his claim to the throne. The fourth and principal pageant of the entry depicted Philip and Mary as descendants and successors of Edward III. Their titles were boldly set in silver and gold, accompanied by the following verse:

Englande if thou delite in auncient men,
Whose glorious actes thy fame a brod dyd blase.
Both Mary and Philip their offspring ought thou then
With al thy hert to loue & to embrace
Which both descended of one auncient lyne
It hath pleased God by marriage to combyne.[4]

Philip never forgot his right to the English throne nor his promises to restore and support English Catholicism. During the reign of Mary and Philip (1554–8), the Spaniards had formed their opinion of the English as a faithless, fickle people; the English reversion to Protestantism under Elizabeth confirmed their judgement. 'The Lord preserve us!' commented a horrified Spaniard, 'these English are a barbarous and heretical people who have no care for their souls or conscience and fear neither God nor his saints.'[5]

Relations between Spain and England were strained during Philip's reign (see Section 1). But over the years, English Catholics looked to Philip for support, and some urged him to invade England and restore the faith. Philip was willing to help individuals and finance seminaries, but he was never convinced by the wild claims of the exiles that the majority of English people were Catholic and merely waiting for his arrival to overthrow the Protestants. The king mistrusted leading Englishmen while he was their ruler and saw no reason to change his opinion when most of them readily adapted to Elizabeth's Protestant regime. Consequently, while he believed that God had chosen him to bring England back to the Catholic fold in 1554, and expected him to play an important role in this cause subsequently, Philip never had any illusions that there would be a spontaneous uprising in support of an invasion. Indeed, there was every indication that the English, Catholic or Protestant, would take up arms against him. One of Philip's companions in England had commented during his stay that 'the English like us Spaniards as much as they like the devil – and they treat us accordingly.'[6] There was ample proof of English xenophobia during the Elizabethan period. Hostility was naturally most marked among committed Protestants, but English propaganda also displayed a virulent racist streak, lashing out against the Moorish and Jewish origins of many Iberians. According to a pamphlet of 1589, the 'Spanish' – often a generic term for all Philip's subjects, or at least those of the Iberian and Italian states – were 'unfaithful, ravenous, and insatiable above all other nations'. They were 'the most loathsome, infected, and slavish people that ever lived on earth'.[7] While such extreme opinions were rare, the horde of English pirates and corsairs who preyed upon Philip's subjects certainly behaved as if they were superior and destined to vanquish the might of Spain. Their constant raids and evident malice were like a sore that would not heal.

1. I am most grateful for the encouragement and support of Dr Maarten Ultee. His helpful comments did much to improve this text. My thanks also to the staff at the Archivo General de Simancas, and to Lynn Young for their help during this project.
2. AGS EK. 1448, f.202, 18 August 1588. This was one of several false reports. AGS EK. 1567, f.126; 1567, f.120.
3. Biblioteca Nacional, Madrid Mss 1451, Philip III's exercise book; AGS E.165 f.147 Philip to Medina Sidonia.
4. BL. C.8.b.9, *The Copie of a Letter Sent in to Scotlande, of the arriual and landynge, and moste noble marryage of the moste Illustre Prynce Philippe, Prynce of Spaine, to the most excellente Princes Marye Quene of England.* London, 1554.
5. Muñoz, 1887, Tercera Carta, 102. See also M. J. Rodríguez-Salgado, 1988; Loades, 1979.
6. Muñoz, 1887, Tercera Carta, 102.
7. This and many other examples of such anti-Hispanic literature can be found in Powell, 1971; Maltby, 1971.

An Introduction by M. J. Rodríguez-Salgado

Yet people who remembered Philip's rule in England still marvelled at the radical change of fortune and alliances. Now that it had come to open war, there was a sense of shock and surprise on both sides. How could two states bound for so long by dynastic, political and commercial interests have come to this? Why, as Lord Burghley mused, was England supporting her traditional enemies, Catholic France and Calvinist Scotland, and opposing her old allies in Spain and the Netherlands?

The answer has less to do with the traditional explanations of an extended religious and commercial conflict than with complex internal and international pressures. Philip and Elizabeth were caught in the maelstrom of political and religious tensions of the second half of the sixteenth century. They struggled to maintain their states and strengthen their faiths even when these two objectives proved irreconcilable. The conflict that culminated in the 1588 Armada campaign had been building up for over three decades. English seamen had plundered the ships of Philip's subjects and allies, and Elizabeth had sent money and soldiers to strengthen the armies of Philip's enemies. Yet these hostile acts did not lead to open war until the 1580s.

Proposals for an Invasion of England and Ireland

It would be wrong to suppose that Philip was eager to initiate an open war with Elizabeth. Indeed, he had tried to avert it. For years Philip had considered and rejected invasion plans. Fears of a French invasion of England and a Spanish war with France deterred Philip from taking Catholic plots and proposals seriously. Each time the question was raised, the king and his councillors would carefully note England's strategic importance – particularly for the safety of the Netherlands – and express fears of French expansion. They would discuss the dynastic implications of deposing Elizabeth and conclude that Mary Stuart, Queen of Scots, had the best claim to the throne, but she was 'French'. Under her rule, England might become hostile to Philip. Moreover, as France itself veered violently from militant Catholicism to toleration of Protestantism, there was no guarantee that Mary's accession would bring England back to Rome. The expansion of Protestantism during her chaotic reign in Scotland was certainly no triumph for the Catholic faith. If Philip did invade England, English Catholics might reject his rule and elect to follow Mary or a French candidate. In view of these and other uncertainties, the many proposals were set aside and Philip would return to treating Elizabeth with kid gloves.

Doing nothing was an appealing policy to an impecunious monarch in a difficult international situation, but it was fraught with danger. In order to prevent the French from building up a strong party in England, Philip II had to retain the favour of the English Catholics. They required proof of his commitment, not just sympathy. They wanted Philip to put pressure on Elizabeth to grant toleration. Some urged her assassination and the reintroduction of Catholicism by force. Moreover, the papacy pressed Philip to act in England and diminished his reputation by claiming that he was interested only in consolidating his states and power. In order to keep English Catholic hopes alive and bolster his reputation as defender of the faith, Philip was forced to give some aid. For example, at the time of the Ridolfi plot in 1571, he ordered the Duke of Alba to invade England. His lack of genuine commitment to the enterprise was amply proved by his failure to provide Alba with money or resources and his qualification of the order: Philip told Alba not to invade if he thought that this move would endanger rather than help the English Catholics. Since the king knew that Alba was utterly opposed to the plan, the result was a foregone conclusion.[1] After the rebels took the chief deep-water ports in the Netherlands in 1571–2 and destroyed Philip's scarce naval resources in the north, the invasion of England became more remote, or at least much more difficult to execute.

Philip had tried to avoid commitment to the papal invasions of Ireland in 1579 and 1580. But three years later he decided to seek papal support for a similar venture. The king's shift from peace to war was provoked by Elizabeth's challenge to his rule in Portugal and the Azores. In 1580 Elizabeth received the Portuguese pretender, Dom Antonio, Prior of Crato, despite Philip's warning that he considered this a *casus belli*. She also supported Dom Antonio's attack on the Azores, 1581–2. These islands were vital for Spanish commerce with the New World. The safety of the Indies treasure fleets, that lifeline of the Spanish empire, was a primary concern, practically an obsession for Philip. After 1580, the number of English attacks in the New World and Spain itself grew. More importantly, the nature of their threat to Philip's empire changed. Whereas earlier attacks consisted mostly of irregular buccaneering raids, English attempts to establish settlements in the New World directly challenged the Iberian monopoly. If the English established a base either in the Americas or the Azores, they could destroy the New World trade.

Meanwhile in European affairs, Elizabeth's role in the revolt of the Netherlands was changing,

1. This is the convincing argument in Maltby, 1983, 199–203.

moving towards greater involvement with the rebels (see Sections 5 and 6). Elizabeth was afraid of Philip's power and determined to curb it. Yet she certainly hoped to avoid an open war, which she could ill afford. Philip had a similar reluctance to invest vast sums in this effort. Even in the later 1580s, as the two states prepared for war, they were holding peace negotiations. In 1587 neither the Council of War in Madrid nor the Spanish judiciary had decided whether English corsairs should be treated as mere robbers or prisoners of war.[2] The road to war and invasion was tortuous in the extreme.

As Spanish military expenditure escalated to counter the English threat, Philip became more receptive to proposals that would rid him of an increasingly dangerous enemy. In 1583, after the Spanish had defeated the Portuguese pretender's attempt to capture the Azores, the Marquis of Santa Cruz took the opportunity to propose an attack against England. He was aware of the problems of such an enterprise, especially the lack of funds, the likelihood of provoking an Anglo-French alliance and the danger of limiting Spanish resources in the Netherlands. But he assured Philip that the French had lost a great deal of reputation with this defeat, and that God would ease all difficulties for this just war. Santa Cruz shared Philip's concern that English raids threatened the safety of the New World treasure fleets and damaged his reputation. Philip was tempted. He wrote to the Duke of Parma asking for his opinion and received an encouraging response in late December 1583 or early January 1584. Parma thought the campaign worthy of Philip's greatness and strong faith. He knew that it was difficult but it was not impossible if certain precautions were taken, beginning with secrecy. This meant that the Spanish Monarchy would have to act alone, without allies or aid.[3]

Unilateral action would place a heavy burden on a monarchy already suffering the effects of prolonged warfare. It is frequently asserted that once Philip acquired Portugal he had the means to launch an attack against England, but the war had been costly and he gained few ships. Only three of the thirty-five major ships in the fleet sent against the Azores in 1583 belonged to him.[4] An invasion of England would require even more ships and provisions. Philip started by ordering more ships' biscuit from Italy and sent reinforcements to the Netherlands. He assured Santa Cruz this would facilitate the campaign, since they would be so much nearer the target. More importantly, Philip urged all haste in the construction of new ocean-going vessels being built in the northern provinces of Vizcaya and Cantabria.[5]

In November 1583, however, Philip informed the pope that the campaign was too difficult and could not be pursued at that moment.[6] Philip may have been influenced by his lack of funds, but it is possible that he was once again looking southwards. The Azores venture had forced him to cancel preparations for the conquest of the Moroccan port of Larache. The original expedition had been prompted by news that the Ottoman-corsair forces had seized the city. There was considerable fear that they would send out raiders or even invade the Canary Islands and southern Spain. Larache belonged to Ahmad al-Mansur, the sharif of the state of Fez-Morocco, whose interest might be purchased. Philip had been negotiating with him for the cession of this important port over a number of years. Nevertheless the king was eager to maintain his capacity to take it by force if necessary.[7]

There was another reason for delaying an invasion of England. The situation in France was again highly unstable. Ever since 1562 Philip had given priority to the French wars, because if France turned Protestant he would not be able to uphold Catholicism in nearby states. In 1584 the Huguenots were gaining power in France. When the brother and heir-apparent of King Henri III, the Duke of Anjou, died in July 1584, the strongest claims to the throne belonged to the Protestant leader, Henri of Navarre. Philip was adamant that the French Catholics must be given money and men to resist the Huguenots regardless of Henri III's wishes. Philip was always reluctant to give aid to any rebels against legitimate rulers and always preferred to act against the Huguenots with the king's support, but after 1584 he feared that the French Catholic cause would collapse unless he supported them. On the last day of December 1584 long negotiations between Philip and the French Catholics resulted in the Treaty of Joinville.[8] 'In truth we have been moved to negotiate this because it seems to be the only way to remedy matters of religion in that kingdom,' Philip wrote in a private note to his secretary Don Juan de Idiáquez, 'and this means we must suffer the problems that this measure might provoke, for the issue of religion is more important than the rest.'[9] Among the problems and drawbacks of the alliance was the need to provide the Catholic League with large sums of money and the risk that Henri III would ally with the Huguenots and declare war on Philip.

This treaty has been much misunderstood. It did not give Philip the ability to manipulate the French at will. The Guises were always mindful of their dynastic interests and likely to put these before anything else. Philip's lack of trust in his allies is

2. AGS GA.208 f.348.
3. AGS E.590 f.125.
4. Thompson, 1976, 192.
5. Herrera Oria, 1946, 8; Maura Gamazo, 1957, 161–2. Shipbuilding programme: Thompson, 1976, 189–90.
6. A copy of this and other letters relating to the Rome embassy and Armada may be found in the National Maritime Museum, PHB 1A, f.435.
7. Maura Gamazo, 1957, 90 ff; Yahya, 1981, 123–8.
8. Jensen, 1964.
9. AGS Ek.1498 f.43, April 1586.

amply demonstrated by his repeated demands for formal guarantees that the Guises and their supporters would never use their forces against Philip.[10] Relations were often strained because the Guises made war and peace without consulting their Spanish paymasters. Philip was delighted when civil war was rekindled by the manifesto of the Holy League in March 1585, but he neither knew in advance nor approved of the Treaty of Nemours between the Catholic League and Henri on 7 July. While it gave the Guises and Catholics in general greater power, Philip's immediate reaction to this, as to all peace treaties between the Guises and the French kings, was to fear for his lands.[11] In general terms, Philip considered the situation in France ideal when the king and Catholics were fighting the Huguenots; favourable whenever there was open conflict between Catholics and Huguenots; and dangerous when there was peace or when the Huguenots and the monarch were closely allied. The Duke of Parma had somewhat different ideas. He endorsed this assessment, but he often complained that in times of war even greater dangers threatened the Netherlands, from the German and Swiss levies travelling to and from France.

Precipitants of the War

The situation in France continued to worry Philip in the early months of 1585, when the Dutch rebels sent a mission to Henri III, offering him sovereignty of the provinces. Although the Spanish ambassador in Paris, Don Bernardino de Mendoza, assured Philip that Henri would not accept, there was no rest until he turned it down formally in March. Not until the threat of an Anglo-French-Netherlands alliance was dispelled was confidence restored in Madrid. All this time English harassment of Spanish subjects and shipping continued. The first retaliatory actions came in the spring of 1585, when Philip ordered the temporary seizure of English ships and goods in Spanish ports. Since the king had encouraged English merchants to come to Iberia with grain, there was some reason for the English to feel that they had been tricked.[1] Elizabeth was not in a peaceful frame of mind either. She had been planning to send Drake on a punitive raid since the summer of 1584. The seizure of the English ships ensured that Drake would receive strong support. Elizabeth had also tried to establish a closer alliance with Scotland and considered increasing her involvement in the Netherlands. She was also pursuing talks with the Sharif of Fez-Morocco to secure an offensive alliance as well as commercial rights in North Africa. The English were particularly interested in aid against Philip and saltpetre supplies. The sharif wanted armaments, wood and other naval stores, as well as naval experts from England. He sought to create a navy and arm his men to match Christian firepower. The Iberian states had always feared such moves because proximity, winds and currents across the Straits of Gibraltar all facilitated the passage of troops and men. Until now, the threat from the sharif had been considered very serious; naval power and full armament would make it intolerable. Ancient fears of a new Islamic invasion resurfaced in Iberia whenever the sharif talked of navies. Moreover, if the English secured a safe port in Morocco they could disrupt and destroy Iberian trade by blocking off the Straits of Gibraltar, just as the Islamic corsairs did from time to time.

The contacts between England and Fez-Morocco were given more substance by the creation of the Barbary Company in July 1584. A year later, Henry Roberts, ambassador of the Queen of England and agent for the Barbary Company, arrived in Morocco. By September the sharif had agreed to support English commercial exchanges, lend diplomatic aid in the struggle against Philip and contribute to Dom Antonio's renewed attempt to gain the Portuguese throne.[2] It was evident that Philip would need to act quickly to curb the burgeoning friendship. He was even more concerned by the English attempt to form an alliance with the Turks. Since 1582 William Harborne had been Elizabeth's agent in Constantinople. His duties were essentially commercial, but from 1584 he devoted more time to promoting Elizabeth's political interests. In the spring of 1585 he was instructed to procure an offensive alliance against Philip. Sir Francis Walsingham suggested a simultaneous campaign. The sultan should invade from the North African coast, or else send the galley fleet against Philip's Italian or Iberian lands while England and other powers attacked Philip in northern Europe.[3]

Inevitably, fear of the North Africans and Turks increased instability within Spain, where tension between Old and New Christians had grown steadily. The New Christians, converted remnants of the Spanish Muslim community (*moriscos*), were always suspected of subversive activities on behalf of Islamic foreign powers. In Aragon, there were constant clashes between the two groups. The authorities were terrified that Islamic attacks against Iberia would trigger a revolt. These fears recurred periodically, and were no less important for being familiar.

The threat of Anglo-Islamic cooperation paled into insignificance when Elizabeth's alliance with the Netherlands rebels became known (Section **6**). In August 1585, after long and bitter arguments, Elizabeth had formally taken them under her protec-

10. AGS Ek.1448 f.38a. Philip to Juan Bautista de Tassis, 2 January 1586.
11. Jensen, 1964, 57–71.

15

1. See Santa Cruz's comments, Herrera Oria, 1946, 9 and Read, 1925, III. 101–2.
2. Yahya, 1981, 130–33.
3. Read, 1925, III, 225–8.

tion and accepted limited sovereign powers over them. English troops occupied key fortifications and English officers were given commanding positions in the councils of the rebel provinces. Santa Cruz argued that even if this had been her only hostile act, it would suffice to justify Philip's full retaliation, since it was a direct challenge to Philip's sovereignty. The occupation of fortifications by English soldiers in the Netherlands was clearly an invasion of Philip's territory. Furthermore, English support for the rebels had strengthened them and would prolong the struggle. All memoranda dealing with England henceforth stressed that the disastrous drain of money and manpower from Philip's empire would continue for as long as the English supported the rebels.[4] After the assassination of William of Orange in 1584, and the ensuing spectacular successes of the Duke of Parma, the Spanish had been optimistic that the long rebellion would soon be ended. But when they saw how English aid fuelled the fires of rebellion, the Spanish concluded that the only way to recover the Netherlands was by attacking England.

Yet more provocations came in 1585. Elizabeth had approved Walsingham's 'Plot for the Annoying of the King of Spain', which resulted in a destructive expedition against the Newfoundland fisheries. This raid passed almost unnoticed as a result of the furore caused by Drake's attacks against northern Spain and the New World. In September 1585 Drake plundered Baiona and Vigo and attacked shipping at sea. He sailed to the Caribbean and sacked the Cape Verde Islands. Santa Cruz reckoned that the English corsairs between them had caused damages of more than a million and a half ducats to Philip's subjects. He did not try to estimate losses to foreigners trading with the Spanish Monarchy. The marquis rightly pointed out that the English had made other, inestimable gains: while Drake was at sea, financiers feared for the safety of their collateral on New World fleets and were reluctant to lend Philip money. Furthermore, England's reputation had increased and her morale was high.[5] It was certainly time to consider serious reprisals, but Philip would not undertake them unless he was certain of his enemies and allies.

The situation in France was propitious: in September the pope had excommunicated Henri of Navarre and the Prince of Condé, and barred them from the succession. All observers predicted a renewal of war between the Huguenots and the League.[6] The French would thus be too busy to intervene in other wars. Even more important was the attitude of the pope. Having urged Philip to undertake the campaign against England, Sixtus V was now

promoting other projects such as the invasion of Geneva. Philip asked his ambassador in Rome, the Count of Olivares, which of these enterprises the pope favoured most. Once assured that the English campaign still had priority, he worked out a strategy to secure funds and diplomatic support for the war. He instructed Olivares to secure support from William Allen (later cardinal) and other English exiles; they should persuade the pope to make a formal request for Philip to attack England. If this was not feasible, Olivares should tell the pope that Philip had been moved by his entreaties and decided to undertake the enterprise. This matter was of considerable importance. If Philip could show that he had been moved to action by Catholic requests, then Sixtus V and his successors would be bound to give material and spiritual support. Sixtus therefore had an interest in stressing the vengeful and private nature of the war. He argued 'that the main reasons why Your Majesty has responded to this proposal are to avenge the offenses done to you, to facilitate [the recovery] of Holland, and because it would be impossible to ensure the safety of the passage to the Indies in any other way'.[7]

Naturally Philip denied this charge. He could not invade England without papal support to validate his campaign. Moreover, he desperately needed money and the help of other Catholic powers. Yet asking for papal support was risky. Popes invariably wanted a say in those wars they supported, and Sixtus had promised the Guises to consider their claims to command a campaign in England in support of their kinswoman Mary Queen of Scots. The Duke of Guise had the military experience and status to serve as joint commander of the Catholic forces. Since Philip did not trust him, however, the king insisted on his own choice. Philip argued that the Catholic cause in France would be quite lost if the Guises withdrew their forces to England. Yet he had to present a viable candidate for such an exalted command. The man who had a higher status, greater military expertise and more support in the curia than Guise was the Duke of Parma. Even before he had made a final decision whether to declare war against England, Philip was committed to a campaign that Parma would command.[8] The point was of some significance because of the succession problems that would follow on Elizabeth's deposition or death.

Philip always asserted that his primary aim was to 'reduce the kingdom to papal obedience' and establish Mary Queen of Scots on the throne. Mary had scandalized the Christian world during her brief reign in Scotland, and few mourned her captivity. But as the years passed she steadfastly refused to

4. Herrera Oria, 1946, 10 Santa Cruz's letter of 13 January 1586. An extreme but interesting exposition of this view, AGS E.591 f.46.
5. Herrera Oria, 1946, 10. Read, III, 1925, 102, 142–3.
6. Jensen, 1964, 72.
7. AGS E.947 f.102, Philip to Olivares, 2 January 1586; AGS E.947 f.15 Olivares to Philip, Rome, 24 February 1586.
8. AGS E.947 f.102.

convert to Protestantism – which most monarchs believed would have facilitated the recovery of her throne – and she acquired a wholly unexpected reputation for saintliness. Although she was still considered partial to France, by 1585 Philip felt that he could wield sufficient influence over her, particularly if he could persuade her to marry one of his cousins. More importantly, she was well beyond child-bearing age. Philip regarded her elevation to the English throne as a temporary measure. From the outset he sought a formal statement from the pope that her son James VI would not be able to claim his English inheritance, even if he underwent what Philip dismissed as a 'false' conversion to Catholicism. Philip wanted some security for his investment. But what of the future? Philip pointed out that he could claim England for himself, but since he had more than enough lands to rule and protect, he wanted to secure the succession of his eldest daughter and whichever Austrian archduke she married.[9]

Sixtus welcomed Philip's interest in the English project and approved of Parma as the commander. He also appreciated that James VI could not be allowed to succeed while still a Protestant, but he was willing, indeed eager, to secure the young man's conversion. Philip let it be known that unless the pope agreed to allow his choice of ruler after Mary, the campaign might never materialize. He also argued he could not afford to fight without papal aid. Philip asked Sixtus for two million gold ducats – half the estimated cost of the enterprise. Sixtus was staggered. At first he refused to make any financial contributions. Then he offered 200,000 *scuti* (worth somewhat less than ducats) to help launch the campaign, and a further 100,000 on landing. The year after this he would give 200,000 more. Sixtus expected Venice, the Grand Duke of Tuscany and the English Catholics to contribute as well.[10]

While searching for funds, Philip was also canvassing opinions – perhaps it would be correct to say an opinion, since in December 1585 he seems to have written only to the Duke of Parma asking for advice on how to deal with England.[11] A courtier or secretary may have alerted Santa Cruz. The timing of his new letter urging invasion – 13 January 1586 – is too close to be coincidental. Santa Cruz spoke in general terms of the English attacks, and stressed the need to act before the king lost too much money and reputation. He pointed out that since the Turks and the French were deeply preoccupied with other campaigns, this was an ideal opportunity. On 24 January 1586, Philip asked Santa Cruz for a full but secret report outlining what would be needed for an attack against England.

The Santa Cruz Proposal

Philip received Santa Cruz's memorandum at the end of March 1586. Historians have consistently been impressed by the speed with which this detailed report was completed, but a summary of the proposal drawn up a year later specifies that Santa Cruz had cooperated with Bernabe de Pedroso, a financial official with long experience of organizing military and naval expeditions.[1] The expedition they promoted was essentially maritime. There were no details of strategy enclosed but the items listed suggest that they envisaged a mixed naval and land campaign of considerable importance. Details of the plan have been summarized in Table 1 (p. 18). It is worth noting that the size of the army was greater than that employed in the Netherlands in the 1580s (average 60,000), but somewhat smaller than the forces Philip used against France in 1557–8. The number of ships and high manning-levels also imply that they expected the fleet to perform tasks separately and not merely to act as a convoy. The fleet, if it had assembled, would have been the greatest of its age. Clearly the king could provide only a small percentage of the required tonnage; the majority would have to come, as it always did, from ships hired or embargoed by the crown.

The cost of the *c*.800 ships and over 94,000 men, along with their equipment and victuals for eight months, was estimated at three and a half million ducats. This was not the full price of the enterprise, since Santa Cruz and Pedroso deducted the salaries and costs of men and goods Philip provided for ordinary defence expenditure. Philip had already mentioned the figure of four million ducats. Thus he was not shocked by the expense, but he must have blanched at the thought of finding and fitting out so many ships and levying and transporting the required troops. Curiously, there is no proof that Philip circulated this proposal, but it is evident that he was attracted by the notion of a maritime enterprise. The Duke of Parma's plan, on the other hand, was widely debated.

Parma's Proposal[1]

Parma's plan differed greatly from the Santa Cruz–Pedroso proposal. Both agreed that a campaign against England was desirable and possible. But the duke was concerned with strategy and the international situation, not with details of victuals and provisions. His reasons for approving the campaign were simple: Elizabeth had executed many good Christians; she had sheltered and supported the Dutch rebels and other enemies of the faith. Thus she deserved punishment. If Philip won the war, Parma

9. AGS E.947 f.102.
10. AGS E.947 f.15, Olivares to Philip, 24 February 1586. E.947 f.16; Olivares's proposal and Italian annotations with Sixtus's answers.
11. AGS E.590 f.125.

1. AGS GA.221 f.1 (*bis*) The more detailed account was published by Duro, 1884, 250–319. Pedroso later sailed with the Armada and survived.

1. AGS E.590 f.125, Parma to Philip, Brussels, 20 April 1586.

17

The Santa Cruz–Pedroso plan

Front-line ships	Provenance	Tons (Castilian)	Men
40 naves	Ragusa, Venice, Sicily, Naples and Levant coast up to Cartagena	24,000	–
25 galleons	Seville – the city, environs and royal ships stationed there	15,000	–
20 galleons	Portugal	14,000	–
35 naves	Guipúzcoa and Vizcaya	12,250	–
30 naves	Hanseatic and other German ships trading with Spain	12,000	–

Cargo ships

40 hulks	From those embargoed to transport food and men	8,000	–

Small ships

50 saetias and corchapines	Catalonia and Valencia	5,000	–
50 caravels, chalupas and barcones	From the coast of Malaga to Ayamonte	4,000	–
100 caravels	Portugal, up to Oporto	8,000	–
20 small caravels	(For transmitting orders)	500	–
100 zabras, chalupas and pataches	–	8,000	–

Total: 510 vessels		110,750 tons	16,612

Oared vessels

40 galleys	20 Spain; 14 Naples; 6 Sicily	–	11,200
6 galleasses	–	–	2,520
20 fragatas	–	–	–
20 falúas	–	–	–
200 small barcas	–	–	–

Grand total: 796 vessels		Spanish Infantry	28,000
		Italian Infantry	15,000
		German Infantry	12,000
		Cavalry	1,200
		Artillery	4,290
		Adventurers (paid)	400
		Others – Adventurers royal officials etc.	3,000
		Ecclesiastics	140
		Given total	94,222
		Actual total	94,362

had no doubt the Netherlands rebellion would end rapidly. He acknowledged some difficulties, however. The English knew the Channel well, whereas Philip's subjects were ignorant of the dangers. Working together with the Dutch rebels, Elizabeth could muster a large fleet with the best sailors. She could also count on the help of German Protestants and the French, who would obdurately oppose any move Philip made against England.

None of these difficulties was insuperable. Parma was confident the campaign would be successful – if God allowed it. Neither Parma nor his master doubted divine support for an enterprise designed to increase the faith. Nevertheless, it was essential to meet certain conditions, above all secrecy, so that Elizabeth would not have time to organize her fleet or marshal the militia. Above all, she must not have time to levy German troops and bring them to England before the attack. Parma was confident of his superiority over the English militias, even when backed by Flanders veterans, but regular German troops were another matter. In order to guarantee secrecy, Philip must act alone. Second, Philip must ensure that the French were 'busy'. In effect this meant encouraging their civil war, but Parma warned that even if they were fighting each other, Henri III would still support Elizabeth. The final condition was to provide adequate defence for the Netherlands and the Franche-Comté, which might be attacked either by the French or by the Germans.

Parma had no fleet, but he devised an interesting plan. He would transport 30,000 men from Flanders in small, shallow river-boats. These ships could cross the Channel in eight to twelve hours. The infantry would be supported by 500 light cavalry, but without the horses, which could not be transported easily in such vessels. Only a few ships would be armed, and lightly. Parma assumed that these forces could be mustered secretly and that he would have a clear run to the English coast. In order to allay any suspicions, he would organize a suitable feint against a rebel area in the Netherlands. He also thought it wise to prepare a fleet in Spain as a decoy. Parma assured Philip that the English feared only a seaborne attack from Iberia: their concerns about Spain would make them relax their guard in the Netherlands.

Juan Bautista Piata enlarged upon Parma's plan, explaining that the troops would be stationed in the area around Bergen-op-Zoom. At most they would need three days to embark.[2] The flotilla would then head for the English coast between Dover and Margate, 'a fertile strip with good landing points'. It was near London and wooded, favouring an army with little cavalry support. Parma was confident that London would be easily taken. He expected Elizabeth to remove to a safe place – she was a woman after all – leaving her forces in chaos and confusion. Piata explained that they had not decided on which side of the river to march, and would not do so until they knew where the English forces were. He also informed Philip of his intention to leave about 1,000 men at the landing point to build a fort. The small boats could support this action; when it was safe, they would return to Flanders to bring horses and other essentials. Parma reckoned it would take three to four hours to disembark and get the army in formation. He planned to leave the Netherlands at night and arrive at the mouth of the Thames at the crack of dawn, which left him a good part of the day to march towards London. On the second or, at most, the third day after landing, he would be at the gates of the city. Later he would progress to take further ports and fortifications. It is noteworthy that Parma believed few English Catholics would support the invasion, and he made his plans accordingly.

If something went wrong and the English were prepared, Philip would have to 'try to become lord of the Ocean', that is, to secure the Iberian-Indies route while the decoy Spanish fleet would have to draw the English ships away from the Netherlands coast and so enable Parma's transport boats to sail unmolested. Parma recommended a campaign in October 1586. Surprise would be guaranteed with such hasty preparation. October was ideal because the farms would be full of grain, and the army could live off the enemy lands. He estimated the cost of the campaign at 300,000 *escudos* per month, but stressed that monthly provision of 150,000 *es* for the Netherlands must also be maintained and, if possible, increased. Projecting this figure over an eight-month period made it appear cheaper than the other invasion plan, but Parma had not taken into account the costs of preparing the diversionary fleet in Spain or hiring additional soldiers. Later in October, Parma also stated that he expected Philip to provide him with victuals, munitions and other provisions. In a long harangue on the importance of having substantial sums of money, Parma discreetly made a bid for leadership of the campaign.[3] He suggested that if Philip wished him to go on it, the Count of Mansfelt should replace him in the Netherlands.

Philip was cheered by the positive response, but angry that Parma had been so tardy. The duke's proposal did not arrive until 20 June 1586; his specification of the victualling and other provisions came only at the end of November, after the original proposal had been discussed. There was clearly no hope of carrying out the campaign that year, as the

2. AGS E.590 f.126.
3. AGS E.592 f.135 Parma to Philip, 30 October 1586.

Comendador Mayor noted. But if they waited another year the international situation, especially in France, would have altered. Moreover, to fund the war, he thought it necessary to seize merchants' bullion from the Indies, which might alert the enemy that a major campaign was being organized. The Comendador Mayor was also concerned with one aspect of the war Parma had omitted: who would replace Elizabeth if Philip invaded? He thought it essential to solve the matter before embarking on the enterprise. He favoured the succession of Mary Queen of Scots, but advanced the startling proposal that she should marry Parma at once. This would encourage Parma to execute the enterprise with ardour and give Philip an excellent friend and neighbour to help him recover the rebel provinces of Holland and Zeeland. Since the couple could not have children, the English succession would be left open. It is evident, however, that rumours were circulating at court that Parma could not be trusted. His son, Ranucio, had a substantial claim to the Portuguese throne (though weaker than Philip's own), and it was feared that Parma would use his increased power as King of England to challenge Philip in Portugal or even in the Netherlands. The comendador defended Parma's record of loyalty, yet the discussions about the English succession show that Philip was highly sensitive to Parma's dynastic rights.[4] To gain the pope's support, however, the king was committed to appoint Parma as commander of the invasion of England.

In any case, Philip wanted immediate action. He decided on a small- to medium-scale naval expedition against Ireland rather than a major campaign against England. First Philip decided that Santa Cruz and his best galleons must escort the *flota* leaving Seville for New Spain, and chase the corsairs who were raiding there. Santa Cruz complained that this would prevent him from preparing the English attack, but Philip stood by his decision.[5] News filtered through to the Duke of Medina Sidonia, who was in charge of fitting out the New World fleets, that the king intended to embargo the ships in Andalusia and use them to strike against England. Medina Sidonia maintained that it was vital for the New World fleets to sail annually, and bitterly opposed the king's policy. Philip did not deny that he was considering this; instead he instructed his secretary Juan de Idiáquez to 'share his thoughts on the matter' with the duke; i.e., to justify the action. According to Idiáquez, English provocation had forced Philip to take an aggressive position. The English were gradually taking control of Holland and Zeeland and hampering trade with the Indies. 'It is no longer possible to defend everything, we must set fire to their home and ensure it is so dangerous that they will be forced to drop everything and concentrate on putting it out.'[6] Medina Sidonia was unmoved. He argued that Philip would gain more reputation if he sent a small fleet against England *and* another to the Indies. This would prove his power at sea.[7]

While Philip debated what policy to adopt, other opportunities arose. Mary Queen of Scots was in secret correspondence with France; from the English and Scottish exiles she learned of Philip's intentions to invade England. She approved wholeheartedly of the enterprise and offered to persuade her son to join them. Mary also decided to name Philip her successor if James refused to convert to Catholicism. In May 1586 she sent a formal statement to this effect to Don Bernardino de Mendoza, Philip's ambassador in France.[8] Aware of Philip's earlier reluctance to support Mary Stuart, historians such as Jensen have assumed that this gesture made her a 'safe' candidate for the English throne. There is no doubt that Philip was pleased and readily agreed to her demand for protection and financial support in July 1586. But he had already made up his mind to promote her cause, because this was the most acceptable strategy to the Catholic world.

In July 1586 Mendoza was also informed of two plots: one for a rebellion in Scotland led by the Earls of Huntly and Morton and Claude Hamilton; the other came to be known as the Babington plot. These proposals overlapped. Mary, the hope of Catholics on both sides of the border, urged Philip to support Babington's conspiracy. She played on his recent loss of reputation in Christendom due to the exploits of Drake and Leicester in the New World and the Netherlands.[9] The prospect of an English Catholic uprising, coordinated with a Scottish rebellion and invasion, naturally appealed to Philip. But he was rather dubious of the Scottish side. In September he requested Parma's opinion on the matter, later deferring to his advice that it could not be successfully carried out. As for Babington's proposal, Philip had encountered many similar plans earlier, and all were unsuccessful; thus he was wary. It would be convenient if the Catholics started a civil war, as they had in France, but he doubted that they could keep the matter secret. When he heard of the arrest and execution of the Babington conspirators in September, Philip expressed pity for their fate, but added that their carelessness was largely to blame for the outcome.[10] There was no alternative to a Spanish campaign under his own exclusive control.

Preparations for the attack went on throughout 1586. Every event during that year and

4. AGS E.590 f.127, the Comendador Mayor's opinions; on the succession, see cat. no. 6.21 and notes therein.
5. Duro, 1884, I, 325–30.
6. Duro, 1884, I, 167.
7. Duro, 1884, I, 161–74.
8. AGS Ek. 1565 f.147; Jensen, 1964, 83.
9. Jensen, 1964, 80–87; a detailed account of the plot in Read, 1925, III, 1–70.
10. AGS Ek.1448 f.78, Philip to Mendoza, 19 October 1586.

the next confirmed the wisdom of declaring open war against England. In France, the situation was not propitious for the first half of 1586, but it improved thereafter. Peace negotiations between Henri III and various factions dragged on, but by early summer Guise hinted that he would come to terms. Philip's response was to offer more money if the Guises agreed not to make peace without his consent. Elizabeth's intervention changed the situation radically. Like Philip, she subsidized the unrest in France. She gave the Huguenots money and urged them to continue their resistance. She arranged for German troop-levies and tried to involve Denmark and the German princes. In January 1587 her ally, John Casimir of the Palatinate, concluded a treaty with Henri of Navarre and the Huguenots to provide 22,000 German troops for an early summer campaign.[11] Although Philip was angry with the Guises for their lack of secrecy, he advanced them 50,000 ducats in November to help them counter the Protestant invasion.[12] With the money sent by Philip and Elizabeth, the French set to war once again. The much-feared Protestant invasion did not occur until the end of August 1587, but no one could have predicted this while the war was in progress. Paradoxically, it was only after the Catholic victories in October and November that Philip became seriously concerned by the situation in France. Philip did not believe the Guises would continue the war.[13]

Perhaps the most famous event of 1587 was the execution of Mary Queen of Scots on 18 February. Tension in England had grown, with warnings and rumours of Philip's preparations. This was the background against which Mary was judged and sentenced to death. In Mattingly's lively and influential account of the Armada, Mary's death precipitated war. All the previous debates and discussions were mere testing of the water: now that Mary had died, the question of who would succeed Elizabeth could be settled to Philip's satisfaction. Moreover, the Catholic world would look to him to avenge the death of a martyr. The execution was the last barrier to what Mattingly considered an inevitable 'clash of irreconcilables'.[14] This interpretation is open to question. Both her son James VI and her relations the Guises had greater reason to seek revenge than Philip. Parma did write that her death left Philip no choice but to invade England, but he had said this before of other events. In theory, of course, her death should have given Philip an excellent opportunity to put forward his claims to the throne. He felt the agreement of 24 February 1586 in which the pope accepted Philip's right to choose Mary's successor was now superseded. Armed with detailed accounts of his

dynastic rights to the English throne drawn up by William Allen, Robert Parsons and other exiles in Rome and Paris, Philip ordered Olivares to broach the matter openly. But even Allen and Parsons warned him against this. They supported his bid for the throne, and would have happily accepted his daughter, but in view of the pope's jealousy of Philip's power, this should be done after the invasion.[15] Moreover, an official claim might force James to give active support to Elizabeth and prompt the French to action as well. Certainly Philip's lobbying would renew papal assertions that the war was fought primarily to advance the king's interest and could result in the withdrawal of financial backing. In June 1587 Philip accepted this advice and stood by the February 1586 agreement. He would defer his claims until the time was ripe.[16] Curiously, Sixtus V raised the English succession the following month, offering to invest one of the archdukes – whoever married Isabel Clara Eugenia – with the title to England. But the pope wanted Philip to enact legislation to prevent England from being absorbed into the Spanish Monarchy, and that was unacceptable. Philip wanted the throne for his progeny, not for his cousins.[17]

The preparations for the fleet were already well advanced at the time of Mary's death. Ships had been seized, victuals requisitioned, and men dispatched. To facilitate the task, the fleet was gathering and provisioning in three main centres: Seville, Lisbon and Cadiz.[18] There were thirty-five large ships and twenty pinnaces and *zabras* in Lisbon. Medina Sidonia suggested that the king should embargo thirty large Andalusian hulks in order to reinforce the fleet and make it invincible.[19] As Mattingly noted, there was an upsurge in activity in March, but not because of Mary Stuart. Philip had been informed that Elizabeth was fitting out thirty ships and would secure another thirty from Holland. She planned to send Dom Antonio with them, from which Philip deduced that Elizabeth meant to provoke further unrest in Portugal and interfere with his preparations.[20] The news spurred him into action. Several days before he heard of Mary's execution and 'without waiting to hear more *consultas* and opinions', he decided to impound the New World fleet and join these ships to the Armada gathering in Lisbon.[21]

Three weeks later he received a gloomy letter from Parma confirming the English military preparations and Mary's fate. The duke maintained that the international situation was not favourable. He painted a bleak picture of the king's position in the Netherlands, where news of German levies had caused grave alarm. Parma thought that the French also required further encouragement and support.

21

11. Jensen, 1964.
12. AGS Ek.1448 ff.59, 66, 69, 78.
13. Jensen, 1964, 90–2.
14. See 36, 57, 58 and early chapters.
15. See cat. no. **6.21**, and AGS E.949 f.16, f.56, f.57, f.28.
16. AGS E.949 ff.28, 40, 46, 65.
17. AGS E.949 f.83, Olivares to Juan de Idiáquez, 16 July 1587.
18. See, for example, AGS E.165 ff.43, 44, 47, 50, 51; GA.208 f.9.
19. Duro, I, 170.
20. AGS Ek.1565, f.26, July 1587.
21. Duro, 1884, I, 177–8 Idiáquez to Medina Sidonia, 21 March 1587. The Venetian ambassador reported that the news arrived at El Escorial on the night of the 23rd, Mattingly, 1983, 72. Even if he had not prevented the fleet from sailing, only a part of it would have gone since his seizure of wine, oil and other provisions had seriously disrupted commerce for the Indies.

The one scrap of comfort the king must have drawn from this was Parma's enduring commitment to the campaign against England, which he urged Philip to put into effect without further waiting.[22]

Drake's Attack on Cadiz, 29 April 1587

Philip's information of Elizabeth's plans was fairly accurate, but out of date. Drake had been sent to the Netherlands in October of the previous year to canvass support for a new attack. When Dom Antonio heard of Portuguese unrest in January, Leicester, Drake and Walsingham all urged the queen to launch a major Anglo-Dutch-Huguenot expedition. Elizabeth's courage failed her; she thought a major campaign would be open war, so she opted instead for her traditional and relatively inexpensive policy of fostering semi-official raids. Drake sailed on 2 April, narrowly averting being recalled. The queen's change of heart may have been another example of her procrastination, but it could also reflect a shrewd assessment that Drake's attack would have serious consequences if it succeeded, as indeed it did. His brief was to prevent the fleets in Lisbon, Seville and Cadiz from joining; to hamper the transport of provisions between these ports; and to attack all ships that might attempt a landing in England or Ireland. As always, he was encouraged to attack any ships from the West or East Indies.[1] Drake's fleet first made for Lisbon, but quickly decided to attack Cadiz, probably because the entrance to Lisbon was difficult to navigate and better fortified.[2] Cadiz was totally unprepared, although Philip had sent warnings of the English fleet. Drake sailed into Cadiz harbour under cover of French and Dutch flags and proceeded to destroy as many ships as possible. There was only token resistance from a few merchant vessels and the eight royal galleys. Between twenty-four and thirty-seven ships were burnt or sunk: some had been intended to join the campaign, while others were laden with provisions for the Armada in Lisbon and the Indies. The English then went to Lagos and Sagres, which they sacked before sailing toward the Azores in search of the rich New World galleons.

Philip later dismissed these daring raids as not serious, but commented that 'their audacity is intolerable'.[3] The Spaniards and Portuguese felt general relief that the English had not joined the corsairs from Algiers and Larache, as had been feared. They were thankful that the sharif and the sultan had not launched simultaneous attacks.[4] The defenders in Cadiz proudly recalled their attempts to repulse the enemy and congratulated themselves for having prevented a landing, which would have been a more serious taint on their honour than the burning of ships. On the other hand, they also hurled criticism at each other for not acting decisively enough, but that was to be expected. Nevertheless, the attack caused a major upset in the royal council. When the Council of War considered the situation on 4 May, they outlined their suspicions that Drake would head for the Indies while another English fleet would be sent to Portugal, hoping that Philip would concentrate on the Portuguese and leave the Indies fleets defenceless. The Indies treasure-fleets must be given priority, they argued. But then they feared that the English might have planned to divert Philip's forces by pretending to attack the Indies so that they could invade Portugal without hindrance. Moreover, they were concerned by reports that North African corsairs were again raiding the Straits of Gibraltar and the Canary Islands. How could Philip defend these vast areas? His advisers told him to bring more galleys from Italy, but this would naturally upset his subjects there, who would be left without adequate defence. He should also levy 20,000 Spanish and at least 5,000 German troops.[5] Over the next few days they voiced grave fears of revolution in Portugal and the loss of Gibraltar.

By 15 May the councillors had recovered their composure and urged Philip to dispatch Santa Cruz to the Indies immediately, with a fleet large enough to beat Drake. They also wanted the king to organize another fleet to attack England. While acknowledging the difficulty of the task, they felt that Philip's 'faith and greatness' would overcome all problems. With God's help he would be able to 'curb the insolence and sacrilege of the English'.[6] On 25 May, the councillors weighed up the dangers from England and expressed certainty that the Algerian city-state and the Turks would join the affray. They knew that they could not defend all the threatened areas, and concluded that an attack was the best means of defence. Their advice became a strident call for action. They urged Philip to 'satisfy Your Majesty's honour and these realms, which have been so offended and harmed by the Queen of England and the corsairs of that realm who infest these waters'. The world must see that whereas he had been willing to overlook such piracy in the past, he now intended to mete out just punishment to these transgressors. They ended with a reminder that this war would have the inestimable advantage of freeing the poor, oppressed Catholics of England.[7] Parma echoed the warnings over the Indies fleets and reiterated his requests for immediate retaliation and the recovery of lost reputation.[8]

Philip had agreed from the outset that the Indies fleet deserved highest priority, but this deci-

22. AGS E.592 f.47, to Philip, 22 March 1587.

1. Read, 1925 III, 229–33.
2. Duro, I, 181–212, contemporary accounts of the attack on Cadiz; Mattingly, 1983, 95–108, for a lively modern account.
3. AGS GA.208 f.366, to Santa Cruz, 25 May 1587.
4. Duro, I, 1884, 199.
5. AGS GA.208 ff.267–8.
6. AGS GA.208 f.343 *Consulta*, 15 May; ff.282 and 278, 6 and 5 May respectively.
7. AGS GA.208 f.343 *Consulta*, 16 May; GA.209 f.66 *Consulta*, 3 July.
8. AGS E.592 f.20, Parma to Philip, 6 June 1587.

sion would delay the attack on England. He ordered Santa Cruz to take all suitable ships from Lisbon and sail at once for the Indies. If he left immediately he might catch up with the English fleet or at least prevent them from doing much damage. But how could the Spanish merchant ships going to the New World sail without protection? The alternative was to make Santa Cruz wait until these vessels were ready to sail; he could then escort them to their destination. At every turn king and council encountered the insoluble problem of how to stretch Philip's resources to defend his sprawling empire. It seemed incredible that one enemy fleet could threaten so many areas.[9] Santa Cruz was unable to sail for another two months. He could not leave unless he received reinforcements, and the new infantry levies were in Andalusia. They should have been transported, along with victuals and artillery, on the ships Drake had burnt. With soldiers at one end of the country and ships at the other, it was difficult to make much progress. The obvious answer was to send the men on foot, but the overland journey was long and difficult. In the end they had to wait for the Neapolitan galleasses and galleys to take them to Lisbon. However much the king pressed his officials to make haste, they could not overcome the basic problems of distance and insufficient resources. When the reluctant Santa Cruz departed from Lisbon in July, still urging Philip to concentrate on offensive warfare, he expected reinforcements to meet him in the Azores. But Philip revoked these orders and sent the ships and their valuable cargoes of men and provisions to Lisbon, to strengthen his fleet. In a letter clearly intended for public consumption in France, he informed Mendoza that Santa Cruz had taken some forty ships, all well fitted-out with some 6,000 men, many of them seasoned soldiers. Their task was to clear the sea of corsairs and destroy Drake. Philip also revealed that the vessels from Cadiz were heading for Lisbon where he had some eighty sailing ships and four galleys.[10]

The king had not exaggerated. The number of ships available for Santa Cruz's punitive expedition indicates how advanced the preparations for a campaign were by the summer of 1587. Santa Cruz departed with twenty-two galleons and large *naos* (twelve from Portugal; two Levantine and eight probably from Vizcaya); fifteen pinnaces and *zabras*, a total of 13,930 tons. There were 5,415 soldiers, twenty-one gentlemen-adventurers and 149 other hired gentlemen, and 2,300 seamen, all carrying provisions for four months.[11]

The fleet from Cadiz had been prepared under the supervision of the Duke of Medina Sidonia. It set out in July with eighty-two ships: fifteen *naves* from Andalusia; six *naves* that had transported infantry from Sicily; two *naves* and four galleasses from Naples; fourteen *zabras* and pinnaces; thirty hulks laden with victuals and twelve Spanish royal galleys to escort them. The fleet had 3,010 sailors and 6,259 soldiers with 539 bronze and 588 iron guns. Large quantities of military provisions included powder, lead, shot, arquebuses, pikes, helmets and bombs.[12] There were also twenty-four clergymen and one doctor on board.[13] The list of the provisions they took to Lisbon fills ninety-eight folio pages.[14] It includes all the items which had been stipulated in the original proposal by Santa Cruz and Pedroso, fitting out the expedition for land as well as naval warfare. The victuals consisted mainly of biscuit, wine, vinegar, oil, bacon, tuna, salt cod, cheese, beans, chickpeas, rice, salt, sugar, raisins, almonds and beef. Among the items for the kitchens and rations we find 1,775 wooden plates, 563 wooden cups, 34 earthenware pots, 210 earthenware jugs, 6,048 earthenware plates and 6,132 bowls of the same material. For the vital water supplies they took 1,633 casks, 2,156 jugs and 104 wooden barrels. Weights and balances of various sorts were provided; scales in iron and other metals, copper measuring instruments. For lights they took candles, of course, but also lanterns. Wooden spades, buckets, hammers, nails and other common tools can be found, as well as items such as paper, wood, sacks, lead, thread and sails.

Impressive as this was, it did not suffice. At the beginning of August Philip and the Council of War discussed what would be required to put together 'a medium-sized army' of 30,000 soldiers and 10,000 sailors. This was assuming that Santa Cruz would return safely in September and that the ships would not be too badly damaged. Their first concern was to secure sufficient provisions, and in order to supply the victuals they recommended requisitioning goods from Spain once more. Philip agreed and ordered that some grain and salt should be sent to the Netherlands, where his troops were suffering from the dearth that had struck the area.[15] By the end of that month there were already complaints from the supply areas, many pleading their own dearth and poverty.[16] While they waited for the return of Santa Cruz and prayed that he would meet and destroy Drake, Philip and his officials thus continued with the endless task of gathering provisions, scouring all Europe for artillery and organizing the movement of troops across the continent.[17]

Despite the loss of reputation, the king knew he could not act until Santa Cruz returned. Philip could not risk sending all major ships out of Iberian waters.[18] Nor could he afford to send an inadequate

9. AGS GA.208 f.268, f.341; Herrera Oria, 1946, 104–6.
10. AGS Ek.1448 f.131, Philip to Mendoza, 17 July 1587; Duro, 1884, I, 336–7, 339–52, 374–5, 369–72, 375–9, 383–4. Oquendo: Duro, 1884, I, 396–7.
11. AGS GA.221 f.22. GA.221 f.6. The two accounts differ, but I have taken f.6 as more likely to be the final figure. GA.199 f.70 gives the following victuals: biscuit (16,530qq), wine (2,294ps), bacon (1,151qq), cheese (605qq), salt beef (1,089qq), salt cod and sardines (1,170qq), rice (835qq), beans and chickpeas (878fs), oil (1,115ps), vinegar (69ps), salt (261fs), water (3,253ps), wood (9,592qq), flour (137qq); GA.221 f.22 gives different figures, somewhat greater.
12. AGS GA.221 f.2. Further details of the artillery may be found in GA.221 f.39 and f.21. See also Section 8. ii: Spanish Shipping and Shipbuilding, for details of the different types of Spanish vessels. The term *'nave'* is being used as a generic name for sailing ships here.
13. AGS GA.221 f.5.
14. AGS GA.221 f.23.
15. AGS GA.209 f.116, *Consulta*, 8 August 1587; f.15 reply, 16 August. Duro, 1884, I, 237.
16. AGS GA.209 f.145 from Cadiz for example.
17. AGS GA.209 f.249, f.80, f.311.
18. AGS GA.209 f.66.

23

force to England and lose battles there. But these difficulties seemed to make him all the more determined to act quickly. In the lull between the departure of the fleet and its return, Philip pondered over maps and considered invading Ireland or the Isle of Wight. Neither suggestion was new, and both had been mooted at the outset of these discussions in 1585–6. In the summer of 1587 Philip seemed to prefer the Irish plan. He believed it was feasible, and while not as prestigious as a direct attack against England, an invasion of Ireland would have the advantage of dividing English forces. The English might even have to withdraw from conflicts in the Netherlands and France. Ireland would be a useful base for a later invasion of England. Much the same reasoning was applied to the projected attack on the Isle of Wight. Perhaps Philip found it less appealing because of the lack of local support, which he reckoned on in Ireland.[19] Parma objected that these campaigns would detract from '*el negocio principal*' – the primary objective of England itself. He did not approve of diversionary attacks, which would alert Elizabeth to reinforce her defences and make an invasion of England impossible.[20] Similarly, he blocked a plan for a diversion in Scotland by arguing that Scottish Catholics could best rebel when England was attacked.[21] Both Parma and Santa Cruz insisted that Philip must concentrate his forces and attempt a major invasion of England.

Philip's Strategy:
September to December 1587

News of the successful siege of Sluis, which had tied down Parma's best troops throughout June and July, was greeted with much rejoicing at the Spanish court.[1] Parma was at pains to stress how greatly it facilitated the campaign against England. Sluis was at the confluence of numerous canals and waterways; consequently it would be much easier to gather the small boats required for the invasion, as well as to transport provisions and men. It was also a convenient embarkation point for England. Parma's enthusiasm and his determination to 'overcome and surmount all the difficulties that may present themselves' to the English campaign greatly encouraged Philip and determined his new strategy.[2] The king did not even wait until Santa Cruz returned, although he knew that the marquis would soon be back with the fleet intact.

Philip's new plan was to join the forces in Spain and the Netherlands and organize a simultaneous assault. Together they would be strong enough to invade England. Philip expected Parma to march to Ostend with some 30,000 to 40,000 men; he reckoned that Santa Cruz had as many as 16,000 Spanish infantry in Lisbon and perhaps 22,000 fighting men in all. He did not mention the number of ships that could be quickly fitted out for service, but figures oscillated between thirty and forty. The king did not approve of taking horses because he believed most would die on such a long voyage; besides, he needed them in Portugal and Spain. Santa Cruz was given command of the fleet and of part of its forces; Parma would command on land, and was given permission to use up to 6,000 Spanish infantry from the fleet. The two men would decide what strategy to follow after they had landed.[3] Philip ordered Santa Cruz to take the fleet directly to the Channel and proceed to Margate without stopping or even fighting with the enemy if he could avoid it. His principal task was to secure the sea route between Parma's embarkation point in Flanders and the mouth of the Thames. Of course the king was aware of what dangers awaited them. He anticipated criticism of his order to sail in winter, particularly as the Armada would not have a safe port in the Channel. But he was hopeful that God would give them good weather. For Philip it was natural to expect miracles in a campaign intended to remedy 'the injuries done by the English to Our Lord and their persecution of his Church and the faithful'. But there were also practical reasons for this decision to risk a winter crossing. Elizabeth had been negotiating alliances with Protestant powers and levying German troops. The Spaniards needed to act before her preparations were complete.

The Turks were also a source of concern. Philip's anxiety increased when he heard they were negotiating peace with the Sofi of Persia so that they would be free to send a fleet against Italy in 1588. He knew that if he waited he might face a defensive war against several enemies. It was better to take the offensive now.[4] These were cogent reasons and sufficient to account for the king's frenzied attempts over the next three months to ensure that the expedition set out before the end of the year. But there was one other consideration which he did not admit to: finance. Or, to be precise, the papal subsidy.

The negotiations between Philip and the irascible Sixtus V gave the pontiff ample scope to demonstrate his cutting tongue and famous temper. Sixtus remained sceptical of Philip's motives[5] but he finally agreed to give Philip one million *scuti*, half of it payable 'when the army landed in England, or the fleet arrived'. Rightly suspecting that Sixtus would use any variation from the strict letter of the agreement to avoid payment, Philip requested that the second part of the sentence be omitted. He was not certain at that point that he would send a fleet; at this

19. AGS E.592 f.32; AGS Ek.1448 f.122.
20. Ibid. also AGS E.592 f.135 and E.592 f.96.
21. AGS E.592 f.49, Parma to Philip, 22 April 1587; E.592 f.89 ibid, 31 May.

1. As usual, Mattingly provides the most lively account, 1983, 126–40.
2. AGS E.594 f.5 Philip to Parma, El Escorial, 4 September 1587.
3. AGS E.594 f.5; E.165 ff.6–7. There is a general summary of the strategy in Section 7(ii).
4. AGS E.165 ff.6–7.
5. AGS E.947 f.110, Philip to Olivares, 22 July 1586; E.947 f.112, what Olivares said to Sixtus, 29 August.

stage he may have favoured Parma's plan. Later he would regret his decision. The fleet did sail, but the soldiers did not land; Sixtus adhered to the wording of the contract and refused to pay.[6] For the time being, however, Philip was happy to receive this promise of aid in December 1586. He wanted to improve the conditions and, if possible, secure a loan for a further one million ducats. The pope would not lend him any money, but he was willing to make his payments earlier than originally promised if Philip agreed to execute his plan in 1587.[7]

As the months passed and expenditure increased dramatically, Philip became quite desperate to anticipate the papal grant. Ambassador Olivares was instructed to negotiate with Gian Agostino Pineli, the papal banker, who offered to advance Philip 500,000 ducats in the three months following the landing. Since Sixtus had already agreed to give Philip half a million on landing, the king could look forward to obtaining the whole million very quickly. Most, if not all, of this money would be paid in the Netherlands as Philip wanted. But there was one condition: Philip must invade by December 1587. Pineli could not afford to keep such a large quantity of money on hand for very long.[8]

With this mounting pressure, Philip urged his officials throughout October and November to prepare the fleet and set sail. Orders were also sent to the Netherlands, and the difficulty of coordinating two fronts became apparent. Philip ordered Santa Cruz to fit out only thirty-one of his best ships – there was no time for more. Naturally, the marquis resented and resisted these orders. The best ships and men had just returned from the Indies. After an arduous voyage they needed rest, repairs, revictualling and reinforcements. Philip was loath to agree to further delays; he was on edge and accused Santa Cruz of deliberately delaying his departure. The marquis responded in strident tones that the men were ill and the fleet could not sail without more artillery and provisions. A letter from Cardinal-Archduke Albert at the very end of October supported Santa Cruz's statements, and Philip resigned himself to a new departure date – the end of November. Forty-eight ships were now expected to sail, but some were damaged in a violent storm on 16 November.[9]

Philip had reason to suspect that Santa Cruz was dragging his feet. The marquis's enthusiasm for the war against England had evaporated when he was told that he would share command with Parma. He complained that he was being reduced to a pitiful supporting role incompatible with his honour. Santa Cruz made sure that his dissatisfaction was given ample publicity, placing the king in an embarrassing position. Philip sought to persuade him that his role was by far the more important. Unless he secured the seas, Parma could do nothing. Philip also argued that Doria held an analogous position in earlier campaigns and had not been dishonoured by it. He stressed that Parma was his nephew and governor of the Netherlands and must be given a superior command. Finally Philip offered the marquis a choice of accepting his charge as it was or resigning, and Santa Cruz agreed to accept.[10]

Parma was equally hostile to Philip's latest plan. Until the summer of 1587, Parma had been a strong supporter of the campaign, generally optimistic and even at times enthusiastic. He often used the proposed campaign to plead for more resources in the Netherlands, and he repeatedly assured Philip that he was working vigilantly 'night and day' to prepare the invasion. He reported the construction and seizure of boats and provisions – a difficult task due to the severe dearth. Parma also said he was mustering his men near the coast and was confident that all would be ready on time.[11] During the difficult siege of Sluis, Parma wrote again of his strenuous efforts to organize the campaign. If Parma's letter was rather pessimistic, stating that the English would inevitably attempt to block his passage, Philip probably attributed this to exhaustion brought on by the tense situation.[12] The victory certainly raised Parma's spirits. Philip's strategy relied heavily on Parma's cooperation, and he was entirely unprepared for the despondent and negative dispatches from Parma that winter. On 6 November Philip received the first, a letter of 22 August. Now Parma argued that it was impossible to carry out an invasion of England that year.[13] It was too late in the season to campaign and his preparations for the expedition were far from complete. He still needed victuals, powder, cordage, pikes and other ammunition. Sails and rigging had not yet been acquired. Parma was also short of men, both infantry and sailors. His attempts to levy German troops had been hindered by the competition from Elizabeth and the Huguenots, and there were long delays in the land transport of the Italian and Spanish infantry.[14] Apart from internal problems, Parma argued that the international situation was less favourable. Philip should devote more attention and resources to France, where the civil wars had abated and there was talk of peace. Blaming the shortage of funds, Parma assumed that there would be no campaign. He left the coast where he had been making hasty preparations and returned to Brussels.

Philip had been desperately trying to provide him and the Guises with funds: in June and July he had sent money and credit for 2.3 million ducats to

6. AGS E.947 f.113, Olivares to Philip, 9 September 1586; E.947 f.115, Philip to Olivares, 18 November, with the king's interesting marginal corrections; E.949 f.5; E.949 f.4, news of the final concession, 22 December – it had been made two days earlier. For the confirmation of this, see cat. no. **2.2**.
7. AGS E.949 f.14, Philip to Olivares, 11 February 1587; E.949 f.54 ibid., 7 April.
8. AGS E.949 f.87, Olivares to Philip, 30 July 1587; f.86, copy of Pineli's agreement; AGS E.954 f.242.
9. Herrera Oria, 1946, 124–31.
10. AGS E.165 ff.23–5, Herrera Oria, 1946, 122 notes that Santa Cruz accepted the office on Philip's condition on 15 October, but he was not satisfied and still trying to change it later.
11. For example, AGS E.592 f.93 from June 1587.
12. AGS E.592 f.96; 20 July 1587.
13. AGS E.592 f.110.
14. See Section 7(i) and notes therein.

25

the Netherlands, of which 300,000 were destined for the French Catholics. Parma's response to this provision, much to Philip's surprise and annoyance, was to look forward to the next instalment.[15] Without it, Parma insisted that the campaign must be abandoned. In these long tirades, not even God was absolved from blame – Parma maintained that He had not helped them to keep the campaign a secret. Indeed, the duke argued that none of his three essential conditions had been met: the enemy knew Philip's intentions; there were not enough troops to secure the Netherlands and provide soldiers to fight in England; and Philip could not neutralize the French, either. It now looked as if the Scottish rebellion Parma had hoped to organize at the time of the attack would not materialize. Yet somewhat inconsistently Parma proposed on 18 September that if Philip allowed him to anticipate at least 600,000 ds and provide up to 400,000 for the French, then the campaign might still proceed.

The king was angry and confused. He had waited until he was certain of Parma before drawing up his strategy. Now that he was committed, the duke was trying to withdraw and criticizing what he had first praised. Later it became clear that Parma had panicked because he was told that the Armada would sail very soon and, despite his bland assurances, he was not ready to attack. In mid October he sent two envoys to Lisbon, urgently warning Santa Cruz of his situation.

Parma was also realizing the weakness of his strategy. He had taken into account the power of the Dutch rebels on land and requested troops for the protection of the loyal provinces, but he had forgotten to provide for Dutch naval power. The Spanish planners had focused almost exclusively on Elizabethan naval power and made slight reference to the Dutch rebel fleet. Only after Parma had been informed that the rebels had mustered between 130 and 140 ships in the canals beyond Lillo and more in Flushing, did he perceive the danger. Now the duke could not move the essential ships and provisions he had prepared in Antwerp, because the canals were under enemy control. Unless he was able to join all his forces, he could not fulfil his part of the invasion. In such situations Parma showed his mettle. He cut new canals to enable his ships to move without crossing into rebel areas or open sea. But until he had done so, he lived in a state of extreme agitation and remained opposed to the invasion.

Parma had also been too optimistic. Secrecy was impossible in the Netherlands, and he now admitted that English and Dutch ships would oppose his departure whatever the time of year. He had always said that his transport vessels were unable to fight with a well-armed enemy, but not until October 1587 did he declare that they could only sail if the wind and current were entirely favourable. Moreover, in April he had negotiated with Scottish Catholics to send armed vessels to the Netherlands in exchange for soldiers; but none had materialized.[16] He realized now that he was totally dependent on the Armada from Spain. Unless Santa Cruz cleared the seas of Dutch and English shipping, Parma could not sail.[17] This explains why after one tirade condemning the expedition and requesting that it be abandoned, Parma demanded that the Armada execute a diversion to draw off the English fleet 'as planned'. Philip must have been irritated. Either the campaign was viable or it was not. Besides, Parma had recently dismissed proposals for the dispatch of a large fleet on the grounds that there was no deep-water port along the Belgian coast in Spanish hands. As Parma's difficulties in the Netherlands gradually emerged, the king came to understand the duke's sudden change of heart.

But there was another reason why Parma had so unexpectedly turned against the project. When Philip read Parma's scarcely veiled allusions to the need for unitary and undisputed command of so important an enterprise, he must have pondered the evil influence of ambition. The competition between his two leading commanders was at the heart of their allegedly insuperable problems. He did not like Parma's tone, but at least he knew what the duke wanted: sole command of the expedition and immediate provision of 600,000 ducats.[18] In response the king asserted his authority and showered praise on his nephew, in whom he expressed full confidence. Months later he agreed to pay 670,000 ducats Parma had borrowed without permission. These royal praises and signs of favour made Parma more cooperative. But he was in a more positive frame of mind after realizing that he had time to prepare his campaign since the Armada was not ready to sail. Still complaining of insufficient manpower and money, and heaping blame on inefficient officials, Parma assured Philip that preparations for the campaign would be completed by the end of December 1587.

As the new year loomed, Philip's anxiety increased. His irritation was reflected in his terse comments on letters from Parma and Santa Cruz. He blamed the former for consuming most of the provisions gathered for the invasion, and the latter for not making rapid progress. To Parma's complaints that the secret had been revealed, Philip replied that if the duke had followed orders and maintained the siege of Ostend or another feint they would have had a

15. AGS E.592 f.99 Parma to Philip, Sluis, 6 August, with Philip's marginal comments; AGS E.592 f.98 acknowledgement of Philip's order to pay the Guises 300,000 if war broke out in France.
16. AGS E.592 f.73.
17. AGS E.592 f.136, Parma to Idiáquez, 13 October 1587; E.592 f.141, Parma to Philip, 14 November; E.592 f.147 and f.149 ibid., 21 December; E.592 f.152 ibid., 29 December.
18. AGS E.592 f.117, Parma to Philip, 18 September 1587, with the king's marginal comments; E.592 f.118 ibid.

better chance. The king's criticisms and his mistaken belief that Parma had been ready to sail in December provoked Parma to a heated defence of his efforts. Philip was in no mood to take more carping criticism from his commanders after he had assuaged their ruffled feathers over the issue of joint leadership. When Santa Cruz bemoaned the shortage of victuals and the sickness among the men, Philip reproached him and the officials for delaying the fleet's departure.[19]

By mid-December Philip realized that he could not meet the papal deadline and the pace now slackened. In Lisbon, sick men were allowed to disembark and urgent repairs continued. Since Parma still complained that he did not have enough men, Philip decided to send him 6,000 Spanish troops in thirty-five strong ships, referred to as the 'second fleet'. Santa Cruz would remain in Lisbon with the 'main fleet' and complete preparations for the major expedition, which these vessels would quickly rejoin.[20] Before the end of the month, reports from England brought alarming news. Elizabeth had ordered the seizure of all shipping along the English coast and planned to have 15,000 men to oppose the invasion. Philip knew that Elizabeth had thirty-seven large, well-armed ships in October and was certain she had embargoed at least seventeen German hulks since then. Her forces would be superior to Philip's 'second fleet' bound for the Netherlands. Consequently in early January 1588, he decided not to risk this force and cancelled his order. Since Santa Cruz had assured him towards the end of December that he was ready to embark men and provisions, Philip decided to return to his earlier strategy and send one large fleet to meet Parma and invade England.[21]

The Final Strategy

We now understand that the wave of criticism and opposition from Parma and Santa Cruz should be seen in the context of their bid for control of the campaign. But it is pertinent to ask if the strategy was flawed. Philip was severely constrained by circumstances and resources. He had neither deep-water ports nor sufficient ships in the Netherlands to prepare a fleet, and he could not strike against England without these. Thus he had to have a naval commander in Iberia. But he could not think of invading England without the veteran troops in the Netherlands. Some had been sent back to Spain and Portugal, but Philip could not withdraw as many as he required, for three reasons. First, he could not leave the area defenceless; second, it was wasteful to transport troops to Spain and thence to England; and third, he wanted to maintain secrecy. Consequently,

an invasion required a transport flotilla and Parma's cooperation even if the Armada was launched from Spain. Besides, as mentioned earlier, Philip was constrained to appoint Parma as commander of the campaign but must ensure that the duke was not in a position to misuse such power and make a bid for the English succession (p. 20). Dual command was the answer. Moreover, the combined operation outlined by Philip made the most efficient use of his resources. Parma admitted as much in January 1588, when he wrote to Philip that the strategy was 'certainly based on such sound and prudent reasoning it was evident that it had emanated from the royal breast and deep understanding of Your Majesty. I personally, and the few who know of the plan, have not ceased to praise and eulogize it as it deserves.'[1]

The extreme obsequiousness suggests that Parma was in trouble again, having received Philip's reproof for his tardy preparations and failure to have done anything with his men and ships. The duke defended himself by citing Philip's instructions that he should not sail until the Armada could secure his Channel passage, and the Armada had not sailed. Parma was happy with Philip's strategy and henceforth insisted it be kept to the letter. Any suggestion that smacked of his own earlier plan to sail alone was sharply rebutted.

There were still three major obstacles, all of which Philip perceived and sought to remedy. The first proved insoluble: Philip had no deep-water port where the fleet could take refuge if attacked or obtain repairs and shelter. To counter the adverse effects, Philip asked other powers for friendly treatment of his ships. He also urged all haste in the passage across the Channel. The second problem was establishing cooperation between the two commanders. He was well aware that their rivalry might result in uncoordinated actions and cause the operation to fail. Philip warned them repeatedly to cooperate and made certain that they realized they would incur his gravest displeasure if they did not. He also appointed a high-ranking official to monitor their behaviour secretly and ensure that they followed royal commands. This anonymous official would reveal his powers only after the fleet had sailed. He would restrain Santa Cruz from independent adventures, and prevent Parma from taking too many troops from the Armada. After Santa Cruz's death the king revoked his instructions. His need to bridle the marquis had conditioned the strategy, however. Philip added quite severe restrictions on what the fleet could do in the Channel – in effect, they could do nothing but respond to a direct English attack. The king nevertheless appreciated the difficulties of

19. AGS E.592 f.152; E.165 f.25.
20. Herrera Oria, 1946, esp. 134–45.
21. Herrera Oria, 1946, 145–9.

1. AGS E.594 f.8.

27

coordinating the attack and included instructions for the Armada in case Parma was not ready when they arrived or if a fusion of the two forces could not be arranged. Philip preferred an attack against the Isle of Wight, but he also thought Plymouth, Bristol and Ireland good targets. He left the final choice to the commanders, however, since they would need to consider their position, the weather and the situation in the Channel (See Section 7.ii: The Invasion Plan).

The other major difficulty was how to ensure that the Armada fulfilled its mission to cover Parma's landing in England. The king had told Santa Cruz first to notify Parma of his approach, and then either to anchor off Margate or sail up and down the Thames estuary. From this strategic position the Armada would be able to block the departure of ships from the Thames and prevent maritime movements from the north, east and south of England.[2] The fleet could also move quickly against enemy ships hindering the progress of the transport flotilla from the Netherlands. As late as July 1588, Philip considered this the best plan but he had also discussed alternatives with Medina Sidonia. The delays and lack of secrecy enabled Elizabeth to station her fleet along the southern coast well before the Armada appeared. With the English fleet already ahead of them they would achieve little by heading for Margate. Medina Sidonia hoped that Parma would be able to sail to the Isle of Wight and join them there. Parma replied that he could not. The ships were too fragile, and the Dutch rebels had taken up position near Flushing from which they could block his exit from the canals. The Armada would have to come closer.

Parma had always been vague on the crucial issue of how the Armada might 'clear the sea'. Perhaps this was because he could not predict the level or nature of the opposition to his voyage. He had at times hinted that the Armada might need to come right up to the embarkation points. He knew that this was not feasible, since most of the ships drew too much water. There was a serious risk that they would run aground if they made the attempt. Medina Sidonia was willing to come as close as he could, and this accounts for his urgent appeal to Parma to send him Flemish pilots who could guide the fleet through the dangerous shoals of the Flemish coast. It also explains why Medina Sidonia decided to stay put at the exposed anchorage off Calais and return there after the fleet was blown northwards. Calais was the nearest deep-water anchorage to Parma's embarkation ports. Once they had joined together, Medina Sidonia could have taken the boats to the centre of the fleet and protected them with his fighting vessels, much as he was doing with the hulks. Parma agreed

that the duke came 'very near'; indeed near enough to effect the merger of the two forces, but he was not there long enough. There is still some doubt as to whether Parma's ships would have been able to leave the ports without attack from the Dutch rebels.[3]

'La Felicisima Armada'

When he decided to invade England, Philip had paid careful attention to the international situation. Apart from making sure of France, he had sought to neutralize his enemies and acquire new allies. He attempted to win over James VI and John Casimir of the Palatinate, as well as leading royalists in France. He had offered his Habsburg cousins help in Poland. The Archduke Maximilian had been elected king by a small faction of Polish nobles in August 1587. Philip gave money and lent some troops when Maximilian's election was challenged by Sigismund of Sweden. Philip had always suspected his Austrian cousins of having designs on the Netherlands – and with reason. Now relations were close, and German soldiers engaged in Poland and France. Philip knew that the Netherlands had nothing to fear from Germany.[1]

As the months passed, these calculations lost all contact with reality. By the beginning of 1588, disorders in France, rumours of warlike preparations in Constantinople, Algiers and Fez-Morocco, and even the fear of a *morisco* uprising could not shake his determination to attack England. Yet the king could not impose his will arbitrarily. Officials in Lisbon, led by Santa Cruz, repeatedly stated that the fleet was not strong enough and refused to sail. At first Philip made every effort to meet their demands. He ordered further requisitions of victuals; he sent officials to borrow and seize cannon and munitions from fortifications and ships throughout his empire. Whereas many of his agents had initially regarded the Armada as a mere supporting player in the drama of the invasion of England from the Netherlands, the fleet's role grew in importance; between 1586 and 1588 it emerged as the first line of the attack. Spanish commanders had always maintained the importance of parity with the enemy, but it would be hard to achieve. Indeed, Elizabeth's fleet was constantly growing: by the end of January she reportedly had sixty ships under Drake and a further sixty under Howard.[2] And the Dutch might well add their forces to hers. Philip decided that his Armada must sail before the enemy fleets could unite; he believed that his own forces were superior, but Santa Cruz and Parma disagreed. They argued that Philip should further strengthen his forces.

It was a dialogue of the deaf. Philip maintained relentless pressure on Santa Cruz to embark

2. This is more clearly stated in the first draft of the instructions to Santa Cruz than the subsequent ones, AGS E.165 ff.6–7; it can be compared to the vaguer wording of the January one, E.165 f.29. Medina Sidonia was similarly ordered to make for Margate without fighting with the English if it could be avoided, and once there 'you will know where the duke, my nephew, wishes you to disembark the men you must give him'. E.165 ff.113–14.

3. AGS E.594 f.105, Parma to Philip, 18 July; E.594 f.125, ibid., 10 August; E.594 f.107, Parma to Philip, 21 July; E.594 f.79 ibid., 21 June.

1. AGS E.949 f.123, f.100; E.693 ff.11, 17(2), 18, 34, 108, 121, 131, 143; E.694 f.85.

2. AGS E.594 f.7.

and the marquis tried every possible delaying ploy while the Armada was building. The problem was that as it grew, it required more men and supplies. Finding troops and food might be difficult, but it was much harder to produce artillery. At the end of December 1587, Santa Cruz reckoned that he still needed 150 large guns. Yet in January he was still embargoing ships from Cadiz which would require more cannon.[3] Foundries were hastily set up in Lisbon, and to speed up the process Philip allowed them to produce large guns without ornamentation or royal arms.[4] On several occasions Santa Cruz and Medina Sidonia delayed their departure in the hope of receiving such vital supplies. For example Juan de Acuña Vela had arranged for forty cannon to be cast in Lisbon in early February 1588. Despite his earlier promise to sail, Santa Cruz would not have left without them.[5] Other less costly but important items took time to produce. So much wood was used for gun-carriages, boxes, ship repairs and household items that it became a scarce commodity. The special bombs and fireworks Philip requested for the fleet, as well as the casks needed for wine and water, could not be made because all available wood was green.[6]

Every day the Armada stayed in port meant additional expenditure. Philip may have spent over ten million ducats on the Armada during 1587; contemporary estimates reported monthly expenditure of 700,000 ds.[7] By January 1588, the king had lost patience. He pressed Santa Cruz for a definite day of departure, hinting that refusal would be regarded as rank disloyalty. In the end, Santa Cruz announced that the Armada would sail on 1 February.[8] This time he meant it. Already on 20 January he had sent some vessels down the channel to Belem. The fleet was impressive, but some observers noted grave weaknesses. Francisco Duarte, who was in charge of purveyance, thought there were too few men for so many ships.[9] The contradictory reports puzzled Philip, so he sent the Count of Fuentes to Lisbon. Fuentes found the Armada in good state, but suggested that Santa Cruz was procrastinating in the hope of getting more ships from Seville. Fuentes told everyone that the king would not tolerate further delay. With a great deal of fuss, the officials buckled down to work. In a flurry of activity, small boats ferried victuals, men and artillery from shore to the waiting ships. Not all the delay could be blamed on Santa Cruz, however: Philip had not yet sent money to pay the troops before departure. Half of the required sum had left Seville, but the rest was still to be found.[10] On 4 February, Fuentes was able to report that the fleet would sail in the next few days if Santa Cruz's health permitted. Unfortunately, the marquis died five days later.[11]

The king was saddened but undeterred. He had already considered replacing Santa Cruz during the wrangle over the marquis's role in the campaign. Indeed, Philip had been convinced for a time that Santa Cruz would resign the command. Thus he was ready to appoint the Duke of Medina Sidonia immediately after Santa Cruz died. The duke's refusal on grounds of ill-health, inexperience and poverty is well known and much misunderstood. The king did not take it seriously; he dismissed it as mere modesty and a plea for financial aid. Medina Sidonia accepted the post after being assured of favour and a sizeable gratuity of 20,000 ducats apart from his salary of 1,000 ducats a month.[12] He was highly experienced in the business of fitting out fleets and of the requisite social status. Although he had not held maritime command before, Medina Sidonia could rely on seasoned commanders such as Juan Martínez de Recalde, Miguel de Oquendo, Hugo de Moncada, Diego and Pedro de Valdés.[13] Medina Sidonia's very experience led him to demand changes in the size and structure of the Armada. He knew what provisions had been used in the conquest of Portugal and the Azores, and he was not prepared to sail without adequate supplies. On his arrival in Lisbon, Medina Sidonia declared that large quantities of powder, water, lead, artillery and many other items were needed, as well as more soldiers.[14] Don Alonso de Bazán, Santa Cruz's brother, confirmed that the fleet was short of 1,700 casks of water; the 4,000 barrels for transporting water had not been made and they lacked staves as well. Among the long list of items requested we find sacks, candles, lights, clothing and shoes, tents, weights and measures, plates and jars. The hospital was already short of supplies.[15]

In order to provide the fleet with these vital commodities, Philip was generous with licences to requisition goods and ships, and he ordered officials throughout the empire to send aid. All the staves, casks and anchors that could be found along the coast of Vizcaya were seized. Butts of cider and large quantities of bacon were taken. Other areas were scoured for meat and cheese. The shortage of such basic commodities as cheese was blamed on the recent seizures of Dutch ships along the Iberian coast.[16] Philip was intent on destroying Dutch commerce with Iberia during these years and had succeeded in reducing the volume of trade. Now he needed the items that they usually brought. Foreign merchants everywhere were encouraged to bring naval stores and provisions to Spain during these years. Prices were high, as were profits. But they ran the danger of

29

3. AGS E.429 f.41, 29 December; E.431 f.18, 2 January.
4. See cat. no. **9.27**.
5. AGS GA.220 f.9, Don Juan de Acuña to Philip, 6 February 1588.
6. AGS GA.220 f.7.
7. Thompson, 1969, 202. Ulloa, 1977, esp. 807–14. For monthly expenditure on wages, see Table 2(b), p. 36.
8. AGS E.165 f.37, Philip to Santa Cruz, 11 January 1588; E.429 f.30, Santa Cruz to Philip, 27 January, confirming the date. Many of these documents have been printed in Herrera Oria, 1946, 149 ss.
9. AGS GA.220 f.49 to Philip, Lisbon, 16 February 1588 – 14,000 men for seventy-eight ships.
10. Herrera Oria, 1946, 160–64.
11. AGS GA.220 f.7.
12. See cat. nos. **13.4** and **13.5**; Duro, 1884, I, 454–70, 480–81.
13. Pp. 219–20, 222, below. AGS E.165 ff.79–84, E.165 f.85; Thompson's article on the subject (1969) settled the matter of the duke's suitability. Further documentation about the appointment and Medina Sidonia's initial activities in Maura Gamazo, 1957, esp. 241–50.
14. AGS GA.222 f.4, GA.222 f.12; Duro, 1884, I 435–7; 475–80, 481–5.
15. AGS GA.221 f.84, 15 March 1588.
16. AGS GA.220 f.104, E.165 f.53.

being seized by the crown as well. Philip took the best ships in his ports, using them to transport men and provisions or incorporating them into the fleet. Many of the supply ships of the Armada were German hulks belonging to Hanseatic merchants. Philip had encouraged them to come, hoping they would replace the Dutch. He promised not to seize them but, as pressure built up for ships and supplies, he broke his word. Lübeck, Hamburg and Emden complained on behalf of their merchants but to no avail. The Armada was a motley collection of vessels, provisions and men – ships and sailors from all over the globe. Once a ship had been chosen for the fleet, it had to be unloaded and the crown normally insisted on compulsory purchase of its cargoes. For instance, the two Venetian ships Philip embargoed in February 1588 were laden with 2,000 casks of wine, and the royal officials bought them.[17] Some of the provisions for the fleet came there by very circuitous routes, such as the twenty-five casks of Irish fish which had been taken by French pirates and sold at Bayonne.[18]

Medina Sidonia also increased the number of guns and ammunition aboard ship. Whereas before the commanders had been happy with thirty shot per cannon, Medina Sidonia ordered Acuña to increase the supply to fifty per piece. He demanded more artillery in general. Acuña also had to provide for the forty-six new cannon that were ready by 12 March. The king and Medina Sidonia told him to have several thousand arquebuses and muskets for the pikemen to use in an emergency.[19] All these demands were simple enough, but nothing could be done without money. Before the fleet sailed, shipping in Lisbon was searched and some artillery was taken. Consequently, the Armada's collection of artillery was as varied as its food. English, Italian, German, French, Portuguese and Spanish guns of different calibres were now on board.

Philip ordered Medina Sidonia to sail before or on 1 March, but this was impossible if he was to remedy what he considered the more urgent and vital deficiencies. The weather in March was cold and stormy, making it difficult for work to proceed. Fortunately for Medina Sidonia, more anchors from Vizcaya arrived. There was a severe shortage even before a violent storm caused the loss of many anchors and cables.[20] The duke hoped also that Philip would relent and let him take at least twelve more galleys. The king had allowed some galleys to join the fleet, but revoked this order on 7 March when disturbing news from North Africa and Constantinople reminded him of dangers to his Iberian and Italian states.[21] After Medina Sidonia examined and declared a good many ships unfit for service, Philip

became thoroughly alarmed. It seemed that all his officials were blind to the dangers of delay. The longer they waited, the more powerful the enemy became; the Spanish fleet would never be strong enough to assure them of victory. None the less on 20 March he capitulated and told Medina Sidonia to fit out as many ships as possible, despite shortages of men. It was essential for his reputation to send a large fleet, even if some part of it might be poorly fitted out.[22] The king still expected the enlarged fleet to sail by 6 April at the latest.[23]

The evolution of the Armada during these months can be seen in the Table on p. 31. It is a tribute to the persistence of the commanders and the willingness of Philip to respond that so much was done to strengthen the fleet. It is also proof of the efficiency of the regime that secured provisions to fit out the ships and sustain vast numbers of men.

The Departure of the Fleet

On 25 April the royal standard was blessed in Lisbon Cathedral. Most of the soldiers and provisions were already on board and the 1,250 men chosen for the guard of honour had to be taken ashore in small boats. A tremendous roar of cannon and arquebus heralded the formal opening of the campaign. The Archbishop of Lisbon as papal legate blessed the standard carried through the gaily decorated streets by Don Luís de Córdoba, mounted on a white horse.[1] The splendid ceremony was a brief interlude in the final stages of repair and embarkation. On 9 May the Armada again made its way down from Lisbon to Belem, but strong winds prevented its progress. Several times the ships hoisted their sails but failed to clear the cape in heavy gales. Medina Sidonia became despondent. Yet on 30 May when the fleet at last sailed out of Lisbon, the duke and his men were jubilant, predicting a happy outcome.[2]

At the Escorial Philip waited anxiously, unable to understand why his campaign should now be prevented by nature. On 2 June he read a draft letter to Mendoza in which his secretary had written that the Armada had been waiting to sail for almost a month; Philip noted drily, 'There is no need for "almost" here.'[3] Adverse weather and the slow supply ships hindered the Armada's progress. Medina Sidonia was enervated by the slow pace of the fleet, and becoming seriously concerned at the shortage of drinking water. When they reached La Coruña on 19 June, the duke decided that the situation was critical and ordered the fleet to anchor. Only fifty ships were able to enter port before nightfall. The rest anchored outside the harbour or sailed nearby. After midnight a terrible storm scattered them. For two days the

17. AGS GA.220 f.37.
18. AGS E.165 f.69.
19. AGS GA.222 f.57, GA.222 f.54; Duro, 1884, I, 452.
20. Duro, 1884, I, 432–3; AGS GA.222 f.59, Oquendo's report of the storm.
21. AGS GA.220 f.4, E.165 f.86, Duro, 1884, I, 445–6.
22. Duro, 1884, I, 452.
23. Ibid., 470–75, Philip to Medina Sidonia, 25 March 1588.

1. AGS E.165 f.98, Medina Sidonia's account of the day.
2. See AGS GA.223 f.74 – compare it with some of the earlier letters in May, AGS GA.223 ff.67, 68, 71.
3. AGS Ek.1448 f.188, dated 2 June 1588.

Development of the Spanish fleets, July 1587–July 1588

Date	Ships	Tonnage	Mariners	Soldiers	Guns (B = bronze) (I = iron)	Round Shot	Powder (quintals)	Lead (quintals)	Match (quintals)
July 1587[1] Santa Cruz	37	13,930	2,762	5,054					
July 1587[2] Andalusia	82	(>11,879)	4,218	6,259	539 B 588 I	45,341	4,355	364	1,758
December 1587[3]	–	–	4,898	11,571					
February 1588[4]	114	–	5,124	12,604					
April 1588[5]	131	–	8,986	19,168	(>804 B)[6] (>946 I)	(>52,000)	(>1,625)		
May 1588[7]	141 (+10)	62,278	7,666	18,539	1,497 B[8] 934 I	123,790	5,179	1,238	1,151
July 1588[9]	131 (+7)	(c.58–59,000)	7,050	17,097					

There are many accounts of the fleet, often partial, at times extremely detailed. They are invariably contradictory, even when dealing with a small fleet such as that of Santa Cruz in July 1587. Musters were often found to be innacurate by the government because of corruption and inefficiency. Even allowing for this, it may be that the Armada was at its peak in men and ships in April, just before the men embarked and began their ordeal. But it was low on shot and powder (see n. 6). Tonnage is in Castilian tons.

1. AGS GA.221 f.6 and f.22; earlier account with variants, GA.199 f.71. This fleet was all that could be fitted out in time to sail against the English.
2. AGS GA.221 f.2. Most of these ships from Andalusia were embargoed and used subsequently, but some were too old or not appropriate and were released after they unloaded. The tonnage given was for the largest ships only.
3. AGS GA.221 f.46; note that there are fewer soldiers than in the October listing – a loss of 646 men. It could be owing to the tightening up of muster procedure or losses in the epidemic of November–December. There are only slight variants in the January figures (AGS GA.221 f.56).
4. AGS GA.221 f.59 for the naval details; GA.221 f.71, soldiers. By February there were several squadrons: under Santa Cruz; Recalde, Oquendo, Pedro de Valdes and Antonio Hurtado de Mendoza; the Levantine ships, hulks and galleasses were noted without commanders. There were already 1,123 cadets and pages and a larger number of pikemen than in other accounts. The reduction is balanced by an increase in harquebusiers, and shows the effectiveness of the marquis's attempts to turn all pikemen into harquebussiers.
5. AGS GA.221 f.139; variants in f.145.
6. They omitted the Portuguese squadron, the most substantial in the fleet. These accounts are nevertheless interesting, because they prove that 35,000 extra shot and nearly 2,500 quintals of powder were needed for the 120 or so ships of the other squadrons, now that Medina Sidonia demanded 50 rounds of shot per gun. Although I normally prefer given figures, I did alter these ones since the accountant got into a hopeless muddle over addition – AGS GA.221 f.127.
7. AGS GA.221 f.158 They did not count caravels (10).
8. *Ibid.*; AGS GA.221 f.143 – The 14 May accounts and the published version are very similar.
9. AGS GA.221 f.181 They did not count the falúas.

31

winds raged and Medina Sidonia could not get news of the fate of his ships. Over the next few weeks he heard that all were safe, but dispersed along the coast of Galicia, Asturias and Vizcaya. It would take some time for them to regroup, but when Philip heard of this latest setback, he ordered Medina Sidonia to sail as soon as the first-line ships were ready and simply leave the rest behind. The king was becoming desperate;[4] but this was unwise. Hulks or pinnaces might be of little use in battle, but they were laden with essential provisions which the heavily armed first-line ships could not carry. Furthermore, the hulks carried items that would be needed once the men landed in England, including wheels for the gun-carriages and victuals. Among the ships dispersed by the storm was the hospital hulk, which had to be recovered.[5]

Medina Sidonia therefore ignored Philip's order to sail and methodically set about remedying some of the worst deficiencies of his fleet. The water shortage – due to corruption in Lisbon and poor quality casks which leaked, rather than to Drake's raid, as Mattingly supposed – was top of the list.[6] Many vessels had suffered damage in the storm and needed repairs. Medina Sidonia was under great pressure from the king and reluctant to oppose the royal will. He became deeply depressed about the campaign. On 24 June he reported that thirty large ships and 6,000 men were still missing. The weather was bad, more like December than June. His forces were inadequate: he was convinced the hulks and Levantine ships could not weather the storms and were too slow; victuals were in short supply and of bad quality – not enough, he thought, to last two months, never mind the expected six. He told Philip that foreign seamen were sabotaging the expedition and claimed to be surrounded by incompetent officials. He begged the king to withdraw from the conflict or else remedy the shortcomings of the Armada.[7]

The news from the Netherlands was scarcely more cheerful. Parma faced serious problems of famine and plague. By March he reported that he could not provide the planned army of 30,000, but only some 17,000 men.[8] In view of the multiple delays and accidents, the reduction of the land forces in the Netherlands and the unexpected bad weather, why did Philip not abandon the campaign as Medina Sidonia suggested?

A Catholic Crusade?

A much favoured explanation for Philip's determination to attack England was his zealous support of the Catholic Church. He always declared that the main reason for the Armada was his desire to restore Catholicism in England. He did not say it was his sole motive, but it was certainly given prominence. However, the king's instructions to his commanders do note other considerations such as reputation, the cost and difficulty of defence and the need to retaliate. Philip's perception of the war as a crusade to release English Catholics from persecution and bondage affected all the men in the Armada. 'Victory is a gift from God: He gives it or takes it away as He wills. Since you are in charge of executing His work, we can expect Him to favour and assist us, unless we become unworthy of this through our sins.'[1] So began the king's formal instructions to the commanders. To secure divine favour, Philip demanded that everyone on board go to communion and confession before embarkation. He prohibited swearing and blaspheming on board ship. No women were allowed, whether prostitutes or wives. This would have upset many soldiers accustomed to taking wives and families with them on campaign. All men in the fleet were instructed to venerate God and do everything in their power to avoid displeasing Him; otherwise He might withdraw His favour. Feuds and fighting among the participants were forbidden. Similar conditions had been imposed when Christian fleets sailed against the Turks.[2] Prayers were to be said daily on board, and the many clergymen attached to the fleet ensured its spiritual health before tackling the task of reconverting the English. As pressure mounted, Philip developed a veritable obsession with sin and moral laxity in the fleet, particularly blasphemy. He wrote repeatedly to Medina Sidonia to suppress it, and to impose rigorously all other prohibitions.[3]

News of the English campaign reached many corners of Iberia as a result of military requisitions, but the king directly involved the kingdom through the Church. He requested monasteries and convents to pray for the campaign. In some instances they received special gifts. For example, Philip made donations to the Carmelite and Flemish nuns of Lisbon in February 1588. When his officials delivered the money, they asked the nuns to offer prayers for the Armada's success, and were assured of their fervent cooperation.[4] In this way, and later through the concession of plenary indulgences by Sixtus V, people of all stations were involved in the spiritual preparation of the Armada.[5]

Even the pragmatic Parma and Santa Cruz referred to God's will, particularly when their frailty or inadequacies were revealed. Medina Sidonia was far more pious, even credulous, and fully in agreement with Philip on the need for moral behaviour by the troops. He reported to the king the visions of victory retailed by nuns and monks. He made careful

4. AGS E.165 f.126.
5. See cat. no. **11.11**.
6. AGS E.165 ff.265–6, Marques de Cerralbo to Philip, 6 July 1588.
7. Maura Gamazo, 1957, 258–61, Medina Sidonia to Philip, 24 June; AGS E.165 f.134, Philip to Medina Sidonia, 5 July 1588.
8. AGS E.594 f.26.

1. AGS E.165 f.29.
2. Díaz-Plaja, 1958, 593–603, Lepanto instructions; Duro, 1884, I, 380–83 (Santa Cruz, July 1587); cat. no. **14.44** Medina Sidonia. The king's instructions to Medina Sidonia, AGS E.165 ff.106–108, ff.113–14, Duro, 1884, I, printed selected documents relating to this.
3. Ibid., also AGS E.165 f.87, GA.222 f.7, Duro, 1884, I, 426–8 correspondence between the duke and king, February and March 1588.
4. AGS GA.223 f.33.
5. Sixtus had been extremely reluctant to grant this, maintaining to the last that Philip would not launch the Armada against England. See, for example, Olivares's clashes with Sixtus in March 1587 and 1588, AGS E.949 f.39; E.950 f.37. But he renewed the grant in 1589, AGS GA.221 f.192.

arrangements to ensure that all men went to communion and confession before sailing. On 15 July he wrote with deep emotion after 8,000 men had received the sacraments: 'this is of such inestimable value that I consider it the best jewel I am carrying in the fleet.'[6] Even after the Armada's return, Philip declared that any good fortune it had encountered 'must be attributed to the public and private prayers that have been offered so devoutly and consistently'.[7] And along with most of the participants he considered the Armada's escape from destruction on the Flemish shoals as a miracle.[8]

The Spanish commanders knew they had to exert themselves in the campaign, if they were to prove worthy of divine help. The leading figures were traditional Catholics who believed that God worked miracles for the faithful but at times confounded their expectations. The unusually bad weather in 1588 was interpreted by some as a sign from God, telling Philip to desist from this war. Philip dismissed this suggestion and later the legend that these storms were caused by witches. For the time being, the king reserved judgement. But he realized that if he disbanded the fleet the Protestants would say that God had sent storms to destroy the Armada in order to save them. Consequently their heresy would be reinforced rather than suppressed.[9]

Philip also believed that the campaign would achieve his goals. His faith ensured that the Armada, whatever the drawbacks and delays, would sail. Although his confidence was partly religious, it also had a firm practical foundation: he was certain that his forces were superior to those of Elizabeth. He admitted that on land the English would muster more troops, but these were of lesser quality, still giving him the advantage.[10] Parma's forces had been reduced, but he was likewise confident that his seasoned veterans would ensure the success of the invasion.[11]

Philip's faith was boosted by the international situation in 1588. The French were once more embroiled in civil war, with the Catholics encouraged by Philip's subsidies. Ambassador Bernardino de Mendoza in Paris tried to coordinate their efforts with the Armada, and largely succeeded. The timing of the Paris uprising in May 1588 (the Day of the Barricades) also owed much more to the balance of power within France than has recently been supposed. One has to make due allowance for the repeated announcements that the fleet was on its way – nothing indicated this latest sailing date would be certain. While Philip did influence the situation, he was not in full control of Guise or other Catholic leaders. If he had been, he would not have allowed them to make peace in July 1588, when the campaign was underway.[12] Else-

where in Europe conditions were also encouraging. The English had quarrelled with the Dutch, and Philip was certain the latter would concentrate on defending themselves rather than helping Elizabeth. The Germans were still involved in Poland, and to everyone's surprise Elizabeth had not hired German soldiers. At most some Protestants might attempt a minor diversion. The King of Denmark, Elizabeth's closest ally, had died, and James VI of Scotland was unlikely to help Elizabeth while the memory of his mother's execution was still so fresh. There was no news of the Ottoman fleet, and the relationship between the sharif and Elizabeth had not developed further.

The king's reputation was perhaps the most important reason for pressing ahead with the campaign. Philip realized that the world was observing his preparations and assessing his strength. If he withdrew the loss of face would be grave, not only for him personally but also for his states and Catholicism in general. The corsairs would sail in droves and attack his lands, and Catholics in areas dominated by Protestants would lose heart. Above all, Philip was terrified that the English might launch further raids against the Iberian and New World coasts. 'An intolerable shame and disaster' was how Philip described this danger.[13] These motives: religion, reputation and defence, are found in all the proposals for invasion submitted to Philip during this period. They are also in evidence in the sermons and poetry which the campaign gave rise to; for example, in the exhortation to the troops by Pedro de Ribadeneira. Most historians cite only the paragraphs referring to the war against England as a crusade, but the Jesuit devoted two-thirds of his exhortation to explaining the economic reasons for the attack, and the damaging results of English raids on Philip's reputation.[14] Even at the lowest levels of society we find mixed expectations of religious and financial gain. In the words of a rather poor contemporary poet:

> My brother Bartolo
> Is on his way to England
> To kill Drake
> And capture the Queen.
> He will have to bring me
> Back from the war
> A little Lutheran boy
> With a chain
> And a Lutheran girl
> For our lady grandmother.[15]

By nature pessimistic, Philip apparently calculated that even defeat would bring benefits. There were degrees of disaster to consider. If the invasion failed because Parma and Medina Sidonia were

33

6. Maura Gamazo, 1957, 276, Medina Sidonia to Philip, 15 July 1588.
7. Op. cit., 278, Philip's circular to the Spanish bishops, 13 October 1588.
8. See pp. 241–2.
9. AGS E.165 f.128.
10. In March he wrote to Medina Sidonia: 'I consider this campaign so important that if my presence was not so necessary here to provide for what is needed there and in other parts, I would be happy to take part. And I would do so with great confidence that it would succeed.' Maura Gamazo, 1957, 247–8, 11 March 1588. While meant to encourage his commanders, such statements are also found in his private correspondence, as in the scribbled note written at the end of that month in which he said that unless the shortage of money caused serious impediments, he had hope in God that all would go well. AGS E.594 f.24.
11. AGS E.165 f.128, Philip's reply to Medina Sidonia's doubts.
12. Jensen, 1964, esp. 137 ff.; Constant, 1984, 166–209, and Mattingly, 1983, 204 ff., have argued that Mendoza planned the Day of the Barricades, and that Guise did not act earlier because of it, but the uncertainty over the Armada sailing date and lack of specific proof suggests that, at most, there is a strong probability of coordination.
13. AGS E.165 f.40, to Santa Cruz, 18 January 1588.
14. Díaz-Plaja, 1958, 747–64.
15. Díaz-Plaja, 1958, 746.

unable to meet, all was not lost, since each force could still achieve conquests on its own. If they failed to make a significant impact but still gave the English a severe drubbing, or a bad fright, then Philip thought a favourable peace was possible. Since November 1585, several peace initiatives had originated in England and the Netherlands. The King of Denmark attempted to mediate in 1586 and again in May 1587. Neither side was persuaded that the other was serious, yet the negotiations continued.[16] Elizabeth wanted to keep contacts open and to observe Philip's preparations in the Netherlands. At times she panicked and pursued peace ardently, hoping to avert the Spanish attack and withdraw from her commitments to the Dutch rebels. She almost persuaded Parma of her sincerity, perhaps because he wanted peace also. In April 1587, Parma was convinced that God in his mysterious way had brought her to the negotiating table. More than a year later, his optimism was fuelled by the death of Christian of Denmark, the renewed civil wars in France and the divisions between the English and the Dutch.[17]

Philip appreciated any move that would deepen the rift between the English and the Dutch, which these negotiations did very effectively. Only rarely did he take them seriously. In May 1586 he thought Parma should pursue the talks to see whether the English were willing to hand over Holland and Zeeland. When he learned they were not, Philip used the talks as a cover for his offensive. If the invasion failed, however, he would still have to consider peace; his instructions to Parma, Santa Cruz and Medina Sidonia listed his conditions. If the campaign went well, Philip told them to press for toleration of Catholicism in England and in the rebellious provinces of the Netherlands; if they were less successful, he would settle for toleration in the Netherlands only. Philip was particularly interested in the return of the fortifications and ports taken by the English. Even if he regained only Flushing, his position in the Netherlands would be greatly improved. Besides, Flushing was a good deep-water port, where another Armada might be fitted out or sheltered.

Philip's order of priorities in case of defeat is illuminating and shows his realism, for he tailored his demands closely to strategic concerns. His officials would begin negotiations by demanding Flushing, then proceed to seek compensation for English attacks and end with the issue of toleration for Catholics in England.[18] But Philip utterly rejected Elizabeth's conditions, particularly the demand for toleration of Protestants in the Netherlands and withdrawal of the Spanish army of Flanders. Although Philip had empowered Parma to conclude a treaty, he

did not wish peace while there was a chance of winning the war. Cautious to the last, neither side withdrew from the negotiations until the Armada was in the Channel. Even then Philip would have preferred the English plenipotentiaries to stay and continue the talks.

Failure of a Campaign

'Cowards! . . . Chicken-hearted Lutherans! . . . Come back and fight!'[1] The taunts of the men aboard the battered and bloodied galleon *San Felipe* had no effect on their English attackers. Having refused calls to surrender, the *San Felipe* was subjected to lethal broadsides from the powerful English guns. The ship was crippled and casualties were high, but the English still did not dare to board her. To the frustration of Philip's commanders, this pattern had been repeated throughout the battle. The Armada campaigners boasted that this proved the enemy's lack of courage, but it really proved the superiority of English ships, much more manoeuvrable than the motley Armada vessels, and of their seamanship in home waters. It also showed the wisdom of their tactics. The English knew that the troops were the Armada's greatest strength. Both sides believed that if it came to boarding, Philip's men had the advantage. The English commanders refused to take the risk and did as much damage as possible at a distance with their guns. A detailed account of the battle and its aftermath is provided in Sections 14 and 15. What we are concerned with here is an assessment of how Philip reacted to its failure.

The king had been aware of what his men could expect. In his instructions to Santa Cruz, Medina Sidonia and Parma, he had warned that the English would avoid boarding, and use their longer-range guns, which shot lower than others. But no one found a way to overcome this problem. Medina Sidonia's hastily improvised plan to use small Flemish boats to hold the English still long enough for his slower ships to board them, could not be put into effect at such short notice. There was no guarantee that it would work, either.[2] The answer to these problems was to build better-designed ships, and to procure a nearby port so as to avoid having to sail with a cumbersome supply fleet. Philip learned his lesson and attempted to remedy these deficiencies after 1588. A major shipbuilding programme was initiated and Parma was encouraged to take a deep-water port.

Spanish accounts reveal sentiments that range from exasperation to outrage. There was a distinct feeling among Philip's subjects that the English had cheated and did not deserve the prize of victory. As Don Fernando de Ayala, who was wounded in the

16. Wernham, 1966, 374–5, 387–8, 393–5 and, especially, Read, 1925, III, 125–8, 141–53, 174–7, 235, 256–8, 260–78, 284; MacCaffrey, 1981, 382, 391 ff., give a good account of the English part of the negotiations. There are numerous Spanish documents in AGS E.590, E.592, E.594 dealing with this in particular, some of the more informative can be found in E.592 ff.16 and 17; E.590 ff.47, 68, 88, 123, 143, 141, 136, 137, 139, 130, 132, 134–5; E.594 ff.83–103 (1586), E.592 ff.1, 7, 13, 21, 59, 100, 105, 134; Ek.1565, ff.54, 67 (1587); E. 594 ff.16, 28, 39, 53, 57 (1588). The end of the talks, E.594 f.113, Parma to Philip, 7 August 1588. Denmark's mediation, AGS E.592 f.5, f.6; E.592 f.105.
17. AGS E.592 f.15, Parma to Philip, 12 April 1587; E.594 f.72. ibid., 8 June 1588.
18. See for example AGS E.165 ff.174–5, E.165 ff.181–2; E.165 f.128.
1. Words reported by Coco Calderón, AGS GA.221 f.190.
2. AGS E.594 f.117, Medina Sidonia to Parma, 5 August 1588; E.594 f.120.

battle, commented, the English success 'was not due to virtue or valour, so they cannot be said to have had a victory'.[3] Contemporary English accounts readily acknowledged that there were important non-human factors which accounted for their success. In the words of the writer and propagandist Richard Hakluyt, 'never was any nation blessed of JEHOVAH, with a more glorious and wonderfull victory upon the Seas, then our vanquishing of the dreadfull Spanish Armada, 1588. But why should I presume to call it our vanquishing; when as the greatest part of them escaped us, and were onely by Gods out-stretched arme overwhelmed in the Seas, dashed in pieces against the Rockes, and made fearfull spectacles and examples of His judgements unto all Christendome?'[4] As far away as Bohemia, Protestants celebrated the deliverance of their fellows and looked for the day when Catholic powers would be vanquished.[5] It was a boost to Protestants in general and English morale in particular.

The impact of the battle was lessened by various factors, apart from the unusual weather. The campaign was prolonged and the outcome uncertain. In England there were fears that the fleet would return for months afterwards. The Spanish Monarchy was flooded with contradictory accounts ranging from the most spectacular victory to the most abject defeat. The king and his subjects were in utter confusion. By mid-October a clearer picture had emerged, but no clear-cut judgement: with more than half the fleet safe, was it a terrible disaster or a replaceable loss?

At a meeting of the Council of War on 7 September, the councillors told Philip that it did not really matter what had happened, 'what matters is that we should show great courage and continue what we have started.'[6] If the fleet had been lost, Philip must fit out another; meanwhile, he should not allow the collection of provisions to slacken and ensure that Iberia was able to withstand an attack if the campaign had failed. The councillors were under no illusions as to Elizabeth's wish to retaliate. Later that month they urged the king to improve defences throughout the empire. But they were more concerned with events in North Africa for a time than in the north. They suspected that the Turks and the Algerian corsairs would try to take advantage of Philip's temporary weakness and attack. When the Armada's long voyage around Scotland and Ireland became known, the council reiterated the need to uphold the king's reputation by mounting another campaign.[7] The tone of these exchanges between the king and his officials was stoic. There was no repetition of the panic and defeatism that emerged after the 1587 Drake raid.

Philip set to work to refit the fleet. Orders were dispatched to all parts of the empire requesting support. Galicia, Asturias and Vizcaya had to provide medicines and supplies. Officials requisitioned food and provisions, but there were also many spontaneous gifts such as those from the city of Valladolid to the sick in Santander.[8] Philip had resolved to send out another Armada as soon as possible, so all survivors of the 1588 expedition were ordered to remain where they landed. Since the ports of northern Spain were ill-equipped and small, many men had to remain aboard the battered and filthy ships. Many who had survived the nightmarish journey died of hunger and disease. 'It is pitiful to behold,' said one of the royal officials in Santander.[9] If the men were caught trying to return to their homes, they were liable to the usual penalties for desertion. Even the gentlemen-adventurers, whether waged or not, found themselves pressed into service.[10] Day after day Philip read and annotated reports, counting the number of ships lost.[11] He was overwhelmed by petitions from injured men and destitute families. The owners of ships lost in the campaign also clamoured for compensation.[12] Philip's capacity to respond to these demands would have been greatly enhanced if the pope had fulfilled his promise and paid him the one million *scuti*. But Sixtus gleefully insisted the contract was only valid if the king's troops landed in England. Olivares argued that the spirit and the letter of the agreement were in conflict. The pope had offered aid to encourage and support a holy enterprise, but Spanish pleading was to no avail. Philip had to meet the costs of the war alone. The expenses were reflected in the increase of borrowing – over 11 million ducats between 1585 and 1588. Many extraordinary financial expedients were put into practice, and taxation was drastically increased. The crown also seized bullion shipments.[13]

But the royal purse had not covered all costs. Many of the provisions taken by the fleets during the period 1585 to 1588 had not been paid for. Numerous complaints had been arriving about the excessive and unfair seizures of grain and other food by royal officials throughout Iberia. Philip had established a quota system in some areas, particularly for the provision of basic items such as grain. Nevertheless, under pressure from the central government or due to the arrival of troops, for instance, these officials had frequently overstepped the limits of what peasants and cities could provide. The Spanish writer-soldier Miguel de Cervantes was among those singled out for reproof and punishment. The town of Ecija in Andalusia complained that they had been forced to give up a large quantity of grain in 1587 and had not

3. BN Madrid, mss.5489.
4. Preface to the second edition; London, 1912–13, I, 35.
5. AGS E.694 f.6. See also Section **16**, particularly the counters and pamphlets.
6. AGS GA.235 f.71.
7. AGS GA.235 f.87, *Consulta*, 18 September; AGS GA.235 ff.90–91, 27 September. See also Section **16**.
8. AGS GA.227 f.204, but note that some 'gifts' were sent in response to the king's specific commands, AGS GA.244 f.112.
9. AGS GA.227 f.227, 4 October 1588.
10. AGS GA.245 f.146; GA.242 f.147; GA.227 f.83.
11. For example, AGS E.594 f.130, on one of Parma's letters.
12. See also AGS GA.242 ff.30–32, f.108, GA.242 f.86, petition of Pedro de Miranda and company, whose ship had been taken.
13. Ulloa, 1977, 808–12.

35

Comparison of Spanish accounts

May and July

	28 May	15 July	Missing
Ships	151	138	(13)
Mariners	7,666	7,050	358
Oarsmen	2,065	n/a	–
Cadets and pages	n/a	1,310	–
Soldiers: Total	18,539	17,097	1,191
Pikemen	–	(2,032)	–
Musketeers	–	(2,764)	–
Harquebussiers	–	(10,787)	–
Gentlemen:			
Adventurers	304	254	–
Entretenidos	282	219	–
Servants	604	450	–
Ancillary corps			
Artillery	99	124	–
Higher Officials	75	41	–
	(includes servants)		
Officers of Justice	10	9	–
Clergy	154	198	–
Hospital	93	93	–
Given total number of men	27,847	25,535	–
Given total effectives	24,615	22,436	–
Wages (per month)	182,247 ducats	n/a[1]	–

[1]250,000 ds cash
aboard the fleet

Only 8 ships were reported missing and their men counted: 3 naves, 4 hulks and 1 zabra. It is evident that 3 falúas and 1 caravel were also missing, and perhaps another small ship. Falúas and caravels were often included in the lists, but not counted in the total because they were very small and had only a few mariners apiece. There are many contradictory accounts of the fleet in May and July. I have chosen these two official accounts because they were likely to have been regarded as the final ones at court. Yet the May one in particular has some discrepancies which account for the difference in the number of soldiers and gentlemen in the fleet. By comparing it with other May accounts it is clear that it over-estimated the number of men and underestimated the number of clergy (which should be *c*.180). Nevertheless, the death toll and missing ships account for a loss of over a thousand fighting men. The published account (Lisbon, May 1588 cat. no. 8.38) formed the basis of the lists given by many historians and can easily be consulted in Martin, 1975, 266–79 and Laughton, 1981, II 376–81, among others. The figures here are taken from AGS GA.221 f.143 (14 May); GA.221 f.158 (28 May); GA.221 f.181 (15 July); other July variants, GA.221 f.179; f.188; GA.225 f.69; E.165 f.92 details of the 'royal chest'.

been paid for it before falling foul of the 1588 campaign. Cervantes had licence to commandeer all their wheat and rye, and the townsmen rightly complained that they would starve. Similar scandals shook the king and councils and led to investigations, and officials were indicted for fraud and extortion. This may have been the most widespread and lasting repercussion of the Armada campaign in Philip's kingdoms. Thompson has argued that the impact of purveyance on the economic and demographic development of certain regions like Galicia and Andalusia after 1588 was very serious, but the large-scale requisitions of the 'Armada' campaign from inception to end were highly damaging.[14] Philip also ordered an investigation into the more serious issue of rotten and spoiled victuals. A good many of the Armada casualties were due to food poisoning, and the king wanted to punish those responsible. Since rations for eight months had been provided, there should have been plenty of food for the home journey. But spoilage led to reduced rations, under-nourishment and ultimately famine on a number of the ships.[15]

It was not just fraud that Philip wanted punished. As the Armada returned he was determined to find out what had gone wrong and to mete out rewards and punishments. Philip ordered secret investigations into the conduct of all the officers. Don Ordoño de Zamudio was already at work on this task at the beginning of October 1588, questioning arrivals, trying to piece together the events. When his secret enquiry produced meagre results, Philip sent Don Juan de Cardona also. In these investigations Medina Sidonia came out fairly well. Some criticisms levelled against him were unlikely to impress Philip: for example his refusal to divert the fleet and attack the English at Plymouth or the Isle of Wight. The king knew that the duke was merely following orders when he refused. His heavy reliance upon Diego Flores de Valdés had aroused adverse comments, but was also in accord with Philip's recommendations. The one incident from which Medina Sidonia did not emerge with credit was the loss of Pedro de Valdés in the *Nuestra Señora del Rosario* on 1 August.[16] Until then the only casualties had been due to bad weather, but when the damaged ship drifted and later fell victim to Drake, the blow to morale was immense. Valdés was an aristocrat and a respected military adviser. He had clashed repeatedly with the Duke of Medina Sidonia before the Armada sailed, disagreeing with most of the war council on essential matters of strategy. The so-called crescent formation of the fleet was his idea.[17] It was easy to suspect that jealousy and revenge might have led

Medina Sidonia to act in uncharacteristic style and allow the destruction of the ship. This was a view both Pedro de Valdés and Don Gonzalo de Eraso promoted. But the case rested on slim evidence and the duke's subsequent activities show that he assiduously protected and salvaged all ships. Moreover, Medina Sidonia was known to have followed the advice of Diego Flores de Valdés on this issue and it was he who was punished, with eighteen months imprisonment.

Parma's actions were more open to criticism and have remained controversial. He declared that he had followed Philip's orders: as soon as he heard from Medina Sidonia, he ordered the soldiers to proceed to the embarkation points. Alas, he was prevented from sailing and joining the fleet by the Dutch ships and by the short period of time the Armada was in Calais. He admitted that he had not left Bruges and had delayed the embarkation of his troops until Monday 8 August. But he justified these actions on the grounds that it would not take him long. The men could not be aboard ship for long without risks of infection and illness. These arguments had a hollow ring. Medina Sidonia's messengers found Parma's transport boats lacked sails, oars and artillery. He did not have enough ships and his cavalry was not ready to leave. When he was accused of having failed to provide water casks, he claimed they were not required because it was a short journey and there was plenty of beer. When hard pressed, Parma repeated what he had always said: the expedition was not feasible unless certain conditions were met.[18] Parma hastened to assure the king that he had no more obedient and humble servant, and that it was not his fault if the campaign had failed. 'These are the works of Our Lord, who knows what He is doing and has the power to provide a remedy and compensation, by giving Your Majesty many more victories and the fulfilment of your desire.'[19]

To quell mounting criticism of his actions, Parma also sent a trusted servant to Rome, ostensibly to visit his sick uncle, Cardinal Farnese, but in truth to justify his actions in the curia. He wrote letters to leading personages in Europe giving his account of the event.[20] Philip found his actions extremely objectionable and said so. Yet despite evidence of negligence and suspicions of sabotage, Philip did nothing, and even expressed his confidence in Parma's loyalty.[21] He could not spare Parma from the Netherlands.

The king was as disappointed with the second investigation as with the first. Juan de Cardona finally plucked up the courage to say that apart from what was common knowledge and the printed reports,

14. AGS GA.226 f.42 (Ecija); GA.209 f.127, *Consulta* on the activities of commissaries, 21 August 1587; GA.208 f.11, an example of wine requisitions in 1586. The problems were the same. Thompson, 1976, 207–27.
15. AGS E.165 f.210; E.165 f.250. See cat. no. **10.5**; p. 263.
16. See pp. 237–8, below, and cat. nos. **15.4** and **15.5**.
17. AGS GA.225 f.55.
18. AGS E.594 f.113, Parma to Philip, 5 August 1588; E.594 f.124 ibid., 8 August; E.594 f.125, ibid., 10 August; E.594 f.163, Parma to Idiáquez, 30 December 1588.
19. AGS E.594 f.125; see also, AGS E.594 f.139, Parma to Philip, 29 September, E.594 f.146, to Juan de Idiáquez, 1 October 1588.
20. To judge by the copy of his letter to the Duke of Terranova, BN Madrid, mss.979 ff.96–102, the details did not vary from those he had initially reported to Philip.
21. Parma's delighted reply is in AGS, E.594, f.157.

37

little more could be extracted from those who took part in the expedition. Having dealt with the Armada survivors for a time, Cardona (and perhaps Zamudio before him) was more struck by pity for their plight than by a desire to condemn their actions. He reported: 'I have not found trustworthy evidence to name any one person other than in the incident that led to the loss of Don Pedro de Valdés, which in my view was very important.' This and the report of some financial irregularities for relatively small sums was as far as he would go. He candidly recommended to Philip not to stir up trouble. 'The high mortality rate since the return [of the fleet] – not only among the common soldiers and mariners, but also among the gentlemen – has prompted me to advise Your Majesty not to search for things that can cause the survivors further pain, but instead to praise God for the campaign. He will give Your Majesty victory as He has done in the past.'[22] Philip resigned himself to this.

The English had emerged with a greatly enhanced military reputation. They had successfully faced the enemy alone. Their ships had handled well. Philip had not expected Elizabeth to put together such a large fleet. While reading the account of the battle sent by Don Jorge Manrique in August, Philip counted the number of English ships carefully. He noted what appeared to be discrepancies in the narrative as the fifty-odd English ships first sighted grew to a hundred, then 130, and finally up to 160, with another forty vessels in Flushing.[23] Surprise, even awe, can be detected in the surviving reports of the event, as the English fleet grew daily from the medium-sized fleet the Spanish had expected to a larger, formidable force. An excellent spy network and the mercantile power of England had allowed Elizabeth to prepare a force that matched, and surpassed, that of her rival.[24]

Not all was gloom and loss for Philip II. On the positive side of the ledger, he could count on the generosity of his Castilian subjects, who were deeply affected by the tragedy. Moreover, as he had realized, even a defeat brought him some dividends internationally. Despite the rejoicing of Protestants, his reputation had increased, especially in the north. The Spanish Monarchy had been regarded as a Mediterranean and Oceanic power, not capable of substantial naval actions in northern Europe. Philip had proved his ability to launch a major campaign in the Channel and aroused considerable fear among Protestants there. Would the 'Spanish fleet' now become as redoubtable as the Army of Flanders? A further cause of satisfaction for the king was Elizabeth's isolation during the campaign. It augured well for a future attempt.

In the aftermath of the Armada neither Philip nor Elizabeth could claim to have substantially advanced their faiths or increased their power. And for both monarchs, the encounter had been costly in human and financial terms. They faced similar financial problems, but were under great pressure to raise enough money for the next campaign, which everyone agreed must be decisive.[25] But as can be seen in Section 16, new preoccupations in France would soon deflect the two antagonists to other fields and battles. Meanwhile, Philip acknowledged that the campaign against England had come to a tragic and unexpected conclusion. He was not alone in wondering why God had seen fit to give the Protestants victory. In a circular of 13 October, he informed the Spanish bishops of the event, noting that the weather had been so bad, it was surprising that so many ships had survived. He asked them to commend him to pious souls willing to pray for him, because he wished always to guide his actions according to God's will. And he added: 'I thank God for whatever He is pleased to do, and I have duly thanked Him for what has happened.'[26]

22. AGS E.165 ff.255–66.
23. AGS E.594 f.180 (2).
24. It is worth noting the surviving account of the Spanish fleet in PRO SP94/3, 13.
25. See Section 16 and notes for details of their subsequent involvement in French affairs.
26. Duro, 1884, I, 278–9.

Abbreviations

AHPGO   Archivo Histórico de Guipúzcoa en Oñate
AGS   Archivo General de Simancas
APC   *Acts of the Privy Council*
arr.   *arroba*
BN   Biblioteca Nacional, Madrid
CSPD   *Calendar of State Papers, Domestic*
CSPF   *Calendar of State Papers, Foreign*
CSPI   *Calendar of State Papers, Ireland*
CSPSc   *Calendar of State Papers, Scotland*
CSPS   *Calendar of State Papers, Spanish*
fan.   *fanega*
HMC   Historical Manuscripts Commission
IJNA   *International Journal of Nautical Archaeology*
MM   *Mariner's Mirror*
MN   Museo Naval, Madrid
NMM   National Maritime Museum
NS   New Style
NRS   Navy Records Society
OS   Old Style
PRO   Public Record Office
V & A   Victoria and Albert Museum

16th century Spanish weights and measures

Arroba   liquid measure, approx. 16 litres or 3.5 gallons.
fanega   dry measure, approx. 55.5 litres or 1.5 bushels.
quintal   weight, 100 Castilian pounds, approx. 46 kg or 101.5 lb.
codo   linear measure, 0.57 m or 1.87 ft.

All dimensions are in millimetres, height × width × depth

Note on Dates

In 1588, England was using the Julian calendar (OS, or 'old style') which was ten days behind the Gregorian calendar (NS, or 'new style') adopted by Spain and the Catholic Netherlands in 1582. Thus, for example, 21 July by the English calendar of the time was 31 July according to the Gregorian calendar (which is now in universal use). All dates after 15 October 1582 given in this catalogue are NS unless indicated otherwise.

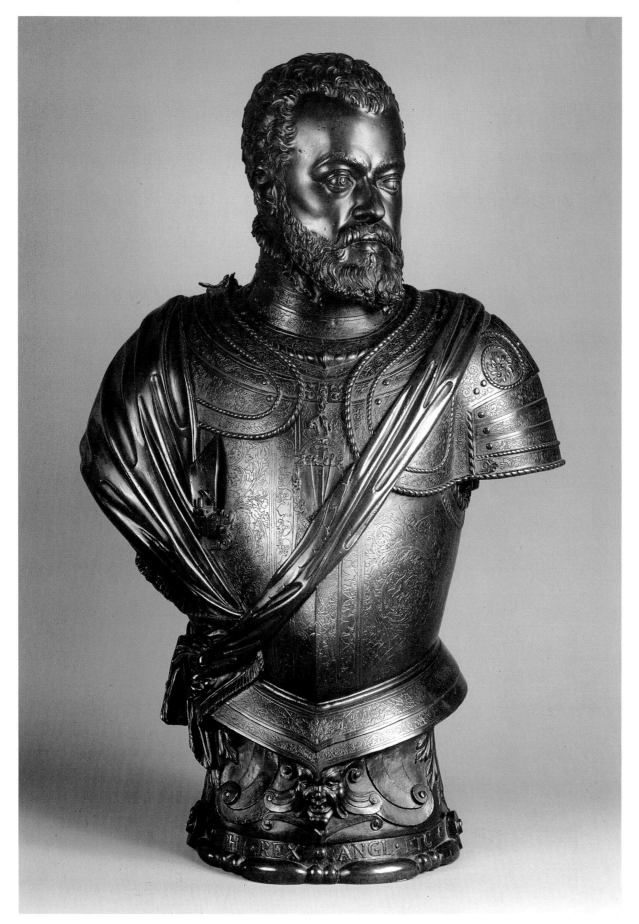

1.18 Bust of Philip II (1527–98), Attributed to Leone Leoni

1. England and Spain before the War

The marriage between Philip, heir to the Emperor Charles V, and Mary Tudor, Queen of England, took place on 25 July 1554.[1] The match was the third between the houses of Tudor, Trastámara and Habsburg in half a century. Catherine of Aragon had married two sons of Henry VII – Arthur in 1501 and Henry VIII in 1509. Mary, her only surviving daughter by Henry, had twice been betrothed to her cousin, Charles V. There were cogent reasons for these marital alliances. First, the Tudors needed support and legitimization, which marriage with the most powerful house in Christendom offered. Close commercial ties bound England to Spain and the Netherlands; the political alliance strengthened them. The greatest benefit was joint defence against the common enemy: France. The French kings had been steadily consolidating their position by marriage and war. In 1453 they dismembered Burgundy and in 1491 incorporated Brittany. These formerly independent states had provided England and Spain with allies and easy access to the French heartlands. Now they had to look further afield for support against the most populous and wealthy monarchy in Christendom.[2] The old alliance between France and Scotland was an added incentive for the English to secure support against France. But the union of England and the Habsburgs was also offensive. The English longed to reconquer Guyenne and the ports of northern France, while the Spanish wanted support in their quarrels over Navarre and Roussillon-Cerdagne, as well as a free hand in Italy. The Netherlands sought the return of the Burgundian lands.

Nevertheless, the Anglo-Spanish alliance was often uneasy. Each side used the other to gain concessions from France. There were constant complaints about privateering and piracy, frequently leading to seizures of ships and suspension of trading concessions. Henry VIII's divorce from Catherine created a long rift, yet by 1543 Henry and Charles were again fighting together against France. Since amity between their states was considered natural, their antagonism in the 1570s later provoked comment. As Lord Burghley noted, 'the state of the world is marvellously changed, when we true Englishmen have cause for our own quietness, to wish good success to a French king and a king of Scots.'[3]

Religious divisions and English fear of Philip II's overwhelming power go far to explain the revolution, but relations were also strained as a result of the marriage between Philip and Mary. At first both sides had benefited considerably. Mary gained a husband who protected her and her realm, who helped restore Catholicism and increased her prestige. But she was devastated by Philip's failure to return her love and

bitterly resented his frequent absences – he lived in England only from July 1554 to September 1555 and for a few months in 1557. The English disliked their inferior rank within a large empire. Relations with Philip were good during his initial stay, but later they felt ignored by the busy monarch. Above all, they opposed his conduct of the war against France (1557–9). Having grudgingly agreed to declare war, they demanded support for campaigns against Scotland and the Hanseatic League. Philip refused to divide his forces and gave priority to the commercial interests of the Netherlands. When the English lost Calais,

1. Loades, 1979, esp. Chapters 4 and 7. Rodríguez-Salgado, 1988.
2. Wernham, 1966; Suárez Fernández 1966 and Suárez Fernández and Fernández Alvarez 1969.
3. Russell, 1971, 229.

Family tree, illustrating the claims of Elizabeth I and Philip II to the throne of England

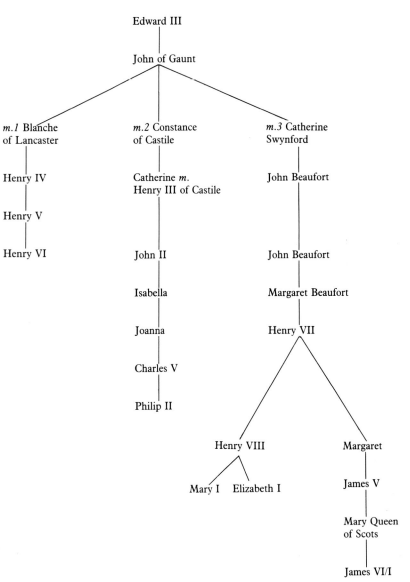

their last possession in France, in 1558, they blamed Philip, although he had offered to defend it and tried to recover it. By the time Mary died in November 1558, Philip was blamed for all the misfortunes assailing England.[4]

For Charles V and Philip II, the marriage was a diplomatic triumph. Since 1551 the emperor had suffered one defeat after another. His lands were torn by rebellion and invasion; he was too weak to support Mary's bid for the throne. Thus the incorporation of England when the empire was at its nadir was hailed as a miracle. 'The evil spirits have been dispersed!' declared Philip's favourite.[5] The psychological impact of England's adhesion to the imperial cause endured for decades. Philip and his advisers could not conceive of survival, let alone victory over France, unless England was on their side. But during the war against France the notion that England was incompatible with the rest of the empire took root. Philip saw the war as a life-or-death struggle, and he regarded the reluctance of the English government to support his strategy as almost treasonous. Meanwhile Philip's other realms, pressed beyond endurance, complained that England was not making sufficient contributions, particularly as the second campaign (1558–9) was prompted by the loss of Calais. The Count of Feria wrote to Philip: 'at a time when all your majesty's other kingdoms and states have supported the war effort with all their might, they [the English], who should have outshone the others, have done the least.'[6]

Philip was left with the indelible impression that the English were ungrateful, difficult, prone to rebellion and opposed to integration with his empire. Furthermore, he distrusted the nobility and thought that religion sat lightly on English hearts. Yet Philip had a strong conviction that God had chosen him to restore and protect English Catholicism, a policy he knew most of England would oppose.

After Mary's death, Philip's councillors were divided on how to retain the English alliance. One group pressed Philip to marry Elizabeth, whom Philip had prudently helped during his stay in England. He refused, largely because he feared it might renew the war with France; but he also felt dishonour would follow marriage to an illegitimate Protestant. None the less, a combination of French negotiations for her hand and arguments that only the marriage could save English Catholicism persuaded him to propose to her in January 1559. He confessed afterwards he felt like a man sentenced to death. As soon as the French suggested that the peace treaty must be sealed by Philip's marriage to Henri II's daughter, Elizabeth de Valois, Philip agreed and immediately

dropped Elizabeth Tudor. She was furious. Philip was then under pressure to impose a military solution. Some of his advisers believed that owing to England's internal weakness and the superior claim of Mary Stuart, Queen of Scotland and Dauphine of France, Henri II would soon lead a successful invasion of England. The Netherlands would succumb to a French attack, and the rest of Philip's empire would fall to the enemy.[7] The pope also assured Philip that his conquest of England would be easy, profitable and most pleasing to God.[8] But Philip rejected all proposals that might lead to war; he had no territorial ambitions and could not afford it. He decided to help Elizabeth build a powerful regime to deter or withstand French assault.

Henry VIII had tried and failed to promote England as the key to the balance of power between the Habsburgs and Valois. After 1559 the two great rivals concluded that the side that took the island would acquire hegemony. Thus each pursued policies to prevent the other's success. Conscious of her position, Elizabeth exploited the rivalry between Philip and France for the rest of her reign. Her successful intervention in Scotland during 1559–60 proved that a weak state could be effective when supported by Protestant ideology and surrounded by neighbours whose main preoccupation was stemming each other's aggrandizement. With Scotland friendly and France weakened by civil strife, England and Spain could afford to quarrel.

M. J. Rodríguez-Salgado

4. Rodríguez-Salgado and Adams, 1983.
5. AGS E.100 f.177.
6. Codoin, Vol. 87, 52.
7. AGS E.137 ff.95–6.
8. AGS E.884, ff.134, 135, 263.

1.1
Allegory of the Tudor Succession,
*c.*1572
**Attributed to Lucas de Heere
(1534–84)**

Oil on panel
Inscribed *The Quene to Walsingham this
Tablet sente/Marke of her Peoples and her owne
contente*, with additional inscriptions on frame
1295×1803
Amsterdam, 1984, 86; Washington, 1985,
82–3; Strong, 1987, 71–7
*Trustees of the Sudeley Collection, Sudeley
Castle*

This eulogy to peace, Elizabeth and her Protestant heritage was probably painted after the
Anglo-French Treaty of Blois (April 1572).
The inscription records that it was a gift
from the queen to her ambassador in France,
Sir Francis Walsingham (1530–90), later secretary of state. The picture makes a didactic
comparison between English fortunes during
the reigns of Henry VIII's two daughters. To
the left of Henry, Mary's bond with Philip II
draws in Mars (the god of war) from Rome,
a reference to the war with Henri II of
France. On the right, Elizabeth is linked
with the figures of Peace – who tramples on a
burning sword – and Plenty, who bears the
fruits of prosperity from an English garden
in the background. Later versions of the picture were produced in the post-Armada years
in celebration of Elizabeth's maintenance of
domestic peace: an engraved adaption by
William Rogers, *c.*1590, noted, 'Plenty and
peace throughout hir dayes are seene/And all
the world admyr's this mayden Queene.'

43

1.2
**Flemish *sacre*, or saker, 1555
Remigy de Halut (*fl.*1536–68)**

Bronze
Inscribed *OPVS REMIGY DE HALVT/
ANNO 1555* (base ring); *PHILIPVS REX*
(on first reinforce); *2082* (weight in Castilian
libras, on reinforce moulding); Turkish
inscription behind dolphins, part of which
reads *QITAR 187*
2959 lgth
Royal Armouries, 1976, 204–5
*Trustees of the Royal Armouries, London
(XIX–304)*

This *sacre*, made shortly after Philip and
Mary's marriage, was discovered in Scotland.
Its previous history appears to have been
chequered. At some time a short Turkish
inscription has been added, while the scar on
its lower right side was possibly caused by a
glancing hit in action. The gun has a stone
shot lodged in its barrel, although it was
designed to fire an iron projectile weighing
about five pounds. Remigy was *fondeur royale*
at the great gun-foundry at Mechelen, near
Antwerp, and cast many pieces for the
Spanish crown. His decorative work in this
instance includes a representation of the arms
of Spain impaling those of England.

44

1.3
Mary I of England and Philip II of Spain
English School, 17th century

Oil on canvas
Inscribed *A°1558/ETANNIS REGNEY PHELIPPI/ET MARIE DEI GRACIA REGIS./& REGINE. A.H.F. UTRIUSO & C.I./ET.H. FIDEI DEFENSOR ARCHIDUCU/AU.DU.B.M. & BRA COUNTU. H.F.F. & T/QUARTI/& QUINTO*
990×762
Scharf, 1890, 10–12
National Maritime Museum (BHC2952)

A modest copy of the well-known panel painting at Woburn Abbey traditionally ascribed to Lucas de Heere. Philip and Mary are portrayed in a room overlooking St Paul's and the Thames. They are flanked by two thrones: that on the left beneath the arms of Spain, that on the right beneath the arms of England. Unlike cat. no. **1.1**, there is no attempt to criticize the union: indeed, the inscription celebrates the extent of the sitters' combined domains: *A.H.F.* stands for '*Angliae Hispaniarum Francie*', *C.I. ET. H.* for '*Cicilie Jerosolymi et Hibernie*', *AU.DU.B.M & BRA* for '*Austrie, Ducum Burgandie, Mediolani et Brabanti*' and *FF & T* for '*Flandrie et Tirollis*'. The composition has the air of a wedding portrait, and it is conceivable that the Woburn picture was itself derived from an earlier work produced at the time of the sitters' marriage in 1554.

1.4
Medal of Philip II, 1555
Jacopo da Trezzo (*c*.1514–89)

Bronze
Inscribed (obv.) *PHILIPPVS.REX. PRINC.HISP.AET.S.AN.XXVIII* (around); *IAC TREZZO F 1555* (below); (rev.) *IAM.ILLVSTRABIT.OMNIA* (above)
67 dia.
Forrer, VI, 1916, 132–9; Forrer, VIII, 1930, 240–42
The Board of Trustees of the Victoria & Albert Museum, London (6759–1860)

Trezzo, a Milanese sculptor, was highly esteemed as a gem engraver and his medals were modelled exquisitely with great delicacy of detail. He entered the service of Philip II *c*.1553–4 and may have been a member of the first embassy sent with gifts to Mary Tudor in December 1553. He was in the Low Countries from 1555 to 1559, going to Spain with the king. In the Netherlands he made a group of medals of Philip and Mary in silver, bronze and lead, and cat. nos. **1.4** and **1.5** were probably designed as a pair.

1.5
Medal of Mary Tudor, 1555
Jacopo da Trezzo (*c*.1514–89)

Bronze
Inscribed (obv.) *MARIA.I.REG.
ANGL.FRANC. ET.HIB.FIDEI.
DEFENSATRIX* (around); *IAC.TREZ*
(below); (rev.) *CECIS.
VIVVS.TIMIDIS.QVIES*
67 dia.
*The Board of Trustees of the Victoria & Albert
Museum, London (A271–1910)*

1.6
Counter of Philip II and Mary, 1557

Copper
Inscribed (obv.) *PHS.D.G.
HISPANIARUM.REX;*
(rev.) *GECT.DE.LA.CHAMBRE.DES.
COPT.A.LILLE*
28 dia.
Hawkins *et al.*, 1885, 85–6; British Museum,
1979, pl. VI, 1
*Trustees of the British Museum, London (Med.
Ill. VI, 1)*

Cat. nos. **1.6–1.10** are from a series of
counters struck for the use of the Chamber
of Accounts at Lille. The counters continued
to be issued until 1560, despite Mary's death
in 1558; the reverse of cat. no. **1.9** has
portraits of Philip and Mary, but the arms of
Philip and his third wife, Elizabeth.

1.7
Counter of Philip II and Mary, 1557

Copper
Inscribed (obv.) *PHS.ET.MARIA.
HISP.ANGL. REG.sFLANDR:COM.s;*
(rev.) as cat. no. **1.6**
29 dia.
Hawkins *et al.*, 1885, 86; British Museum,
1979, pl. VI, 2
*Trustees of the British Museum, London (Med.
Ill., VI, 2)*

1.8
Counter of Philip II and Mary, 1560

Copper
Inscribed as cat. no. **1.6**
30 dia.
Hawkins *et al.*, 1885, 86–7; British Museum,
1979, pl. VI, 3
*Trustees of the British Museum, London (Med.
Ill., VI, 3)*

1.9
Counter of Philip II and Mary, 1557

Copper
Inscribed (obv.) as cat. no. **1.6**;
(rev.) *QVI:BIEN:GECTERA:SON:
COPTE:TROVE*
28 dia.
British Museum, 1979, pl. VI, 4; Hawkins *et
al.*, 1885, 87
*Trustees of the British Museum, London (Med.
Ill., VI, 4)*

1.10
Counter of Philip II and Mary, 1558

Copper
Inscribed (obv.) as cat. no. **1.7**;
(rev.) *G.POVR:CEVLX:DES:COMPTES.
A.LILLE*
29 dia.
Hawkins *et al.*, 1885, 87; British Museum,
1979, pl. VI, 5
*Trustees of the British Museum, London (Med.
Ill., VI, 5)*

45

1.11
**The Great Seal of Philip II and
Mary,** 1554–8

Wax
Inscribed (obv.) *PHILIP'.ET.MARIA.
D̄.Ḡ.REX.ET.REGINA.ANGL'.
HISPANIAR̄.FRANC.VTRIVSQ'.
SICILAE.IERVSALEM.ET.HIB.
FIDEI.DEFENSOR'.;*
(rev.) *ARCHIDVCES.AVSTRIE.DVCES.
BVRGVNDIE.MEDIOLANI.ET.
BRABANCIE.COMITES.HASPVRGI.
FLANDRIE.ET.TIROLIS*
150 dia.
Wyon, 1887, 74–6 and pl. XXI
British Library, London (437)

Great Seals were held by the Chancery and
used to authenticate royal orders and other
documents. This is one of only two Great
Seals (the other being that of William and
Mary) to show a husband and wife.

46

1.12
Flag with the arms of Philip II, 1554–8

Silk damask
1355×1115
Valencia de Don Juan, 1898
Patrimonio Nacional. Real Armería de Madrid (L11)

One of three pieces of a large standard bearing the arms of Philip II on the right and those of Mary Tudor on the left, with a single crown above. Made during their marriage, the blue-and-red band round the shield represents the Order of the Garter as it appears on the Great Seal of England at this time (see also cat. no. **1.11**).

1.13
Dispatch or document chest, 1567

Wood and leather
Embossed with Philip II's coat of arms
315×533×325
Archivo General de Simancas, Valladolid

Philip's determination to organize his government and increase efficiency prompted him to establish a repository for all important documents in the castle of Simancas (near Valladolid). Documents were sent there in boxes such as this one, even during his brief stays in England.

1.14
Martyrdom of English reformers, 1555–6

Engraving
264×194
British Museum, 1870, 4–5
Trustees of the British Museum, London

This print is a piece of Protestant propaganda from the period of Philip's reign in England, depicting the Marian persecutions as a massacre of the innocents, and Bishop Gardiner, one of the leading persecutors, as a wolf devouring sheep. Philip's presence in England was widely resented.

1.15
Two imported Spanish polychrome tiles, *c.*1500–20

Pottery, glaze
142×140 each
Frothingham, 1936, 9–11; Ainaud de Lasarte, 1952
Museum of London (L223/1 & L223/4)

There were long-established trade links between England and Spain. Cat. nos. **1.15** and **1.16** give some idea of the range of items traded. The tiles show the *cuenca seca* technique of decoration: designs include zoomorphic, anthropomorphic, botanical and geometric patterns. They were recovered from the chancel site of All Hallows Church, Lombard Street, in 1939.

1.15

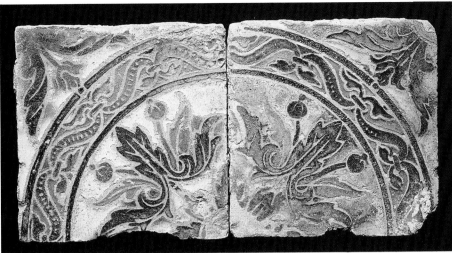

1.18
Bust of Philip II (1527–98), *c.*1554
Attributed to Leone Leoni (1509–90)

Bronze
Inscribed *PHI.REX.ANGL.ETC.*
889 ht
Plon, 1887, 297–8, 301–302; Forrer, III, 1907, 398–411; Middeldorf, 1975, 84
Her Majesty the Queen

47

1.16
Spanish olive jar, 16th century

Earthenware
Inscribed *W.C.* underneath lugs
510 ht; 220 dia.
Goggin, 1960; Martin, 1979b, 279–302
Museum of London (A17024)

Excavated in Gardeners Lane, Putney, March 1916. Jars of this kind were commonly used for the carriage of foodstuffs.

1.17
Letter from Philip II to the Count of Feria, 28 January 1559

MS
310×220
Fernández Alvarez, 1951; Rodríguez-Salgado, 1988
Archivo General de Simancas, Valladolid (E.812, f.15)

The Count of Feria was an ardent promoter of Philip's marriage to Elizabeth Tudor. He was the only Spaniard in Philip's household to have an English wife – Jane Dormer – and was deeply committed to English Catholicism. He argued that it was important to maintain close bonds with England, contain France and protect the Catholic Church: all could be achieved by the match. The king found the proposal distasteful. He opposed it on the grounds that it might provoke the French and so ruin the peace negotiations then in progress. But he was finally persuaded to propose to Elizabeth. In this letter he is adamant that he has not allowed political or personal reasons to influence his decision to pursue the match. He declares that even if Mary Stuart and the French were to take over England at once he would not be moved to propose to Elizabeth, to whom he feels no attraction. Only the prospect of saving Catholicism is irresistible. In a resigned tone, Philip placed himself in God's hand and left it up to Him to decide whether the marriage negotiations should succeed. Shortly after, Philip dropped Elizabeth without warning, having accepted the hand of Elizabeth de Valois in order to seal the peace of Cateau-Cambrésis with France.

Both this bust and its probable pair, the portrait of the Duke of Alba (cat. no. **6.2**), are said to have come from the Spanish royal collections. The technique used in both busts differs from that of Leoni's other sculptures, which have their whole surface inlaid or incised with ornament. The shallow ornamentation of these pieces suggests they originated from Flemish factories. As the inscription indicates, cat. no. **1.18** was produced at the time of Philip's marriage to Mary Tudor. The source for the head may have been the full-length bronze of Philip II (Museo del Prado), believed to have been first cast by Leoni in 1551. Vasari records that Leoni made heads of Philip II and Charles V for Alba, and it is known that busts of Philip II as King of England, Charles V and the Duke of Alba were in the Alba palace, Alba de Tormes, in the early nineteenth century. It is therefore possible that cat. nos. **1.18** and **6.2** are from a set commissioned by Alba himself.

2.1 Pope Sixtus V (1521–90), Venetian School, 16th century

2. Political and Religious Divisions in Europe

Fear, anxiety and insecurity were pervasive characteristics of the European mentality at the turn of the sixteenth century. Christians believed the devil was omnipresent, his powers now far greater than in earlier times. They sought to avoid his temptations by increasing the number of good works prescribed by the Church, thereby hoping to earn salvation. Since the priest was the mediator through whom God transmitted his grace, much depended on the effective intervention of the established Church to ensure salvation. Rife with corruption, the late medieval Church was considered by many to present a veritable danger to souls of the faithful. There was much talk of the Antichrist and the end of the world.

The call for reform was loud in the late fifteenth century, but the papacy seemed deaf to all pleas and the initiative inevitably passed to others. Rulers such as Isabella and Ferdinand reformed the worst abuses, developed institutions such as the Inquisition to eradicate dissent and encouraged religious orders to educate the people. Lay activity is evident also in the humanist movement, which refused to succumb to the general gloom, cast aside despair and promoted new models of Christian living and education to enable human beings to fulfil their potential.

The reformer Melanchthon once asked: 'What do we ask of religion?' and concluded it was two things, the 'teaching of moral and manners' which the humanist Erasmus had provided for and, more important, 'consolation in the face of death and of the Last Judgement'. This, he claimed, 'is what Luther gives us'. Luther's attack upon indulgences in 1517 developed into a general debate about papal authority and the means to gain salvation. Although he was excommunicated in 1520, many Christians were slow to condemn him. They endorsed his call for reform and reacted with emotion to his message that humanity would be saved by divine grace and not by its puny efforts on earth.

Luther and more radical Protestants broke away from the established Church, where reform was also taking place, albeit in a less spectacular fashion. During the 1530s and 1540s a number of influential religious orders were established, most notably the Theatines, Capuchins, Ursulines and Jesuits. In 1545 the general council of the Church met in Trent. Although it failed to heal the divisions in Christendom, when it closed in 1563 it had clarified many points of dogma and set out a programme for the improvement of the clergy and teaching that would later bear fruit. By then the survival of Protestantism had been assured, not because of superior theology but because of the armed resistance of its followers. The Reformation was as much a political as a religious phenomenon.

Protestant movements flourished in areas of extreme political fragmentation, such as the Holy Roman Empire and Switzerland, or where royal authority was weak, such as the border with the Ottoman Empire. Religious divisions were incorporated into existing disputes for control – the cities that sheltered Zwingli and Calvin were in conflict with the local bishops and lords from whom they sought independence; they naturally inclined to creeds that strengthened and justified their resistance. Protestant theology was invaluable to Henry VIII and Gustav of Sweden when they quarrelled with the pope. The temptation to despoil the Church of its massive wealth and thus strengthen the dynasty doubtless encouraged some rulers to embrace Protestantism, but it would be wrong to think that the change was purely due to greed. Princes were prey to the same doubts and fears of eternal damnation that coloured the lives of their subjects. Even more, their belief that sovereignty was entirely dependent on divine validation made it essential for them to have a close relationship with God and his Church.

Lutheranism was initially the most successful of the Protestant creeds. It spread in many parts of the Holy Roman Empire, Bohemia and Hungary; Denmark, Sweden and Finland were also Protestant by the 1540s. But Calvinism was to prove a far more effective rival to the Catholic Church, particularly in central and western Europe. Calvin's form of protest was more radical than Luther's and less dependent on the support of secular authority for its survival. This is natural: Luther had long regarded his movement as one of reform within the established structure and sought the help of secular princes to make his attack on the papacy more effective. Calvinism developed slightly later, when it was evident that there were many rulers as well as leading ecclesiastics who would not accept the reformed message. Neither reformer was in the least inclined to challenge the existing social order, but Calvin, conscious of the importance of urban magistrates and the need to promote the faith in areas where princes opposed it, stressed the importance of lay participation at all levels of the ecclesiastical structure, placing particular weight on 'the magistrates'. The Calvinists were well organized and quickly secured noble and urban support in France and the Netherlands. Their hierarchical structure allowed for tight control of theology and effective marshalling of resources. More importantly, Calvinists gradually developed new theories of resistance to 'ungodly' rulers that justified rebellions in Scotland, the Netherlands, Switzerland and France. The Catholics followed suit. By the 1570s both creeds justified resistance to royal authority in the name of God. The wars of religion in the second half of the sixteenth century changed the political as well as the religious structure of Europe.

Genuine calls for toleration were rare. It was the cry of the weak and oppressed during this period, and considered a transient and unfortunate position, rapidly revoked when the annihilation of the enemy was possible. Both Catholics and Protestants believed that there was only one God and one truth, and the enemies of the Lord had to be destroyed. Inevitably, these views affected the conduct of foreign policy. While all agreed that the opposing creed must be destroyed, internal problems prevented them from launching an all-out attack on the enemy abroad. It was difficult to decide whether dissent should be dealt with by tackling the internal manifestations first, even if it meant compromise abroad, or if it required the extermination of dissent abroad before the internal problem could be solved. It was an insoluble conundrum.

Catholicism and Protestantism were fairly well matched by the mid sixteenth century. No one state could assume the role of champion of the faith alone – they needed allies to defeat the enemy. Talk of leagues was rife in both Christian camps after 1559, but rulers were deterred by the general fear that once Christendom split into two opposing camps, Armageddon would follow. Moreover, traditional alliances and strategic and commercial interests cut across religious lines. United by faith, Spain and France were nevertheless still divided by their struggle for supremacy in Europe. England and the Netherlands were natural allies against the French; the Catholic emperor needed the Protestant princes against the Turks; mercenaries were hired irrespective of religion. Everywhere we find confusion and guilt as ideology conflicted with other basic requirements.

The Protestants had one further problem: knowing who was on their side. Lutherans and Calvinists deeply distrusted each other, and both were suspicious of the Anglicans. The alignments in 1588 give ample proof of the complex situation in Christendom. The pope had long advocated attacking Elizabeth and could not refuse aid, but he was afraid of increasing the power of Philip II, who already controlled much of Italy. Regarding the Spanish monarch as a threat to papal authority, successive popes allied with the emperor and the King of France to counterbalance the Spanish monarch. Consequently, they tolerated – even when they officially condemned – the alliances of these

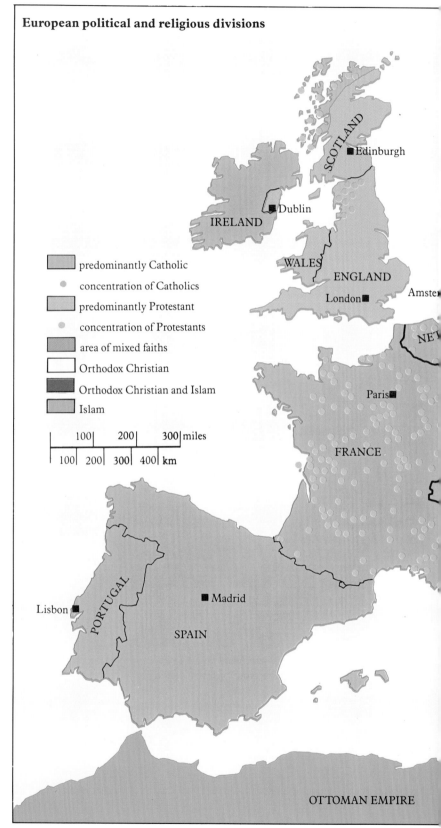

European political and religious divisions

predominantly Catholic

concentration of Catholics

predominantly Protestant

concentration of Protestants

area of mixed faiths

Orthodox Christian

Orthodox Christian and Islam

Islam

| 100 | 200 | 300 | miles |
| 100 | 200 | 300 | 400 | km |

rulers with Protestants. Sixtus V offered Philip one million *scuti*, but never paid it. Henri III of France regarded the invasion as another step towards the aggrandizement of Spain and wished to support Elizabeth, but he was held in check by the Catholic League, who were Philip's allies. The Emperor Rudolf II should have helped his uncle, but insisted on neutrality for fear that intervention would lead to renewed conflict between Catholics and Protestants in Germany. Moreover, Habsburg forces were involved in the war for the Polish succession against Sigismund of Sweden. Denmark was sympathetic to Elizabeth and willing to help if she paid, but was overtaken by a succession crisis. In Scotland, James wavered between his desire to avoid retaliation and eagerness to safeguard his claim to England. Although Elizabeth increased her pension payments, James was neutralized by the struggles between competing dynastic and religious factions at home. John Casimir of the Palatinate, who had frequently acted for Elizabeth in the Netherlands and France, would not intervene after his disastrous invasion of France in 1587, for which he blamed Elizabeth, as she had encouraged him and then withdrew support. Other German Protestants were eager to keep their commercial and financial interest in the Spanish monarchy. Moreover, it was generally believed that Elizabeth and Philip were fighting for financial and defensive motives, not out of religious zeal, so there was little temptation to use valuable resources in support of either side. Contrary to general expectations, their war did not cause general European strife. Christendom preferred to watch and wait.

M. J. Rodríguez-Salgado

(i) THE PAPACY

2.1
Pope Sixtus V (1521–90), *c*.1588–90
Venetian School, 16th century

Oil on canvas
1608×1090
Ranke, 1908, 112–59
The Vatican Museums (456)

Felice Peretti was Cardinal of Montalto before his election as successor to Pope Gregory XIII. His humble birth, eccentric manner and considerable self-confidence in international politics are aptly suggested in this notably direct portrait. Sixtus's excommunication of Henri of Navarre in support of the Catholic League was the first sign of his determination to restore and extend the scope of Catholic control – an ambition which even embraced the overthrow of the Turkish Empire and the conquering of Egypt. He constantly urged action against Protestantism, though he refused to give direct financial support to Philip II's enterprise against England, promising him instead a million *scuti* should it succeed. Curiously, the pope expressed great personal admiration for the Protestant Elizabeth I. In Rome his assiduous patronage of art and architecture aimed to enhance the splendour of the papal city: among his many projects was the erection of obelisks originally brought there by Caligula, one of which is portrayed in the top left of the picture.

2.2
Letter from Sixtus V to Philip II, 7 August 1587

MS (2ff.; holograph)
each page approx. 215×300
Archivo General de Simancas, Valladolid (E.950, f.289)

Sixtus announces that he has made William Allen a cardinal, as Philip had requested. All Rome now thinks that this signals the beginning of the war against England. He alludes to the new conditions he has attached to the grant of one million *scuti*, which in effect imposed financial penalties if Philip did not act during 1587. As he was suspicious of Philip, the pope urged him to launch the campaign immediately, and not for selfish reasons.

2.3
Cardinal William Allen (1532–94)
Edme de Boulonais (*fl.*1682)

Engraving
185×135
O'Donoghue, I, 1908, 39
Trustees of the British Museum, London (1871–12–9–2)

A Lancashire-born Catholic, Allen went into exile in 1561 and was ordained a priest at Mechelen in 1565. He founded a college for

GUILIELMUS ALANUS, S.R.E.CARDINALIS, S.T.D.
Duac.·Archiĕpus Mechlin.designatus; obiit Romæ
Aº MDXCIV.

2.5
***The Holy Bull and Crusade of Rome*,**
1588

Publ. John Wolfe, 1st ed., London

the training of missionary priests at Douai in 1568, and its graduates played a vital role in maintaining Catholicism in England. An active propagandist and leader of the English Catholics in exile, he supported military action to put Philip II on the throne and convert England back to the Catholic faith; but, paradoxically, his writings may have strengthened the loyalty of English Catholics at home to Elizabeth's government.

2.4
Medal of Pope Sixtus V; naval defence, 1588

Bronze
Inscribed (obv.) *SIXTVS . V. PONT . MAX . ANN . III.*; (rev.) *TERRA MARI SECURITAS* (Security by land and sea) 1588
34.5 dia.
National Maritime Museum (D.19)

In 1588 Pope Sixtus V (obverse) equipped five galleys to defend the coast of the States of the Church, shown at their base in the harbour of Civita Vecchia (reverse).

Printed book
185×260
Shaaber, 1929, 126–9
British Library, London (G.6068.(1))

This book, which appeared in October or November 1588, is an English translation of a Dutch work published the previous September in Middelburg. It contains a copy of the papal indulgences for the Catholic forces and a German description of the Armada, and served as a propaganda piece deriding the papacy, Catholicism and the Armada. John Wolfe was perhaps the most prolific English printer of books and pamphlets connected with the Armada: between June 1588 and March 1589 he put out at least sixteen different works on this theme.

(ii) RELIGIOUS CONFLICT

2.6
The St Bartholomew's Eve Massacre, 1572, *c.*1575–80
François Dubois (1529–84)

Oil on panel, signed
940×1540
Amsterdam, 1984, 92–3
Musée Cantonal des Beaux-Arts, Lausanne (729)

54

The massacre of 3,000 Huguenots by a Parisian mob on the night of 23–24 August 1572 followed the assassination of the Huguenot leader, Gaspard de Coligny, by royal agents led by the Duc de Guise and encouraged by Catherine de Médici. Catherine's decision to abandon her strategy of mediation and conciliation was prompted by Coligny's growing influence over her son, Charles IX, and his plans to lead France (in alliance with William of Orange and Elizabeth I) into war with Spain. This painting by Dubois, a Huguenot who fled to Geneva after the massacre, portrays the entrance to the Louvre in the background,

2.7

Coligny's house in the middle distance and uncompromisingly graphic scenes of slaughter around them. A wounded Coligny is ejected from his window (this occurred at 2 a.m.; he was later hung from a gibbet in the street) whilst his son-in-law Charles de Téligny attempts to escape across the roof-tops behind. The figure in black in the left background leaning over a pile of bodies represents the queen mother. The event sparked off similar massacres in the provinces, killing many thousands more Protestants before the end of the year, forcing the Huguenots to temper their political aspirations.

2.7
Massacre of Huguenots at Vassy, 1 March 1562

Engraving
460×620
Museum of London, 1985, 30–31
French Protestant Church of London

The massacre of French Protestants in a church at Vassy by the Catholic troops of François, Duc de Guise, signalled the beginning of civil war in France. Guise is shown here (marked *B*) supervising the massacre. Many of the congregation of 1,200 died.

2.8
The sack of Mechelen, 1–4 October 1572

Engraving
263×345
Parker, 1977, 140–41
Trustees of the British Museum, London (1948–4-10-2-81)

Mechelen briefly declared for the Prince of Orange on 30 April 1572, but surrendered to Alba when Orange retreated. Alba allowed his unpaid troops to sack the town, and the atrocities committed induced many other rebel towns to submit to the Spanish. Sufferings such as those depicted were often the lot of the losers in sixteenth-century political and religious conflict.

2.9
Martyrdom of Franciscan friars at Gorkum, 25 June 1572, ?c.1580
After J. Nolin

Engraving
Inscribed *MARTYRIOS YVARIA SVERTE DE TORMENTOS QUEIAIDISCIERONLOS FRAYLES DEL ORDEN DE S FRANCISCO*

ENFIANDES PEREL NOMBRE DE CHRISTO NOS S
335×415
Trustees of the British Museum, London (1870–10-8-2869)

A crude adaptation of an earlier print, commemorating a massacre by the Sea Beggars. An inaccurate Spanish inscription and some changes have been added.

P. EDMONDVS CAMPIANVS *vande Societeyt* Iesv, *ghehanghen ende ghevierendeelt voor het gheloof binnen* Londen.

56

P. EDMONDVS CAMPIANVS ROBERTVS SHERWINVS, *ende* ALEXANDER BRIANTVS *van de Societeyt* Iesv *worden te* Londen *voor het gheloof ghehanghen ende ghevierendeelt.*

2.10
Edmund Campion (1540–81)
J. M. Lerch (*fl.*1659–84)

Engraving
266×168
O'Donoghue, I, 1908, 331
Trustees of the British Museum, London (1862–2–14–486)

While at Oxford, Campion was admired for his eloquence and patronized by Leicester. Later he became a Jesuit and was sent by Allen to England as a missionary, but he was quickly betrayed and executed for treason.

2.11
Martyrdom of Edmund Campion, Robert Sherwin and Alexander Briant at Tyburn, 1 December 1581
Frederick Bouttats the Younger (d.1676)

Engraving
277×184
National Portrait Gallery, London

Campion, Sherwin and Briant trained together at the English College at Douai and shared a brief career on the English mission. This engraving is an example of martyrdom propaganda popular with Catholic exiles abroad and shows Campion praying for the queen as the cart is driven away.

P. ROBERTVS PERSONIVS ANGLVS
Soc. Iesu Socius et Superior P. Campiani in priā Missione Anglicana obiit 15. Ap. 1610 Ætatis suæ 64.
Ascendit ex adverso et opposuit murum pro domo Israel Ezech.13.

2.12
Robert Parsons (1546–1610)
Carlo Gregori (1719–59)

Engraving
Inscribed *ROBERT PARSONS ENGLISHMAN/Society Jesus companion and Superior to Campion/within English Mission:died.approx.1610 Aged 64/He Ascends from adversity and is placed near the Lord. Ezech.13*
205×146
O'Donoghue, III, 1912, 420
Trustees of the British Museum, London (1863–2–14–547)

A convert and able pamphleteer, Parsons was ordained in 1578 and travelled with Campion as a Jesuit missionary to England, where he set up a secret printing press and published tracts on piety. In 1581 he escaped to France and was involved in various plots against Elizabeth.

2.13
***The second Volume of the Ecclesiasticall Historie, conteining the Acts and Monuments of Martyrs**, 1583*
John Foxe (1516–87)

Publ. John Day, 4th ed., London
Printed book (2,154 pp.)
385×250
Maltby, 1971; Oastler, 1975, 26–8
British Library, London (4824.k.2)

The Martyrdome of Iohn Cardmaker, and Iohn Warne Martyrs.
The Martyrdome of Iohn Cardmaker, and Iohn Warne,
Philosopher. An. 1555. May.30.

Foxe's book was a Protestant martyrology based on existing documentation. It was first published in its complete version in 1563, and many editions followed. An immensely popular work, it soon took its place beside the Bible as the staple reading of Protestant England. Day and Foxe collaborated closely from the beginning, although the earlier editions were not always well printed. The fourth edition was of better quality and was produced, despite Day's bad health at the time, at an estimated cost of £850.

2.14

A discovery and playne Declaration of sundry subtill practises of the Holy Inquisition of Spayne, 1569
Reginaldus Gonsalvius Montanus. Transl. V. Skinner

Publ. John Day, 2nd ed., London
Printed book (99 pp.)
190×130
Maltby, 1971, 32–43
British Library, London (G.11738)

The Elizabethan view of the Spanish Inquisition was based largely on this work and Foxe's *Book of Martyrs* (cat. no. **2.13**). Montanus was in some way associated with the Lutheran community of San Isidro in Seville, destroyed in 1557–8. His book, meant as a warning to Englishmen, was an instant success in Latin and was immediately translated into English, French and Dutch.

2.15

Historia Ecclesiastica del Scisma del Reyno de Inglaterra . . ., 1588
Pedro de Ribadeneira, S. J. (1527–1611)

Printed book, publ. Madrid
145×100
Fuente, 1868
British Library, London (4707.a.33)

Ribadeneira was a favourite of St Ignatius Loyola, who trained him. He travelled to England with the Count of Feria in 1558. In this book, dedicated to the future Philip III, he traces the growth of Protestantism in England from Henry VIII to 1587. His avowed aims were, first, a desire to teach control of the 'libertine passions' he believed motivated Henry VIII; second, to praise Spain by telling the life of Henry's 'saintly' Queen Catherine; third, being a Jesuit, he wished to recount the suffering of his fellows in England. Official support for the work can be detected in its simultaneous publication in Madrid, Zaragoza, Lisbon and Antwerp in 1588.

2.16

An admonition to the nobility and people of England, 1588
William Allen (1532–94)

Printed book (60 pp.)
160×100
Wood, I, 1813, col. 615ff.
British Library, London (G.6067)

To further his aim of restoring England to the Catholic faith, Allen published a number of works, of which the present one is perhaps the best known. Few copies have survived; most were destroyed shortly after publication.

2.17

A Declaration of the Sentence and deposition of Elizabeth, the usurper and pretensed Queene of Englande, 1588
William Allen (1532–94) or Robert Parsons (1546–1610)

Printed broadsheet
Publ. Antwerp
490×340
British Library, London (C.23.e.14.)

This broadsheet was drawn up by either William Allen (see cat. no. **2.3**) or Robert Par-

sons (cat. no. **2.12**), both committed to military intervention in England by Philip II. It was intended for promulgation by Parma's forces in the event of a successful invasion of England.

2.18

Crucifix from the *Girona*

Bronze
Inscribed *INRI* on a horizontal band near the top of the cross
81 ht
Crédit Communal, 1985, 10.2
Ulster Museum, Belfast

A simple bronze cross, whose arms and foot

terminate in points; there is a suspension-loop at the top. Just above the foot there is a skull. The figure of Christ is missing.

2.19

Ring from the *Girona*

Gold
Inscribed *IHS*
27 dia.
Sténuit, 1974, 241; Crédit Communal, 1985, 10.4
Ulster Museum, Belfast

Large, heavy gold ring with circular bezel on which is engraved the sacred monogram *IHS*, surmounted by a cross; beneath the monogram is a symbol resembling a widened *fleur-de-lys*. The shoulders of the ring bear linear ornament. This ring may have belonged to a member of the Society of Jesus, for in 1541 Ignatius Loyola adopted the *IHS* sigma in his seal as General of the Society and it subsequently became the mark of the order.

2.20

Agnus Dei* reliquary from the *Girona

Gold
39 ht
Sténuit, 1974, 242; Crédit Communal, 1985, 10.5
Ulster Museum, Belfast

A lidded gold receptacle in the form of a book; the cover lifts to expose a hollow container in which are five small circular compartments and a large rectangular block. The cover, elaborately decorated overall, has a central area, framed with columns, in which is engraved a representation of St John the Baptist, bearing an oriflamme cross. The back has a rectangular compartment where, presumably, a relic was protected by a crystal or glass cover. When found the reliquary contained a small wax tablet – an *Agnus Dei*. These tablets, made of the wax of paschal candles and blessed by the pope on the Wednesday of Holy Week, were supposed to possess miraculous protective properties. Frequently they were impressed with the image of the Lamb of God, carrying a cross or flag. On the reverse was often the image of a saint or the name or arms of the reigning pope.

2.21

Religious medal from the *Trinidad Valencera*

Copper
Inscribed *SALVAM TE*
31 ht
Crédit Communal, 1985, 10.7
Ulster Museum, Belfast

Small, oval religious medal of copper, with a representation of the Madonna and Child on one side; on the other is a head of Christ in profile and the inscription *SALVAM TE* (that I may save thee). There is a suspension-loop at the top and three small lugs.

2.22

Religious medal from the *Trinidad Valencera*

Pewter
32 ht
Crédit Communal, 1985, 10.8
Ulster Museum, Belfast

Small, oval, pewter religious medal with a representation of the Madonna and Child on one side; on the other the head of Christ in profile and an indecipherable inscription. There is a small suspension-loop at the top.

2.23

Cover of ewer or altar cruet from the *Girona*

Silver-gilt
40 dia.
Crédit Communal, 1985, 10.9
Ulster Museum, Belfast

Small circular lid, the flat top of which is decorated with engraved concentric circles;

the lid is surmounted by an *A* in a circle; the *A* stands for *Aqua*, and the existence on board of an altar cruet for water suggests the existence also of one with a *V* for *Vinum*; in turn the presence of these two implies the existence on board of the minimal requirements for the mass, i.e., at least a chalice, paten and pyx.

(iii) FRANCE

2.24

Catherine de Médici (1519–89), *c*.1560

Studio of François Clouet (before 1522–72)

Oil on panel
239×191
Musée Carnavalet, 1979, 17–18, 20–21
Musée Carnavalet, Paris (P2127)

Born in Florence, Catherine married Henri II in 1533. After the king's death in 1559 she acted as chief adviser and regent to her sons, François II, Charles IX and Henri III. She struggled to uphold the authority of the monarchy in the face of religious strife, rival networks of noble families and foreign interference. Although she remained a Catholic, she was not dogmatic and promoted compromise between the warring religious factions at home. After 1572 she was less influential, but still played an important role in the negotiations between Henri III and Guise in 1588. The portrait is one of several from the hand or studio of Clouet, who shared some of his sitter's enthusiasm for Florentine culture and its dissemination in France. The striking marquetry frame is Flemish, and dates from the early seventeenth century.

60

Le peintre n'a pourtraiƈt que la beauté des Yeux
De ce Roy magnanime & non pas sa vaillance
Car il la doiƈt grauer luymesme dans les Cieux
Mille fois plus au vif par le fer de sa lance.

·1587·

Honeruogt

2.25
Henri III (1551–89), 1587
Léonard Gaultier (1561–1641)

Engraving
Inscribed *LG* and *Honervogt* (Jacques
Honnervogt the Elder), plus verses
244×172
V & A, 1966, 254
*The Board of Trustees of the Victoria & Albert
Museum, London (E.1265-1960)*

This engraving is after a drawing, now in the
Bibliothèque Nationale, Paris, by an unidentified French artist. It was published as propaganda for the sitter's cause at the height of
the 'War of the Three Henris' (1585–9) during which Henri III lost control of most of
his kingdom. Henri's attempts to impose
royal authority over the competing religious
and noble factions ended with his assassination (see cat. no. **16.21**).

2.26
**Henri III and his court at a ball
celebrating the marriage of Anne,
Duc de Joyeuse to Margaret de
Lorraine-Vaudémont**, *c*.1581–4
Attributed to Hermann van der Mast
(1550–1604)

Oil on canvas
1220×1850
Colliard, 1963, 147–51
*Musée National du Château de Versailles (MV
5636)*

The ball was held in the Louvre on 24
September 1581 to mark the marriage
between the king's sister-in-law and one of
his court favourites, the Amiral de France,
the couple portrayed in the centre. To the
left sits Henri III beside his mother
Catherine de Médici and his wife Louise, and
behind them stand the Dukes of Guise,
Mayenne and d'Epernon. The painting thus
records the main groupings of the royal
entourage – ones which remained in harmony

only until 1584. The Valois court's
enthusiasm for fêtes and its patronage of the
arts is well documented; a number of com-
positions similar to the exhibited picture are
in existence (e.g., at Château de Blois;
Musée de Rennes; Gaasbeck Castle).

2.27
François, Duc d'Anjou (1554–84)

Line engraving
140×121
National Maritime Museum (F1242)

This engraving is from *Les Guerres de Nassau* . . . by Willem Baudart (2 vols, Amsterdam, 1616), a history of the Dutch revolt. Anjou was a younger brother of Henri III, and actively involved in the French civil wars, not always on the side of the crown.

62

2.29

2.29
Henri IV of France (1553–1610)
Attributed to Guillaume Dupré (1574–1647)

Bronze
210 ht
Migeon, 1904, no. 215
*Musée National du Château de Pau
(DP53.3.6; on loan from Musée du Louvre)*

As with most images of Henri IV, this fine portrait bust in miniature aimed to present the king as a spirited, humorous individual of evidently sharp intelligence. As a leading Protestant noble he had been closely involved, from 1568, in the Wars of Religion. Marriage to the king's sister in 1572 – part of Coligny's shortlived programme of Protestant–Catholic reconciliation – was followed by his imprisonment after the Massacre of St Bartholomew and temporary conversion to Catholicism to save his life. Though subsequently recognized by Henri III as heir to the throne, he had to fight for his inheritance. The death of both the king and Guise in the War of the Three Henris (1585–9) brought him to the throne without serious challenge. He was to pursue a vehemently anti-Habsburg foreign policy, cultivating both French patriotism and his own authority, and worked at the same time to defeat or reconcile leaders of the Catholic League.

2.28
Henri de Lorraine, Duc de Guise (1550–88), known as 'Le Balafré', *c.*1576–88

Engraving
Inscribed *Voicy l'Amour du peuple . . . et trembler l'univers; par le blond; Avec preuileie de la sainte union*
380×258
*Trustees of the British Museum, London
(R.6–41)*

Guise, a member of the most powerful Catholic family in France, became leader of the Holy League formed in 1576 in reaction to growing Huguenot influence. Motivated by religious fervour and ambition, and with Spanish support, Guise drove Henri III out of Paris in 1588. The king took revenge later in the year by having Guise murdered. The engraving is a piece of League propaganda, the poem celebrating Guise as a champion of France and the Church, 'Behold the Beloved of the people . . . Behold this fearless Mars . . .' Guise's nickname, 'Le Balafré' (Scarface) came from the facial wound he received in battle in 1575.

2.28

2.30
Henri IV of France (1553–1610), 1595
Antonio Tempesta (1555–1630) after Nicolaus Van Aelst (1525–1612)

Etching
482×359
V & A, 1966, 766
The Board of Trustees of the Victoria & Albert Museum, London (E.3608–1960)

One of many likenesses of Henri IV on horseback (others include the Victoria & Albert Museum's equestrian statuette by Le Sueur) representing the king as a man of action and military hero. The print was published during a significant period of his reign: having re-converted to Catholicism in 1593, he was finally admitted to Paris in 1594, and received absolution from Pope Clement VIII in 1595. In October 1595 he forced the submission of the Duc de Mayenne, leading to the dissolution of the Catholic League.

HENRICVS IIII REX GALLIÆ ET NA VARRÆ

Nicolo van Aelst formis Romæ 1598.

64

2.32

(iv) THE OTTOMANS AND CHRISTENDOM

2.31
The Siege of Malta: *Zeitung aus der Insel Malta . . . und zum hefftigsten belegert hat . . . 1565 jars*

Publ. Hans Wolff of Nuremburg
Hand-coloured woodcut
355×477
Bradford, 1961
National Maritime Museum (70 G 1565C)

In March 1565 Suleiman the Magnificent sent an expedition of 40,000 men to capture Malta. The island was the headquarters of the Knights of St John, a crusading order dedicated to the war against Islam, whom Suleiman had already evicted from Rhodes. The resistance of the 700 knights and their retainers from May to September against an overwhelming force became a legend which inspired Europe and stemmed the Ottoman advance into the western Mediterranean.

2.32
Battle of Lepanto, 7 October 1571, *c.1572*
Signed 'H. Letter' (?South German School)

Oil on canvas
Inscribed *IL.GIO.ANDREA.DORIA; LA CAPITANIA DENEGRNI; OCHIALLRE.DALGIERIFUGE DALLABATTA.GLIA.HLETTER*
1265×2338
Royal Academy, 1983, 401
National Maritime Museum (BHCO261)

On 25 May 1571 Pope Pius V proclaimed a Holy League with Venice, Spain and other Christian allies to check expansion of the Ottoman Empire. Over 200 galleys and other vessels under Don Juan of Austria attacked the slightly larger Turkish fleet about forty miles from its base at Lepanto (Navpaktos) on the western coast of Greece. The Turks lost 180 vessels and over 25,000 men, including most of their commanders. Christian losses were about 7,000. This contemporary painting highlights the encounter between the Christian right wing under the Genoese admiral Gianandrea Doria, with the Turkish left under Uluj-Ali (Ochiali), King of Algiers. It is based on a Venetian engraving of 1571–2 and may have been executed for the Genoese Negroni family whose *capitana* or flagship appears beside Doria on the left. To the right Uluj-Ali makes his escape. Don John and the Turkish commander Ali Pasha are in the middle distance.

2.33
Don John of Austria (1547–78)
Jan van Belcamp (*fl.c.*1624–52)

Oil on panel
712×584
Lord Sackville, Knole

One of the heroes of his age, Don John was the illegitimate son of the Emperor Charles V and half-brother to Philip II of Spain. His successful suppression of the *Morisco* revolt in 1570 in Spain won him command of the Holy League fleet against the Turks. Its victory at Lepanto in 1571 owed much to his leadership. After further distinction in North Africa and Italy he was sent as governor to the Spanish Netherlands in 1576 (see cat. no. **6.3**). This idealized picture, one of a series at Knole, probably based on engravings, is by a well-known early copyist of historical portraits for the English court. Don John wears the insignia of the Golden Fleece, the highest order of Burgundian chivalry.

2.33

2.34
Standard of Don John of Austria, 1571

Silk damask embroidered with gold and silver thread and coloured silk
Inscribed *SOLI DEO GLORIA*
600×560
Valencia de Don Juan, 1898; Calvo Pérez and González, 1983, 74
Patrimonio Nacional. Real Armería de Madrid (L16)

The standard depicts the crucifixion on one side and the Virgin Mary on the other. It is one of five standards embroidered for use during the campaign leading up to the Battle of Lepanto in 1571.

65

2.35
Votive model of the *Real* galley of Lepanto, late 16th century
Unknown Spanish maker

Wood
1140×660 (over oars)
Martínez-Hidalgo, 1971, no. 100;
Guilmartin, 1974
Museu Marítim de Barcelona (Diputació de Barcelona)

The large crucifix – the Santo Christo – carried by the *Real* of Don John at Lepanto is preserved in a chapel of Barcelona Cathedral. This model was also placed in the chapel after the battle as an *ex-voto*, or thank-offering, and is presumed to have been intended as a representation of the *Real* herself. Modern ideas of scale and accuracy rarely apply to such votives and any actual resemblance is probably slight. The *Real* would have had two masts, but also had at least thirty banks of oars and was highly decorated. None the less, the model shows the general arrangement of galleys as a type; the one- or two-masted lateen rig, the rowing

frame or *apostis*, the central *corsia* or gangway and the disposition of the main artillery under a forward fighting platform or *arrumbada*.

2.36
Lantern from the galley of Mahomet Bey, 1572

Painted wood with metal frames and glass panels
2070×720×720
Valencia de Don Juan, 1898, 383;
Guilmartin, 1974, 72
La Marquesa de Santa Cruz

This lantern was captured by the Marquis of Santa Cruz from a Turkish galley of Mahomet Bey, the son of Hassan Pasha, the Bey of Algiers. Lanterns of this kind were mounted at the stern of a flagship. See also cat. no. **8.29**.

2.37
Blade of the scimitar of Ali Pasha

Steel with gilded inlay
Arabic inscription
885×43
Valencia de Don Juan, 1898
Patrimonio Nacional. Real Armería de Madrid (M.18)

Ali Pasha was the supreme commander of the Turkish fleet at Lepanto, and his death in the battle helped to ensure the Turkish defeat. This scimitar was among the many prizes taken by the Christians.

2.36

(v) CENTRAL AND NORTHERN EUROPE

2.38
Emperor Rudolf II (1552–1612)
Unidentified artist, 17th century

Oil on panel
620×510
Her Majesty the Queen

The sitter was Archduke of Austria (1576–1608), King of Hungary (1572–1608), King of Bohemia (1575–1608) and Holy Roman Emperor from 1576. Eccentric to the point of alleged insanity, Rudolf pursued his interests in alchemy and the occult arts with rather greater consistency and renown than he was to achieve as a European ruler of considerable and troubled domains. He sought conciliation between Protestants and Catholics with a view to the overthrow of the Ottomans, and failed on both fronts, quarrelling bitterly with his ambitious younger brother Matthias, to whom he was forced to give up all but his emperorship by 1611. The portrait is one of several extant likenesses conveying something of Rudolf's notable flamboyance in old age; there is a full-length version at Apsley House. Individualistic to the end, he refused the last rites of the Church on his deathbed.

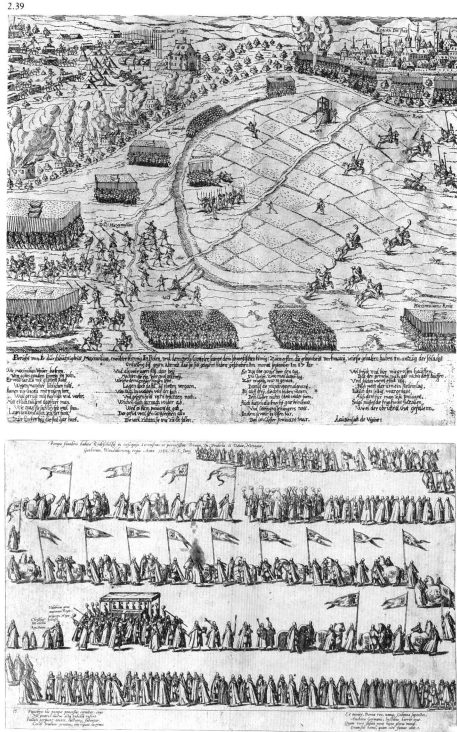

2.39

68

2.41

The Siege of Cracow, 1587

Engraving
238×269
Trustees of the British Museum, London (52-4-24-83)

A propaganda print in support of the Archduke Maximilian's claim to the Polish throne. It depicts the unsuccessful siege of Cracow which had to be lifted in December 1587. Maximilian is shown with his camp and the mixed squares of German cavalry, pike and arquebus.

2.40

The situation in Poland, 1587–8: *Puntos de papeles que (h) an benido en el despacho de Don Guillén de San Clemente* (Summary of the papers sent with Guillén de San Clemente's dispatch), 24 February 1588

MS
311×211
Archivo General de Simancas, Valladolid (E.694, f.8)

Guillén de San Clemente was Philip's ambassador at the Imperial court. Among the papers he sent was a letter from Archduke Maximilian to Rudolf II (25 January 1588) announcing his defeat and capture by the Polish forces, and requesting assistance. Philip II had supported his cousin's bid for the Polish throne but could spare no more resources. The struggle tied down Imperial, Swedish and Polish forces in 1587–8.

2.41

Funeral procession of Frederick II of Denmark, 15 June 1588

Engraving
Inscribed Titles of Frederick II; Latin poem, *Funebris hic pompe . . . cito fumus abit* (eight lines)
212×340
Trustees of the British Museum, London (1861–11–9–431)

The death of Frederick II deprived Elizabeth of the possibility of immediate aid from Denmark. This engraving depicts all the pomp of a royal funeral of the period, the horses shrouded in mourning, halberds and the ceremonial sword carried reversed, and the king's bier borne by courtiers. Frederick's successor, the young Christian IV, can be seen following the bier.

(vi) SCOTLAND

2.42

John Knox (1505–72), from *Icones, id est Verae Imagines, Virorum Doctrina et Pietate Illvstrium . . .*, 1580
Theodore Beza (1519–1605),
apparently after Adrian Vanson

Publ. I. de Laon, Geneva
Wood engraving in printed book
335×225
SNPG, 1975, 26
British Library, London (611.e.3)

John Knox was a major figure in the Protestant Reformation in Scotland. He was condemned as a galley slave and later exiled to England and Geneva for his part in a rebellion against the Catholic French Regent of Scotland, Mary of Guise (1547). His revolutionary Calvinism embraced radical theories of resistance to ungodly rulers, and these were once again put into practice on his return to Scotland in 1559. By this time

IOANNES CNOXVS.

Mary of Guise had succeeded in alienating the Scottish aristocracy, and Knox's renewed calls for rebellion thus found crucial support from the nobility in the ensuing civil war. In 1560 he persuaded the Scottish Parliament to accept the Calvinist faith. Beza was Calvin's successor at Geneva, and this woodcut is thought to have been based on a portrait of Knox by Vanson, sent to Beza from Scotland.

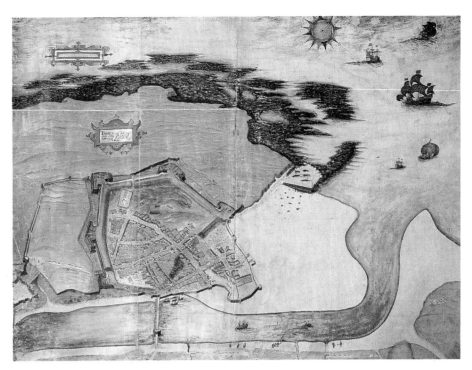

69

2.43

Plan of Berwick-on-Tweed, *c.*1570

Pen and watercolour
Inscribed *THE true description of her Maigties towne of Barwick*
550×745
Colvin *et al.*, 1982, 607–64 and pl. 41
British Library, London (Cott. MS Aug.I.ii.14)

The fortified garrison town of Berwick was the most important English stronghold on the Scottish border. The fortifications were modernized between 1558 and 1570 at a cost of almost £130,000, making it the most expensive defensive project of Elizabeth's reign, and a mark of the continuing English fear of attack from Scotland. While the defences were superficially impressive, they were criticized by contemporaries as militarily ineffective and poorly constructed. Perhaps fortunately, they were never put to the test.

2.44

The Memorial of Lord Darnley,
*c.*1568

Livinus de Vogelaare (*fl.*?1551–68)

Oil on canvas
Extensive inscriptions
1397×2210
Jacques, 1822, 101–27; Buchanan, 1958,
116; Millar, I, 1963, 76–7
*Trustees of the Goodwood Collection, Goodwood
House*

This allegorical picture is an indictment of
Mary Stuart's complicity in her husband's
murder. Set in a chapel, the composition
portrays in the centre an effigy of Lord
Darnley; on the sarcophagus are two reliefs
describing his murder (probably organized by
Mary's lover and subsequent husband, the
Earl of Bothwell) on 9 February 1567.
Darnley's brother and their parents – the
Earl and Countess of Lennox, for whom the
painting was conceived – are depicted on the
right praying for vengeance, and in the
centre kneels his infant son, James VI.
Mary's subsequent surrender at Carberry Hill
to the insurgent Scots lords, whose banner
shows Darnley's corpse and the inscription
*JUDGE AND REVENGE MY [CAUSE]
O LORD*, is represented (bottom left) along
with Bothwell's flight. The artist is known
only through this and a possibly earlier version of the picture in the Royal Collection.

2.45
The Regent Morton, 1577
Unidentified artist

Oil on canvas
Inscribed *Regint Morton 1577 Nec Temere Nec Timide*
551×459
Mackie, 1978
Scottish National Portrait Gallery (PG 839)

James Douglas, 4th Earl of Morton, was one of the leading figures of the Protestant faction which gained control of Scotland after the fall of Mary Queen of Scots. He conspired to murder Lord Darnley and to depose Mary and Lord Bothwell (1567). He helped to secure the coronation of the thirteen-month-old James VI in 1568. Morton was regent from 1572 to 1578 and suppressed the Catholic nobles. They in turn accused him of Darnley's murder and secured his execution in 1581.

2.46
Mary Queen of Scots and her son James, 1583
Attributed to Arnold von Brounckhorst (*fl.*1565–83)

Oil on panel
546×762
Auerbach, 1961, 265–71
Duke of Atholl, Blair Castle

This is the earliest life-sized portrait of Mary, although there are some early full-lengths of James. The source of this depiction is unknown, but a similar portrait-type of James VI has recently been attributed to his Flemish court painter, Arnold von Brounckhorst, who was appointed in September 1580. The cap and jewels are identical, the face type matches perfectly and both are inscribed with the date 1583. The portrait aims to stress James's legitimacy and strengthen his authority through the visual link of mother and son.

2.47
The Babington plot, 1586
Mary Queen of Scots (1542–87)

MS (4ff.; contemporary copy)
295×204
CSPSC, 1585–6, 525–30
Public Record Office, London (SP53/18, 51)

The unsuccessful plot by Anthony Babington, to assassinate Elizabeth and release Mary Stuart, furnished proof of the latter's complicity in Catholic conspiracies and helped to build the case for her execution. This is a copy of Mary's last letter to Babington, authenticated by three of the chief plotters, Babington, Nau and Curle, some two weeks before they were executed.

72

2.48

**The execution of Mary Queen of
Scots (1587),** *c.*1613
Netherlandish school, 17th century

Watercolour
219×264
SNPG, 1987, 51–2
Scottish National Portrait Gallery

This drawing was originally part of an album
illustrating the history of the period, compiled by a Delft magistrate. It shows Mary
before her execution on 18 February 1587,
clutching a crucifix, while outside her garments are burned to prevent their use as
relics. The costume and architecture are dis-
tinctly Dutch.

(vii) IRELAND

2.49
Seal-matrix of George Dowdall, Archbishop of Armagh

Silver
Inscribed + *SIGILLV GEORGII + DOWEDAL DEI GRACIA + ARCHIEPI ARMACHALL TOCI HIBI PMATIS*
105 ht
Ulster Museum, Belfast (A60:1906)

Silver seal-matrix of George Dowdall, Archbishop of Armagh and Primate of all Ireland between 1543 and 1558. The seal shows the archbishop seated between St George and St Christopher beneath an arcade, with the archbishop's arms below.

2.50
Sword from Lough Neagh, 16th century

Iron, steel and copper
926×149
Halpin, 1986
Ulster Museum, Belfast (A1:1970)

The blade of this sword bears an inlaid copper-alloy cross pomme, which suggests that it is an import from Germany (the cross pomme is considered a German mark imitating an Italian one). However, the open ring-pommel of the hilt-form is characteristically Irish.

2.51
Pair of Irish spurs

Bronze and iron
112×70
Seaby, 1966
Ulster Museum, Belfast (280:1964)

Two similar Y-shaped spurs decorated with a foliate design of raised loops, possibly derived from tongue or ovolo moulding and showing Italian Renaissance influence. The arms bear a series of diagonal grooves, with raised edgings, alternately plain and hatched. Such spurs might be considered the last of the purely traditional Irish form.

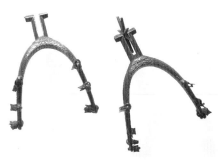

2.52
Irish battle-axe from the River Bann, Cos. Antrim/Derry, 16th century

Steel
182×153
Ulster Museum, Belfast (L46:1934)

This is a characteristic Irish Galloglaigh axe, descended from the 'Lochlann' axes of the Viking period, although the only reference to their manufacture in Ireland is in 1589. In section from shaft-hole to cutting-edge the blade of this axe-head shows a thickening, at its greatest 30 mm from the cutting-edge.

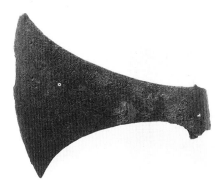

73

74

2.53

Map of the siege of Smerwick Bay, November 1580

Watercolour
452×513
Hickson, 1892, 264; Dunlop, 1905, 322; Jones, 1954–6; Glasgow, 1966; Salisbury, 1966; Dolley, 1967; Public Record Office, 1967, 579
Public Record Office, London (MPF 75)

This map shows the siege by English forces of the 'Golden Fort' erected at Smerwick by a Hispano-papal expeditionary force. The siege ended on 10 November 1580 with the surrender and subsequent massacre of the defenders. The map is a finished copy of an earlier sketch: both were made under the supervision of William Winter, who was captain of the *Achates*. It has considerable importance for it shows named royal ships, naval guns used in a land role, and the tactics employed by the English fleet. The *Swiftsure*, *Aid*, *Revenge*, *Marlyon* (or *Merlin*) and the *Achates* all took part in the campaign against the Armada, and the drawings of them here may be portraits of the actual ships.

2.54
Sir John Perrott, Lord Deputy of Ireland (1527?–92)
Valentine Green (1739–1813), after G. Powle

Mezzotint
170×112
O'Donoghue, III, 1912, 453
Trustees of the British Museum, London (C1.111 P.1)

Perrott was a successful viceroy and highly regarded by the Irish chiefs, but in December 1587, he was replaced by Fitzwilliam as Lord Deputy of Ireland. This eighteenth-century print is after a contemporary portrait.

2.55
Letter from Sir John Perrott to the Privy Council, 15 October 1587

MS (2ff.)
298×210
CSPI, 1586–8, 418–19; Falls, 1950, 162–7
Public Record Office, London (SP63/131, 50)

Perrott's letter encloses intelligence from Spain suggesting that an invasion of Ireland was threatened. He expresses fears about the loyalty of the Irish and says that the English forces in Ireland are too few, too poorly equipped and supplied and too dispersed to be able to resist an invasion. Ireland was not in fact the primary Spanish objective, but fears such as these led to the savage treatment meted out to the Armada survivors.

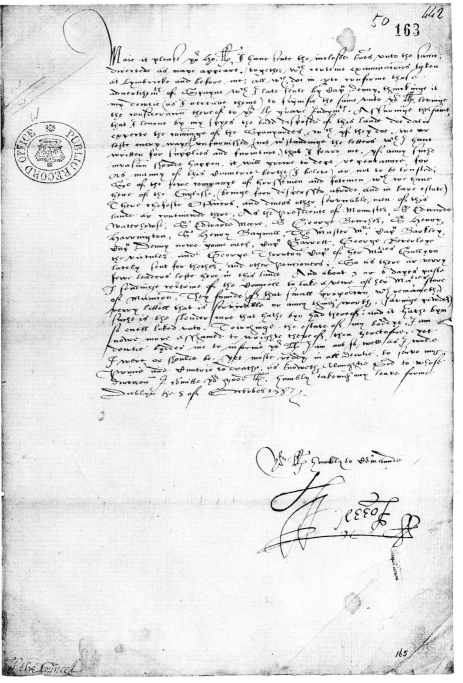

75

3.2 Elizabeth I (1533–1603), Attributed to John Bettes the Younger

3. The Court of Elizabeth I

An effusive pamphleteer recounting Elizabeth's entry into London on 14 January 1559 was moved to write: 'if a man should say well, he could not better term the City of London at that time, than a State wherein was shewed the wonderful Spectacle of a noble hearted Princess towards her most loving people.'[1] The term spectacle is indeed apt. Elizabeth was an excellent actress, always at her best when playing to the gods. Lacking prestigious dynastic connections, she made a virtue of her insularity and loudly vaunted her Englishness, making much of being one with her 'people'. It was just what the realm wanted after their subjection within the multinational empire of Philip II. In that first major ceremony, she was already presented with a role: that of 'Deborah, the judge and restorer of Israel'. The comparison with an Old Testament sovereign was meant to reassure those who doubted the ability of females to rule, as well as to provide her with a model: Deborah had been chosen by God to save His people. Elizabeth was required to do the same – embrace and extend the Protestant faith, and bring justice, peace and plenty. The analogy was also intended to suggest that England was the New Israel.

In the course of her long reign, Elizabeth acquired other famous attributes and images which she accepted and developed. There were comparisons to other biblical figures like Judith and Esther, but also to classical myths – the moon goddess, Belphoebe, Astraea, Tuccia the vestal virgin. The images were all meant to convey sagacity, the dawn of a golden age, and – as she became older and less likely to marry – chastity and virginity.[2]

As in the case of the emergence of Gloriana, the personification of glory and success by which she is still popularly known, the myth-making was most intense when the queen and country were most threatened. It was during the 1570s, after the queen's excommunication and open invitation to Catholics to challenge her, that the Accession Day tilts developed. These colourful pageants were designed to enhance her image and show her power by depicting the subjection of the nobility to the idealized queen in the best courtly-love tradition. The 1580s and 1590s saw the creation of the most striking images: in literature Spenser's *The Faerie Queene*; in painting the work by Gheeraerts and Hilliard, where each image is more distant from reality than the next, until the queen is deified.

Players need costumes and the pageants in which Elizabeth played required glittering ones. She had a great passion for jewels and rich clothing and encouraged her male courtiers, at least, to be equally resplendent. It was important to give outsiders the impression of wealth. Elizabeth did not tolerate female competition and always demanded to be the centre of attention. All the recent studies of her court stress her 'sexual jealousy' which expressed itself in the exclusion of certain females from court and periods of anger with courtiers who married.[3] As the queen aged, the court aged with her and the atmosphere was more claustrophobic than festive. At her accession many offices changed hands; she brought back old Tudor families, but after this there were few changes of personnel. When death removed some official or lady-in-waiting, Elizabeth was likely to appoint their son or daughter to the post or consolidate the office with some other. She was also mean with her rewards and was constantly cutting down court expenditure. The result was a rather closed court with intense rivalry for the restricted number of posts and patronage. The queen prevented her ladies-in-waiting from playing a political role, but their proximity to her allowed them to have some influence in patronage and this was beneficial. It prevented the smaller inner circle in the Privy Council from monopolizing patronage, whilst leaving them unchallenged in political affairs.[4] Court ceremonial was not as rigid as in many Continental palaces, but it became more so in the 1580s, not least because Elizabeth herself wished to stress that access was a great privilege. In this, as in so much else, the myth of 'open doors' to her people proved more enduring than true, especially in the 1580s when her summer progresses were suspended. These progresses stimulated aristocratic building, especially in the south, but the queen did not spend much on palaces and construction.[5]

The pastimes of the queen and courtiers were standard: hunting, hawking, music-making or attending theatrical and musical performances, bowling, cards and dice. Elizabeth also enjoyed reading and dancing and the atmosphere was cultured, even if that culture was rarefied. But there was a darker side to the court: gambling was rife and seemed to have been getting out of control by the 1580s. There was also a high degree of feuding and violence in and around the court, of which the Oxford–Knyvett feud was the most spectacular, featuring illegitimate children, several murders and beatings during 1580–83.[6] Elizabeth may have been adored by her nobility in pageant, but only because she was wise enough to leave them largely unfettered in their localities and willing to protect them from the law when they transgressed.

Since the early 1570s the Protestant tone of the court had been reinforced by the association of religious and political conservatism with rebellion. Addi-

1. Pollard, 1964, 368; see cat. no. **3.12**.
2. Yates, 1977; Strong, 1977; Strong, 1987.
3. The term was used by S. Adams, 'Eliza Enthroned? The court and its Politics', in Haigh, 1984 and by Loades, 1986. See also P. Wright, 'A Change in Direction. The ramifications of a female household, 1558–1603' in Starkey, 1987.
4. Ibid.
5. Adams, 1984, esp. 72–3; Nichols, 1823; Dunlop, 1962.
6. Stone, 1964, 112–13; Loades, 1986, 190–97.

77

tionally, the Earl of Leicester was able to place more of his relatives and associates in important posts, and their leanings were towards a more active and interventionist, even extreme, Protestantism. Inevitably, the threat of war and invasion exacerbated and polarized religious tensions. The queen saw herself as the defender of the faith within Christendom – it was not simply a propaganda ploy. Nevertheless, both Elizabeth and her chief adviser, William Cecil, were at heart cautious and moderate, disliking extremes and risky policies and, above all, spending money. The result of this caution and of England's unique religious development, outside the main currents of Catholicism and Protestantism, was to heighten the sense of isolation in England and to nurture the development of the extraordinarily vibrant, if insular, court culture of her reign.

M. J. Rodríguez-Salgado

78

3.1

Tableau of the Court of Elizabeth I
Designed by Martyn Bainbridge, 1988

The exhibition's first tableau is a composite interior and exterior view of Greenwich Palace in the year 1588. Using John Bettes' portrait of Elizabeth (cat. no. **3.2**) as the source, we see the queen and her attendants in one of the state rooms at Greenwich. A typical sixteenth-century court interior is evoked with the rush-matting floor covering, Turkey carpets and the gilded leatherwork hanging behind a velvet state chair. The diorama behind is shown to give a bird's-eye view of the palace of 'Placentia' at Greenwich, which stood on the site of the present Royal Naval College opposite the National Maritime Museum. On the hill can be seen Duke Humphrey's Tower, which was replaced by the Royal Observatory in the seventeenth century. Greenwich, the birthplace of Elizabeth, was one of a number of palaces used by the queen; others were Nonsuch, St James's and Richmond. Queen Elizabeth's famous review of her troops took place downriver, at nearby Tilbury.

3.2

Elizabeth I (1533–1603), *c*.1585–90
Attributed to John Bettes the Younger (*fl*.1570–d.1616)

Oil on panel
1193×915
Strong, 1987, 117–19
National Maritime Museum (BHC2680)

One of a group of five portraits of Elizabeth I from the studio of a minor English painter. It is unlikely that the queen sat to Bettes for any of them; as with most extant portraits of Elizabeth it tells us more about the image cultivated around her than about her true physical appearance. More a regal icon than a human portrait, the densely bejewelled figure bears a sceptre of office before a background of green tiles decorated with gold. Painted during the years of the greatest political tension with Spain, the picture aims to convey a sense of courtly magnificence and the unstressed authority of the monarch.

3.3

William Cecil, 1st Baron Burghley (1520–98), riding his grey mule
English school, 16th century

Oil on canvas
Inscribed *CORVNUM VIA VNA*
1310×1130
Caw, 1904, 93–4; Poole, I, 1912, 15–16; Strong, 1969b, 32; Auerbach & Adams, 1972, 51–2
The Curators of the Bodleian Library, Oxford

Burghley, Lord High Treasurer and Queen Elizabeth's chief minister from 1572, was the dominant figure in English politics for forty years. He was closely involved in the diplomatic and political manoeuvres leading to the outbreak of the war with Spain, and helped to plan the naval and military campaign of 1588. Burghley well understood the publicity value of portraiture; the queen apart, there are more portraits of him than of any other English public figure. The picture of him on his mule, taken from the earlier of two standard face patterns, is an image unique in English art of the time. It exemplifies his role as elder statesman and man of business. He is dressed in the familiar Tudor black cap with ear flaps and a brown-and-gold brocaded cloak and surcoat, with the lesser George suspended from a chain. He holds a sprig of honeysuckle and pink and his shield of arms hangs from a tree. The appearance of the flowers and tree, and of the mule itself, stand as symbols of constancy, loyalty, fortitude, nobility and humility. Lord Burghley's partiality for riding mules and donkeys is none the less well attested. In 1578 Lady Mason sent him a gift of a donkey, and in 1586 Burghley himself ordered a replacement for the aged mule given to him several years earlier by the French ambassador.

Cor Vnum Via
Vna.

3.4

Sir Francis Walsingham (1530–90)
Attributed to John de Critz the Elder
(1555–1641)

Oil on panel
762×635
Strong, I, 1969a, 321
National Portrait Gallery, London (1807)

80

Although there are other versions, this is the
only extant portrait-type of the sitter; it was
probably painted in the 1580s when de Critz
is known to have been employed by Walsingham on several occasions. Walsingham
began a career in foreign affairs by gathering
intelligence abroad for Burghley. After a later
spell as ambassador in Paris (see cat. no. **1.1**)
he was made a secretary of state in 1573, an
office he held until his death. He was notably
close to the queen during the 1580s (he is
portrayed wearing a cameo of her, set in
gold), but she did not pay immediate heed to
his advice in 1587 to make serious preparations against an impending Spanish invasion
attempt.

3.5

Elizabeth greeting Dutch emissaries
Dutch or German School, 16th
century

Gouache
Inscribed with names of those present,
*Liseter/Amiral/Konigin von Schotland/Vestlan/
Walsbrun/Konigin/Ambassadur*
244×375
Rijksmuseum, 1984, 87
Staatliche Kunstsammlungen, Kassel (10430)

Elizabeth is shown receiving two emissaries
from the Netherlands, Vestlan and Walsbrun,
in her Privy Chamber, *c.*1585. Also depicted
are the Earl of Leicester, the Lord High
Admiral, Mary Queen of Scots and 'Ambas-
sadur' Walsingham. Although its precise subject is not explained, the picture may be seen
as a commentary on the significance of Mary
Queen of Scots's influence in relation to
negotiations regarding Spain and the
Netherlands.

3.6
Cameo pendant of Elizabeth I, *c*.1600

Enamelled gold, diamonds, onyx cameo
58×28
*The Board of Trustees of the Victoria and
Albert Museum, London (M33–1985)*

Onyx cameo pendant of Queen Elizabeth I in
a gold frame enamelled with flowers and set
with diamonds, with a smaller diamond
pendant below. A number of cameo portraits
of Elizabeth are known, but this one is
unusual in being double-sided. The reverse
of the portrait bears personal emblems of the
queen, the imperial column device and the
sun, while the sea and a town are also depicted. The emblematic references which
would remain concealed in normal wear suggest a close association with the queen, and
the cameo was possibly her personal gift.

3.7
The Knyvett Seal and Case, *c*.1580

Sapphire seal with gold and enamel case
45×31
V & A, 1980, 61
*The Board of Trustees of the Victoria and
Albert Museum, London (M52–1980)*

Engraved with the arms and crest of Sir
Thomas Knyvett (1539–1618). The seal is
swivel-mounted in a horseshoe-shaped gold-
and-enamel setting and is unique in retaining
its original oval hinged case of gold and
enamel.

3.8
Phoenix badge of Queen Elizabeth, ?1570–74

Silver
Inscribed (obv.) *ELIZABETHA
D.G.ANG.FR.ET.HIB REGINA* (outer);
*+HEI MIHI QVOD TANTO VIRTVS
PERFVSA DECORE.NON HABET
ETERNOS INVIOLATA DIES* (inner –
Alas! that virtue endowed with so much
beauty, should not uninjured enjoy eternal
life); (rev.) *FELICES ARABES MVNDI
QVIBUS VNICA PHOENIX
PHOENICEM REPARAT
DEPEREVNDO NOVAM.O MISEROS
ANGLOS MVNDI QVIBUS VNICA
PHOENIX VLTIMA FIT NOSTRO
TRISTIA FATA SOLO* (Happy Arabs
whose only Phoenix reproduces by its death a
new Phoenix. Wretched English whose only
Phoenix becomes, unhappy fate, the last in
our country)
44×41
Hawkins *et al.*, 1885, 90–91, 124–5; Strong,
1963a, 135–6; Yates, 1977, 38, 58–9, 65–6;
British Museum, 1979, pl. VIII, 17
*Trustees of the British Museum, London (Med.
Ill., VIII, 17)*

The phoenix is a symbol of Elizabeth's
virginity, royal dignity and the sanctity of
her government. The inscription on the
reverse was composed by Walter Haddon,
Master of Requests, and the medal introduced a new profile image of Elizabeth. It
may have been produced in response to the
papal excommunication of 1570.

3.9
Elizabeth I
Nicholas Hilliard (1547–1619)

Miniature
51×48
Inscribed *ER; Ano Dm. 1572; AEtatis suae 38*
Strong, I, 1969a, 101; Strong, 1987, 79
National Portrait Gallery, London (108)

Hilliard's earliest known portrait, this is one of only two extant miniature likenesses of Elizabeth painted before 1576. The artist did much to raise the reputation of the miniature genre and to nurture the growing demand for images of the queen.

3.10
An Elizabethan Maundy, *c.*1565
Levina Teerlinc (?1483–1576)

Miniature
65×55 (originally rectangular)
Murdoch *et al.*, 1981, 45; Strong, 1987, 55
Lent privately

Daughter of the Flemish illuminator Simon Benninck, Teerlinc came to England in 1546 to enter the service of Henry VIII. This is one of nine limnings presented to the queen as New Year's gifts from 1559 until the artist's death; it shows Elizabeth (lower left), at the traditional Royal Maundy ceremony, wearing a long white apron, advancing to wash the poor women's feet.

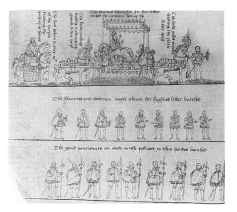

3.11
The Earl of Leicester, 1576
Nicholas Hilliard (1547–1619)

Miniature
Inscribed *Anō Dm. 1576–/AEtatis Sue 44*
45 dia.
Strong, I, 1969a, 194
National Portrait Gallery, London (4197)

Leicester was a patron of Hilliard who, in 1571, prepared for him a 'book of portraitures'. This miniature was painted shortly before Hilliard visited France.

3.12
Elizabeth I's entry into London, 14 January 1559, *c.*1560–70
English School, 16th century

Pen and ink drawings, bound in volume
385×275
Strong, 1963a, 100
College of Arms, London (MS M.6)

This is one of a series of drawings made soon after the event, probably by one of the heralds. The representation of the queen and the litter is taken from an early woodcut of Elizabeth.

3.13
Queen Elizabeth standing in a room with a latticed window
William Rogers (*fl.*1589–1604), after Isaac Oliver (d.1617)

Engraving
258×199
O'Donoghue, 1894, 161, pl. 140; 1910, 88; Hind, I, 1952, 811; Strong, 1963a, 30
National Maritime Museum (P74)

Second state, cut down from a full length of which only one impression is known, this is 'perhaps the most justly famous of all engravings done in England during the Tudor period' (Hind). Probably based on the drawing by Oliver in the Royal Library, Windsor, although it is likely that the setting is Rogers' own invention.

3.14
Treasury account book, 1572–3

MS
364×130
Strong, 1977, 114–16
National Maritime Museum (CAD/A/1)

The book illustrates the liberal expenditure
of the Elizabethan court on liveries for royal
servants. Goldsmiths, embroiderers and
various craftsmen helped to create the cult of
Queen Elizabeth through theatrical and symbolic use of imagery in court ritual and
public display.

3.15
Elizabeth I, *c.*1570–75
English School, 16th century

Marble
495×580×201.5; 1404 dia.
Strong, 1963a, 145
The Earl of Scarbrough, Leeds Castle

This is the only known contemporary bust of
Elizabeth. It was perhaps originally in
Lumley Castle (but it is thought not to be
the same as that depicted in the Lumley
inventory of 1590). Though the sculptor is
unknown, he seems to have been English;
the work was well executed by the standards
of English sculpture of the period.

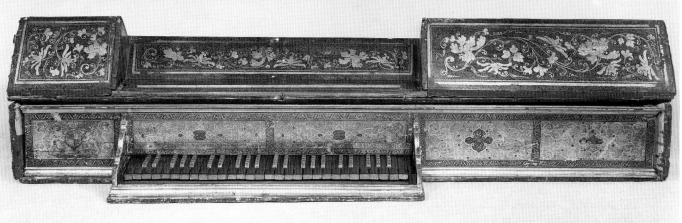

84

3.16
Spinet known as Queen Elizabeth's Virginals, *c.*1570
Unknown maker, possibly Venetian

Wood, gesso, gold, felt, bone and metals
180×410×1520 (spinet); 215×585×1650 (case)
Thornton, 1968; Schott, 1986
The Board of Trustees of the Victoria & Albert Museum, London (19–1887)

This instrument has been associated with Elizabeth because it bears the Tudor royal arms (to the left of the keyboard) and a badge depicting a crowned falcon on a stump, with a sceptre (to the right). This was a device used by Elizabeth and her mother Anne Boleyn, and makes it very likely that this was a possession of the queen. The spinet is very similar to an instrument of 1571, now in Leipzig, made by the Venetian Benedicti Floriani, and the general decorative style of this piece was very popular in Venice at that time. The forward-facing surfaces of the spinet are decorated with moresques in red and blue glazes on a gilded ground (the yellowing of the varnish over the glaze makes the blue now appear green). The keyboard, which has a range of fifty notes, is probably not original, and the outer case of the spinet dates from about 1680.

3.17
H KAINH ΔΙΑΘΗΚΗ NOVUM TESTAMENTUM, 1576
Publ. Henricus Stephanus, Geneva
Printed book (178 pp.)
120×75
British Library, London (C17.a.14)

This New Testament in Greek belonged to Elizabeth I. It has been rebound in leather, but attached to the front and back covers are the remnants of the original white and coloured canvas binding, embroidered with the arms of Elizabeth I and other motifs, including the Tudor rose. Elizabeth was a scholar who read Greek with ease.

3.18
A lead-glazed earthenware candle-sconce

Inscribed *E.R.* and initials *A.M.* behind candle sockets
395×272
Hobson, 1903, B.278; Rackham, 1939
The Trustees of the British Museum, London (MLA 1855, 12–1, 40)

The central panel is decorated in relief, with a large crowned Tudor rose under the royal arms of England, which are supported by pilasters displaying early-Renaissance ornament. A virtually identical sconce in the Brighton Museum and Art Gallery is said to have come from Hampton Court, and it is possible that they were both commissioned by royal or aristocratic clients. This piece was made in the Rhineland or by an immigrant potter in southern England.

3.19
The Burghley Tankard, *c.*1572–5
Probably made at Jacopo Verzelini's glasshouse, London

Glass, silver-gilt, enamel
213 ht
Tait, 1979, 56
The Trustees of the British Museum, London (1897, A.F.3134)

The tankard is a tube of colourless glass, mounted in silver-gilt. The lid is heavily embossed, with a free-standing disc in the centre, containing a medallion enamelled with the arms of William Cecil, Lord Burghley. The escutcheon-shaped thumbpiece also bears his crest and there is a standing figure of Justice on the handle. The shape resembles that of contemporary, tall, narrow tankards of silver and hardstone.

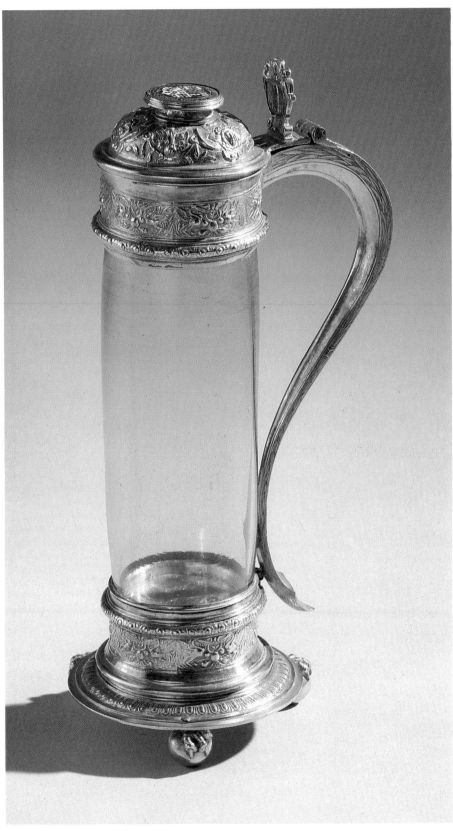

3.20
The Bacon Cup, 1574
?Affabel Partridge (*fl.*1573–4),
London

Silver-gilt
Inscribed *A thyrde bowle made of the Great*
Seale of Englande and left by Syr Nycholas
Bacon knygt Lorde Keeper as an heyreloma to
his house of Redgrave 1574
291×174
Read and Tonnochy, 1928, 46–8
Trustees of the British Museum, London (M &
L.A. 1915, 3–13,1)

85

When Sir Nicholas Bacon (1509–79) became
Lord Keeper of the Great Seal on Elizabeth's
accession, the obsolete silver seal of Philip
and Mary was broken according to custom
and presented to him (see cat. no. **1.11**). The
120 ounces of silver were melted down to
make three matching cups, all still extant,
which he bequeathed to his three houses at
Redgrave, Stiffkey and Gorhambury. The
body of the cup is engraved with three
shields of arms within strapwork surrounds,
being the arms of Bacon, Bacon impaling
Ferneley after his marriage and the arms of
his eldest son Nicholas. The cover is surmounted by an ermine boar, the family crest.

3.21
A Procession of Elizabeth I
Ranelegh Barrett (*fl.*1737–68) after
?Robert Peake (1576–?1626)

Oil on canvas
1370×1692
Ilchester, 1921, 1–20; Strong, 1963a, 87;
Strong, 1987, 153–5
Lent privately

The subject of this eighteenth-century copy
after the well-known picture of *c.*1601 at
Sherborne Castle (attributed to Peake) has
been given various interpretations, including
the suggestion that it represents the queen's
procession to St Paul's in November 1588
after the defeat of the Armada. This cannot
be substantiated. Most recently, and most
convincingly, it has been taken as a celebration of the fourth Earl of Worcester's
appointment as Master of the Horse in 1601.
It shows the queen attended by her Knights
of the Garter (among them, in the foreground second from left, the Lord Admiral,
Howard of Effingham). Whatever the precise
occasion, the presentation of Elizabeth, carried in a manner reminiscent of a Roman
triumph, aimed to promote her as a monarch
both fêted by and involved with her subjects
– a combination of other-worldly aloofness
and public accessibility through which her
popular image was conventionally cultivated.

3.22
Elizabeth I: the 'Sieve' portrait,
1583
Quentin Massys the Younger
(?1543–1589)

Oil on canvas
Inscribed *STA[N]CHO/ RIPOSO / &
RIPOS/SATA / AFFA/NNO* (left) and *A
TERRA ILBEN / MAL DIMORA IN
SELLA (on sieve).1583.Q.MASSYS/ANT.*
1245×915
Yates, 1977, 115–18; Strong, 1987, 101–107
Pinacoteca Nazionale, Siena

Between 1579 and 1583 a number of portraits
were painted of the queen holding a sieve, a
symbol of chastity (derived from the story of
the Roman vestal virgin Tuccia who carried a
sieve full of water from the River Tiber to
the Temple, without spillage, as proof of her
virginity). The Siena portrait, discovered in
the last century in an old Medici palace, is
the finest and iconographically the richest of
the group. Elizabeth's chastity is presented as
the basis of her godliness and personal
mystique through which she is divinely and
practically equipped to build an empire.
Strong has pointed to the importance of John
Dee's treatise of 1577, *General and Rare
Memorials Pertayning to the Perfecte Arte of
Navigation*, in proclaiming the queen's just
pretensions to imperial power through
mastery of the seas, a notion keenly supported by the chancellor, Sir Christopher
Hatton (who is portrayed in the centre of the
right background group). The column on the
left incorporates a series of medallions depicting the story of Dido and Aeneas, implicitly
comparing Aeneas' choice of imperial power
over personal love with Elizabeth's own
political course. The imperial crown at the
base of the column alludes to Aeneas' destiny
and to the queen's rightful expectation – one
whose fulfilment, expressed by the globe on
the right patrolled by English ships, is none
the less dependent on the continuing maintenance of her chastity and sense of discern-
ment. To this degree the portrait, like its
companions, argues firmly against the
queen's marriage negotiations with the Duc
d'Alençon, conducted since 1579. The picture
was formerly attributed to Cornelius Ketel,
but cleaning in February 1988 (just before the
catalogue went to press) revealed the signature
of the younger Massys, an Antwerp painter
whose work is little known, on the lower right
of the canvas.

4.2 Philip II (1527–98), Alonso Sánchez Coello

4. The Court of Philip II

'The new temple of Solomon' was how a number of contemporaries described Philip II's magnificent building of San Lorenzo el Real de El Escorial. The drawing owned by William Cecil of the half-completed monastery-palace calls it simply 'The king of Spain's house' (see cat. no. **4.12**). Sometime between 1557 and 1560 Philip conceived this ambitious project which took from 1563 to 1584 to complete. It was dedicated to St Lawrence, on whose feast day the king had won his first major victory over France, and his primary reason for building the monastery was to thank God for his guidance and favour in the difficult early years of his reign, as well as to ensure constant divine support in the future. This was not unusual: the novelty of the Escorial was that it incorporated a permanent royal residence with all this entailed in terms of administrative personnel and rooms. The palace, the monastery, a school and a seminary were integrated into the same building. Additionally, the monastery had responsibility for a hospital in the town. Nor was this all: Philip II had been charged by his father to provide a grand tomb where prayers would be continuously offered for him and his wife, the Empress Isabel. Several other members of the family also awaited suitable entombment, including Philip's wives and children, so it was decided to construct a grand mausoleum as well. This multiplicity of functions and Philip's fondness for good singing led to the choice of the Hieronimites to run the monastery. The order spent much of the day in prayer, study and contemplation, and were much favoured by Charles V and Philip. Philip hoped 'that all these works will honour the worship of God and the saints, and will bring eternal benefits for the Christian people, for our soul and for the souls of our royal forefathers and successors'.[1]

The desire to ensure that his creation should last led to the choice of granite for the structure. Much debate surrounds the king's choice of shape and the plain façade. Philip may have wanted it to suggest the shape of the grill on which St Lawrence was martyred, but this was not his sole inspiration. At the time of the building of the Escorial, there was much interest in reconstructing the Temple of Solomon. Several treatises were published, at least one of which was financed by Philip and supported by his architects. The building resembles some of the partial reconstructions of what was considered the most perfect building ever to grace the earth.[2]

The simplicity and grandeur of the outside of the building also satisfied the king's taste. Throughout his life Philip detested vanity. He did not invite panegyrics. He had a preference for elegant but simple clothes, and tried to reduce protocol whenever he could, using ceremony and symbol to enhance his authority only where necessary. He was at pains to ensure that the rigid ceremonial of the Burgundian court, introduced by Charles V, did not distance him unduly from his people. In 1585 he decreed that he should be addressed simply as Sir, not with the traditional title of Sacred Catholic Royal Majesty. For Philip, true nobility and authority did not require excessive symbolism, it emanated from within. This deliberate disdain of vainglory was both a personal and a courtly attribute. Philip was raised in a court culture which prized stoic virtues of restraint and moderation in all things. The severe public demeanour, the control of emotion and gesture, the outward calm the Spaniards call *sosiego* were characteristic of Philip and other members of his family. Outside Spain it was usually interpreted as haughtiness, pride and coldness, although after 1554 the king was generally praised for his exquisite manners. Philip made a clear distinction between public demeanour which, like his monastery-palace, must create an impression of regal magnificence, and his personal relations, which were full of warmth and affection. After the death of his fourth wife, Anne of Austria, in 1580, he devoted more time to his children. During his absence in Portugal in 1581–3 he wrote to them frequently and sent them gifts such as fruits and colouring books.[3] He fretted because his little boy had not yet cut his first tooth at the age of two, worried when his daughter fell and asked them to measure themselves in coloured ribbons so that he could see how much they had grown. The king and his children exchanged stories and details of their dwarfs and their outings to gardens, palaces and woods. He told them of the flowers that decorated his rooms and how he missed the song of the nightingale. Their shared love of nature is evident in the care Philip took of his gardens and woods. He brought gardeners from the Netherlands and plants from all over the world.

Like most of his contemporaries, Philip loved hunting and attended in a carriage when unable to ride. But the bulk of his pursuits were indoors. He was, above all, a great collector. From the 1540s he was a regular purchaser of books of all types and in all languages. Thousands of them were donated to the magnificent library he built in the Escorial. The painters he employed also varied greatly, although he never wavered in his great love of Titian, Hieronymus Bosch and other Flemish 'primitives'. He had a good selection of portraits and sensuous allegories, but the bulk of his purchases after 1562 were religious paintings, prints and views of nature to decorate the Escorial. His own cell-like bedroom had

1. The charters and codicils were published in Zarco Cuevas, 1917.
2. Two of the latest theories and suggestions of the meaning of the Escorial are Osten Sacken, 1984 and the controversial article by Taylor, 1967.
3. Gachard, 1884.

many small pictures of saints so that he could meditate on their virtues and sufferings and be inspired by their example. He used Bosch's pictures, especially the *Seven Deadly Sins*, to prompt meditation and reform. Other pictures were Patinir's peaceful *Flight from Egypt* and the pictures of the Holy Family by Jan Gossaert (Mabuse).

This belief in the power of an image to instruct as well as to delight was evident in the decoration of the other rooms. The king's great audience chamber was filled with nearly seventy maps, many from Ortelius's *Theatrum*. The antechamber, also used as a dining or banqueting room, was decorated with views, flora and fauna from the Spanish colonies. The sheer number of paintings on a theme, or even the detailed enumeration of saints within the monastery, also attest to the king's passion for collecting. Aside from books, paintings and maps, Philip loved to collect relics. By 1598 he had 7,500 of these; many inherited, others purchased, but mostly gifts – such as the foot of St Philip, smuggled out of England to Brussels in the 1560s. It was not until December 1588 that the papers certifying its authenticity came from Rome and the relic was ready to join the rest.[4] Philip kept a cabinet of relics near his bedroom in the Escorial. From this and the position of his bedroom next to the high altar – designed to enable him to listen to the choirs and participate in divine services during his frequent bouts of illness – it appears that he needed physical proximity to sources of divine power as well as their support.

The sobriety of the ruler naturally influenced the atmosphere of the court, but this is not to say that Philip's court lacked splendour or laughter. The king's room might be no bigger than a monk's cell, but the rest of the palace was grand and colourful, as were the other palaces where the king lived. Although the Escorial was both monastery and palace, the courtiers did not live like monks; they whiled away the time there, as elsewhere, hunting, gambling, reading, talking, working at their government or courtly posts and, above all, struggling for positions and power. The frequent presence of children also enlivened its atmosphere. The court, like the king's tastes, was orderly, varied and cosmopolitan.

M. J. Rodríguez-Salgado

4. AGS E.593, f.63.

4.1

Tableau of the Court of Philip II
Designed by Martyn Bainbridge, 1988

In the exhibition's second tableau the exterior and interior of the Escorial Palace is revealed and we see King Philip of Spain, depicted working on papers of state, in his cell-like room in the royal apartments adjacent to the basilica. It was from this tiny chamber that Spain's mighty empire was run during Philip's frequent visits to the palace. The ascetic atmosphere contrasts with the opulence of the other parts of El Escorial, which is depicted in a diorama within the tableau. In a whitewashed room, with its blue and white 'Dutch-style' tiled dado, the only furnishings are a simple desk and chair, a pre-Copernican armillary sphere and, on the table, a small painting depicting the martyrdom of San Lorenzo. It was to these rooms that news of the fate of the epic venture would have been relayed to the king.

4.2

Philip II (1527–98), c.1570
Alonso Sánchez Coello (1531/2–88)

Oil on canvas
1095×924
Buttin, 1914, 195–7; Caw, 1936, 24; Tower of London, 1960, 22
Glasgow Museums and Art Galleries (PC159)

Sánchez Coello was a pupil of the portraitist Anthonis Mor (1517–74) and later a favourite of Philip II. He was introduced to the Spanish court by Philip's sister Juana of Portugal (his country of origin) and followed Mor as principal portraitist to the Habsburgs. Though lacking the flair of his predecessor's best work, this picture combines accuracy of detail with a sense of formality and austerity aptly reflecting the rigidity of court etiquette. He portrays the king wearing the Order of the Golden Fleece and dressed in black splinted armour similar to that made for him by Desiderius Colman of Augsburg, 1549–50 (with gold damascene work designed by Jorg Sigman), now in the Real Armería de Madrid.

4.3

Anne of Austria (1549–80), c.1570
Alonso Sánchez Coello (1531/2–88)

Oil on canvas
1093×930
Caw, 1936, 24
Glasgow Museums and Art Galleries (PC137)

The death of Philip's third wife in 1568 without male issue prompted an urgent search for a new queen, and the choice fell

90

on his young niece, daughter of the Emperor Maximilian II. This portrait and its pair (cat. no. **4.2**) were probably painted to celebrate the sitters' marriage at Segovia in 1570. Anne fulfilled her ten-year child-bearing role with mixed success: though four of her five children died young, her fourth son Philip survived to accede to the throne in 1598. The queen is portrayed here wearing an elaborate black-and-gold costume with rich pearl-and-gold tracery.

92

4.4
Don Fernando (1571–8), 1577
Alonso Sánchez Coello (1531/2–88)

Oil on canvas
Inscribed *Alfonsus Sancius F. 1577*
1199×998
Patrimonio Nacional. Monasterio de las Descalzas Reales

Painted shortly before the young sitter's death, the picture bears out the artist's reputation as a subtle and penetrating portraitist of royal children. Don Fernando was then the eldest son of Philip and Anne of Austria and had been sworn in as successor to the throne. The suggestion of his commitment to assuming the responsibilities of state despite his youth and delicate health is poignantly made. The picture is from the important art collection of the Descalzas Convent and Monastery, an institution founded by Philip's sister Juana.

4.5
Infanta Catalina Micaela (1567–97), *c*.1580
Attributed to Teodoro Felipe de Liaño (d.1625)

Oil on paper, laid on canvas
102×102
Caw, 1936, 15
Glasgow Museums and Art Galleries (PC28)

Catalina Micaela and Isabel Clara Eugenia were Philip's favourite daughters. The former was to marry Charles Emmanuel, Duke of Savoy, helping to maintain the alliance between the Habsburgs and the House of Savoy.

4.6
Infanta Isabel Clara Eugenia (1566–1633), *c*.1580
Attributed to Teodoro Felipe de Liaño (d.1625)

Oil on paper, laid on canvas
102×102
Caw, 1936, 15
Glasgow Museums and Art Galleries (PC30)

The sitter was Philip's eldest daughter by his third marriage. She became her father's confidante, not marrying until the year of his death, when she was thirty-three. Her husband was her cousin, Archduke Albert of Austria. Philip left them the Netherlands, which she ruled until her death.

4.7
Philip II (1527–98), *c*.1580
Attributed to Sofonisba Anguisciola (*c*.1530–1626)

Oil on canvas
880×720
Prado, 1985, 15–16, 616
Museo del Prado, Madrid (1036)

This portrait reflects the virtues of restraint and austerity encouraged at the Spanish court. The king is shown dressed with great simplicity, holding a rosary, and his sole ornament is a pendant of the Order of the Golden Fleece. The picture has been conventionally identified as the work of Sánchez Coello on the grounds of its evident stylistic relationship with the artist's portrait of Anne of Austria (Prado no. 1284). More recently, however, it has been tentatively attributed to Sofonisba Anguisciola, one of six painter sisters from Cremona. She worked at Philip's court, painting the king and his family, and also produced portraits of other major figures, including Pope Pius IV.

4.8
Medal of Philip II as ruler of the New World, 1559
G. P. Poggini (1518–c.82)

Silver
Inscribed (obv.) *PHILIPPVS.*
HISPANIAR.ET.NOVI.ORBIS.
OCCIDVI.REX-I.PAVL.POG.F;
(rev.) *PACE.TERRA.MARIQ.*
COMPOSITA.MDLIX
40 dia.
Trustees of the British Museum, London

This medal portrays on the obverse a bust of
Philip II wearing armour, and on the reverse
Peace burning arms before the Temple of
Janus, probably to commemorate the Peace
of Cateau-Cambrésis.

94

4.9
Medal of Philip II with two of his children, c.1586
?Italian

Silver
Inscribed (obv.) *PHILIP.HISP.REX.*
PRINCEPS.ET.INFANTIS.SVIS;
(rev.) *TRIVMPFVS*
31 dia.
Armand, 1883; Pierson, 1975
Trustees of the British Museum, London

The obverse of this medal portrays Philip II
with his son Philip (later Philip III) and the
Infanta Isabel Clara Eugenia. The reverse
shows Philip's triumphal entry into Madrid
after his conquest of Portugal.

4.10
Medal of Philip II, c.1585

Silver
Inscribed (obv.) *PHILIPP.II.HISP.ET.*
NOVI.ORBIS.REX; (rev.) *NON*
SVFFICIT ORBIS (One world is not
enough)
50 dia.
Trustees of the British Museum, London

This medal was struck to celebrate Spanish
overseas conquests.

4.11
Philip II (1527–98)
Jonas Suyderhoef, c.1613–86, after
Anthonis Mor, c.1517–76/7

Etching with engraving
Inscribed *Philippus II Catholicus,*
Hispaniarum rex . . .
400×275
National Maritime Museum

No. 10 from the series of portraits *Duces*
Burgundiae.

4.12
The Escorial under construction,
*c.*1575
?Juan de Herrera (*c.*1530–97)

Pen and wash
Inscribed *Por esta parte tiene 575 pies Por esta*
parte ques poniente tiene 645 pies; Endorsed by
Lord Burghley *The Ki of Spanyes Hows at*
508×775
Skelton and Summerson, 1971, no. 100;
Patrimonio Nacional, IV, 1986, 55–67
The Marquess of Salisbury, Hatfield House

Juan de Herrera was the chief architect of
the Escorial after 1567. This isometric
perspective drawing shows in the foreground
the main façade; left, the completed monastery; right, the college and seminary in progress. Behind the partly built palace walls projecting from the east front, the site of the
Church of San Lorenzo swarms with workmen and mechanical devices. It has been tentatively dated by comparison with accounts
of the progress of construction. How it came
into Lord Burghley's possession is unknown.

96

4.15
Philip II (1527–98), 1590
Attributed to Juan Pantoja de la Cruz
(1553–1608)

Oil on canvas
1575×1029
Albèri, 1851, 422–4; Martínez Sierra, c.1921
Museo del Prado, Madrid (6181)

Pantoja de la Cruz was a pupil and follower
of Philip II's favourite court portraitist,
Alonso Sánchez Coello. Using a dark background and simple props, he brings out the
sobriety, austerity and majesty of the king in
old age. The picture is close in conception to
Pantoja's better-known full-length portrait of
Philip which hangs in the Escorial. The artist
suggests Philip's love of solitude and plainly
depicts his lack of ostentation – the insignia
of the Golden Fleece, of which Philip was
Grand Master, hangs from a simple ribbon.
The king holds a letter, a suitable symbol for
a man who spent much of his day working
on state documents. This devotion to the
affairs of his realms was well known. The
plain black suit was Philip's habitual attire –
it was thought at once elegant and simple.
Having resided at the Spanish court for some
time, the Venetian Tommaso Contarini commented in 1593 on Philip's firm control of
emotion and impassive countenance: 'neither
the news that the enterprise against England
had come to its sad conclusion, nor details of
the many defeats suffered by his troops in
Flanders have shattered the calm and composure of his visage.'

4.13
Armchair from the Escorial, 16th
century

Walnut and velvet
1080×620×490
Patrimonio Nacional, IV, 1986, 122
*Patrimonio Nacional. Monasterio de El
Escorial (1.317)*

This *sillón frailero* comes from one of the
Escorial's bedchambers. The fabric is richly
coloured and braided and includes on the
seat back the arms of Castile and León.

4.14
Banqueta de cordobán

Leather and wood
550×535×225
*Patrimonio Nacional. Monasterio de El
Escorial*

One of a number of austere sitting stools,
made from sixteenth-century leather around a
wooden frame, that were placed against the
walls in the less formal apartments of the
Escorial.

4.16
Philip II's invalid chair

Modern reproduction in walnut
1610×780×940
Patrimonio Nacional, III, 1986, no. 63
Patrimonio Nacional. Monasterio de El Escorial

Philip had his first attacks of gout when he was only thirty. As he grew older they became more frequent and prolonged and he had a number of chairs designed to support his swollen limbs. This is a reproduction of the most famous, designed by the Flemish Jehan l'Hermite, to allow maximum movement and comfort. The arms, back and legs can all be adjusted.

4.17
Books from Philip II's library

Patrimonio Nacional. Monasterio de El Escorial

The two books exhibited, *La tercera parte del Vita Christi Lartutano* and *La filosofia geometrica de Arquimides*, were both acquired by the king for the Escorial Palace. Each is normally housed within the desk in his private room (reproduced in the exhibition tableau, cat. no. **4.1**) which contains a representative selection from the wide subject areas covered by his considerable library.

4.18
Writer's set, 16th century

Bronze
140×350×100
Patrimonio Nacional, IV, 1986, no. 8
Patrimonio Nacional. Monasterio de El Escorial

The set comprises three bronze containers placed on a modern base of red velvet-covered wood. The side containers were for ink, that in the centre for blotting powder. They are decorated with engravings of Philip's arms and the gridiron, the symbol of St Lawrence. This *escribanía* is normally kept today on the desk in Philip's study in the Escorial.

4.19
The Banquet of Monarchs
Follower of Alonso Sánchez Coello
(1531/2–88)

Oil on canvas
Inscribed *ASC ANNO 1596*
1100×2020
Evans, 1973; Conselho da Europa, 1983, 169–73
National Museum, Poznań (776)

This allegorical banquet was a celebration of Habsburg rule in the Netherlands. Despite the inscribed date, it is likely to have been commissioned on the betrothal (1597) or marriage (1598) of Philip's eldest daughter, Isabel Clara Eugenia and her cousin, the Archduke Albert, appointed joint rulers of the Netherlands after Philip II's death. They share the honour of sitting at the table with the Emperor Charles V, his wife Isabel of Portugal, Philip II and his fourth wife, Anne of Austria. Nothing can be said about the male figure with his back to the viewer, but the female at the centre has the coat of arms of Elizabeth de Valois, Philip's third wife and Isabel Clara Eugenia's mother. The other identifiable figures were all governors of the Netherlands during Philip's reign. Behind Charles V stands his illegitimate son, Don John of Austria (governor, 1576–8); the Duke of Alba (governor, 1567–73) is shown bowing low between the Empress Isabel and Philip. On the extreme left of the canvas, bearing a curious tree with the imperial Habsburg emblem is Alessandro Farnese, Duke of Parma (governor, 1578–92). At the back, right, are two other Habsburg princes, brothers of Albert, the Archdukes Ernest (governor 1593–5) and Matthias (who ruled for the rebels during 1578–81). All have been copied from early to late sixteenth century portraits.

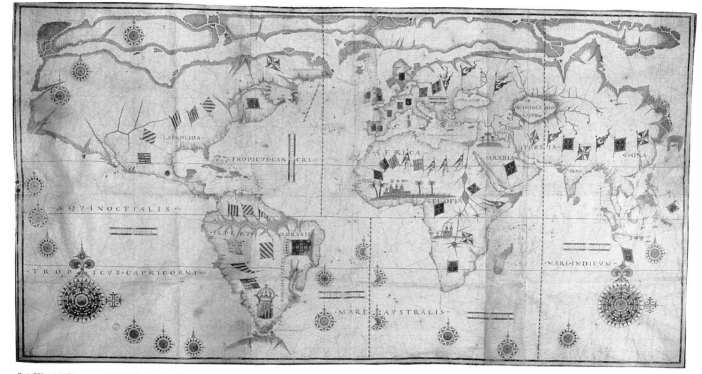

5.1 World Chart, *c*.1585, ?Sebastião Lopes

5. The Spanish Empire

The extent of Philip II's empire was awesome. In Iberia he possessed the kingdoms of Castile, Aragon, Navarre and, after 1580, Portugal. Across the Pyrenees he had Roussillon-Cerdagne; in North Africa he held a number of ports: Oran, Mers-el-Kebir, Melilla, the Peñón de Vélez, La Goleta and, later, the Portuguese fortifications, including Mazagan and Ceuta. The Balearic and Canary archipelagos, Sardinia, Sicily, Naples and Milan belonged to him, and he occupied a number of fortified positions in western Italy. The Franche-Comté and the Netherlands were his only 'northern' states in Europe. Vast territories were subject to him in the New World: the Caribbean islands, Mexico, the Isthmus, Peru and the Pacific coast. In 1565 the Philippines were added and named after him; the Azores, Brazil and a string of Portuguese posts in Africa, India and Japan followed in the 1580s.

Contemporaries acknowledged that he ruled the greatest land mass in the world, but did not grant him the accolade of being the 'Greatest Prince in Christendom' for some time. Size did not guarantee power. They were conscious of the many weaknesses of Philip's empire. It was far-flung, almost impossible to govern given the distance separating the king from the periphery. Countless sea and land routes had to be maintained in order to keep communications and contacts open. The conflicting defence requirements of the many states posed insoluble problems and ensured that commitments regularly outstripped resources. Since there was no common language, culture or law, the only element binding the empire was the sovereign himself. There was no collective responsibility or pro rata division of the burdens of empire: each state accepted the need to provide its own defence, and to give some help to the king if he were attacked, but no more. Moreover, Philip inherited a bankrupt state in 1554–6. Although he increased taxation and received ever-growing sums from the Indies, expenditure on administration and war forced him to re-schedule his debts in 1557, 1560, 1575 and 1597. The foundations of this colossus were weak. Attempts to consolidate the empire by separating the Netherlands and Franche-Comté foundered repeatedly since Philip was determined to maintain his 'God-given' inheritance intact. He shared the common belief that if he ever lost one dominion, the rest of the monarchy would collapse.

Two states held the Spanish monarchy in check and constantly threatened its survival: France and the Ottoman Empire. France, a compact, fertile, populous territory with easy access to all routes, could match the might of Spain. Although the French monarchy was seriously weakened as a result of the civil wars from 1562 onwards, it did not cease to challenge and undermine Habsburg power. The Huguenots were particularly active, encouraging dissent and rebellion in Navarre, Catalonia and the Netherlands, forcing Philip to ally with his erstwhile enemies, the Guise, and constantly divert resources to intervene in France. Philip and his counsellors rejected accusations of opportunism, arguing that this intervention was essential in order to preserve his dominions from heresy and invasion. France also received support from other Christian powers in this period, particularly when following an anti-Spanish policy. The Christian states habitually intrigued – and acted – against any power which threatened to establish hegemony.

The Ottoman Empire had cooperated with France during the first half of the sixteenth century, expanding steadily in eastern Europe and along the Mediterranean. For the Spanish and Italian states, the huge Ottoman-corsair fleets (200–350 ships) posed a direct threat, but so did the Algerian and other corsair bases. In Spain fear of invasion grew as tension increased between Christians and *Moriscos*, the remnants of the Hispano-Muslim communities. In 1568 the *Moriscos* of Granada rebelled and called upon their Ottoman and Algerian allies to invade. They received little support, yet order was not restored until 1571. To counter the Islamic threat, Philip concentrated his resources for much of the 1560s on building a Mediterranean fleet. The outbreak of the revolt in the Netherlands prevented him from continuing with his plan to conquer Algiers. It is no coincidence that the Netherlands rebels should have chosen 1566 and 1572 to launch their invasions. Philip was too enmeshed in the Mediterranean to attend to events in the north. During 1570–73 he was committed to the Holy League, an alliance with the papacy and Venice against the Ottomans. The celebrated victory of Lepanto brought him no strategic or political gains, however. The conquest of Tunis (1573) did, but it fell again to the Ottomans in 1574. Bogged down with the rebellion in the Netherlands, Philip could do little to arrest the advance of the Ottoman-corsair forces in the Maghreb. When they took the Sa'di state of Fez-Morocco in 1576 hysteria swept through the Iberian realms. The neighbouring coast was now in the hands of the Ottoman-corsair forces: in a few hours they could make the crossing and invade Iberia once more.[1]

Philip could only attend to one major threat at a time. When the unpaid army ran amok in the Netherlands and caused the States to unite in 1576, he decided to eliminate the Mediterranean front by suing for a truce. His nephew, King Sebastian of

1. Braudel II, 1972.

100

Portugal, decided to face the threat and made urgent appeals for Philip to join his crusade in the Maghreb. He intended to recover Fez-Morocco first and then Algiers. Philip pursued peace and gave minimal aid to the expedition, which sailed in June 1578. Sebastian and his motley crew of Christian and Maghrebian supporters were annihilated by the superior Ottoman-backed forces.[2]

After this, Philip maintained peace in the Maghreb, concentrating his attention on the Portuguese succession. When Sebastian's successor, Cardinal Henrique, died in January 1580, he claimed the throne. Although his title was indisputable, it was challenged by Dom Antonio, the illegitimate son of Henrique's older brother, Luis, who was supported by powerful anti-Castilian groups. Philip promptly invaded Portugal. By 1581 he was in control there, but two more years elapsed before he won the key islands of the Azores from Antonio's supporters.[3] Since Philip regarded Portugal as his due inheritance, he warned fellow monarchs that support of the pretender would be construed as a *casus belli*. Although they ignored the warning, Elizabeth was sufficiently concerned to make her support of Antonio conditional on equal French involvement. Having urged joint action, she characteristically failed to fulfil her promises when Henri III sent his troops to the Azores in 1582.[4]

The hostile activities of the English were of little importance when set beside these conflicts. Privateer and piratical activity was usual; so was meddling in rebellions. Philip's honour was wounded when Elizabeth seized money destined for Alba's troops in 1568, and he was insulted by the manner in which she rewarded Drake after his triumphant and destructive voyage around the world (1577–80). Yet these actions did not seriously threaten the security of his states or cause much damage to his reputation. The situation altered in the 1580s. The number of expeditions and raids against New World shipping and colonies increased sharply, not least because Elizabeth's leading ministers – Leicester, Burghley, Walsingham, to name but the most prominent – actively encouraged it. The success of Drake and others encouraged emulation and awakened greed. Elizabeth had no power to control these ventures, although she could have restrained them. After 1580, however, she was determined 'that the King of Spain's greatness should be impeached'.[5] As Cecil stressed, now that Philip was temporarily free from the Ottomans and much more powerful than France, he could impose his will upon Christendom and must be prevented from doing so. All methods were acceptable, but Elizabeth concentrated on unofficial intervention in the Netherlands and privateer raids, because they could be disowned and so would not provide a legitimate cause for war.

The primary aim of the English was to take the rich convoys of the New World trade.[6] After 1564 Philip had reorganized the system and provided strong armed guard for these valuable ships.[7] He normally paid for war by arranging large loans, of which a sizeable proportion was payable in bullion. Moreover, in times of crisis he would take the money and goods of individuals on the fleets, offering compensation in government bonds. This convinced his contemporaries that taking a convoy would deprive him of the means to wage war for one or two years. Furthermore, it would provide such encouragement to pirates that they would infest the seas and put an end to his lucrative commerce. Elizabeth ordered her seamen to attack the convoys in 1585, 1586 and 1587, but they failed. Instead, they raided isolated ships and vented their frustration on the defenceless coasts of Galicia and America. These attacks forced Philip to increase expenditure on fortifications, particularly of the underpopulated ports where the convoys gathered in the New World. In 1587 the English succeeded in destroying ships and supplies intended for the Armada, which had to be delayed in order to provide protection for the convoys whilst the English navy prowled. More importantly, perhaps, the raids against Galicia and Cadiz seriously damaged Philip's reputation, while those against the colonies assumed a far more threatening aspect when Raleigh and Grenville attempted to establish English settlements in Virginia (1585–7). The cumulative impact of these multiple attacks, and the potential the English now displayed for establishing hostile colonies, inclined Philip to act against England. Elizabeth's direct challenge to his dominion in Portugal and the Netherlands finally decided the issue in favour of war.

M. J. Rodríguez-Salgado

2. Ibid., also Danvila, 1954.
3. Danvila, 1956.
4. Wernham, 1966, 360–64; MacCaffrey, 1981, 281–2.
5. MacCaffrey, 1981, 289.
6. The literature dealing with English voyages is abundant but the following will give a sound introduction to the subject: Wright and Fowler, 1968, especially Gilbert's proposals to damage Spanish interests (17–20) and Hakluyt's support for plantations (22–6); Quinn, 1974, especially Chapters 7, 10, 11; Andrews, 1984.
7. Parry, 1966, especially 134–5.

5.1
World Chart, *c*.1585
?Sebastião Lopes (*fl*.1558–96)

Four-coloured manuscript sheets assembled
as one chart
2180×1145; scale *c*.1:1,850,000
Cortesão and Texeira da Mota, IV, 1960, 17–
19; Mollat *et al.*, 1984, 242
*Bibliothèque Nationale, Paris (Cartes et Plans,
S. H. Archives, 38)*

This chart shows the world-wide nature of
Philip II's empire after his conquest of Portugal in 1580. Its handwriting and style
strongly suggest manufacture by Sebastião
Lopes in the Armazém da Guiné e India in
Lisbon, then Europe's leading hydrographic
agency. The chart incorporates fresh
Spanish, Portuguese and Asian information,
notably in representations of the new Spanish
colony in the Philippines, and the Saya de
Malhu Bank, north-west of Madagascar.
Both were major hazards to shipping sailing
between Portuguese commercial and military
outposts. Symbolic depictions of empire like
Elmina Fortress and the church in Africa,
and Castile's arms in southern and central
America, mark Philip's strategic interests
beyond Europe. His concern at Arab power
is illustrated by the fifteen flying crescents.
The northern passages postulated here
illustrate the perceived threat to Philip's
Pacific interests from contemporary English
and Dutch exploration of Arctic waters.

5.2
Mining of precious metals in the New World (from *Americae pars quinta*, 1595)
Theodore de Bry (1528–98)

Engraving
Inscribed *NIGRITAE IN SCRUTANDIS
VENIS METALLICIS/ab Hispanis in
Insulas ablegantur*
300×218
British Library, 1977, 30
National Maritime Museum

Gold was the lure for the first *conquistadores*.
Negro slaves were brought from Portuguese
East Africa to work in the mines established
by the Spanish. This stylized scene is of gold
mining in Hispaniola. The Milanese Giralmo
Benzoni, on whose *Historia del Mundo Nuova*
de Bry based his text, took part in a treasure-
hunting expedition from Panama in 1540.

NIGRITÆ IN SCRUTANDIS VENIS METALLICIS
ab Hispanis in Insulas ablegantur.

101

5.3–5.8
Gold and silver bullion from the Padre Island wrecks, 1554

5.3
Gold ingot, 149 lgth, 0.182 kg (ref. 1437)
Inscribed *AV/S* (possibly *AVREVS*, 'gold',
or an owner's or assayer's mark); *XV*:
(assayed value of VIII, possibly a tally mark)

5.4
Silver disc, 246 dia., 2.444 kg (ref. 1418)
Inscribed with two scallop shells (probably the Shell of St James, used as an official mark); three rectangles on reverse.

102

5.5
Silver disc, 120 dia., 0.449 kg (ref. 1410)
Inscribed with a wheel with four knobbed spikes; *PLVS VLTRA.M* (Mexico City); Pillars of Hercules and possibly a profile of Charles V; *A. . .CA. . .*

5.6
Silver disc, 117 dia., 0.849 kg (ref. 1412)
Inscribed with two arcs, possibly part of stamps.

5.7
Silver disc, 395 dia., 12.183 kg (ref. 1417)
Inscribed *PLVS ULTRA M* (Mexico City); Pillars of Hercules with possibly a profile of Charles V (marked twice); *X* (possibly a royal taxation mark); *TASCO+* (mine or mining district in Mexico); *LVIS* (possibly Luis Rodríguez, royal assayer).

5.8
Silver disc, 304 dia., 4.868 kg (ref. 1424)
Inscribed *PLVS ULTRA.M* (Mexico City); Pillars of Hercules and possibly a profile of Charles V; shield with possible owner's mark; two rectangles.
Olds, 1976, 119–21, 122, 124–7, 177, 178; Arnold and Weddle, 1978
Texas Antiquities Committee: Corpus Christi Museum and The Harris County Heritage Society

In April 1554 three Spanish ships, from a fleet *en route* from Vera Cruz in Mexico to Spain, were wrecked on Padre Island in what is now Texas. This bullion is a sample of the forty silver discs and two gold ingots excavated from two of the wrecks. Gold, silver and other treasure made up the major part of the cargoes lost, some carried as payment for goods supplied to colonists in the New World, and some as part of the 20 per cent revenue collected for the king. Gold was usually transported in ingot form, and silver in crude discs, although coins minted in the New World were also taken to Spain. Other countries were envious of Spain's lucrative monopoly of trade with the New World, and tried to break it, resorting to raids and piracy. They also traded indirectly with the Spanish colonies, using Spanish or loyal Flemish middlemen. By these means, and by the activities of the Spanish government and its subjects, American bullion was spread throughout Europe.

5.9
Eight-*real* piece from the *Girona*
Silver
Inscribed (obv.) *PHILIPPVS D G HISPANIARVM REX*; (rev.) *INDIARVM REX*
38 dia.
Oliva and López-Chaves Sánchez, 1965, Philip II, type II, no. 118; Crédit Communal, 1985, 5.26
Ulster Museum, Belfast

Round silver eight-*real* piece of Philip II with the arms of Spain on obverse with *P* and *B* on left-hand side, star and *D* on right; arms of Castile on reverse. Lima mint, assayer Diego de la Torre. This coin and cat. nos. **5.10, 5.11** and **5.12** are representative of the immense wealth in gold, as well as silver, from the New World, which often yielded over a million *pesos* a year from 1586. This was a small percentage of the total and it is likely that bullion from the New World during the sixteenth century exceeded 180 million *pesos*.

5.10
Eight-*real* piece from the *Girona*
Silver
Inscribed as cat. no. **5.9**
40 dia.
Oliva and López-Chaves Sánchez, 1965, Philip II, type II, no. 118; Crédit Communal, 1985, 5.27
Ulster Museum, Belfast

Round silver eight-*real* piece of Philip II; arms of Spain on obverse, with *P* and *B* on left-hand side, *D* and star on right; Lima mint, assayer Diego de la Torre.

5.11
Eight-*real* piece from the *Girona*
Silver
Inscribed as cat. no. **5.9**
39 dia.
Castan and Cayon, 1978, Philip II, type 64, no. 4232; Crédit Communal, 1985, 5.28
Ulster Museum, Belfast

Round silver eight-*real* piece, with arms of Spain on obverse, with star and *D* to left, *P* and *B* to right; arms of Castile on reverse. Lima mint, assayer Diego de la Torre.

5.12
Four-*real* piece from the *Girona*

Silver
Inscribed (obv.) *PHI*; (rev.) *REX
HISPANIARVM ET . . .*
31 dia.
Castan and Cayon, 1978, type 58, no. 4095;
Crédit Communal, 1985, 5.35
Ulster Museum, Belfast

A rather badly eroded round silver coin;
arms of Spain on obverse; arms of Castile on
reverse.

5.13
Medal of the Wealth of the Indies,
*c.*1560
Italian work, after G. P. Poggini
(1518–*c.*82)

Silver
Inscribed (obv.) *PHILIPPVS.II.SPAN.ET.
NOVO.ORBIS.OCCIDVIREX*; (rev.)
RELIQVVM PATVRA; Ex: INDIA
39 dia.
*Trustees of the British Museum, London
(M.1994)*

The reverse of this medal has a female figure
representing the Indies (the New World),
holding a globe. This symbolizes the
abundance of the New World and the vast
territories of the Spanish Empire.

5.14
***Book of Intelligence of Spain and
Portugal***, 1582
William Lyllestone (or Lytlestone)

MS
194×130
Read, III, 1925, 218
National Maritime Museum (REC/40)

Philip II's acquisition of the Portuguese
crown in 1580 greatly increased Spanish
maritime resources, and an invasion of England now seemed a real possibility. Lyllestone may well have been working for Walsingham as the book is dedicated to Dr
Valentine Dale (*fl.*1541–89) who served on
several diplomatic missions under Walsingham. The book was based on information
gathered while Lyllestone was at the Spanish
court, perhaps on the ambassador's staff. It
contains a great deal of miscellaneous information arranged in tabular fashion, including
lists of ports, ships and galleys in Spain and
Portugal. Before the Armada, Walsingham
relied for information largely on the chance
observations of English merchants in Iberian
harbours. This book would have been a useful addition to such intelligence.

5.15
Sir Francis Drake (*c.*1540–96), 1620
Willem and Magdalena van de Passe

Engraving
Inscribed *FRANCISCVS DRAKE MILES
AVRATVS* (Francis Drake, the golden
warrior)
219×154
Hind, II, 1955, 145; Strong, I, 1969a, 71
National Maritime Museum (10 I 1596)

Henry Holland's *Herwologia*, of which this is
a plate, depicted notable reformers and
opponents of the papacy. This idealized post-
humous portrait of Drake is related to several
authentic earlier engravings, all of which may
derive from the same unknown original. The
globe commemorates Drake's circumnavigation, a voyage which aimed to undermine
Spanish economic interests world-wide.

5.16
The arrival of English colonists in Virginia in 1584, 1590
Theodore de Bry (1528–98), after John White (*fl.c.*1545–93)

Engraving
155×215
Quinn, 1955; Quinn, 1985
National Maritime Museum

Raleigh's unsuccessful attempts to establish a colony at Roanoke (now in North Carolina) between 1584 and 1590 were a direct affront to Spanish sovereignty in the New World. A short-term aim of the project was to create a base for English privateers attacking Spanish shipping.

5.18

5.17
Attack on Santiago, 27 November 1585
Theodore de Bry (1528–98)

Engraving
Inscribed *QVOMODO DN.FRANCISCVS/ DRACO CIVITATEM ET INSVLAM/ S.JACOBI expugnatam obtinuerit*
330×230
National Maritime Museum

On 27 November 1585 Drake attacked Santiago in the Cape Verde Islands with more than a thousand men organized into three companies. As no treasure was found, the English burnt down the town.

5.18
View of San Domingo, 1586, 1595
Theodore de Bry (1528–98)

Engraving
Inscribed *QVOMODO FRANCISCVS DRA/CO, CIVITATEM S. DOMINICO IN IN-/sula Hispaniolasitam expugnauerit*
330×230
National Maritime Museum

On 10 January 1586, with the help of a Spanish pilot, Drake landed his fleet at the mouth of the river Hayna and captured San Domingo in Hispaniola (Haiti), one of the largest settlements in the West Indies.

VI.
QVOMODO DN. FRANCISCVS
DRACO CIVITATEM ET INSVLAM
S. IACOBI expugnatam obtinuerit.

Nſula S. IACOB, ex omnibus quæ Africam contingunt celeberrima eſt, ſita è regione CAPO
VERDE. Et ab hac Inſula, reliquæ omnes, etiamſi aliquot miliaribus inuicem diſtent, nomen ſuum
acceperunt. Ciuitas S. IACOB, idem habet nominis cum ipſa Inſula, & mercaturam exercet cum
GVYNEA, & aliis vicinis regionibus Africæ, vnde omnis generis merces per mercatores in Portugaliam ſiue Luſitaniam transvehuntur.

Explicatio numerorum præcedentis tabulæ.

1 Locus eſt vbi claſſis Britannica primò ſubſtitit, & anchoras firmauit.   2 Locus quatuor ferè
miliaribus à ciuitate diſtans, vbi Anglicani milites ex nauibus egreſſi ſunt.   3 Via qua Angli, montes ſuperârunt.   4 Campus latus & vndique patens, vbi Angli aciem inſtruxerunt, ad oppugnandam ciuitatem.   5 Acies Anglorum.   6 Propugnaculum extra ciuitatem S. IACOB, per quod Angli ciuitatem ingreſſi
ſunt. Erat autem in loco editiori ſitum, vt ex eo ciuitas luſtrari commodè, & iter quæ ad eam duceret eligi poſſet, ſita eſt enim
ciuitas inter duos montes, & valles habet arboribus fontibuſq́, ſaluberrimis maximè conſpicuas & iucundas.   7 Vallis ipſa,
in qua ſalutarium herbarum, & ſuauiſſimorum fructuum, vtpote Dactylorum, Chyſomelorum, ſaccari & aliorum, maximus
eſt & vberrimus prouentus.   8 Forum in ciuitate.   9 Templum ciuitatis.   10 Propugnaculum medium verſus mare,
omni munitione inſtructum.   11 Propugnaculum verſus occaſum, tormentis probè munitum.   12 Propugnaculum verſus
ortum, tormentis munitum.   13 Locus apertus in cacumine montis verſus occaſum, armis æquè vt propugnacula cætera in
ſtructum, per quem Angli ſunt ingreſſi.   14 Sacellum, verſus occaſum ciuitatis extructum, quò ex foro peruenitur.   15 Incolæ Portugallenſes, ex ciuitate S. IACOB fugientes.   16 Via qua Angli ad locum S. DOMINIGO profecti ſunt, quem
ipſi vnà cum præcipuis Inſulæ proceribus, tenuerunt, qui adueniente Anglorum exercitu, in fugam verſi ſunt.   17 Locus S.
DOMINIGO, qui in medio Inſulæ ſitus, 12000 paſſibus à ciuitate S. IACOB, abeſt.   18 Locus mari vicinus, Prayo dictus,
quem Angli ſub diſceſſum ſuum, quemadmodum etiam ciuitatem S. DOMINIGO, igne perdiderunt.   19 Piſcis volans (ſeu
auis potius) ad viuam expreſſus, quales in mari Atlantico innumeri inueniuntur, ita vt aliquando in naues cadere ſoleant, cum
enim ad 200 paſſus volârunt, in mare rurſus decidunt. Aliquando magna copia conuolant, vt Delphino vel BONITO, qui etiam marinus piſcis eſt, & ipſis inſidias ſubinde ſtruit, reſiſtant, vltra dimidiam vlnam in longitudine non habent.

b 3

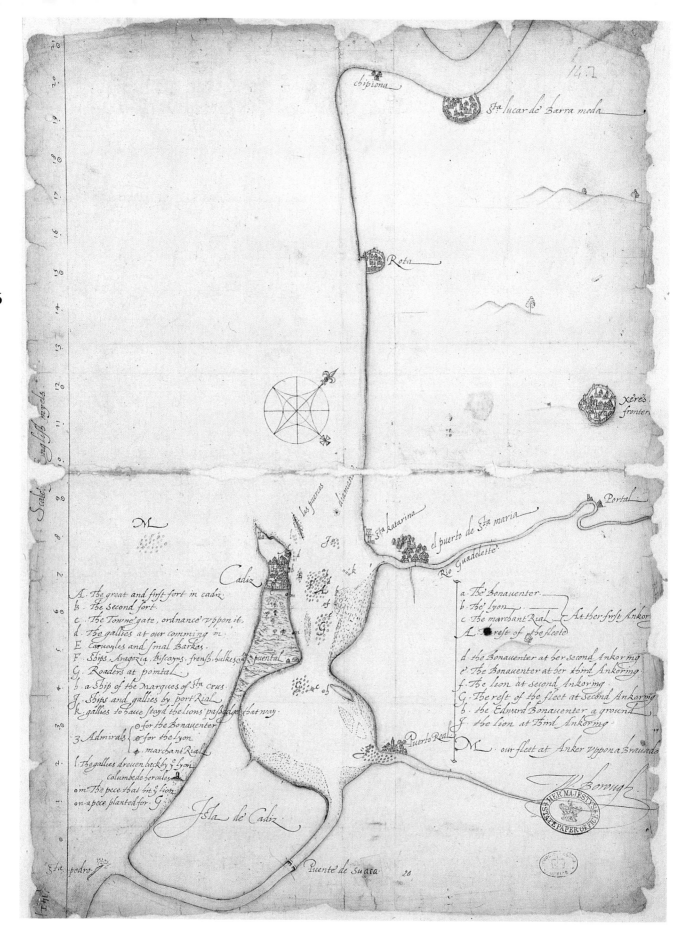

5.19
Plan of the attack on Cadiz, 29 April 1587
William Borough (1537–99)

Pen and watercolour
460×360
Corbett, I, 1898, 142–5; British Museum, 1977, 114; Quinn and Ryan, 1983, 98–102
Public Record Office, London (MPF 318)

Drake's attacks on the Spanish and Portuguese coasts in 1587 were aimed at destroying or dispersing the Armada, but they did not seriously weaken the fleet. After the Cadiz raid, in which twenty to thirty ships were sunk or captured along with supplies, Santa Cruz was forced to spend three fruitless months at sea hunting Drake. This delayed the Armada's sailing for several months, by which time Santa Cruz was dead. Borough was Drake's vice-admiral, and drew this map as part of his successful defence against capital charges made by Drake of cowardice and other crimes. The map is intended to show that Borough, in the (*Golden*) *Lion*, did not stay out of danger at Cadiz as Drake claimed. The *Lion* is shown in three positions (marked 'b', 'f' and 'J' in black) between the English ships and the Spanish coastal guns, one of which (marked 'm' in red) is said to have hit the *Lion*.

ANTHONIUS de 1. Coninck van Portugael en Algarben.

107

5.20
Dom Antonio, Prior of Crato (1531–95), *c.*1600

Engraving
Inscribed *ANTHONIUS de 1. Coninck van Portugael en Algarben*
185×140
National Maritime Museum (P74)

In 1580 the last direct male heir to the Portuguese throne died. Dom Antonio, illegitimate son of the Infante Dom Luis and head of the Order of St John in Portugal, was proclaimed king by a small faction. He was quickly crushed by Philip II and fled first to France and later to England.

6.1 An Allegory of the tyranny of the Duke of Alba, Netherlandish School, late 16th century

6. War and Rebellion in the Netherlands

The revolt of the Netherlands began, as did so many contemporary rebellions, with divisions at the centre of government: an old-fashioned conflict between an absentee monarch and an impecunious, aggressive aristocracy. The existence of an organized religious opposition, and widespread social and economic grievances quickly complicated the issue. For different reasons, nobles and Protestants – few could claim to be both – attempted to reduce royal authority and opposed Philip II's new ecclesiastical structure. When tension gave way to violence in 1566, Philip II did not trust the élite to put down the unrest, and sent 10,000 men under the command of the Duke of Alba.[1]

Alba's severe suppression of dissent became legendary. While modern scholarship has shown many of the wilder claims to be mistaken, it has confirmed that the iron duke largely deserved his epithet.[2] He was a stern disciplinarian, and under instructions to restore royal authority, renew the flow of taxation (which had all but ceased since Philip's departure in 1559) and impose religious conformity. The king had tried conciliation and failed; now he wanted obedience. Alba made considerable headway, but aroused much resentment and fear. The decision to impose sales taxes proved the final straw and provoked a new wave of unrest in 1572.

The rebels justified their resistance to a legitimate sovereign in traditional terms: they purported to act for the best interests of king and country; they accused his evil counsellors of misleading him, and alleged that privileges had been ignored. The defence of privileges played a particularly important role, forming the basis for claims of tyranny, yet the allegations were seldom substantiated. It was a rallying cry rather than a specific grievance.[3] As for complaints about taxation, the rebel governments later imposed the same taxes they denied Alba and Philip.

The role of religion in the Netherlands conflict is hard to define. Philip was consistent: he demanded conformity and insisted that the call for toleration was false. He accepted traditional dogma that he was entrusted by God to preserve his faith and would be called to account for the souls lost as a result of his actions. Furthermore, he could not conceive of loyalty to the crown if subjects rejected the divine authority which sanctioned the exercise of sovereignty. 'If the faith is lost,' he wrote, 'I will lose my states and the nobles will lose theirs; since these [heretics] do not wish to acknowledge the authority of God, they will similarly reject that of their lords.'[4] The situation in France, Scotland and the Holy Roman Empire confirmed his fears and suggested that tolerance might lead to protracted civil war and the emasculation of monarchical power.

The rebels were divided on the issue, but ultimately intractable. William of Orange and the moderates appear to have sought genuine toleration and had no qualms about inviting Catholics (the Archduke Matthias, the Duc d'Anjou and Henri III), or Protestants (Elizabeth, the Earl of Leicester) to be their sovereign. For the small but powerful Calvinist groups toleration was anathema. Wherever they could they established their creed as the sole religion and they rejected Catholic leaders, particularly Anjou. When the provinces united against the monarch in 1576–9 they had a chance to impose their own religious settlement. Significantly, they rejected toleration and finally agreed that each province should be free to choose its official religion.

The Dutch revolt was never simply a civil war. Foreign powers, especially France and England, intervened from the start, but all sovereigns were careful to preserve the fiction that they were not meddling in Philip's affairs. Thus the emperor disowned his brother when Matthias was appointed governor of the rebel provinces in 1577, and the king of France pretended he neither knew nor cared for his brother's adventures first as defender (1578) and later as sovereign of the Netherlands (1580–83). Unable to fight on all fronts, Philip accepted their lame explanations, along with the unconvincing denials of Elizabeth. Centuries of rivalry inclined him to consider the French monarchs as the graver threat, and indeed they would have been but for the civil war in France. The Netherlands rebels were allied to the Huguenots and fought on their side in several wars, consequently support for the Dutch affected the balance of power within France. Even without Spanish prompting, French Catholics opposed major intervention in the neighbouring state. The most notable example of this was the Massacre of St Bartholomew in 1572, precipitated by Charles IX's decision to invade the Netherlands.[5]

But it was England, not France, that directly challenged Philip's sovereignty in the Netherlands. There was a powerful Protestant group at court headed by Leicester, Walsingham and (often) Burghley, consistently urging intervention. The desire to weaken a powerful neighbour tempted Elizabeth to offer covert help to the rebels: she sheltered the exiles and allowed them to send armaments and other vital supplies from English ports. Yet she resisted pressure to intervene more directly, chiefly because she had no desire to spend money on risky enterprises which might embroil her in a major war. She also disliked rebels and had a particular

1. Parker, 1972 and 1977; Lagomarsino, 1973.
2. Maltby, 1983.
3. Woltjer, 1975.
4. AGS E.527, ff.4–5.
5. Sutherland, 1973. The links between Huguenots and Dutch rebels can be further explored in Coligny, 1974.

aversion to radical Protestants who embraced resistance theories. Nevertheless, opportunism and fear drew her inexorably towards intervention. It was an axiom of English politics that if France gained control of the Netherlands, the safety and commerce of England would be seriously endangered. When the French, led by Anjou, were on the point of taking control – for example in 1572 and 1577–8 – she offered money and troops to the rebels. Once the immediate threat was over, parsimony and caution would reassert themselves and she quickly went back on her promises. By 1580 it was clear that Anjou could not be prevented from controlling the Netherlands, and her fear of Philip had increased. Although he had not been unduly hostile, there was growing concern about what he might do to England if he established a firm government in the Netherlands. Elizabeth decided to support, and thereby control, the Duc d'Anjou.[6]

It was not until August 1585 that she took the calculated step of supporting the rebels officially. The Treaty of Nonsuch was a direct challenge to Philip's authority and an act of war. Elizabeth was motivated by her fear that the revolt would collapse after the deaths of Anjou and William of Orange in the summer of 1584, and the spectacular progress of the Duke of Parma and loyal forces, who had already reconquered much of the southern Netherlands. Moreover, news of Philip's treaty with the French Catholic League and his seizure of English ships in Iberia provoked new fears of his intentions towards England. Elizabeth justified the treaty in a pamphlet which argued that she was merely preempting danger to English security, and rescuing an ally from tyranny. Not a word was said about religion. But her occupation of Brill and Flushing (demanded as security for the money she was lending) smacked of invasion, and when Leicester – against her wishes – accepted the governorship of the rebel provinces, it was difficult to prove that this was not usurpation.

Elizabeth promised the Dutch 6,400 infantry, 1,000 horse and loans of £126,000 per annum. The Earl of Leicester and his men arrived to enthusiastic acclaim; lavish propaganda was produced hailing him and Elizabeth as the saviours of the Dutch and Protestantism in general. Within months there was nothing but acrimonious disputes and calls for his resignation. There were three main sources of tension. First, the English soldiers proved undisciplined and troublesome. Their pay was poor and irregular, owing to massive peculation and financial incompetence. Such was their behaviour that they were refused quarters by the hostile population. Their reputation plummeted when William Stanley

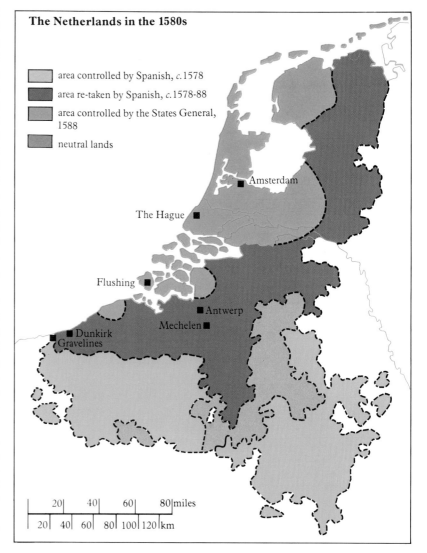

The Netherlands in the 1580s

area controlled by Spanish, c.1578

area re-taken by Spanish, c.1578–88

area controlled by the States General, 1588

neutral lands

Amsterdam

The Hague

Flushing

Antwerp

Mechelen

Dunkirk
Gravelines

20 40 60 80 miles
20 40 60 80 100 120 km

and Rowland Yorke betrayed Zutphen and Deventer and went to serve Parma. The English commanders were busy quarrelling, particularly with Leicester, who also clashed with the Dutch. The earl tried to gain control of taxation and advanced extreme Calvinists. This was bad enough, but his decision to prohibit trade with the enemy was considered intolerable by the Dutch burghers. Their truculence, and the restrictions they imposed, exasperated him and, like Anjou, he attempted a *coup d'état*. Both failed miserably. The Dutch were now convinced that Elizabeth intended to seize control of the provinces. Amidst cries of English tyranny, Leicester returned to England and resigned his office in January 1588.

Elizabeth had no desire to control the Netherlands directly, and assured them so repeatedly. But her constant shifts of mood and policy raised doubts about her commitment to the revolt, which were

6. Neale, 1930; Wernham, 1966; Wilson, 1970; MacCaffrey, 1981.

reinforced by her peace negotiations with Parma during 1586–8.[7] At first she kept them secret. When she finally informed the States of her actions it was to put pressure on them to agree to a reconciliation with Philip. Confronted with proposals to end their substantial independence and reintroduce Catholicism as the official religion, many Dutchmen concluded that Elizabeth intended to abandon them; perhaps even betray them in order to avert Philip's wrath against England. As a result of these tensions, the Dutch made no contribution to England's defence. Elizabeth did not even trust them to block Parma's exit and kept part of her fleet at the Straits of Dover, although Maurits of Nassau assured her they would if she promised not to meddle in their internal affairs again. Having risked war with Spain over the Netherlands, Elizabeth had failed to secure Dutch support when the inevitable reprisals came.

M. J. Rodríguez-Salgado

7. Ibid.; see also the copious correspondence in AGS E. *legajos*, 950, 952, 954.

111

6.1

An allegory of the tyranny of the Duke of Alba

Netherlandish School, late 16th century

Oil on panel
1200×1920
Stedelijk Museum Het Prinsenhof, Delft (PDS 121)

Philip II sent the Duke of Alba with an army to restore order in the Netherlands. Alba's rule was bitterly unpopular and became a crucial element in rebel propaganda. Thousands of pamphlets and prints amplified tales of Alba's cruelty. In this allegory, Alba is seen enthroned on the left, being crowned by the devil. He holds on a heavy chain a group of kneeling figures representing the seventeen provinces. Behind them members of the nobility and the States watch mutely. Cardinal Granvelle, who was thought to have influenced the king's policies towards the Netherlands, is shown with Alba. The devil holds a papal crown for him. In the background are scenes of torture and hangings. Through the archway the public square of Brussels is seen, where the executions of the Counts Egmont and Horn are taking place. Paintings of this subject continued to be made for several decades.

6.2

Fernándo Alvarez de Toledo, 3rd Duke of Alba (1507–82)

Leone Leoni (1509–90)

Bronze
Inscribed *FER.DVX./ALB/AE*
946 ht
Plon, 1887, 297–8, 301–302; Forrer, III, 1907, 398–411; Middeldorf, 1975, 84
Her Majesty the Queen

Probably produced as a pair to cat. no. **1.18**, although Leoni is known to have cast a head of Alba for Vespasiano Gonzaga, and this one could conceivably be it. The sitter was one of Philip's principal ministers from the mid 1560s until his downfall in 1573, notorious for his ruthless attempts to suppress the Netherlands revolt whilst governor there from 1567. His policy of open religious persecution and autocratic rule alienated him from most of the old nobility, north as well as south, and he thereby inadvertently helped to turn the revolt into a patriotic war against Spain. He had managed in 1569 to persuade Philip against invading England during the rebellion of the northern earls, but had lost his master's confidence by 1573. Only after seven years' political exile was he entrusted with power once more; he successfully led the Spanish forces against Portugal, taking Lisbon in 1580.

6.3

Don John of Austria (1547–78)

Unknown artist

Etching
Inscribed *Quartus Regius Gubernator ab anno
1577 ad cal: Octobris anni 1578 imperavit.
Cum Privileg. Ord Fed*
257×161
V & A, 1966, 852
*Board of Trustees of the Victoria and Albert
Museum, London (E.4332–1960)*

IOANNES AVSTRIACVS CAROLI V. IMPERATORIS FILIVS
·*Quartus Regius Gubernator ab anno 1577 ad cal:
Octobris anni 1578 imperavit·*

Hero of Lepanto (see cat. no. **2.32**), Don
John was Governor-General of the Netherlands from 1576. Despite instructions from
Madrid to pursue with conciliation and caution the continuing goals of Spanish
sovereignty and Catholic monopoly, he had
firm ambitions of his own. He adopted an
aggressive military stance in the north and
lost the confidence of the south; the episode
depicted in the background of the print may
refer to his capture of Namur in 1577. His
broader international aims included marriage
to Mary Stuart and usurpation of Elizabeth's
throne. Though essentially loyal to Spanish
interests, he had aroused Philip's mistrust by
the time of his death from typhus at Namur
in 1578.

6.4

William of Nassau, Prince of Orange (1533–84), *c.*1579

Attributed to Adriaen Thomasz. Key
(1544–*c.*89)

Oil on panel
480×340
Stedelijk Museum, 1984, 23
*Royal Cabinet of Paintings, Mauritshuis, The
Hague (225)*

William of Orange began his career as a supporter of the status quo in the Low
Countries, accepted at the Habsburg court,
and ended it – condemned by Philip as an
outlaw – as a defender of the independence
of the United Provinces. He was drawn into
the conflict with the Spanish monarchy over
Philip II's attempts to reform the Church in
the Low Countries in the early 1560s, which
introduced harsh measures of religious persecution. He led the aristocratic opposition to
these measures, but his equivocal position in
the 1566 rebellion served to make him
unpopular with both the government and the
Calvinist rebels. He retreated to Germany,
but returned in 1572 when, following the Sea
Beggar rising, the Estates of Holland invited
him to be their stadtholder, nominally in the
name of Philip II. In fact he was to become a
symbol of opposition to Spanish rule, and the
leading figure of what in 1579 became the
United Provinces. It is a mark of his political
sense that he did not attempt to make himself their sovereign ruler. Realizing the need
for a sovereign who could provide outside
support, he persuaded the Provinces to
accept the Duc d'Alençon in this role (see
cat. no. **6.11**). Orange died at the hands of a
Spanish-hired assassin, at a time when Holland and Zeeland were proposing to make
him their hereditary count. He had managed
to hold the disparate forces of the Dutch
revolt together through crucial times, when it
might have collapsed as a result of local
rivalries.

6.5

William the Silent as St George, *c.*1577

Marcus Gheeraerts the Elder (*c.*1516/
21–?90)

Engraving
354×268
Hind, I, 1952, 104–107, 121–2; Wernham,
1966, 329–32
*Trustees of the British Museum, London (1873–
7-12-143)*

This print was probably published between
February 1577, when Philip II accepted William as Stadholder of Holland and Zeeland,
and the following October when Orange
became Ruward of Brabant. William is
shown as St George, saving 'Belgium' from
the dragon of (Spanish) tyranny, restoring
peace and justice. Different parts of the
figures stand for different ideas: William carries a shield of Faith and wields a sword of
Hope; his horse represents the alliance
between Holland and Zeeland; the dragon's
right front leg denotes the Spanish Inquisition, which lays a claw of Avarice on a bag of
money.

114

6.6
Maurits of Nassau, Prince of Orange (1566–1625)
Daniel van den Queborne
(*fl.c.1570–c.1620*)

Oil on canvas
1100×850
The Mayor and Aldermen, Gemeente Arnemuiden

The second son and heir of William of Orange, and Stadholder of several Netherlands provinces, Maurits played a key role in Dutch politics from 1587, particularly in the campaigns against the Spanish (1590–1609).

His achievement, however, fell short of unifying the whole of the Netherlands. This portrait may be dated to the mid-1590s; during this period Daniel van den Queborne was appointed court painter to the sitter.

6.7
Maurits of Nassau, Prince of Orange (1566–1625)
Jan Pietersz. Saenredam (1565–1607)

Etching and engraving
Inscribed on oval frame centre *I. Saenredam Sculp. BELGIADAE . . . AMOR, plus verses*
360×455
Hollstein, 1980, 128
Trustees of the British Museum, London (1872–1-13-579)

Maurits is shown here before the landing at Philippine, in the Netherlands (1600).

6.8
Justin of Nassau (1559–1631)
Studio of Jan Anthonisz. van Ravesteyn (1572–1657)

Oil on panel
Inscribed *JUSTINUS. NASSOU*
250×300
Rijksmuseum, 1976, 700
Rijksmuseum, Amsterdam (A536)

Justin of Nassau was the illegitimate son of William I of Orange. After studying at the new university of Leiden he served under his father in Zeeland. In 1588 he was appointed Lieutenant-Admiral of Zeeland and blockaded the Flemish coast, particularly Dunkirk, to prevent Parma's transport fleet from joining the Armada. Several of the retreating Spanish ships fell into his hands. The portrait is one of many from van Ravesteyn's studio, which was based in The Hague, of contemporary Dutch dignitaries.

6.9
Hat badge of a Dutch sailor, 1574

Silver
Inscribed (obv.) *LIVER TURCX.*DAN
PAVS* (Rather Turk than Papist); (rev.) *EN
DESPIY.DELAMES* (In spite of the Mass)
32×17
Milford Haven, 1921, 232–3
Nederlands Scheepvaart Museum, Amsterdam

Badges of this type were worn by sailors taking part in the relief of the Spanish siege of Leiden. The inscriptions sum up popular Protestant religious antagonism.

116

6.10
François, Duc d'Alençon (1554–84), 1561
François Clouet (before 1522–72)

Oil on panel
350×229
Duke of Westminster

François Clouet was the son of Jean Clouet, court painter to François I and Henri II. Most of the French court portraiture of this period is in the form of crayon drawings, usually from life. Clouet was a miniaturist, whose technique was based on the soft style of the chalk drawings. The sitter, who later became Duc d'Anjou (see cat. nos. **2.27** and **6.11**), is portrayed here aged seven.

6.11
The Duc d'Anjou's arrival at St Michael's Abbey, Antwerp, 1582
Netherlandish school, 16th century

Oil on panel
520×470
Rijksmuseum, 1984, 78
Lent privately

On 19 February 1582 François, Duc d'Anjou (Henri III's younger brother and formerly Duc d'Alençon), arrived in the Netherlands at the invitation of the Estates-General, who had in 1580 offered him sovereignty over the Netherlands. After the formal rejection of Philip II's sovereignty in 1581, the offer was renewed. The picture treats his ceremonial entry into the gate of St Michael's, where he was to reside as Duke of Brabant; he is accompanied by Orange (the figure in black to his left) and watched by the people of the city. Above the gate, three allegorical figures representing Courage, Victory and Honour offer him an olive branch and a crown. The artist took an optimistic view of the event and all it promised, but Anjou soon quarrelled with the Dutch and left after his attempted *coup d'état* in 1583.

6.12
Queen Elizabeth as Diana with Time and Truth disclosing the pregnancy of the Pope as Callisto, *c.*1585
Peter van der Heyden (*fl.*1551–85)

Engraving
215×260
British Museum, 1870, 6–7
Trustees of the British Museum, London

Based on Titian's *Diana and Callisto*, which Philip II owned, this print celebrates the alliance between Elizabeth and the Dutch. They are represented by four naked figures bearing the arms of Holland, Gelderland, Friesland and Zeeland. It also represents the triumph of Protestantism over the pope, who here personifies deception and corruption. Among the eggs he has hatched are the Inquisition, the murderer of William of Orange (Balthasar Gérard), the Spaniards and the Capuchins.

6.13
The Prince of Orange milking the cow of the Netherlands, *c.*1583–4
English School, 16th century

Oil on panel
Inscribed with English verses
520×670
Rijksmuseum, Amsterdam (A2684)

This version of a popular satirical motif was produced from within the group of pro-English radical Protestants in the Netherlands. Elizabeth is depicted as the only disinterested supporter of the Dutch (represented by six men), who provides them with essential sustenance. Philip is ridiculed for trying to do the impossible – ride and thus control the cow. The use of the term 'malcontent' in the inscription is significant. Malcontents were Catholic Walloon troops who repudiated the Pacification of Ghent in 1578 and renewed the war against the Protestants. However, the Calvinists denounced the limited religious toleration which William of Orange had introduced with equal vehemence. Their hostility towards him increased when he openly supported the Catholic Duc d'Anjou, first as Defender of Netherlands Liberties (1578–9) and later as their sovereign (1580–83). Orange was suspected of pursuing personal interests at the expense of the reformed faith. The contempt generally felt for the Duc d'Anjou is evident. Unable to tolerate the restrictions they imposed, he tried unsuccessfully to seize power over the Netherlands in 1583. The main object of the allegory is to show Protestant opposition to religious compromise.

117

6.14

**The Earl of Leicester as governor of
the Low Countries**, *c*.1585–7
C. van Sichem (*c*.1546–1624)

Line engraving
Inscribed *ROBERTVS DVDLEVS
LEYCESTRIAE COMES REGINAE
ANGLIAE MISSV BELGARVM
PRAEFECTVS*
188×144
National Maritime Museum (F1231)

118

This engraving celebrates Leicester's
presence in the Low Countries, and is
unlikely to post-date his departure in 1587,
by which time he had caused political chaos
there. The crown on the ground to his right
may symbolize the sovereignty offered to
Elizabeth by the Dutch, which she refused.

6.15

Map of Flushing, 1585
Robert Adams (1540–95)

Ink and colour wash
310×390
Motley, II, 1884, 348; Skelton and
Summerson, 1971, 65
*The Marquess of Salisbury, Hatfield House
(CPM II.43)*

In 1572 Flushing ejected the Spanish garrison that had built its *trace Italienne* fortifications. This plan was prepared for Sir
Francis Walsingham and shows this Dutch
naval base garrisoned by English forces.
Located at the mouth of the Scheldt, the
port was used to deny shipping access to
Antwerp and to prevent the seaborne
reinforcement of Spain's army in Flanders.

6.15

6.16
Opposition to Leicester in the Low Countries, 1587

Silver counter
Inscribed (obv.) *FVGIENS.FVMVM. INCIDIT.IN.IGNEM.1587* (Avoiding the smoke he falls into the fire);
(rev.) *LIBERTAS.NE.ITA.CHARA.VT. SIMILAE.CATVLI* (Let not liberty be as dear to us as its cubs to an ape)
30 dia.
Hawkins *et al.*, 1885, 138–9; British Museum, 1979, pl. X, 3
Trustees of the British Museum, London

6.17
Leicester unwillingly leaves the Low Countries, 1587

Silver medal
Inscribed (obv.) *ROBE.CO.LEIC.ET.IN. BELG.*; (rev.) *INVITVS DESERO* (I quit unwillingly); *NON.GREGEM.SED. INGRATOS.* (Not the flock, but the ungrateful)
49 dia.
Hawkins *et al.*, 1885, 140–41; British Museum, 1979, pl. X, 5.
Trustees of the British Museum, London

6.18
Support for Leicester in the Low Countries, 1587

Silver counter
Inscribed (obv.) *TRAHITE.AEQVO.IVGO.* (Draw with equal yoke) *1587*;
(rev.) *FRANGIMVR.SI.COLLIDIMVR.* (We break, if we clash)
29 dia.
Hawkins *et al.*, 1885, 143; British Museum, 1979, pl. X, 10
Trustees of the British Museum, London

This counter was issued by Leicester's adherents in the town of Hoorn.

119

This is one of a number of counters produced in the Low Countries expressing opposition to Leicester as governor. The Netherlanders are shown falling into the fire of Leicester's rule whilst attempting to evade the smoke of Spanish government.

This rare medal was issued by Leicester to his friends on his return to England and expresses his unwillingness to leave the Low Countries.

6.19

The 'Hell-Burners' of Antwerp, 5 April 1585

Netherlandish School, 17th century

Etching
Inscribed *Pontis Antuerpiani fractura*
290×412
Fyers, 1925, 50–53
National Maritime Museum

The Italian engineer Federigo Gianibelli constructed two floating bombs for use in attacking the great bridge that formed part of the Duke of Parma's siegeworks around Antwerp. Only one of the bombs, later called 'Hell-Burners' by the Spanish, reached its target, but it blew a great hole in the bridge and killed 800 Spanish troops. However, this success was not followed up: Parma rebuilt the bridge and Antwerp later surrendered.

6.20

Report of a Dutch attack at Dunkirk, April 1588

David Cabreth

MS
310×230
CSPF, 1586–8, 567; Herrera Oria, 1929, 222
Public Record Office, London (SP78/18, 51)

The attack on this Spanish-held port was made by means of a Dutch merchantman carrying a 'large and concealed gunpowder charge. The ship's crew brought the vessel into Dunkirk and then escaped: the ship exploded, causing great damage and terror. Shortly afterwards, Medina Sidonia was warned that a similar attack might be made on the Armada. It is likely that this event, rather than the 'Hell-Burners' episode, helped to inspire fear in the fleet during the English fireship attack.

120

Pontis Antuerpiani fractura.

A . *Pons.* B . *Flotta ante pontem.* C . *Arx S. Mariæ.*
D . *Naues septendecim Antuerpia in pontem immissæ.*
E . *Quatuor ex his maiores ignem foris, intus cuniculos portantes.*
F . *Vna ex maioribus, extincto aquis igniario, in fumum abit.*
G . *Altera, et tertia, ad ripam uento impulsæ, ruinam euomunt.*

H . *Quarta ponti impacta magnam pontis, atq; hominum stragem edit.*
I . *Pr. Parmensis, Caetanus, et Vastius humi strati, à relabentibus saxis, trabibusq; sauciantur.* K . *Tuccius Centurio sublimis elatus, demissusq;, ad ripam enatat.* L . *Adolescens prætorianus ex medio ponte in alteram ripam uiolenter infertur.*

6.19

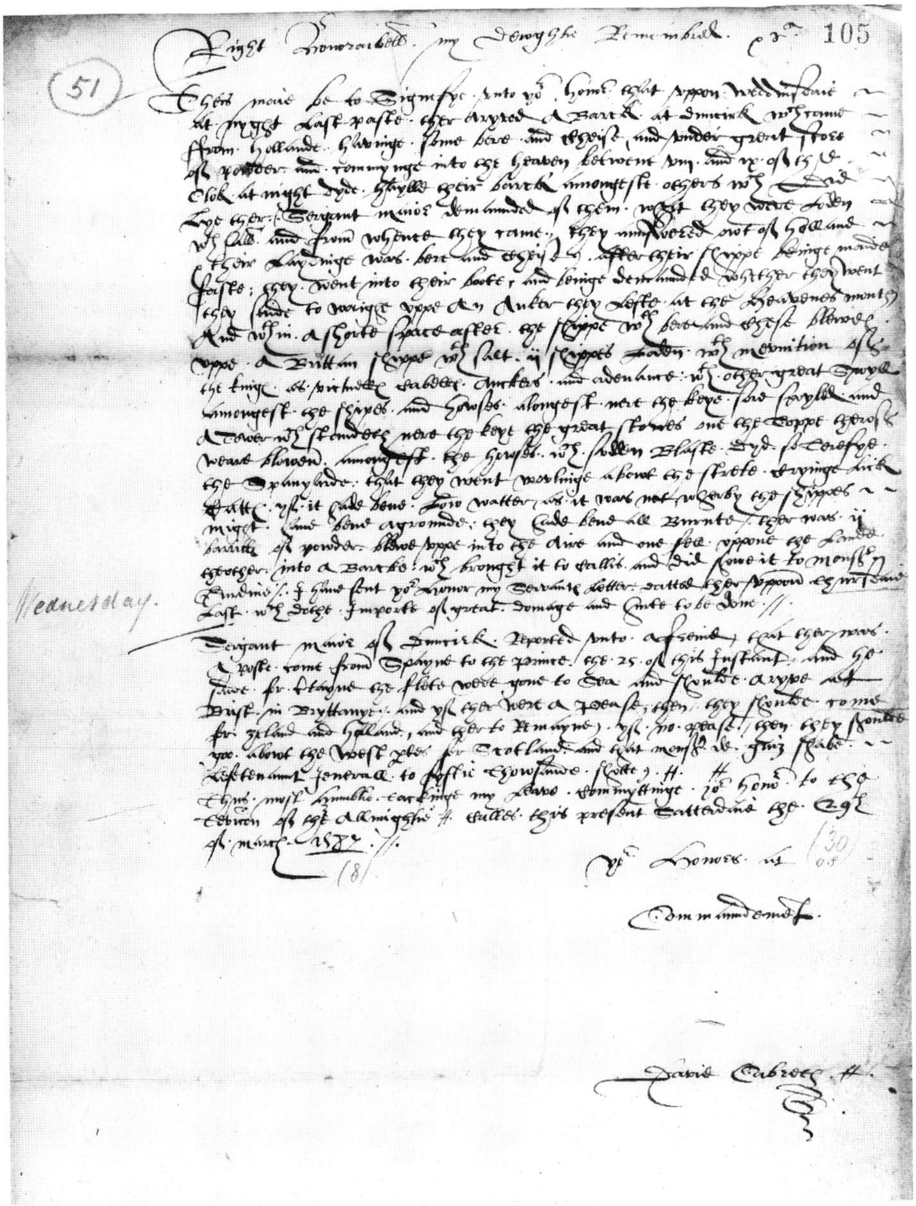

using the Armada to clear the Channel, landing between Dover and Margate. The area was fertile, wooded and near London. He reckoned it would be possible to march on from there to take the city.

6.23
Letter from Philip II to Parma, San Lorenzo de El Escorial, 4 September 1587

MS
310×213
Archivo General de Simancas, Valladolid
(E.594, f.5)

Having received Parma's advice, Philip announced his strategy for the invasion of England in this draft letter. He expressed his joy at Parma's conquest of Sluis, which would facilitate the invasion by allowing the duke to collect flat-bottomed boats from the nearby canals. These would serve to transport an army of 30,000 men to England. The king was even more delighted by Parma's enthusiasm which was overcoming the problems of mounting the expedition. This was the first time Philip clearly stated his plan to send the fleet first and foremost to protect Parma's passage. Once Parma had landed his troops, the two commanders could jointly decide what the fleet should do next.

6.24
Cardinal Allen's plans for the English Church and government, *c*.1587–8

MS
308×212
Archivo General de Simancas, Valladolid
(E.950, f.22)

William Allen listed the major posts available and requested for himself the Archbishopric of Canterbury and the grand chancellorship should the invasion succeed. There was already a dispute over the appointment of Archbishop of York – the Welsh Bishop of Cassano challenged Allen's candidate for the post. Also of interest is the marginal comment in Spanish advising Philip to win popularity by abolishing the system of royal wardship when the fleet landed.

THE ROAD TO WAR

6.21
Philip's claim to the English throne, *c*.1587: *Arbol de la succession de Inglaterra, despues de la vnion de las lineas de Lancastre y de York*

MS
572×430
AGS E.949, ff.25, 26, 40, 56
Archivo General de Simancas, Valladolid
(E.949, f.57)

Mary Stuart is shown as the legitimate successor, deprived by the 'usurper' Elizabeth. Bastardy and heresy exclude all but Philip II (heir to the house of Lancaster) from the throne after Mary Stuart. William Allen and Robert Parsons championed Philip's claim and provided the information.

6.22
Letter from the Duke of Parma to Philip II, 20 April 1586

MS
311×216
Archivo General de Simancas, Valladolid
(E.590, f.125)

This is Parma's response to the proposed invasion of England. He thought the campaign would be difficult, but highly desirable both to stop the rebellion in the Netherlands and to contain Protestantism. Three conditions were essential, however; (1) secrecy – Philip must act alone and catch Elizabeth unawares; (2) France must be neutralized; (3) adequate provision for the defence of the Netherlands and Franche-Comté must be made. Ideally, he wanted to invade from the Netherlands in small boats,

7.3 Alessandro Farnese, Duke of Parma (1545–92), Otto van Veen

7.43 Robert Dudley, Earl of Leicester (1532?–88) as Governor-General in the Netherlands, English School, 16th century

(i) The Armies of Philip II

The Duke of Parma referred to the Spanish soldiers in the Netherlands as 'his right arm', and even as the nerves of war, an accolade usually reserved for that vital commodity, money. Like money, Spanish soldiers – reckoned to be the finest infantry in Christendom – were in short supply. They withstood hardship and fought with discipline and bravery which few could match. One of the reasons for their success was the training they received: it was usual for the Spanish infantry to serve in the fortifications and outposts of North Africa and Italy before being sent to war. But after covering the garrisons in the peninsula and the colonies, there were not many available or willing to serve in Italy and the Netherlands. During Philip's reign, Spanish soldiers made up only 9 to 15 per cent of the troops he employed in the Netherlands. In 1588, for example, out of 63,455 men serving there, 30,211 were local troops – often the proportion was even higher. The next largest group was the German contingent, although at 11,309 it was less that half its usual strength. There were 9,668 Spaniards, more than double the number for much of the decade. The 5,339 Italians, 1,556 Burgundians, 1,722 English, Irish and Scottish soldiers made up the rest.[1]

Parma thought that he would need 30,000 infantry for the campaign in England, with 500 cavalry as support.[2] He specified their provenance: 6,000 Spaniards, 6,000 Italians, 6,000 Walloons, 9,000 Germans and 3,000 Burgundians. He was eager to gather as many pikemen as possible and the best arquebusiers. The cavalry would be mixed and go without horses, as these were plentiful in England. Additionally, Philip was asked to send troops to strengthen the garrisons in the Netherlands and the Franche-Comté. Philip tried to comply in full.

It would have been relatively easy to levy raw recruits, but the core of the army had to be seasoned soldiers, and these were scarce. Following the pattern of previous years, Philip moved experienced soldiers to the front and replaced them with new levies. A few companies from Sicily, Naples and Milan were sent to the Netherlands, but 3,000 of their men went directly to Lisbon. Their places were taken by 7,000 new Spanish infantry.[3] Experienced troops from the North African, Spanish and Portuguese fortifications, as well as those from the Azores, were also ordered to join the fleet at Lisbon.[4] To reduce risks and expenditure, most of the Spanish reinforcements Parma had requested for the Netherlands went with the expeditionary fleet. When Medina Sidonia suggested that these 6,000 men were necessary for the campaign, Parma complained and Philip reiterated his order that the men should be left to defend the Netherlands.[5]

Philip ordered new levies of 11,000 Spanish infantry to join the fleet in Lisbon, while Italian recruits were sent to the Netherlands. He asked for 3,000 to 4,000 men from Naples, and 4,000 to 5,000 from Urbino, Romagna, Parma, Ferrara and Corsica. The Neapolitans passed into history for their colourful costumes and plumes, which earned them Parma's soubriquet of 'the theatrical *tercio*', more suited to a mock battle than real war. Altogether some 10,000 Italians were sent to the north. Philip also empowered Parma to levy Netherlanders and Germans, but recruitment by Casimir of the Palatinate and the Huguenots during 1587 drained the area and made his task difficult.

The Spanish and Italian troops were levied largely by royal officials. Throughout his reign, Philip sought to impose direct control of military organization. But at times of crisis, the rudimentary state organization could not provide sufficient numbers, and more men had to be raised by military entrepreneurs. German troops were always raised by such contractors, who were asked to provide a specific number of men at prearranged prices. They often agreed to transport and provision them as well. Frequently they loaned large sums to the crown. After 1586, Spanish recruitment went through a new phase: a large proportion of the infantry recruited came from Andalusia, in the form of contributions from towns and lords who retained a great deal of control over the appointment of officials and areas of recruitment.[6] Despite many problems, Philip successfully raised the required number of men, but conditions in the Netherlands led to the death of many soldiers, especially raw recruits. The famine of 1587 was followed by plague; this, together with the bitterly cold winters and the rigours of the journey, took a heavy toll. Additionally, there was large-scale desertion – more than the usual one-sixth among the Spanish and Italian troops in the Netherlands.[7] By the spring of 1588 only 6,562 remained of the Spanish reinforcements, and 5,339 Italians were registered in the whole of the Netherlands. In March Parma abandoned hope of taking 30,000 men. He settled for 17,000 for the campaign against England, and he felt that even this was excessive in view of the requirements for the defence of the Netherlands. The invasion force was now composed of 8,000 Germans and Walloons, 4,000 Spaniards, 3,000 Italians, 1,000 Burgundians and 1,000 from the British Isles.[8]

In Lisbon 16,000 men, mostly Spanish, were ready to embark by December 1587. Like all Philip's armies, this one included a number of royal officials

1. Parker, 1972, Appendix A; AGS E.590 f.7; O'Donnell y Duque de Estrada, 1986a and b.
2. AGS E.590 f.125, cat. **6.22**.
3. AGS GA.208 f.83.
4. O'Donnell y Duque de Estrada, 1986a, a study of the Spanish contingents; id., 1986b for the Italian infantry.
5. See, e.g., AGS E.594 f.49 and E.594 f.79.
6. AGS GA.208 f.83, GA.221 f.8, Thompson, 1976 for a clear account of Spanish military organization, 110, 123–4 for Andalusia. Redlich, 1964, is the best authority for the German military enterprises.
7. O'Donnell y Duque de Estrada, 1986a and 1986b. Parker, 1972.
8. AGS E.594 f.26, Parker, 1976, 359.

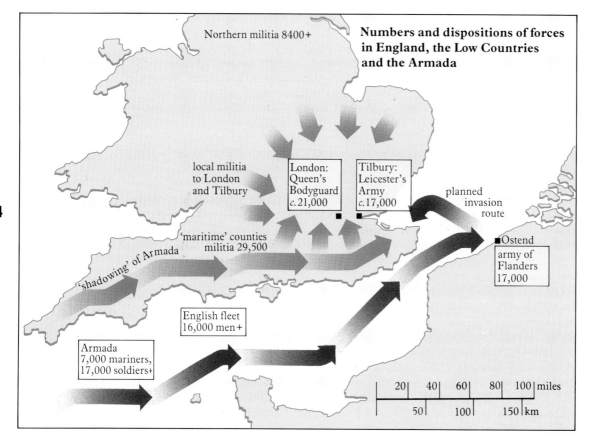

Numbers and dispositions of forces
in England, the Low Countries
and the Armada

Northern militia 8400+

local militia
to London
and Tilbury

London:
Queen's
Bodyguard
c.21,000

Tilbury:
Leicester's
Army
c.17,000

planned
invasion
route

'maritime' counties
militia 29,500

'shadowing' of Armada

English fleet
16,000 men+

Armada
7,000 mariners,
17,000 soldiers+

Ostend
army of
Flanders
17,000

	20	40	60	80	100	miles
		50		100		150	km

124

and medical staff, but the unusual number of ecclesiastics – between 158 and 180 – reflected the king's intention to begin the process of conversion immediately. The number of regular and irregular troops in the fleet grew as the delays gave them time to gather. By mid-May 1588 there were nearly 19,000 regular infantry on board the fleet. They were supported by an impressive array of unpaid *aventureros* (aristocratic adventurers) with their retinues, and *entretenidos* (some aristocrats, but mostly lower nobility), who received support from the king. Figures vary in the multiple accounts produced, but the *aventureros* increased from 116 (14 May) to 224 (28 May). Their retinues, all capable of fighting, were estimated at *c*.450. There were 220–30 *entretenidos*, and 163 of their servants could fight as well. These men were, again, mostly Spanish, but there were also forty Portuguese noblemen, a number of Italians and some English, Irish and Scots. Taking into account the number of seamen, which remained steady at 8,000, the effectives of the invasion fleet in May 1588 were just under 29,000 men.[9]

A new muster was taken in July 1588, after the storms and the epidemic which affected the fleet in La

Coruña. It includes a number of men (*c*.200–300) taken from the garrisons of Galicia, but omits the 2,000 combatants in the eight missing ships. There were now 25,535 men on board and the effectives were reckoned at 22,436.

The well-organized, professional army which served in the Netherlands and in the Armada campaign contrasted sharply with the ill-equipped and untrained militias which were called upon to defend Spain during raids or invasion. In some areas – especially the south and east – constant corsair activity had sharpened these groups into effective forces. However, in Galicia and Portugal, where the English attacked with impunity in 1585–9, the men pressed into service were so poor that even the desperate Medina Sidonia decided to send them back home rather than take them on the campaign against England.[10]

M. J. Rodríguez-Salgado

9. These figures were culled from the numerous summaries of the fleet, but particularly from AGS GA.221 f.143, GA.221 f.158, E.431 f.45 and B.L. 192 f.1.
10. Thompson, 1976.

(ii) The Invasion Plan

The main task of the Armada was to protect the passage of the Duke of Parma and his men to England.[1] The fleet was to proceed without delay to 'cape Margate' avoiding all diversions. There was good anchorage there, and both current and tide favoured contact with the Netherlands.

Philip accepted that if Drake's ships or any other English squadron chased the fleet and got too close, then they must give battle. He did not stipulate the order of battle because he realized he could not predict the conditions, so he left the decision to Medina Sidonia and the experienced captains in the Armada. Credit for the powerful and effective formation of the fleet thus belongs entirely to them. Philip did warn them that the English, with their faster ships and longer-range guns, would try to avert close encounters, and that they would use fireships. He hoped that his ships would not have to fight the English until they reached Margate, where the numerical and qualitative superiority of the Armada (and divine aid) would surely give him victory. There was another reason for lifting the ban on combat at this point – it might distract and engage the English fleet and so serve as a useful cover for Parma's voyage. Once the fleet had reached Margate or – if the wind pushed it further – the mouth of the Thames, Medina Sidonia had to wait until Parma's flotilla landed safely. Parma had been gathering ships and men in Dunkirk and Nieuport. On receiving news of the Armada's arrival in the Channel, he was ordered to embark his men and sail for England. It was a task he predicted would be accomplished in less than three days: two days for embarkation and the journey in eight to twelve hours.

The instructions are vague as to what port or area had been designated for the attack. At one time or another the Isle of Wight, Southampton and Dover had been seriously considered and rejected as too difficult or not of sufficient importance (in the case of the Isle of Wight). Parma favoured a direct march on London, but had not decided upon which side of the river it was best to land. They hoped to gain information as to the disposition of the defending troops on arrival and then choose. Moreover, the exact place of landing could not be accurately predicted since both the Armada and the flotilla would be at the mercy of the winds and the English and Dutch fleets. It was usual in this period for the sovereign to discuss strategy and decide upon a number of likely targets, deferring a final choice until the last moment or leaving it up to the commanders.

When the army of the Netherlands had landed, Philip ordered Medina Sidonia to give Parma most of the soldiers and some of the artillery from the ships. There is no doubt that the land campaign was the primary one. The two generals were then to decide jointly what role the fleet should play. The king had some suggestions and expected them to discuss these seriously when the time came. The Armada might simply patrol the Channel and keep communications between the invading forces and the Netherlands open. This would be essential if, as was suspected, the English withdrew inland taking victuals and horses with them. Once a major English position had been taken, and if there was no other urgent need, Philip wanted Medina Sidonia to take the fleet – supported by Italian and German troops – to Ireland.

If Medina Sidonia failed 'to join hands' with Parma, Philip ordered him to 'take some enemy port' where the fleet could shelter and repair, preferably at the mouth of the river Thames. Alternatively, the fleet might turn back and attack the Isle of Wight. The king was adamant that this was the secondary target and it must not be attempted until the primary objective had failed. It might be possible to coordinate with Parma's troops later from the island. Philip decided against ordering Medina Sidonia to take both Southampton and the Isle of Wight on the grounds that 'the whole of England' would turn out to recover the port but they could not easily recover the island.[2]

Finally, should the attack fail completely – something which the king and his councillors found inconceivable since they saw it as God's work – they consoled themselves with the thought that the mere threat of invasion would have made the English more amenable to peace.

M. J. Rodríguez-Salgado

(iii) The Defence of England in 1588

There was considerable uncertainty as to where the Spanish might land, and there were a number of plans both for national and local defence. Thousands of men were brought into London to act as bodyguard for the queen, and a force of about 17,000 was gathered at Tilbury Camp under the Earl of Leicester. It was feared that the enemy might either land in the south-east or attempt to force its way up the Thames, and Leicester's army was to be the main force to meet them in battle. Other areas were regarded as vulnerable: the southern 'maritime' counties contributed militia, nominally 29,500 strong, to follow the Armada's progress up the Channel, and forces from East Anglia northwards were ready both to defend the coast and guard the Scottish border.

1. Instructions for Santa Cruz: AGS E.165 ff.6–7, ff.23–5, E.594 f.1, f.2; for Medina Sidonia: AGS E.165 ff.106–108; ff.109–11; ff.113–14; Additional instructions to Parma, E.165 ff.174–5; ff.179–80 and Medina Sidonia, E.165 f.144. Parma's strategy: AGS E.590 f.125 and E.594 f.127. **2.** AGS E.165 ff.113–14.

125

Plans also existed to reinforce major ports if they were attacked, along with other possible landing-places such as the Isle of Wight, Anglesey and Milford Haven. The main strategy was to delay the Spanish on the coast using small forces, to allow time for the main army inland to organize a counter-attack, although some favoured the idea of massing troops on the coast and attempting to prevent a landing.

Numbers of seamen and soldiers

	Seamen	Troops
English	16,000+	76,000?
Spanish	7,000	34,000+

In 1588 England did not possess a standing army, but did have a large body of militia, backed by small numbers of veteran troops who had served in the Low Countries and elsewhere. The exact size of the militia is difficult to ascertain, for despite the profusion of figures relating to troop musters in 1588, it is clear that conflicting requirements for soldiers could lead to the same men being counted twice. Also, some troops were not recorded, as they were still on the march to their places of duty when the order to return home was received, and the government did not have to pay them.[1]

Local militia had existed for centuries, but in 1573 the government stipulated that each county was to select a sufficient number of able men to be trained and armed as militia. This is the origin of the 'trained bands'. Training was particularly required in the use of pikes and muskets, and the policy met opposition on grounds of cost. Weapons such as the bill and the obsolescent bow (see cat. nos. **7.40** and **7.57**) were generally cheaper than the newer arms, and the bow in particular had special significance for moralists and traditionalists. Regular archery training was seen by some (including, on occasion, the government) as a way of curbing gambling and similar pursuits, and the myth of the bowman as the backbone of English military force still held great appeal in the late sixteenth century. However, by 1588 the great majority of the militia seems to have been armed with pike and musket, apart from the cavalry, who carried either lances or handguns such as petronels.

Training appears to have involved both instruction in the use of particular weapons and the performance of the many manoeuvres needed to put bodies of troops in battle array. These manoeuvres could even include mock battles. When the Earl of Derby visited Liverpool in 1577, the civic celebrations included a military display in which the town

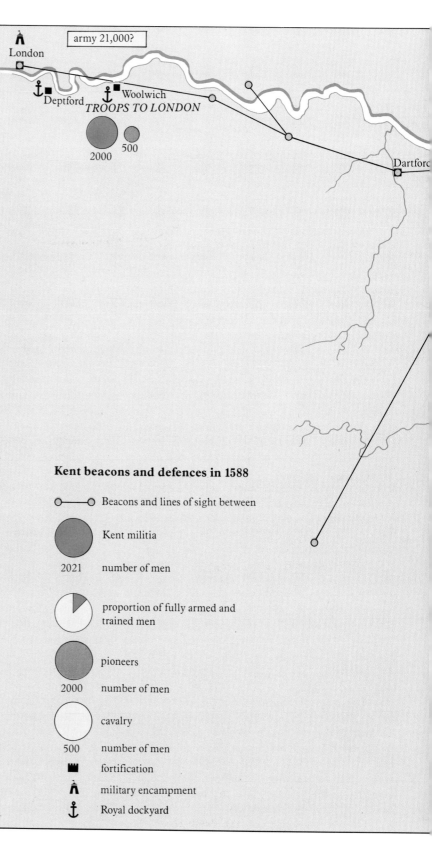

army 21,000?

London

Deptford

Woolwich

TROOPS TO LONDON

2000

500

Dartford

Kent beacons and defences in 1588

○——○ Beacons and lines of sight between

⬤ Kent militia

2021 number of men

◔ proportion of fully armed and trained men

⬤ pioneers

2000 number of men

○ cavalry

500 number of men

▪ fortification

⋀ military encampment

⚓ Royal dockyard

126

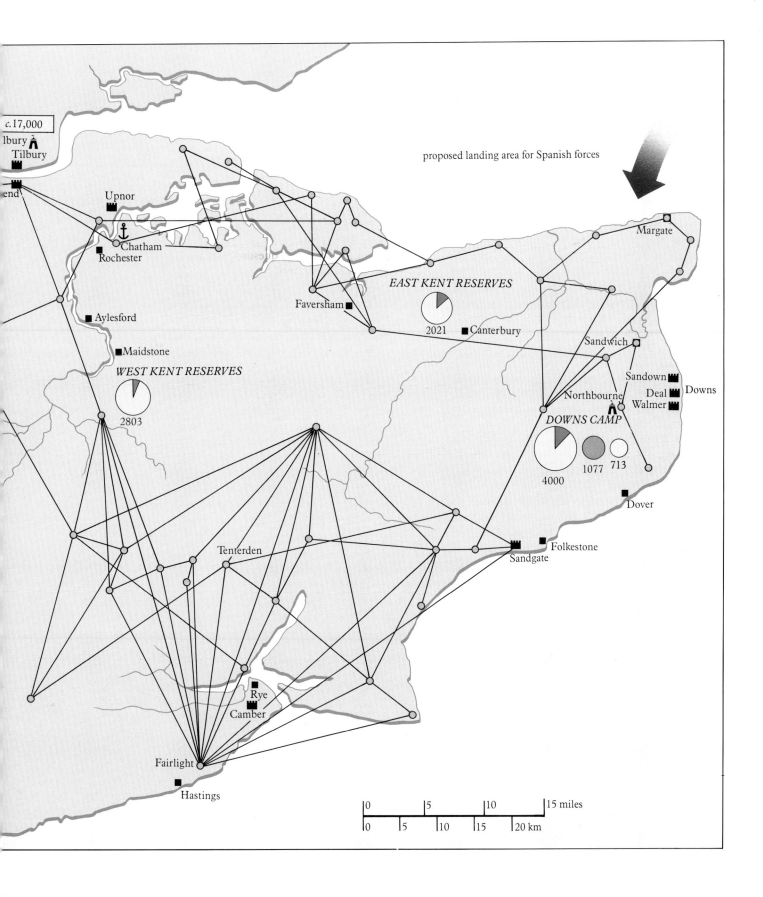

*c.*17,000

Tilbury

end

Upnor

Chatham

Rochester

Aylesford

Maidstone

WEST KENT RESERVES

2803

Faversham

EAST KENT RESERVES

2021   Canterbury

proposed landing area for Spanish forces

Margate

Sandwich

Sandown

Northbourne   Deal   Downs

Walmer

DOWNS CAMP

4000   1077   713

Dover

Tenterden

Sandgate   Folkestone

Rye

Camber

Fairlight

Hastings

0		5		10		15 miles

0	5	10	15	20 km

company 'skirmished very bravelie and orderlie'.[2] It is difficult to assess exactly how widespread or effective the training was, or how generally well-equipped the English militia were. It has been estimated that the Kent militia, defending the county in which the Spanish might have landed, had only 2,958 fully armed and trained infantry out of a force of some 10,824 foot-soldiers. Furthermore, 2,000 of the trained men were due to join the queen's army in London.[3]

Warning of the invasion threat was conveyed across the country by means of the beacon system, complemented by post carried by horsemen or conveyed in small, fast ships. Sir Thomas Scott's letter to Burghley of 5 August 1588 (see cat. no. **7.67**) was carried through the night to London, passing through Sittingbourne at 4 a.m., and Drake's warning to Seymour that the Armada had been contacted was taken up the Channel in a caravel (see cat. no. **14.46**). The beacons, however, were the most important means of alerting the county forces. They were sited on high points, within sight of one or more other beacons, as the map of the Kent beacons shows (cat. no. **7.69**). The system was not always well-maintained, but efforts were made to see that watchers were stationed at the beacons in the dangerous period between spring and autumn. The flickering of beacons on the Cornish coast was seen by the Armada when it sighted the Lizard and beacons are prominent in both English and Dutch representations of the campaign (see Section 14). The general success of the beacon and post systems can be judged from the extent of the mobilization in 1588, which at its peak may have involved as many as 76,000 men.

Although they greatly outnumbered the potential Spanish invasion forces, it is difficult to know just how effective the English troops might have been. The main army in any battle with an invader would have been commanded by Leicester, who had shown himself to be a poor general in the Low Countries and in any case was seriously ill, dying shortly after the Armada campaign. More experienced and competent men such as Sir John Norris and Sir Roger Williams were entirely subject to his authority and not exalted enough to act as more than important advisors. Most militia officers and soldiers, no matter how well-trained, had no actual experience of war, whereas the Spanish forces included many veteran troops, schooled in the hard campaigns of the Low Countries and elsewhere.

Land warfare would have inevitably involved some sieges, as happened in the Netherlands, but here there was a fundamental weakness in the English defences. A major programme had been started in about 1583 to repair and improve fortifications, including essential works at Dover and Portsmouth, but royal forts and blockhouses were too few and too scattered to be of much more than local importance. The most important inland towns and cities had only their medieval walls, which would have been little use against contemporary siege techniques. A considerable effort was made to create earthworks and trenches on the coast in 1588, but these would not have hindered the enemy for long.

Successful defensive action on land would in the end have depended on the ability of the English either to defeat the Spanish in a pitched battle, or to so wear down the Spanish forces that they would be obliged to make a truce. The question as to whether an invasion would have been defeated or not is of course unanswerable.[4] The few instances of the militia's response to Spanish raids in the 1590s are insufficient for any generalizations to be made about the qualities of the local forces. When 400 Spanish troops landed on the Cornish coast in 1595 and burned some settlements, the local men at first ran away, but later rallied and prevented the raiders from landing again.[5] Determined as many Englishmen doubtless were in 1588, there would have been no easy victory for them over an invading force, and the strain of a prolonged land war would have been considerable. The men marching to Tilbury or their other places of duty in 1588 were fortunate that they did not have to face the kinds of horrors witnessed in the Low Countries by the poet and one-time soldier, George Gascoigne, who died in 1577:

My promise was, and I record it so,
To write in verse (God wot though little worth)
That war seems sweet to such as little know
What comes thereby, what fruits it bringeth forth . . .
I set aside to tell the restless toil,
The mangled corpse, the laméd limbs at last,
    The shortened years by fret of fevers foul . . .
The broken sleeps, the dreadful dreams, the woe,
Which one with war and cannot from him go.

Ian Friel

1. The principal works concerned with the defence of England and English military forces in 1588 are Webb, 1965; Cruikshank, 1966; McGurk, 1970; Boynton, 1971 and Colvin *et al.*, 1982.
2. Twemlow, 1935, 244–5.
3. McGurk, 1970, 88.
4. The matter is discussed at length in Parker, 1976.
5. Rowse, 1947, 403–406.

7.1
Cañon de batir, Mechelen, 1556
Remigy de Halut (*fl.* 1536–68)

Bronze
Inscribed with the arms of Spain and
England surrounded by collar and insignia of
the Golden Fleece with *PHILIPPVS REX*
in cartouche; *IOANES.MARICVS.A.
LARA.FIERI.CVRAVIT/OPVS.REMIGY.
DE.HALVT/ ANNO 1556* (base ring); *5316*
(weight mark, Castilian *libras*)
2900 lgth; 183 cal.; *c.*2500 kg
Crédit Communal, 1985, 110
Ulster Museum, Belfast

The inscription on this siege-gun shows that
it was cast on the orders of Don Juan
Manrique de Lara, Captain-General of the
Artillery (1551–74). It was part of a fourteen-
strong siege-train shipped with the Armada.
This piece and two others were loaded
aboard the transport *Trinidad Valencera*, a
converted Venetian grain ship later wrecked
in Kinnagoe Bay, County Donegal. These
were the heaviest guns used on either side,
throwing an iron shot of forty pounds, and
their job was to batter down fortifications
from close range. At sea their dismantled
field-carriages (two sets for each piece) were
stowed in the hold, and the guns themselves,
mounted on makeshift sea-carriages, were
expected to serve as naval ordnance, but
were very difficult to use in this role.

7.2
Gun-carriage wheel from the
Trinidad Valencera

Wood and steel
1095 dia.; 120 wdth
Ulster Museum, Belfast

This is a large, composite wooden wheel, fitted with an iron tyre 110 mm wide. The
wheel has ten spokes, each morticed in place,
meeting at a hub 240 mm in diameter. The
hub is 110 mm deep, and would have taken
an axle 88 mm in diameter.

7.3
Alessandro Farnese, Duke of Parma
(1545–92), *c.*1585–90
Otto van Veen (1556–1629)

Oil on canvas
Inscribed *EXAND. FARNESI / PARMAE.
DUX*
580×480
Musée de l'Art Wallon, 1966, 57
*Musées Royaux des Beaux-Arts de Belgique,
Brussels (1327)*

Grandson of Charles V, educated at the
Spanish court, a veteran of Lepanto, governor of the Netherlands from 1578 and a

notable patron of the arts, the Duke of
Parma was a statesman of eminent social
standing and high military renown, as this
richly decorated portrait pointedly suggests.
The painter's training in Italy (from 1576)
may have endeared him to his Italian sitter,
and in 1585 he was appointed court painter
to Farnese in Brussels. By this stage Parma's
campaign to regain Spanish control of the
Netherlands was proceeding with considerable success: the south was in harness, and
by 1588 his preparations for the reconquest
of Holland and Zeeland were well advanced.
He was to command the Spanish military
forces in the invasion of England, and was
blamed by some when the scheme failed. His
intervention in the French wars from 1590–
92 was also at Philip's bidding and against
his own inclination.

7.4
Alessandro Farnese, Duke of Parma
(1545–92)
Gisbert van Veen (1562–1628) after
Otto van Veen (1556–1629)

Engraving
Inscribed *Victor Alexandro Magno . . .
Relligio Parmae tegmine tuta tuae;
EXPVGNATIO ANTVERPIAE;
EXPVGNATIO TYRI*; shield with *Relligio,
Lex, Grex, treis, vos Farnesia Iesu Christi
fulminea, Parma tuetur ope*
438×241
National Maritime Museum (G.1592)

129

This engraving surrounds the figure of Parma
with scenes and symbols of victory, and
shows him as a defender of religion and
truth. The Latin poem associates him with
his namesake, Alexander the Great, perhaps
linking with the theme apparently shown on
his parade shield (cat. no. **7.6**).

130

7.5
Parade helmet of Alessandro Farnese, Duke of Parma (1545–92)

Steel damascened and embossed with gold and silver
300 ht; 240 wdth
Blair, 1958, 176–7
Kunsthistorisches Museum, Vienna

Parade armour of the sixteenth century was usually decorated in the classical manner, and intended to imitate the splendid armours of antiquity. This helmet and the shield (cat. no. **7.6**) are exquisite examples of parade armour of the period, which was made for public display rather than use in battle.

The helmet is of the burgonet type, and its decoration is a mixture of classical and Christian symbolism. On both sides of the helmet are scenes which appear to have been taken from the legend of Hercules, and show him fighting with a Triton and a half-dog, half-water-serpent Hydra. The cheekpieces are embellished with angels holding palms and laurel wreaths, with spears over their shoulders.

This headpiece was formerly in the armoury of Archduke Ferdinand II of Tyrol (1529–95), who acquired it from Parma.

7.6
Parade shield of Alessandro Farnese, Duke of Parma (1545–92)

Steel damascened and embossed with gold and silver
650 ht; 500 wdth
Blair, 1958, 176–7
Kunsthistorisches Museum, Vienna

Like Parma's parade helmet (cat. no. **7.5**), this shield was formerly part of the armour collection of Archduke Ferdinand II of Tyrol, purchased by him from the Duke of Parma.

The shield is replete with classical motifs. It is quartered by figures of the many-breasted goddess Diana of Ephesus, a symbol of fertility, and between these are scenes representing the seasons. The central panel of the shield appears to show Alexander the Great receiving the keys of Babylon, and in this perhaps links Parma's Christian name with the theme of military conquest. The figure holding the keys is crowned with the laurel leaves of victory.

7.7
Field cuirass of the Duke of Parma, late 16th century

Steel and leather
Front: 390 ht, 400 wdth; back: 410 ht, 400 wdth
Grosz and Thomas, 1936, 134; Blair, 1958, 124 and 170
Kunsthistorisches Museum, Vienna (A117)

Part of Parma's field armour comprising collar, breastplate with scalloped waist-flange, and backplate, closed over the shoulders and round the waist by straps. The surface of the cuirass has been left 'rough from the hammer', that is to say, the marks from the armourer's hammer have not been polished off and can be clearly seen. The heavy roped and turned edges at the neck and arms are not only decorative but also prevented a weapon glancing off into the throat or limbs.

7.8
Letter from Dr Valentine Dale (*fl.*1541–89) to Burghley, 22 July 1588

MS (2ff.)
299×215
CSPF, 1588, II, 35–6; Wernham, 1966, 393–5
Public Record Office, London (SP77/4, 260)

Dr Dale was one of the commissioners sent by Elizabeth to negotiate peace with Parma. The discussions, held at Bourbourg near Ostend between late May and July 1588, were futile, and had the unfortunate effect of making the Dutch fear possible English betrayal. This induced them to keep their ships on their own coast for most of the Armada campaign. The negotiations allowed the English to gain some first-hand information regarding Parma's preparations. In this disturbing report Dr Dale describes seeing more than 15,000 Spanish, Italian and German troops, the latter well-equipped and in good order despite having made a twenty-two-day march from the Tyrol. Flat-bottomed invasion barges were being gathered at Gravelines and Dunkirk to transport men and horses. However, Dale reports that Parma is worried about the sea crossing: his naval forces are weak and the crossing could only be made by stealth or with the support of the Armada.

7.9
Map of Ostend, 1590
Simon Basil (*fl.*1590–1608)

Pen and colour wash
Inscribed *Simone Basilio Authorie De Rob: Adami famulo, 1590*
316×411; scale 1:824000
Strada, 1635, 9, 537–58; Skelton and Summerson, 1971, 66
The Marquess of Salisbury, Hatfield House (CPM II. 46)

Ostend's long defiance – until 1600 – forced Parma to construct canals in 1588 to move his flat-bottomed craft safely around Ostend to Nieuport, where the troops embarked (marked 'D' on the map) for England. Elizabeth's Privy Council subsequently ordered Robert Adams to improve the fortifications of Ostend. In June 1590, Adams was joined there by Simon Basil, who succeeded him as Surveyor of the Queen's Works in 1595.

7.10
The Arte of Warre . . ., 1588
Niccolò Macchiavelli (1469–1527), trans. P. Whitehorne

Publ. Thomas East for John Wight, 3rd ed., London
Printed book
198×295
Webb, 1965, 13–15, 28–9; Hale, 1983, 247–8
British Library, London (1140.h.2)

Niccolò Machiavelli, Florentine statesman, was influenced by classical writers. His *Libro dell'Arte della Guerra*, written in popular dialogue form, emphasizes ancient Roman models. The book was first published in Florence in 1521, and the first English edition was printed in 1560. Whitehorne served with Charles V's army and, like Machiavelli, rejected mercenaries and claimed that satisfactory troops were to be found only

7.9

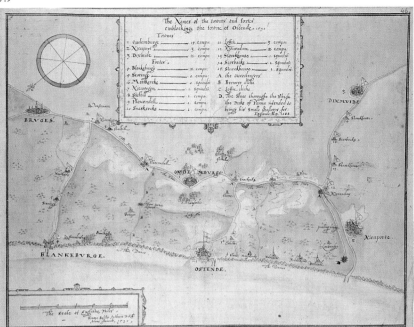

131

among one's own countrymen. First published in 1560, this popular and influential book includes Whitehorne's own work, *Certain waies for the ordering of soldiers.*

7.11
The Pathwaie to Martiall Discipline . . ., 1581
Thomas Styward (*fl.*1580)

1st ed., London
Printed book
189×287
Webb, 1965, 42–50
British Library, London (G.2329)

This book was one of the most popular military treatises in Elizabethan England, appearing in three editions in the 1580s. Styward derived some of his ideas from his own experience and that of his contemporaries but, like most military writers of the time, he was much influenced by classical precedent, particularly that of the Roman army. Some professional soldiers scorned this reliance on antiquity, but it is likely that those English militia officers who read about warfare found themselves imbibing classically based military theory: little else was available in print.

7.12
Dialogos del Arte Militar . . ., 1588
Bernardino de Escalante

Publ. Brussels, 1595 ed.
Printed book
AGS E.165, f.223 (Treatise 1588)
200×157
British Library, London (534.e.7(2))

Escalante, a commissioner of the Inquisition of Seville, drew up two lengthy memoranda urging Philip II to attack England in 1587–8, with details of the best strategy to adopt. His treatise, approved in 1588, included information on the basic items needed for a naval campaign. His book was aimed at the educated and experienced soldier, and deals with the major offices in the army, describing the duties of each in order to improve military discipline and efficiency. This copy is bound with the 1589 editions of two earlier military treatises, by Sancho de Londoño and Francisco de Valdés, which cover similar themes.

7.13

Three drawings of musket and pike drill from *Wapenhandelinghe van Roers Musquetten ende Spiessen*, 1607
Jacques de Gheyn II (1565–1629)
No. 6 . . . *the right use of all what a souldier needeth to know in handling of the Pike*
No. 9 . . . *touching the right use of calivers*
No. 41 . . . *the right use of muskett*

Pen and brown ink with grey washes
264×172; 263×135; 266×188
Boon, II, 1978, 68–74
National Maritime Museum (M109, M96, M108)

These drawings are part of a large set designed for engraving as plates for the manual of the exercise of arms, *Wapenhandelinghe van Roers Musquetten ende Spiessen*, published in Amsterdam and London in 1607. Jan van Nassau-Seigen commissioned the drawings about ten years prior to publication. The manual was dedicated to Prince Maurits of Nassau and was intended to serve as a training guide for officers and commanders. The drawings illustrated here are taken from three sections which describe in detail the commands and movements associated with the use of the caliver, a light military gun; the musket, a heavier gun requiring the use of a rest; and the pike, used in formation as a defence against cavalry. De Gheyn was probably assisted by one of his pupils. Despite the repetitive nature of the subject, the figures have been invested with a lively quality and show a fine eye for details of dress.

7.14

Italian or Flemish corselet, *c*.1580

Steel
710 ht (body); 190 ht (helmet)
Trustees of the Royal Armouries, London (III.2275–80)

'Flanders corselets' were used in very large numbers by the heavy-infantry pikemen during the second half of the sixteenth century. This example is composed of elements from several, including a gorget of a later form. The cheekpieces are modern restorations.

7.15

Italian or Flemish corselet, *c*.1580

Steel
710 ht (body); 190 ht (helmet)
Trustees of the Royal Armouries, London (II.37)

Composed of a 'Spanish' morion and cuirass, worn with tassets at the thighs and pauldrons and vambraces protecting the shoulders and arms. This example is unusual in having gorget plates fitted to the neck of the cuirass, rather than as a separate defence. The cheekpieces are modern restorations.

7.16

Buff jerkin, *c*.1570–90

Ox-hide leather
675 front; 1185 chest
Halls, 1970, 10; Cruikshank, 1966, 116
Museum of London (57/127.1)

Buff jerkins were sleeveless protective garments made from thick leather, of similar shape to the doublets over which they were worn. The thickness and durability of the ox-hide made it especially useful for military clothing, and a jerkin such as this would have helped to protect the body of the wearer whilst leaving the arms free. Jerkins could also be worn underneath armour as padding and supplementary protection, although the ones used for this purpose were sometimes made of fustian cloth or canvas. Military buff jerkins were in use in the later part of the sixteenth century.

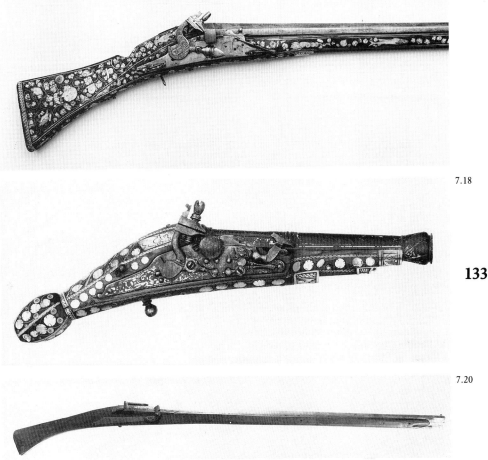

7.17

7.18

133

7.20

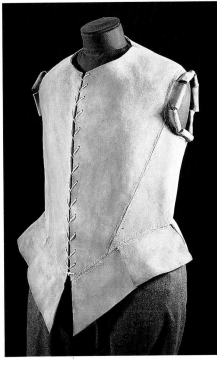

7.17
English snaphance musket, 1588

Wooden stock inlaid with engraved bone
Inscribed *R.A.* (gunmaker's initials on
barrel); *R.I. D.I.* (stockmaker's initials on
stock); *1588* (on butt plate)
1620 lgth (barrel 1237); 21 cal.
Hayward, 1959
*Board of Trustees of the Victoria and Albert
Museum, London*

According to tradition, this gun was captured
from one of the ships of the Spanish
Armada. However, it is English, and the
legend probably originated from the date
1588 on the butt plate. The cock of the
musket is engraved with a dolphin, and the
lockplate with scroll-work, but the barrel is
plain. The ornament on the stock consists of
floral scrolls with Tudor roses, hunting
scenes, birds, insects, snails and fish. The
musket is fired by an early form of flintlock
known as a snaphance. The flint is held in
the jaws of the cock which is pulled back
(cocked) against the force of a spring. When
released by pressing the trigger the cock
snaps forward striking the flint against the
steel, sending a shower of sparks into the
priming powder in the pan and igniting the
charge.

7.18
English snaphance pistol, *c.*1600

Metal damascened with gold; walnut stock
inlaid with engraved bone and
mother-of-pearl
286 lgth (barrel 159); 11.4 cal.; 0.538 kg
Norman and Wilson, 1982, 75–6
*Trustees of the Royal Armouries, London
(XII.1823)*

One of the first decorated English pistols, of
a type known as a 'pocket dag' because of its
small size.

7.19
Matchlock musket, *c.*1560–70

Wood and iron
1345 ht; 16.5 cal.
*Trustees of the Royal Armouries, London
(XII.8)*

Matchlock muskets delivered a heavy short-
range shock, and could be used with lead
balls, small shot, penetrating arrows called
'sprites', or fire arrows. They were loaded
from the muzzle with black powder, a wad
and the projectile. Priming powder was placed in the pan and the cover closed until
needed. Shortly before use, the 'match', a
cord treated with saltpetre and held in the
serpentine, was lit. To fire the musket, the

pan cover was moved aside, and a squeeze on
the trigger pulled the match into the pan.
The resultant flash was transmitted to the
main charge via the touch-hole. The system
was vulnerable to wind or rain which could
extinguish the match or blow away the priming powder. (See cat. nos. **7.20** and **7.21**.)

7.20
Spanish matchlock musket,
15th–16th centuries

Wood and iron
Inscribed *E.I.* (on stock)
1360 lgth (barrel 980); 16 cal.
Museo Arqueológico Nacional, 1980; cf.
Crédit Communal, 1985, 4.1
Museo Arqueológico Nacional, Madrid (41.991)

The stock of this musket has certain similarities with the stock of a 16 mm-calibre
musket recovered from the wreck of the galleass *Girona*.

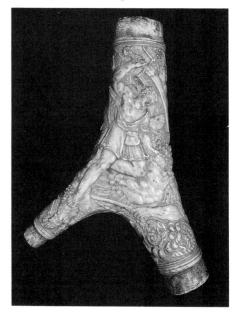

7.21
Spanish matchlock musket, late 16th century

Wood and iron
2046 lgth; 21 cal.; 9.2 kg
Museo del Ejército, Madrid (1.955)

The barrel of this musket is figured and carved near the chamber and has fore and rear sights. It has a straight trigger, a reversed spring and an inlaid iron ramrod. There is a maker's mark near the fore sight.

7.22
Spanish wheel-lock musket

Wood and iron
1870 lgth; 8 cal.; 4.2 kg
Blair, 1983, 33–42
Patrimonio Nacional. Real Armería de Madrid (K.8)

One of the greatest problems in producing an effective firearm was to ensure reliable and near-instantaneous ignition. The wheel-lock was a step in this direction which appeared early in the sixteenth century. In essence it worked like a modern cigarette-lighter. A wheel, rotated rapidly by a spring mechanism released when the trigger was pressed, set off a shower of sparks from a lump of iron pyrites. These sparks then ignited gunpowder 'priming' in the pan, which in turn set off the main charge. Though reasonably effective, the wheel-lock was complicated, difficult to make, delicate and expensive, and therefore comparatively rare in military use.

7.23
Spanish wheel-lock spanner, late 16th century

180×30
Valencia de Don Juan, 1898; Blair, 1983, 33–42
Patrimonio Nacional. Real Armería de Madrid (K.12)

This spanner was used to wind up the mechanism of a wheel-lock musket.

7.24

7.25

7.24
Spanish priming flask, late 16th century

Iron and leather
130×90
Museo Arqueológico Nacional, Madrid (52004)

This flask held the fine gunpowder used for priming firearms, and was fitted with suspension-loops.

7.25
Spanish powder flask, late 16th century

Iron, mounted with leather cover
272×193
Museo Arqueológico Nacional, Madrid (52602)

This flask has a belt-hook, and a spring lever to deliver a single charge of gunpowder.

7.26
Powder flask, probably German, 16th century

Made with antler horn
221×155
Museo Arqueológico Nacional, Madrid (52447)

Carved in relief with a representation of David and Goliath in classical dress. Flasks of this type were often made for sporting use, and frequently carved with biblical, mythological or hunting scenes.

134

7.27

7.28

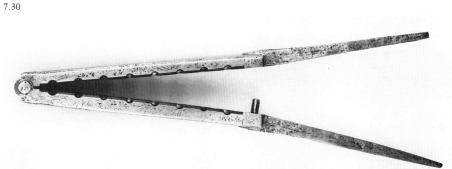
7.30

7.29

7.27
Powder flask, Pamplona, 16th–17th centuries

109 lgth
Museo Arqueológico Nacional, Madrid (1976/89/14)

This has a fluted body and loops for suspension; it lacks its original simple nozzle top.

7.28
English powder flask, late 16th century

Red velvet-covered wood with gilt-brass mounts and enamel medallion
248 lgth
Norman and Wilson, 1982, 101–102
Trustees of the Royal Armouries, London (XIII.149)

This powder flask bears the arms granted to the London Goldsmith's Company in 1571. It is unlikely that such an elaborate piece would have been the property of an ordinary soldier, and it is possible that it belonged to either Richard or John Martin, who were goldsmiths and captains of London militia companies in 1588.

7.29
Priming flask, *c*.1600

Wood and iron
137 lgth
Trustees of the Royal Armouries, London (XIII.12)

The musketeer carried the gunpowder for his musket in two types of flask, the main charge in a powder flask and the finer grained powder for filling the pan of the gun in a smaller priming flask. These were often suspended from a leather or fabric belt called a bandolier.

7.30
Shot mould

350 (closed)×45
Valencia de Don Juan, 1898; Blair, 1983, 512–13
Patrimonio Nacional. Real Armería de Madrid (K.263)

This is a shot mould of the pincer-type, with handles incorporating cutting blades to shear off the lead tail or sprue left on the ball when the mould was opened. The molten metal was poured into the closed mould. This particular mould was for shot of 15–17 mm calibre.

7.31
Boat-shaped lead ingot from the *Gran Grifón*

Lead
648×140×148; 51.075 kg.
Martin, 1975, 104–105, 169–70
Shetland Museum, Lerwick (G4/70)

Ingots of this type were carried to supply lead for the soldiers' bullets. Their boat-like shape made them easier to handle.

7.32
Thirty musket balls from the *Gran Grifón*

Lead
19.05 cal.
Martin, 1975, 182
Shetland Museum, Lerwick (G74/77)

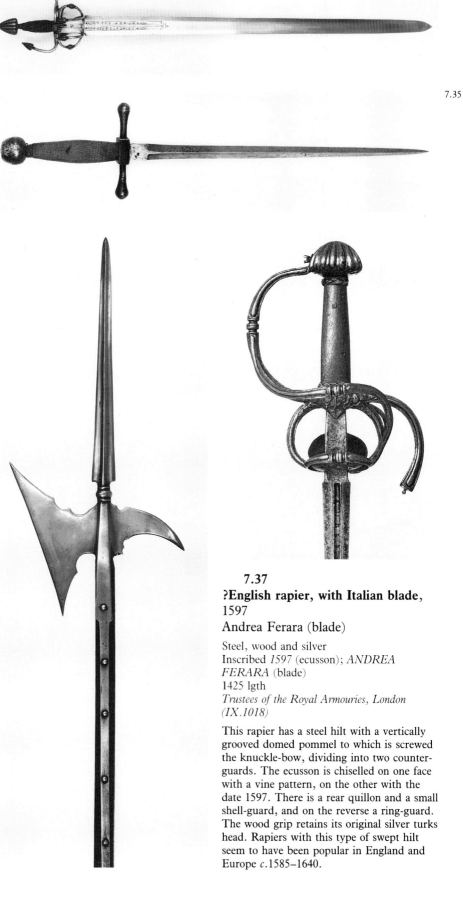

7.33
Fifty-four arquebus balls from the *Gran Grifón*

Lead
12.7 cal.
Martin, 1975, 182
Shetland Museum, Lerwick (G73/77)

More than 4,000 musket and arquebus balls were recovered from the wreck of the *Gran Grifón*, part of her large cargo of military stores.

136

7.34
Spanish sword, 1567
Lopus Aguado

Iron, steel, gold
Inscribed *GREGORIO DE ARRIETA-IN DOMINO CONFIDO-LV-PVS AGVADO-ENSAN CLEMENTE*; *1567*
1190 lgth (blade 940×50)
Valencia de Don Juan, 1898; Norman, 1980, 86
Patrimonio Nacional. Real Armería de Madrid (G.54)

The quillons of this sword are recurved in the plane of the blade, the forward one almost becoming a short knuckle-guard. The two projections are joined by a C-shaped bar near their roots. Supposed to have been owned by Philip II, but more likely the property of Gregorio de Arriéta, whose name is inscribed on the blade.

7.35
Dagger, 16th century

Steel and wood with modern cotton braiding
400 lgth (blade 280; hilt 90)
Valencia de Don Juan, 1898
Patrimonio Nacional. Real Armería de Madrid (G.149)

Daggers were carried by most sixteenth-century soldiers, and were also a common civilian weapon.

7.36
Halberd head, early 16th century

Steel head with modern wooden haft
451 head lgth
Trustees of the Royal Armouries, London (VII.970)

This halberd has an axe-blade with straight cutting-edge and a down-curving fluke at the rear. The top blade is of a hollow diamond section.

7.37
?English rapier, with Italian blade, 1597
Andrea Ferara (blade)

Steel, wood and silver
Inscribed *1597* (ecusson); *ANDREA FERARA* (blade)
1425 lgth
Trustees of the Royal Armouries, London (IX.1018)

This rapier has a steel hilt with a vertically grooved domed pommel to which is screwed the knuckle-bow, dividing into two counter-guards. The ecusson is chiselled on one face with a vine pattern, on the other with the date 1597. There is a rear quillon and a small shell-guard, and on the reverse a ring-guard. The wood grip retains its original silver turks head. Rapiers with this type of swept hilt seem to have been popular in England and Europe *c*.1585–1640.

7.38
Pike, 16th century

Iron and wood
2520 lgth
*Trustees of the Royal Armouries, London
(VII.1227)*

However proficient, musketeers were vulnerable once their muskets had been discharged, and men armed with pikes were used to fend off the enemy until they had reloaded. According to Gervase Markham in his *Souldiers Accidence* (1625), 'the strongest men and best persons to be pikes; the strongest and squarest fellows wilbe fitt to carrie musquettes and the least and nimblest should be turned to the harquebuses.'

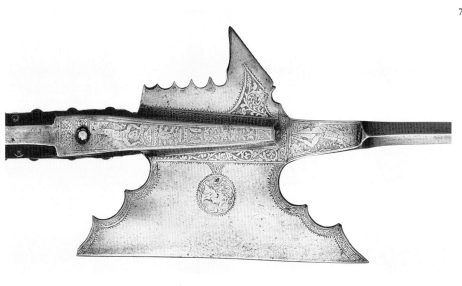

137

7.39
Italian halberd

Steel head, etched and gilded, wooden haft
2324 lgth (head 521)
Webb, 1965, 91–2, 105; Boynton, 1971, 117; Borg, 1976, 347; Norman and Wilson, 1982, 67–8
*Trustees of the Royal Armouries, London
(VII.962)*

The halberd developed from the long-handled axe and was widely used throughout Europe by the early sixteenth century. English authorities generally advised that halberdiers should be used only in small numbers, for tasks such as guarding a company's ensign. Decorated or gilded examples such as this one also served as the arms of ceremonial guards, and twenty 'Holberts guilte' were issued to Drake's *Revenge* in 1588 (cat. no. **9.31**).

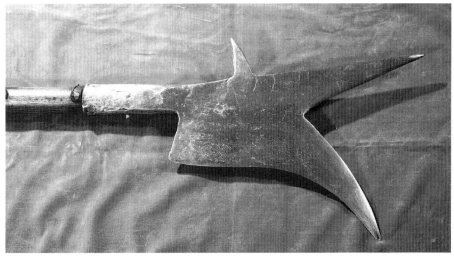

7.40

7.40
English bill, 16th century

Iron head with recurved cutting-edge, modern wooden haft
2045 lgth (head 488)
Webb, 1965, 90–91; Boynton, 1971, 107, 112, 170–71, 261; Norman and Wilson, 1982, 68
*Trustees of the Royal Armouries, London
(VII.1493)*

Military bills derived from agricultural implements. This is a good example of the somewhat crude but functional form favoured by the English for close-quarter fighting against cavalry. In late-sixteenth-century England, bills were generally regarded as obsolete weapons, fit only to be used by clumsy labourers. They began to be phased out of the militia, but later underwent something of a revival.

7.41
Tent toggle from the *Trinidad Valencera*

Wood
38 lgth
Crédit Communal, 1985, 7.5
Ulster Museum, Belfast

Small, turned wooden toggle with median groove and small swellings at the ends, originally thought to be from a duffel-coat, but actually a fastening from one of the two campaign tents carried in the *Trinidad Valencera*.

7.42

Armour for the tilt of Robert Dudley, Earl of Leicester, *c*.1575
Under Master Armourer John Kelte (*fl*.1552–76), Royal Workshop at Greenwich

Steel
Inscribed *RD*
1778 ht; 32.66 kg
Norman and Wilson, 1982, 37–8
Trustees of the Royal Armouries, London (XI.81)

138 This armour was possibly made for the entertainment given for the queen by Leicester at Kenilworth in 1575. Only the pieces for the tilt survive with this armour, and its surface, formerly blued or russet, has etched sunken bands that were originally fire-gilt. The bands have narrow strapwork which encloses allegorical masks, figures and trophies. The badges of the bear and ragged staff of Warwick are found in three places with the Order of the Garter, and in three others with the badge and collar of the French royal order of St Michael. The areas between the bands are crossed diagonally by sunken ragged staves charged with crescents, alternating with scrolled leaves. The badge of the Order of the Garter is found at the centre of the upper part of the breastplate, where it is shown as if suspended on a neck chain and flanked by Leicester's initials. Leicester served as commander of the English army in the Low Countries from 1585 to 1587 and on 24 July 1588 was appointed Lieutenant and Captain-General of the Queen's Armies and Companies. He was in charge of the forces mustered at Tilbury Camp in July and August and died shortly afterwards, whilst returning to Kenilworth.

7.43

Robert Dudley, Earl of Leicester (1532?–88) as Governor-General in the Netherlands, *c*.1586
English School, 16th century

Oil on canvas
2060×1345
Strong, 1969a, 191–6; Clarke, 1981
The Collection at Parham Park, West Sussex

Leicester was Elizabeth's favourite from 1559. He was an ardent supporter of the Netherlands rebels and was appointed commander-in-chief of the English forces in the Netherlands in 1585. But his adoption of the title of governor-general in 1586 angered the queen and seriously strained their personal relations. Leicester spent a great deal of

money on the venture and felt that Elizabeth had not supported him adequately, while she in turn believed that he had challenged and compromised her authority. They were reconciled on his return in 1588, when he was appointed to command the forces based at Tilbury, which would have been used to meet the invading army in pitched battle. The queen was distraught when he died.

The face type of this portrait resembles a 1586 medallion engraved by Hendrik Goltzius (1558–1617), a Haarlem engraver much admired by Hilliard. Leicester is shown with the accoutrements of an aristocrat and military commander: a rapier or dress sword; a wide-bladed polearm or partizan in the background (a symbol of military rank); and a petronel gun in his hand. Leicester was a cultured patron of the arts and many portraits of him survive. In his own portrait collection, depictions of foreign monarchs and contemporary figures such as William of Orange predominated. Surprisingly, he had no pictures of English monarchs, yet a portrait of a pope and one of the Duke of Alba hung in his London home.

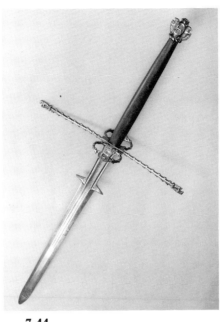

7.44
The Earl of Leicester's bearing sword, *c.*1550–75

Steel and wood
1285×185×525
Viscount De L'Isle, Penshurst Place, Kent

This sword would have been carried in procession before the Earl of Leicester, the royal badge probably indicating that it was connected with one of his royal offices. The decorative motifs relate to the royal crest of England, the Order of the Garter and the arms of Warwick. It may be the sword recorded in the inventory of Kenilworth, Leicester's principal castle, in 1583. The blade has been damaged and subsequently repaired.

7.45–7.57
The Mendlesham Parish Armoury

Parish Church of St Mary the Virgin, Mendlesham, Suffolk (1; 5; 7; 8; 14 and 9; 11; 16; 17; 18; 28; 26; 27; 29)

The Mendlesham Parish Armoury (cat. nos. **7.45–7.57**) is perhaps the most complete surviving militia armoury of the sixteenth and early seventeenth centuries. The armour and weapons are usually stored in the timber-lined village armoury over the porch of the church of St Mary the Virgin. The armoury is recorded as far back as 1593, and is probably of somewhat earlier date. With its barred windows and iron-bound door it typifies the many town and village militia armouries that once existed. The Mendlesham church-wardens' accounts for 1588 mention swords, daggers, calivers, shot moulds, sheaves of

arrows and other items being in the armoury. The extant pieces range in date from *c.*1520 to *c.*1630. This remarkable collection gives an excellent idea of the miscellaneous and sometimes aged gear with which some English militias were equipped at the time of the Armada.

7.45
German or Flemish Almain rivet, *c.*1520

Steel and leather
763×510
Blair, 1958, 119

Light half-armour comprising breastplate, tassets to protect the thighs and splints for the arms. A complete Almain rivet, a cheap form of corselet worn by the infantry, was described in the sixteenth century as 'accounting always a salet (helmet), a gorjet (collar), a breastplate, a backplate and a pair of splints for every complete harness'.

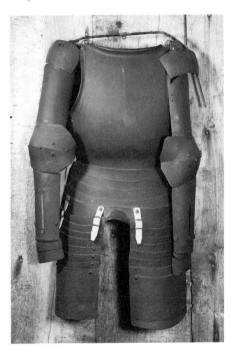

139

140

7.46
Italian corselet, *c*.1520

Steel and leather
469×352

Corselet or half-armour worn by infantrymen comprising breastplate, backplate and vambraces. The armour would have been worn with a gorget at the neck and a helmet probably of sallet type. The tassets which protected the thighs are missing. The breastplate has a broad band of vertical flutes with horizontal flutes above and below, and the main plate of the backplate is recessed to fit between the shoulder-blades, with additional plates rivetted on at the sides.

7.47
Corselet, probably Flemish, in the Italian fashion, *c*.1550–80

Steel and leather
788×650
Blair, 1958, 44–5; Stone, 1961, 192

This comprises a long-waisted cuirass, two skirt-plates with associated tassets of six plates to fit the thighs closely, and pauldrons (not a pair, *c*.1580) to protect the shoulders. A light half-armour, corselet was the name usually given to the armour of a pikeman.

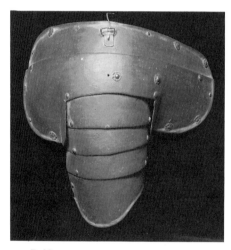

7.48
Pair of pauldrons, probably Flemish, *c*.1590

Steel
353×362 and 335×335
Blair, 1958, 44–5

Pauldrons were the plates of armour which protected the shoulders. These ones have six plates and had buckles to connect with the collar.

7.49
Infantry armour, probably German, *c*.1550

Steel and leather
825×650
Blair, 1958, 119–20

This armour consists of breastplate, tassets and Almain collar (that is, with the shoulder-defences permanently attached). The tassets (plates attached to the skirt of the armour to protect the front of the hips and thighs) are not a pair. The left belongs to the breastplate, whilst the right, of Italian pattern, *c*.1550, does not.

7.50
Vambrace for left arm, 16th century

Steel and leather
700×210 (max.)

The component parts of this vambrace range in date from *c*.1520 to the late sixteenth century: the pauldron, for example, is the earliest piece, whilst the turning joint and upper and lower cannons are from *c*.1570.

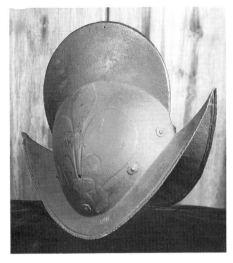

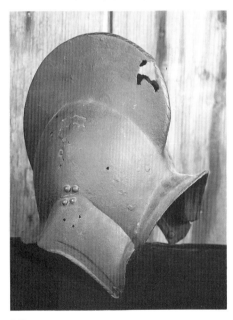

7.53

7.51
German comb morion, *c*.1590

Steel
373×411×231
Blair, 1958, 138

This helmet type was made in two halves and shaped with a high comb. Each side of the skull on this example is embossed with a large *fleur-de-lys* and the cheekpieces are missing. The morion was a development from the open-faced helmet called a kettle-hat, which was used throughout Europe in the Middle Ages. Morions were worn by infantry arquebusiers and pikemen until the early years of the seventeenth century.

7.52
Burgonet, possibly Flemish, *c*.1590

Steel
360×323×205
Blair, 1958, 135–41

This is an open helmet with hinged cheekpieces and a high comb. Burgonets were often fitted with an additional face defence called a buffe and were popular with light cavalry, infantry and pikemen during the second half of the sixteenth and early seventeenth centuries.

7.53
Burgonet, possibly Flemish, *c*.1590

Steel
333×360×205
Blair, 1958, 135–41

This helmet is decorated with roped edges and rosetted rivets, and is similar to cat. no. **7.53**.

7.54
Powder flask, probably English, late 16th century

Wood and iron
282×233×60

This flask retains its upper cap and long nozzle.

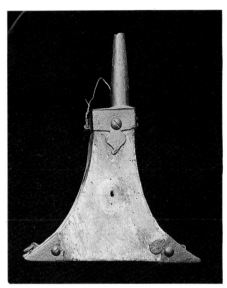

141

7.55
Powder flask, probably English, late 16th century

Wood and iron
Inscribed *mendellshm̃*
181×232×55

This flask lacks its cap, nozzle and spring cut-off. The name of the village has been inscribed on one side, in a late-sixteenth- or early-seventeenth-century hand.

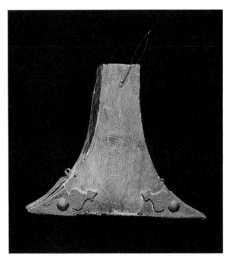

7.56
Powder flask, probably English, late 16th century

Wood and iron
Inscribed *Mendelshm*
288×142×59

This flask still has its upper cap, nozzle, belt hook and spring cut-off, but the iron cornerpieces are missing. There is an iron rosette on the front. Powder flasks were worn on the right side of the body, suspended on cords from the belt or, as probably with this example, hooked over the belt. They normally had a removable cap to act as a measure for one charge of shot.

142

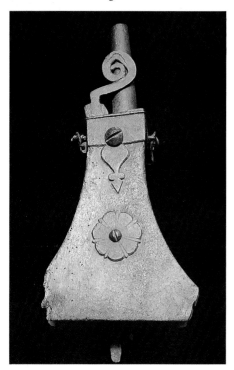

7.57
Longbow, possibly Elizabethan

Wood
1345×30×32
Boynton, 1971, 65–9, 171

One end of this longbow is broken, but its original length was probably about 5½ feet (1680 mm). It is unlikely to date from much later than *c.*1600, making it one of the few early longbows to survive outside of an archaeological context. Elizabethan moralists, nostalgic authors and government legislation claimed that the longbow was the archetypal weapon of the Englishman, recalling the glories of the English archers at Crécy and Agincourt. The longbow was cheaper than the musket, but required much practice to use skilfully, and by 1588 it had been outmoded in warfare by firearms. Even though some English militia (and ships – see cat. no. **9.31**) were equipped with them at the time of the Armada, archers were then very much in the minority.

7.58
Denzil Holles (1538–90), 1585
English School, 16th century

Oil on panel
Inscribed NOT FORGOTTEN (presumably after the sitter's death); other inscriptions
597×482
Hon. Mr and Mrs Clive Gibson

Holles came from Haughton, Nottinghamshire, and was a captain of musters in his county at the time of the Spanish invasion threat. Though such officers were often of humble social station, Holles was himself the son of a knight. His grandson of the same name was one of the Members of Parliament impeached by Charles I in 1642.

7.59
A Drake Colour, *c.*1580–90

Silk-taffeta flag with gold-leaf paint and silk
cord and tassel
2134×2134
Borrett, 1984; Wilson, 1986, 107, n. 150
The National Trust

This is one of eight flags of similar date
preserved at Buckland Abbey and traditionally associated with Sir Francis Drake and
the *Golden Hind*. It consists of a white taffeta
cross on a red taffeta background, with a bel-
led falcon in gold leaf in one corner. Two of
the eight flags are royal banners, whilst five
of the remainder have white crosses (mostly
with devices) and one has an eight-rayed sun
in the centre and no cross. It has been suggested that the flags were the colours of a
militia regiment raised by the Drakes. This
flag may have been the colour of a militia
captain's company; flags of this period,
however, had both military and naval uses.

144

7.60
Sir John Norris (1547?–97)
Attributed to Federico Zucchero (1540/1–1609)

Etching
210×142
O'Donoghue, III, 1912, 344
Trustees of the British Museum, London (75–5–8–644)

'Black Jack' Norris, Member of Parliament for Co. Cork, was a soldier with considerable military experience in Ireland, France and the Low Countries. In 1577 he fought on behalf of States-General in the Netherlands, for which he was knighted by Leicester. In 1588 he was based at Tilbury, acting as marshal of the camp. He was also employed inspecting fortifications in Kent and Essex. Leicester was jealous of his greater experience. This portrait is a plate from John Thane's *Autography*, published in the eighteenth century.

7.61
George Carey, 2nd Baron Hunsdon (1547–1603)
Nicholas Hilliard (1547–1619)

Miniature
Inscribed *Ano.Dni.1601/Aetatis Suae.54*
47×38
Auerbach, 1961, 121
Trustee of the Will of the 8th Earl of Berkeley

Carey went as an envoy to Scotland in 1569 and again in 1582. In 1570 he served against the northern rebels and the Scots. Appointed captain-general of the Isle of Wight in 1582, he fortified the island in anticipation of the Armada in 1587.

7.62
Sir George Carey's seal matrix, 1586

Ivory
Inscribed *SIGIL GEO: CAREY: MIL.CAPP.INS.VECTIS E/// ADMIRALLVS COM. SOWTHAMTO.*
78×88; 78×85
Tonnochy, 1952, 207–208
Trustees of the British Museum, London

This matrix comprises two faces joined by a conical handle. The larger face bears a representation of a three-masted Tudor warship, and the smaller a shield of arms of twenty quarterings derived from the Spencer of Spencercombe and Boleyn marriages of the Carey family.

7.62

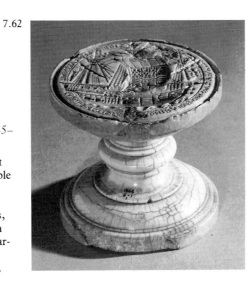

Infelix virtus et mentis vela secundis Extrema Comitem tandem oppressere ruina

7.63
Robert Devereux, Earl of Essex (1567–1601), 1620
Crispin de Passe (c.1565–1637)

Inscribed *ROBERTUS DEUEREUS COMES ESSEXIAE; Virtutis Comes Inuidia* (in oval); inscription below
163×115
Hind, II, 1955, 118, 146, 37?
National Maritime Museum

Essex became Elizabeth's principal favourite in the later part of her life, although their relationship was not always smooth; it ended with Essex's rebellion and execution. His uneven military career had begun with Leicester's expedition to the Low Countries in 1585. He was kept at court during the Armada campaign, but escaped to join the 1589 Drake–Norris expedition. He later commanded the land forces in the 1596 Cadiz expedition (see cat. no. 16.24).

7.64
Orders for the defence of the Queen's ships at Chatham, 28 March 1585 (os)

MS
Inscribed *1585/from the lo of the Counsell for releefe of the navie at Chattam*
300×205
McGurk, 1970, 73
Staffordshire Record Office (Sutherland Papers, D593/S/4/25/1)

This order was sent from the Privy Council to Lord Cobham, Lord-Lieutenant of Kent, and others, and laid out a plan to defend the royal ships moored in the Medway at Chatham. It envisaged that some 2,000 militia from different parts of the county, alerted by the beacons, would converge on Upnor Castle and Chatham Church to be ferried out to the ships. Although never implemented, these projected measures show how detailed Elizabethan defence plans could be.

7.65
List of possible landing places in Kent, 21 July 1588

MS (2ff.)
Inscribed *11 July 1588/Orders for defence for the Sea Coast, And for distribucion/of the forces of y sher July/1588*
310×200
McGurk, 1970, 83–8
Staffordshire Record Office (Sutherland Papers, D593/S/4/19/3)

This list was agreed by the deputy lieutenants of Kent and Sir John Norris when they met to muster the Kent militia at Rochester. The document outlines possible invasion sites and assigns particular groups to defend them. The aim was to use small bodies of troops to delay the enemy on the coast, giving time for the assembly of larger forces inland. The list states that less than half the infantry were trained, an indication that they might not have been able to delay the Spanish for long.

145

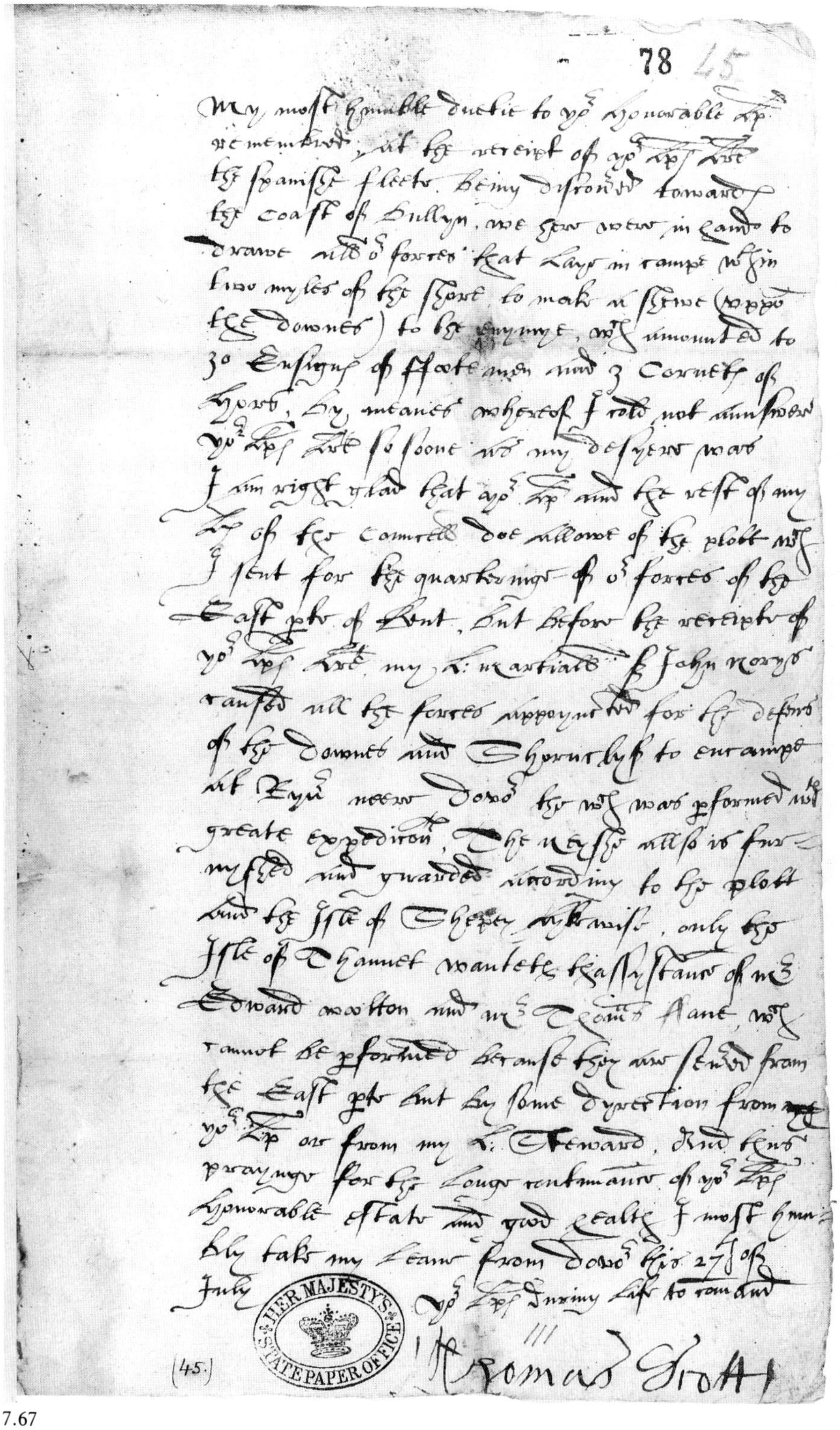

146

7.66
Sketch of existing and proposed fortifications at Gravesend and Tilbury, 29 July 1588
Sir John Norris and others

MS
203×300
McGurk, 1970, 85; Colvin *et al.*, 1982, 602–606, pl. 44
Staffordshire Record Office (Sutherland Papers, D593/S/4/12/13)

The English government feared that the Armada might sail up the Thames, and this made the strengthening of the forts at Gravesend and Tilbury a necessity. Norris inspected them on 28 July, and submitted this rough plan for the positioning of new 'sconces', or earthworks, to the Privy Council. Considerable work on the two forts was undertaken in 1588–9. The line of the elaborate earthworks at Tilbury designed by the Italian engineer Gianibelli resembles that of Norris' 'New Sconce'.

7.67
Letter from Sir Thomas Scott to Burghley, 5 August 1588

MS (autograph)
285×175
McGurk, 1970, 86–7
Public Record Office, London (SP12/213, 45)

Scott was one of the deputy lieutenants in charge of the defence of east Kent. His letter states that when the Armada was seen off Boulogne, thirty ensigns of infantry and three cornets of horse were drawn up on the Downs 'to make a shewe . . . to the Enymye'. He warned that the vulnerable Isle of Thanet lacked its commanding officers Wotton and Fane, who were on duty elsewhere.

7.68
Elizabethan chart of the Medway and the mouth of the Thames

Coloured chart on vellum
655×925; scale 1:15840 approx.
British Museum, I, 1844, 100; Oppenheim,
1896, 150–1
*British Library, London (MS Cott. Aug.I, i,
52)*

This chart was probably drawn between
1567, when Upnor Castle was built to defend
Chatham dockyard, and 1585, when a chain
defence was put across the river at Upnor.
Some twenty-three royal ships are shown
moored in the river between Upnor and
Rochester bridge, in descending order of size
and with their rigging dismantled, as would
have been the case with ships laid up in winter. The beacon on Barrow (now Beacon)
Hill is depicted: this would have alerted the
area in the event of an attack coming downriver, and the local militia would have
mustered at Chatham Church and Upnor
Castle for transport out to the ships. The
dockyard itself can be seen, with its long
storehouses, but lacking (until the seventeenth century) a dry-dock.

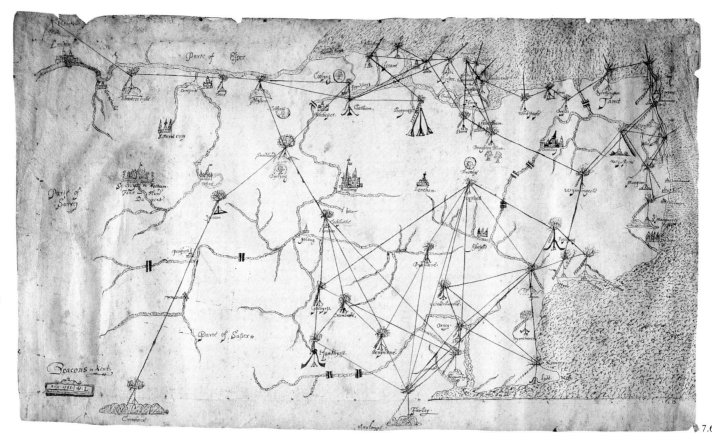

148

7.69

Map of the beacon system in Kent, 1585

William Lambarde (1536–1601)

MS
Inscribed *Beacons in Kent./Aug. 1585. W:L*
325×550
McGurk, 1970, 72–3, 76–8; Boynton, 1971,
132–8
British Library, London (Add. MS 62935)

The beacon system covered most of England,
and was used to alert the authorities and
local forces to the threat of invasion. This
remarkable map, also published in Lambarde's *Perambulation of Kent*, shows the
lines of sight within the Kent beacon system
and their connections with beacons in Sussex, Surrey and Middlesex. The key beacon
for alerting Kent was that at Fairlight
(*Farley*) in Sussex. Although it is not known
exactly how long it would have taken an
alarm raised at, say, Fairlight to reach
London, it is clear that if the system worked
properly it would have been possible to
inform the government and most of the large
towns in Kent within a matter of hours. The
Kent system was put in readiness shortly
after the map was drawn, and the map was
probably used in planning local warning and
defence measures. Lambarde was the first
historian of Kent and served as a justice of
peace and commissioner for musters in the
county.

7.70

Map of coastal defences, Weybourne, Norfolk, 1588

Edmund Yorke

Pen and colour wash
Inscribed *Reason would a Scall, but tyme
permits not, so as necessiti inforceth to make the
distansis upon the places. Mad in hast this fyrst
of May 1588. E Y*
447×588
Tenison, VII, 1940, pl. 21; O'Neil, 1940; *id.*
1960, pl. 21a; Skelton and Summerson,
1971, 52
*The Marquess of Salisbury, Hatfield House
(CPM II. 56)*

The deep water at Weybourne made it a
potential invasion site. Its defences were
strengthened by the addition of the fortifications shown here in red. During the summer
of 1588 Captain Yorke was ordered to make
several surveys of East Anglian defences for
Burghley and, as the inscription shows, this
was done in great haste.

7.71

Map of Great Yarmouth and neighbourhood, 1588

Edmund Yorke

Pen and colour wash
Inscribed *Mad the 30 Apr: 1588*
522×1507
Skelton and Summerson, 1971, 51; Colvin *et
al.*, 1982, 406
*The Marquess of Salisbury, Hatfield House
(CPM I. 37)*

Great Yarmouth's medieval defences were
strengthened in 1569 and later, to Yorke's
plan, between May and September 1588 at a
cost of almost £605. Yorke's alterations
included a southward extension of the town
wall, a bulwark and ravelin on the seaward
side, two gun platforms and three forts. The
map appears to show some of the local militia
in a mock skirmish in front of the town.

7.70

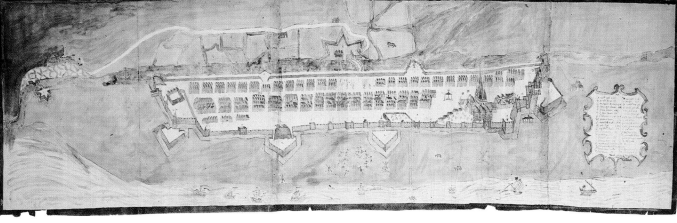

7.71

8.38 *La Felicissima Armada*, Pedro de Paz Salas   **8.30 The** *Ark Royal*

(i) English Ships and Shipping

The English government mobilized thirty-four royal ships and 192 privately owned vessels against the Armada. However, the last figure represents the *total* number of private ships used in the spring and summer of 1588, and not the actual number of vessels in combat with the Spanish. The maximum number of ships under Howard's direct command was about seventy-two, Drake having thirty-nine and Seymour sixty-six, with numerous small volunteer ships that joined the fleet once the Armada was off the coast. Impressive as these figures seem, the actual strength of the English naval forces was much less. Fifteen of Howard's ships were victuallers or store-ships, as were an unknown number of those with Seymour. Nine of Seymour's fleet were discharged for various reasons before the battle began, and one of his royal ships was the useless galley *Bonavolia*. Crucial weaknesses of the English fleet as a whole were that almost half (101) of the ships were of less than 100 tons, and none of the private ships exceeded 400 tons. The government regarded the 100-ton limit as the lowest useful size for a merchant vessel that also might function as a warship, as shown by the tonnage bounty paid on ships built over this limit.[1]

The problem faced by the government was that little else was available. This had been revealed by the series of shipping surveys conducted between 1560 and 1583. The 1582 survey recorded that out of 1,630 ships, only 177 exceeded 100 tons burden (theoretical cargo capacity), and of these a mere nineteen exceeded 200 tons. England was not a great maritime power; its merchant fleet was smaller than those of the major Continental powers. The growth in long-distance trades to the Mediterranean, Africa and other areas in the 1570s and 1580s encouraged the construction of large, defensible merchantmen, but numbers of large ships did not increase sharply until the 1590s, when the continuing war with Spain increased the demand for privateers.

London was the most important shipping and shipbuilding centre in the country. The 1582 survey showed that sixty-two of the 177 ships of more than 100 tons belonged to the port. East Anglia ranked second with forty-three such ships, followed by the Tyne-Tweed area (seventeen), Yorkshire (eleven), Bristol, Essex and Dorset (nine each), followed by some southern and south-western counties. The capital's shipbuilding capacity was likewise far greater than that of any other part of the country: thirty-nine out of ninety-seven ships of 100 tons or more built in the periods 1571–6 and *c*.1580–94 were constructed in London. Only Bristol began to approach London as a builder of large ships, but even

so it produced only ten such vessels between the dates mentioned.[2] London's pre-eminence was reflected in its contribution of at least thirty large ships to the anti-Armada fleet, but the very largest ships in England all belonged to the queen.

The royal fleet was not a state navy as such, for the ships were the personal property of the queen, but it was administered and maintained on a reasonably effective basis for a navy of the late sixteenth century. The core of the administration was a body of officials, created by Henry VIII, to oversee naval expenditure and the equipping and upkeep of the ships. The Admiralty, as it was known (it was not called the Navy Board until the seventeenth century), was created as a group of men of equal authority subject to the Lord Admiral. The administrators were generally people with sea experience or shipping interests, and some, such as Hawkins, Winter and Borough, were seamen and navigators of considerable reputation. The navy had four permanent dockyards, at Deptford, Woolwich, Portsmouth and Chatham, at which there were facilities for the construction, repair and maintenance of the ships. In 1588 Chatham was the most important base for the navy, although it had only recently become a shipbuilding centre: Deptford and Woolwich seem to have been the only Elizabethan dockyards to build many royal ships. The actual design and construction of the ships was overseen by the queen's master-shipwrights, who in 1588 were Matthew Baker, Peter Pett and Richard Chapman. The dockyards had small permanent staffs of officials and workmen, along with mariners to act as shipkeepers. At Deptford in 1588 there were sixteen permanent employees, including three clerks, seven shipwrights and the 'keper of the Plugge and the doche headd'.[3]

Burghley was able to bring the naval administration under his sway in the 1560s and 1570s, and enhanced the authority of one particular officer, the treasurer. This had important consequences when the forceful and aggressive John Hawkins was appointed to the post in 1578. He accused fellow officials of corruption, and his two 'bargains' with the crown of 1579 and 1585 were at least ostensibly aimed at improving the honesty and efficiency of the administration. Hawkins undertook the ordinary (routine maintenance) and extraordinary (new building and heavy repairs) in return for fixed annual sums. He inevitably faced allegations of corruption from his enemies, some of which may have been justified, although it must be remembered that few sixteenth-century administrators operated without making profits or taking some perquisites from their posts.[4] Whatever the relative merits of the individuals

1. Laughton, II, 1981, 324–31, has an almost complete list of the English ships, but appears to omit vessels mentioned earlier in the text on pp. 66, 181, 201, 257, 260 and 287. Oppenheim, 1896, 167–8, for the tonnage bounty.
2. Oppenheim, 1896, 171–5; Pollitt, 1974; Davis, 1972, 1–8; PRO SP12/107, 68; SP12/156, 45; SP12/250, 33.
3. Pollitt, 1980; Quinn and Ryan, 1983, 48–9, 52–3; Oppenheim, 1896, 149–52; PRO E351/2225, m.3v.
4. Laughton, I, 1981, 79–80, 111; Quinn and Ryan, 1983, 66–9.

involved, some idea of the general effectiveness of Elizabethan naval administration can be gained from the state of the navy in 1588.

Of the thirty-four royal ships, twenty-two had been built or re-built since 1577, and of these half had appeared in the three years preceding the Armada. The royal master-shipwrights Peter Pett and Matthew Baker surveyed twenty-six of the warships in the autumn of 1587 and found that only nine did not need major repairs, and a further six were decayed but did not need extensive work in the near future. The remainder were generally judged 'to be of not long continuance', although mostly sufficient for summer service. The majority of these decayed ships were those built between 1562 and 1573, and evidently reaching the ends of their useful lives. However, it should be noted that two of the oldest ships, the *Elizabeth Jonas* (1559) and the *Triumph* (1562) were listed in the middling category, and the strength of their hulls was noted with approval. The picture was not very encouraging, but the eight small vessels omitted from the survey had all been built within the previous four years and were probably in good condition. Also, it must be remarked that even a ship like the *Mary Rose*, built in 1557, after the loss of her more famous namesake in 1545, and listed as 'dangerous' by Pett and Baker, was able to take a continuous and very active part in the Armada battle. Howard was fulsome in his praise of the condition of the older royal ships. Perhaps jealousy of Hawkins caused Pett and Baker to be more damning than they might otherwise have been, but on the whole the evidence of these two master-shipwrights has to be taken seriously.

When twenty-four ships were re-surveyed the following September, the *Mary Rose* was one of four needing major dry-dock repairs (she was in fact rebuilt in 1589). The other twenty were almost all rather leaky and requiring repairs, but could be made seaworthy.[5] The English fleet in 1588 was probably in no worse condition than any other navy of the period, and it is a remarkable fact that out of the ninety-eight or so vessels owned by the crown between 1558 and 1603, only two were lost by wreck.

It is quite possible that the queen's ships were in a much better state than many privately owned ships. The appraisals of 115 ships by the High Court of Admiralty between 1579 and 1590 listed fifty-seven of the vessels as either 'old', 'very old' or of an age of ten years or more. The crews of such ships must have run appalling risks. The men of the privateer *Black Dog*, for example, sailed to the West Indies and back in a ship that was 'very farre out of Reparation' by the time she was appraised in 1590.

Her hull, masts and spars were worth scarcely more than her small armament.[6]

A great deal more is known about English warships of the Armada period than merchantmen, because of the survival of government records. It is clear that the Elizabethan period was one of great change in the design of English fighting ships. There was a movement away from the older type of warship, with large fighting castles fore and aft, towards a vessel with a much lower superstructure. The reduction in castle height entailed a certain loss of fire-power in close-range and boarding actions, but it also reduced wind resistance and thus helped to improve manoeuvrability. This made possible a new style of fighting which took advantage of the improved performance to turn faster than an adversary and manoeuvre into a favourable position for firing from a distance. The sailing qualities of English ships and the stand-off fighting technique were remarked on by adversaries at the time of the Armada (see below, pp. 237, 266).[7]

A comparison of the contract specifications for the *Mary Gonson* of *c*.1514 with those for the *Defiance* of 1590 gives an indication of how much English warship design changed in the course of the sixteenth century. The total superstructure height of the *Mary Gonson*, a ship of some 250 tons burden would have been perhaps ten feet (3.05 m) higher than that of the *Defiance*, a ship only fourteen or so feet longer but with a burden of about 440 tons.[8] The credit for the development of the new type has long been given to the 'mathematical mind' of John Hawkins, both before he became treasurer at the Admiralty and during his period of office. It was suggested that Hawkins' disgust with the performance of the high-castled *Jesus of Lübeck* on his third, disastrous slaving voyage of 1568 led him to develop the idea that low-built warships were better for oceanic voyaging, and should supplant the older vessels in the navy. The suggestion has been oft-repeated, and has almost solidified into fact, but there is no clear evidence that Hawkins was solely responsible for any changes in design.[9]

There is a dearth of information on the process by which ship-design specifications were drawn up, but it is interesting that the dimensions and forms of the three warships built in 1590 were the work of a committee of nine, including Howard, Drake, Hawkins and the shipwrights Matthew Baker and Richard Chapman. Their scribbled notes, much altered and augmented, were the basis of the final contracts.[10] If any individuals are to be singled out as innovators in ship design, one should perhaps look to the royal master-shipwrights.

5. Corbett, I, 1898, 224–9; Laughton, I, 1981, 10–11, 14, 16–17; and II, 1981, 250–54.
6. Anderson, 1974, 6–12; PRO HCA 24/50–HCA 24/57, *passim*; PRO HCA 24/57, f.27r–v.
7. HMC, III, 1889, 344.
8. Anderson, 1960; PRO SP12/224, 46.
9. Corbett, I, 1898, 370–78; Williamson, 1969, 249–50.
10. Oppenheim, 1896, 129; PRO SP12/218, 31, 33; PRO SP12/224, 46, 83, 84.

Many English shipbuilders of the late sixteenth century seem to have relied to a considerable degree on building by eye, making little use of written aids. This is hardly surprising, for most shipwrights were undoubtedly illiterate: out of forty-five shipwrights involved in the High Court of Admiralty appraisals mentioned above, only fourteen could sign their names.[11] The most famous of the queen's master-shipwrights was Matthew Baker (c.1530–1613), a man whose skill in mathematics and geometry was acknowledged even by his enemies, and is demonstrated by a volume of his notes on ship design which survives in the Pepysian Library. Baker stressed the importance of using mathematics, geometry and drawings or 'plots' in the design of ships, basing some of his ideas on Mediterranean practice which he had observed at first hand. He was responsible for the construction of the *Foresight, Vanguard, Revenge* and at least ten other royal ships in the years up to 1588. In his career we can begin to see something of a separation taking place between the ship designer and the practical shipwright, for a private ship was said to have been 'molded' (designed) by him and 'framed' by another shipwright. It is significant that the three warships built in 1590 were all based on the design of the *Revenge*.[12]

Another aspect of warship development, associated with the reduction in superstructure height, was an increase in length relative to breadth. Measured over the distance between stem and sternpost, Baker's ships were almost always longer in relation to their beams than those of his contemporaries. The length to beam ratios in all but two of his ships exceeded 1:4, and in one case 1:5, whilst those of his contemporary Peter Pett only once went beyond 1:4 (Richard Chapman's two ships, the *Ark Royal* and the *Tremontana*, had ratios of about 1:3.9). Narrower lines played a crucial part in reducing water resistance, and so were very significant in improving performance and producing what has become known as the 'race-built galleon'. It is quite possible that Matthew Baker was one of the major driving forces in the development of this new type, but it is also likely that others such as Hawkins played some part in the process. Also, contemporaries did not necessarily see alterations in ships in the same way that we might. A report on the state of the four old 'great ships', the *Triumph, Elizabeth Jonas, White Bear* and *Victory* (built between 1559 and 1562), by Baker, Chapman and others in 1591, described them as 'the cheifest strength and countenance of the navye'.[13]

Merchantmen were shorter and broader than warships, to fit them for the carriage of bulk cargoes. The amount of cargo space restricted the room available for guns below deck. Privateers were effectively warships, and probably had gun decks like those of royal vessels. For example, a ship like the 120-ton *Galleon Fenner*, arrested in 1585 on suspicion of having been used 'pirateously', would have had to carry a substantial part of its armament of more than fifteen guns on a gun-deck.[14] The meagre pictorial evidence available suggests that merchant ships of the period did not have large superstructures.

The typical rig of a European ship in 1588 consisted of three masts, the fore and mainmasts carrying topmasts and square sails and the mizzenmast at the stern with a single triangular lateen sail. Some larger ships had four masts, the fourth mast being called a bonaventure, stepped aft of the mizzen and also carrying a lateen sail. Ten of the English royal ships were four-masters, and all of them were of 400 tons or more, but the other warship in this range, the *Revenge*, was a three-master.[15] The basic equipment of royal and private ships was the same.

The 1588 inventory of the *Elizabeth Bonaventure* gives an idea of how a warship of the period was equipped, although some gear had been lost in the course of the Armada campaign. The ship normally carried eight great anchors (of which five were broken or lost), a sheet anchor, five cables of fifteen- to sixteen-inch circumference, and a wide variety of other cordage. The navigational instruments included five compasses, two running-glasses and two sounding leads (some of the other ships also carried special leads and lines for deep-sea use). The cookroom was furnished with a 'Great Meate Kettell' and a copper furnace, and there would normally have been a supply of bowls and platters. The *Elizabeth Bonaventure*'s flags comprised two with St George's crosses, a silk ensign 'spoiled with shot and gyven to the Capt–', and two streamers. There was also 'a bluddey flagge', probably a red flag used to signify that no quarter would be given. Besides the 'spoiled' ensign, there is other evidence of close-range fighting: the ship's new main topsail was 'full of hooles with shotte'.[16]

The efforts of the English government in maintaining the navy and documenting the private shipping of the kingdom meant that in 1588 England was able to raise a large force to face the Armada. It had more vessels than the Spanish fleet, but most of its ships were much smaller than those of their opponents. However, it had very manoeuvrable, well-armed fighting ships which helped to counter the threat posed by the great Spanish galleons. If the English fleet was not superior to the Armada, it was at least a reasonable match for it.

Ian Friel

11. See note 6, above.
12. NMM PST 20 A, pp. 12, 34–5, 40. This is a photographic copy of the Pepys Library MS 2820, *Fragments of Ancient English Shipwrightry*; Perrin, 1918, 7, 11; Taylor, 1959, 154; PRO SP12/218, 31.
13. Glasgow, 1964; dimensions taken from Anderson, 1957, corrected by reference to PRO SP12/243, 111 and Oppenheim, 1896, 124; PRO SP12/238, 43.
14. PRO HCA 24/53, ff.62a, b.
15. PRO SP12/220, *passim*.
16. PRO SP12/220, ff.49v–50r.

The Spanish fleet, July 1588

		Tonnage	Mariners	Soldiers
Portugal – Duke of Medina Sidonia				
San Martín[1][3] (*capitana general*)	gln (1000)	161	308
San Juan[1][3] (*almiranta general*)	gln (1050)	156	366
San Marco[2][3]	gln (790)	108	278
San Luis[1][3]	gln (830)	100	339
San Felipe[2][3]	gln (800)	108	331
San Mateo[2][3]	gln (750)	110	279
Santiago[1]	gln (520)	80	307
San Cristóbal[1]	gln (352)	79	132
San Bernardo[1]	gln (352)	65	171
Julia[1]	z (166)	48	87
Agusta[1]	z (166)	43	49

		Tonnage	Mariners	Soldiers
Castile – Diego Flores de Valdés				
San Cristóbal[1][3] (*capitana*)	gln (700)	116	187
San Juan[1][3] (*almiranta*)	gln (750)	90	206
San Juan el Menor[2]	gln (?530)	77	207
Santiago el Mayor[1]	gln (530)	103	190
La Asunción[1]	gln (530)	70	170
San Medel y Celedón[1]	gln (530)	75	197
Nuestra Señora del Barrio[1]	gln (530)	81	196
San Felipe y Santiago[1]	gln (530)	81	153
Santa Ana[1]	gln (250)	54	99
San Pedro[1]	gln (530)	90	184
Nuestra Señora de Begoña[1]	gln (750)	81	219
La Trinidad[2]	n. (872)	79	162
La Santa Catalina[1]	n. (882)	134	186
San Juan 'Ferrandome'[2]	n. (652)	57	183
Nuestra Señora del Socorro[2]	pt (75)	15	20
San Antonio[2]	pt (75)	26	20

		Tonnage	Mariners	Soldiers
Biscay – Juan Martínez Recalde				
Santiago[1] (*almiranta*)	nao (666)	106	206
María Juan[2]	nao (665)	93	306
La Magdalena[1]	nao (530)	61	213
La Concepción Mayor (?*de Zubelu*)[1]	nao (468)	58	161
San Juan[1]	nao (350)	49	141
La Concepción (?*de Juanes*)[1]	nao (418)	58	167
El Gran Grín[2][3]	nao (1160)	75	261
Santa María de Montemayor[1]	nao (520)	47	155
La Manuela[1]	nao (520)	48	115
La María[2]	pt (70)	25	19
La María (?*Miguel Suso*)[2]	pt (?96)	25	20
San Esteban[1]	pt (78)	25	10
La Isabela[1]	pt (71)	29	24

		Tonnage	Mariners	Soldiers
Andalusian – Pedro de Valdés				
Nuestra Señora del Rosario[2][3] (*capitana*)	nao (1150)	119	240
San Francisco[1] (*almiranta*)	nao (915)	85	238
La Duquesa Santa Ana[2]	nao (900)	65	207
San Juan Bautista[1]	gln (810)	84	249
La Concepción[1][3] (F)	n (862)	69	191
Santa Catalina[1]	n (730)	69	220
Santa María del Juncal[1]	n (730)	66	221
San Bartolomé[1]	n (976)	56	184
San Juan Gargarín[1]	n (569)	38	165
La Trinidad[1]	n (650)	54	156
El Espíritu Santo[2]	pt (70)	15	18

		Tonnage	Mariners	Soldiers
Guipuzcoa – Miguel de Oquendo				
Santa Ana[1][3] (*capitana*)	nao (1200)	125	275
Nuestra Señora de la Rosa[2][3]	nao (945)	85	238
San Salvador[2][3]	nao (958)	90	281
Santa Bárbara[1]	nao (525)	47	135
San Esteban[2]	nao (936)	73	201
Santa María (or *Marta*)[1]	nao (548)	73	166
San Bonaventura[1]	nao (379)	54	158
La María San Juan[1]	nao (291)	40	95
La Santa Cruz[1]	nao (680)	40	125
La Urca Doncella[1]	nao (500)	29	112
La Asunción[2]	pt (60)	16	18
San Bernabé[2]	pt (69)	17	17
Nuestra Señora de Guadalupe[2]	pz (–)	12	–
La Madalena[2]	pz (–)	14	–

		Tonnage	Mariners	Soldiers
Levant – Martín de Bertendona				
La Regazona[1] (*capitana*)	n (1249)	80	291
La Labia[2] (*almiranta*)	n (728)	71	231
Veneciana (or *Trinidad*) *Valencera*[2][3]	n (1100)	75	338
'Florencia'[1]	gln (961)	89	294
Santa María (or *Rata*) *Encoronada*[2][3]	n (820)	93	355
La Juliana[2][3]	n (860)	65	347
San Nicolás[1]	n (834)	68	226
La Anunciada[2]	n (703)	80	186
La Trinidad de Scala[1]	n (900)	66	342

		Tonnage	Mariners	Soldiers
Hulks – Juan Gómez de Medina				
El Gran Grifón[2] (*capitana*)	(650)	45	234
San Salvador[1] (*almiranta*)	(650)	53	218
La Barca de Hamburg[2]	(600)	30	257
San Pedro el Mayor[2]	(531)	34	110

	Tonnage	Mariners	Soldiers
La Casa de Paz Chica (or Pequeña)[1]	(350)	21	154
Sansón[1]	(500)	31	184
El Ciervo Volante[2]	(400)	39	132
El Falcon Blanco Mayor[1]	(500)	34	182
San Gabriel	(280)	16	31
El Castillo Negro[2]	(750)	46	157
El Perro Marino[1]	(200)	18	80
Santa Barbara[2]	(350)	24	106
Santiago[2]	(600)	33	32
San Pedro el Menor[2]	(500)	22	176
El Gato[1]	(400)	41	30
San Andres[1]	(400)	39	26
La Barca de Anzique	(450)	28	150
La (Buena) Ventura[1]	(160)	15	49
Esayas[1]	(260)	24	23

Patajes, zabras, etc. – Agustín de Ojeda

	Tonnage	Mariners	Soldiers
Nuestra Señora del Pilar de Zaragoza[2]	n (300)	59	114
La Caridad Inglesa	hulk (180)	37	43
San Andrés	hulk (150)	38	27
Nuestra Señora de la Freseneda	pt (–)	20	–
La Concepción[2]	pt (–)	19	–
La Concepción de Juan de Leciaja	pt (–)	21	18
Nuestra Señora del Puerto	pt (55)	27	28
Nuestra Señora de Guadalupe[1]	pt (70)	32	17
Nuestra Señora de Begoña	pt (64)	23	–
La Concepción[2]	pt (60)	18	–
San Jerónimo[2]	pt (55)	40	–
Nuestra Señora de la Gracia[1]	pt (57)	26	17
La Concepción[2]	pt (–)	18	–
El Santo Crucifijo[2]	pt (150)	24	40
La Trinidad	z (–)	24	–
Nuestra Señora de Castro[2]	z (–)	18	–
San Andres	z (–)	17	–
La Concepción[2]	z (–)	18	–
San Juan[2]	z (–)	29	–
La Asunción[2]	z (–)	18	–
Santa Catalina[2]	z (–)	20	–

Galleasses – Hugo de Moncada

	Tonnage	Mariners	Soldiers
San Lorenzo[2] [3] (capitana)	–	124	244
Napolitana[1] [3]	–	100	221
Zúniga[1] [3]	–	102	196
La Girona[2] [3]	–	120	229

	Tonnage	Mariners	Soldiers
Galleys – Diego de Medrano			
La Capitana	–	53	56
Princesa	–	44	37
Diana[2]	–	47	32
Bazana	–	46	26
Falúas (7 ships, no names given)	–	42	–
Caravels			
Nuestra Señora de la Asunción	–	14	–
San Jorge	–	11	–
La Concepción de Antonio Vicente (?)	–	24	–
San Antonio de Pedro Alfonso	–	17	–
San Antonio de Alvaro Rodríguez	–	16	–
San Juan	–	8	–
Jesus de Ayuda	–	11	–
San Lorenzo	–	5	–
Concepción de Ruy de Sea	–	19	–
Concepción	–	–	–

Rejoined the fleet before sailing

	Tonnage	Mariners	Soldiers
Santa Ana[2] [3] (Recalde's capitana)	nao (768)	101	311
Santa María de Gracia y San Juan[2] (Levant Sq.?)	n (800)	53	267
Falcón Blanco Mediano[2]	hulk (300)	23	57

May have gone

	Tonnage	Mariners	Soldiers
Santa María de Visión	n (666)	70	255

155

The names and effectives are taken from GA.221 f.181, and the tonnage from Martin, 1975, 266–79. The figures for the number of soldiers in the Guipuzcoan, Levant, Hulk and Patajes squadrons differ considerably in the May and July accounts. The names were apt to change from one account to another.

Abbreviations: glns (galleons); n, ns (nave(s)); pt (patache(s)); z (zabra(s)); M (mariner); O (oarsmen).

Note that Agustín de Ojeda replaced Antonio Hurtado de Mendoza as commander of the Patajes, Zabras etc., squadron and played an important role in the Armada.

1. ships known to have returned
2. ships lost
3. front-line ship

The English fleet

The tonnages of the royal ships are given in tons burden; those of the privately owned vessels are as given in various contemporary lists, collated in Laughton, II, 1981, 324–31, and appear to equate roughly with tons burden.

Queen's ships

Ship	Tonnage
Ark Royal	540
Revenge	441
Rainbow	384
Triumph	760
(White) Bear	732
Elizabeth Jonas	684
Victory	565
Mary Rose	476
Vanguard	449
Elizabeth Bonaventure	448
(Golden) Lion	448
Hope	403
Dreadnought	360
Nonpareil	357
Antelope	341
Swallow	308
Galley Bonavolia	300?
Swiftsure	232
Foresight	231
Bull	229
Aid	225
Tiger	156
George Hoy	100
Tremontana	132
Scout	120
Achates	90
Brigantine	90
Charles	70
Merlin[1]	50
Moon	59
Spy	42
Advice	42
Sun	39
Cygnet	29

Privately-owned ships

Ship	Home port (if known)	Tonnage
200 tons plus		
Galleon Leicester	–	400
Merchant Royal	–	400
Edward Bonaventure	–	300
Roebuck	–	300
Hercules	London	300
Sampson	–	300
Toby	London	250
Golden Noble	–	250
Galleon Dudley	–	250
Centurion	London	250
Samaritan	Dartmouth	250
Minion	Bristol	230
Violet	London	220
Susan Parnell	London	220
Mayflower	London	200
Minion	London	200
Ascension	London	200
Primrose	London	200
Margaret and John	London	200
Tiger	London	200
Red Lion	London	200
George Bonaventure	London	200
Griffin	–	200
Minion	–	200
Bark Talbot[1]	–	200
Thomas Drake[1]	–	200
Spark	–	200
Hopewell	–	200
Virgin God Save Her	–	200
Hope Hawkins	–	200
100–199 tons		
Edward	Maldon	186
Gift of God	London	180
Anne Frances	London	180
Bark Potts	–	180
Hope[1]	Plymouth	180
Solomon	London	170
Bark Burr	London	160
Brave	London	160
Bark St Leger	–	160
Bark Mannington	–	160
Royal Defence	London	160
Vineyard	London	160
Nightingale	–	160
Daniel[4]	Newcastle	160
Bark Bond[1]	–	150

Ship	Home port (if known)	Tonnage	Ship	Home port (if known)	Tonnage
Bark Bonner	–	150	*Jonas*	–	–[3]
Bark Hawkins	–	150	*Solomon*	–	–[3]
John Trelawney	–	150	*Richard Duffield*	–	–[3]
Galleon Hutchins[4]	Newcastle	150	*John*	Barnstaple	–[3]
Bark Lamb[4]	Newcastle	150	*Charity*	Plymouth	–[3]
Marigold[4]	Aldeburgh	150			
Grace	Great Yarmouth	150	*Less than 100 tons*		
Mayflower	–	150	*Jacob*	Lyme	90
Cure's Ship[1]	–	150	*Elizabeth*[1]	Lowestoft	90
Frances	Fowey	140	*Diana*	London	80
Golden Lion	London	140	*Passport*	London	80
Thomas Bonaventure	London	140	*Unity*	–	80
Samuel	London	140	*Bark Buggins*	–	80
Bear Yonge[1]	–	140	*Elizabeth Founes*	–	80
White Lion	–	140	*Disdain*	–	80
Crescent	Dartmouth	140	*Bark Webb*	–	80
William	Ipswich	140	*Handmaid*	Bristol	80
Bartholemew	Topsham	130	*William*	Rye	80
Unicorn	Bristol	130	*Frigate*	–	80
Katharine	Ipswich	125	*Rat*	Isle of Wight	80
George Noble	London	120	*Bark Halse*	Dartmouth	76
Toby	London	120	*Handmaid*[4]	Hull	75
Antelope	London	120	*Bark*	Bridgwater	70
Prudence	Leigh (Essex)	120	*John*	Chichester	70
Primrose	Harwich	120	*Griffin*[4]	Hull	70
Elizabeth	Dover	120	*Bark Sutton*	Weymouth	70
Angel[1]	Southampton	120	*Phoenix*	Dartmouth	70
Golden Ryall	Weymouth	120	*Katherine*	Weymouth	66
William	Plymouth	120	*Elizabeth Drake*	–	60
Jewel	Leigh	110	*Makeshift*	–	60
Salamander	Leigh	110	*Diamond*	Dartmouth	60
Dolphin	Leigh	110	*Speedwell*	–	60
Rose	Topsham	110	*Chance*	–	60
Robin	Sandwich	110	*Moonshine*	London	60
Anthony	London	100	*Release*	London	60
Rose Lion	Leigh	100	*Hart*	Dartmouth	60
Pansy	London	100	*Hearty Anne*	–	60
Jane Bonaventure	London	100	*Revenge*	Lyme	60
Galleon	Weymouth	100	*Aid*	Bristol	60
William	Colchester	100	*Fancy*[4]	Newcastle	60
Grace	Topsham	100	*Ann Bonaventure*	Hastings	60
Mary Rose	–	–[3]	*John Young*	–	60
Elizabeth Bonaventure	–	–[3]	*Heathen*	Weymouth	60
Pelican	–	–[3]	*Bark Halse*	–	60
Pearl	–	–[3]	*Thomas Bonaventure*	–	60
Elizabeth	Leigh	–[3]	*Margaret*	–	60
John	London	–[3]	*Flyboat*	–	60
Bearsabe	–	–[3]	*Grace of God*	–	50
Marigold	–	–[3]	*Golden Hind*	–	50

157

Ship	Home port (if known)	Tonnage
Delight	–	50
Flyboat Yonge	–	50
Lark	–	50
Fancy	–	50
Little Hare[4]	Hull	50
Carouse	–	50
Nightingale	–	40
Little John	–	40
Susan[4]	King's Lynn	40
Elizabeth	–	40
Raphael	–	40
Hazard	Faversham	38
Matthew[4]	Lowestoft	35
Caravel	–	30
Marigold	–	30
Gallego	Plymouth	30
Gift	Topsham	25
Black Dog	–	20
Katharine	–	20
Pippin	–	20
Hearts-ease	–	–[3]
Hope	–	–[3]
Unity	–	–[3]
White Hind	–	–[3]
Gift of God	–	–[3]
Eleven crayers	Hastings	–[3]
Five crayers	Hythe	–[3]
Greyhound	Aldeburgh	–[3]
Jonas	Aldeburgh	–[3]
Fortune	Aldeburgh	–[3]
Solomon	Aldeburgh	–[3]
William	Leigh	–[3]
Tiger	Plymouth	–[3]
Chance	Plymouth	–[3]
Minion	Plymouth	–[3]
Acteon	–	–[3]

1. used as a fireship at Calais
2. estimated tonnage
3. tonnage appears to be within this particular range
4. vessel known to have been discharged from service before the campaign began

158

Comparative tonnages of the English and Spanish fleets

Tons	English ships (tons burden)	Spanish ships (*toneles machos*)
1000–999	–	1
900–999	–	3
800–899	–	3
700–799	2	9
600–699	1	14
500–599	2	14
400–499	8	25
300–399	10	12
200–299	28	12
100–199	74	8
0–99	101	50
Total	226	151

Note: Tonnage ranges and comparisons are approximate: tonnages of vessels in the main list of Spanish ships are in *toneladas*, on which the charter price was calculated. *Toneles machos* were used to measure cargo capacity, and were roughly equivalent to tons burden.

(ii) Spanish Shipping and Shipbuilding

Prior to the 1570s the King of Spain had no permanent Atlantic navy of his own, unlike the galleys he maintained in the Mediterranean. Naval warfare in the Atlantic had been intermittent, and the crown relied on small private squadrons on contract to the king or on armed merchant vessels (generically termed *naos* or *naves*) hired or pressed into service.[1] At that time in Spain the idea of a purpose-built fighting ship had still not been fully developed. All ships were armed with at least some guns and they fulfilled both functions, although for military ventures they were usually more heavily armed, carried a detachment of fighting men, and may have had some changes made to their superstructure.

The owners of commandeered ships received a 'salary' or fee for the use of their vessels, but it is not at all certain that it was sufficient to compensate for the loss of freightage dues. Furthermore, it was common for there to be a delay of many years before shipowners were paid or compensated. Thus, royal embargoes placed shipowners under financial duress and could lead to their bankruptcy.

Despite the drawbacks of the system, it was not until the late 1560s and early 1570s with the

1. Labayru, 1900, 265; Artiñano, 1920, 277.

rebellion of Flanders,[2] that the defence of the Atlantic came to occupy a more important place within Spanish political and military affairs and Philip began to develop a permanent fleet. Even then, the crown undertook the building of fighting ships only in a sporadic manner. In 1570 an Atlantic squadron, the *Armada Real de la Guarda de la Carrera de las Indias*, was established with the specific purpose of defending the *flotas* sailing between Seville and the Indies.[3] This squadron, under the *Adelantado* Pedro Menéndez de Avilés, consisted of twelve small galleons of 230 *toneles* each, built in Bilbao from 1568 onwards.[4] In January 1578, Cristóbal de Barros, who was first 'superintendent of shipbuilding and forests' for Spain's north coast in the early 1560s,[5] laid the keels of two larger galleons in Deusto, on the Bilbao river. These were intended to be the *capitana* and *almiranta* of the Indies Guard (though the original plan had been to build some ten ships).[6] In 1582 nine galleons were begun in Guarnizo (Santander), also under Barros's supervision.[7] These nine ships, which can be regarded as the beginning of Spain's permanent royal fleet, were the basis of the Castilian Squadron in the 1588 Armada.

But these building programmes did not produce enough royal fighting ships; of the thirty-five main ships (excluding galleasses and galleys) that took part in the Azores expedition in 1583, only three belonged to the king.[8] The same held true for the 1588 *Felicissima Armada*. Of the 151 ships that sailed from Lisbon on 30 May, only some twenty-seven belonged to the crown: ten galleons of the Castilian Squadron, nine galleons of the Portuguese Squadron, the four Portuguese galleys and four Neapolitan galleasses. The other large ships, forty-seven *naos* or *naves* and twenty-six hulks, had been drafted into royal service while the remaining fifty-one vessels were small *pataches* (twenty), *zabras* (ten), *caravelas* (eleven) and *falúas* (ten), apparently also requisitioned or on hire.[9]

It was not until after the Armada that the Spanish crown started building galleons in earnest and that purpose-built fighting ships (galleons as opposed to armed *naos*) began to play a more important part in the king's naval forces in the Atlantic. Between 1589 and 1598 the crown financed the construction of some forty galleons beginning with the 'Twelve Apostles' built in Guarnizo and Deusto from 1589 to 1591.[10] This intensive royal building programme represents the success of the view that the Armadas should consist of royal galleons as opposed to private armed *naos*. However, privately owned ships continued to form the greater part of Spain's naval forces into the seventeenth century. For example, in September 1590, the Armada of the Atlantic under Alonso de Bazán consisted of a total of seventy-six ships, forty of which were private (twenty-five *naos*, fifteen *pataches* and *zabras*) and thirty-six belonged to the king: four galleons of the Portuguese crown, eight of the Castilian crown, three small galleons, thirteen *filibotes*, one *patache*, four galleasses and three galleys.[11] In 1597 the king had twenty galleons and, a year later, twenty-seven galleons, but these represented only 25 and 40 per cent, respectively, of all the ships in the Armada.[12]

The mainstay of Spain's Atlantic trading and war fleets during the 1500s was the 'multipurpose' *nao* of Spain's north coast, in particular of the Basque provinces of Guipuzcoa and Vizcaya.[13] The shipyards of the Spanish Basque country also produced a large number of smaller trading and fishing vessels; *pataches*, *zabras* and *pinazas*. During the Middle Ages the Basques, forced to look seaward because of an unproductive hinterland, acquired and developed a high degree of competence in the arts of shipbuilding and navigation. The Basques enjoyed the advantages of plentiful oak timber and iron, a favourable geographical location on the route linking Spain with Northern Europe and ample capital. Guipuzcoa and Vizcaya became the foremost shipbuilding regions in Spain. To quote words used by the Duke of Medina Sidonia in 1582: 'the Biscay *naos* . . . are the strength of these kingdoms.'[14]

Basque shipping dominated the *Carrera de las Indias*. Between 1520 and 1580 Basque ships made up 80 per cent of those sailing from Spain to the New World, but decreased thereafter.[15] They were also predominant in the Spanish Newfoundland cod and whaling enterprises and in the transport of Castilian wool to France and Flanders. Basque ships also played a crucial part in successive royal fleets. In the 1582 battle against the fleet supporting Portuguese pretender Dom Antonio, almost half of the twenty-five Spanish ships actually engaged in the naval action were requisitioned Basque *naos*, while in the attack against the island of Terceira the following year some thirteen out of thirty-five *naos* and galleons in the fleet came from either Vizcaya or Guipuzcoa.[16] In the 1588 Armada at least nineteen of the sixty-six main fighting ships were Basque, the largest contingent from any one region.

The other areas of Spain's Atlantic coast did not boast important shipbuilding industries, due to a lack of either shipbuilding materials, skilled labour or capital. They produced some large ships, though not on a continuous basis, and constructed relatively small trading and fishing vessels. The Cantabrian coastline of the Cuatro Villas (Castro de Urdiales,

2. AGS GA f.101 on the organization of a Hispano-Portuguese armada against corsairs threatening the *Carrera* (1571).
3. MN Madrid, Colección Fernández Navarrete, XXII, doc.76, f.286.
4. AHPGO, Partido de San Sebastian, leg.372, f.84.
5. AGS GA 71, f.227.
6. MN Madrid, Colección Sanz Baturell, art.3, tomo III, f.245, documento 401, and AGS GA 111, f.165. AGS GA 82, f.215.
7. MN Madrid, Colección Fernández Navarrete, XXII, ff.286–328.
8. Duro, 1886, 402; Thompson, 1976, 192.
9. AGS GA 221, f.190.
10. Thompson, 1976, 192 and 304.
11. AGS GA 290, ff.67 and 68.
12. Thompson, 1976, 192.
13. Barkham, 1985.
14. AGS GA 221, f.198.
15. Chaunu, VIII, 1959, 257–9.
16. Duro, 1886, 297 and 402; Labayru, 1900, 502 and 506–507.

159

Laredo, Santander and San Vincente de la Barquera) was the most important shipbuilding region after the Basque country, although it was really only the ports of Laredo and Santander, through which large amounts of Castilian wool was exported, that witnessed the construction of *naos*.[17] Of Asturias and Galicia, Cristobal de Barros reported to the king in July 1571:

> there are no *naos*, only some small vessels which sail to the Basque ports with wine and sardines and towards Portugal and Andalusia with sardines. They are vessels of little or no substance, the biggest ones of thirty-five *toneles*. In Avilés there is usually a *nao* of 100 *toneles* that goes to *Terranova* (Newfoundland and the Canadian east coast), and in Gijón, Ribadesella and Llanes, one and a half dozen *chalupas* of fifty to sixty *toneles* which during this season are in the Irish fishery and during the winter go to that of Cabo Daguer . . . It may be that some of the *chalupas* of Gijón have gone to the codfishery [Newfoundland] and not to Ireland. These *chalupas* are good sea-going vessels and very appropriate for transporting horses and for being fitted with oars.[18]

In Andalusia the construction of *naos* appears to have ceased almost completely by the mid-1500s, because of a scarcity of adequate building materials, particularly of timber. As early as 1505 Martín de Zamudio, a burgess of Bilbao, was engaged as an agent by the Casa de la Contratación (the agency based at Seville which administered Spain's trade monopoly with the Indies) for the purchase of Basque ships and guns for use on the *Carrera* or Indies run.[19] Thus, it is likely that many of the nine *naos* of the Andalusian Squadron in the Armada had been built in Basque shipyards, even though their owners may have been Andalusian.

The shipbuilding capabilities of the ports of Spain's north coast are well reflected in a memorandum sent by Barros to Philip II in November 1588, barely weeks after the return of the *Invincible*. Barros had been asked to advise on the best places to build twenty-four royal galleons. He suggested that they could be built in Guarnizo (Santander) in two consecutive lots over a period of two years; or they could be divided up amongst eleven shipbuilding centres: two galleons in Guarnizo, two in Laredo/Barzena and the other twenty in nine Basque ports. In his opinion, the second option would be quicker but cost more

Home ports of the opposing fleets

and the ships would not be as sturdily built, given the difficulties of supervision. Barros added that, 'in Asturias and Galicia it is not worth attempting this, as there is little timber and that which is lacking would have to be brought from Guipuzcoa and Vizcaya.'[20] However, at this time four *naos* (averaging close to 475 *toneles* each) were being built with the aid of royal loans in the Asturian ports of Villaviciosa, Avilés, Luarca and Tapia.[21]

While Basque *naos* formed the backbone of royal fleets for a large part of the 1500s, there were, of course, ships from other regions that also participated. During the last two decades of the century these appear to have come primarily from two areas: Portugal and the Mediterranean. The annexation of

17. AGS GA 75, f.24 and f.168.
18. AGS GA 75, f.24.
19. Chaunu, 1955–9.
20. AGS, GA 227, f.286.
21. Ibid.

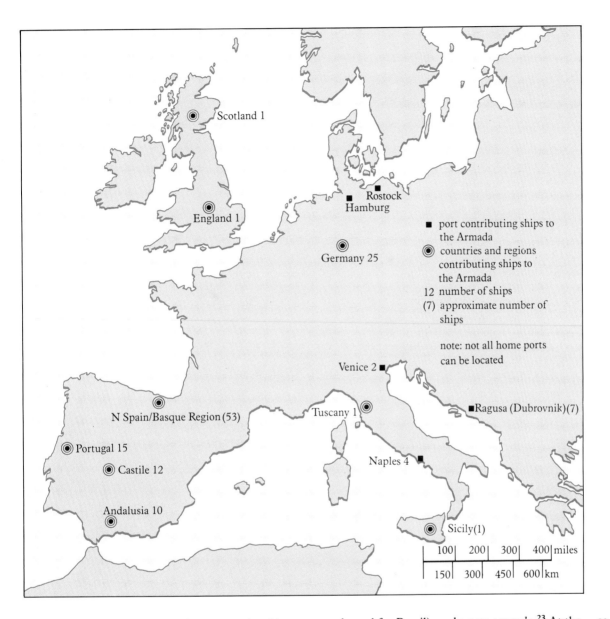

Scotland 1

Rostock
Hamburg

England 1

Germany 25

- port contributing ships to the Armada
◎ countries and regions contributing ships to the Armada
12 number of ships
(7) approximate number of ships

note: not all home ports can be located

Venice 2 ■

N Spain/Basque Region (53)

Tuscany 1 ◎

■ Ragusa (Dubrovnik) (7)

Portugal 15

Castile 12

Naples 4

Andalusia 10

Sicily (1)

| 100 | 200 | 300 | 400 | miles |
| 150 | 300 | 450 | 600 | km |

Portugal in 1580 gave Philip II access to that kingdom's shipping which, from all accounts, was of a high standard. Escalante de Mendoza, experienced seaman and author of one of the earliest-known but unpublished treatises on shipbuilding (1575), noted that 'the Portuguese built their *naos* very strong, large and powerful [for their trade to Brazil and the East Indies]', but he added that 'they build no great number'.[22] In March 1581 Philip II had ten Portuguese royal ships at his disposal: the galleons *San Martin* (600 Portuguese tons), *San Matheo* (450 tons), *San Sebastian* (400 tons), *San Francisco* (300 tons), *Santo Antonio* (220 tons), *San Rafael* (200 tons), *San Pedro* (400 tons, bound for Malaca), *San Christobal* (300 tons, bound for 'La Mina') and *San Miguel* (200

tons, bound for Brazil), and a new *caravela*.[23] At the same time six out of nineteen *naos* from Lisbon, Aveiro and Villa do Conde had been embargoed by the king in Lisbon.[24] The *San Martin* and *San Matheo* took part in the 1582 Azores campaign, the first as *capitana* of the fleet[25], and in the 1588 Armada the *San Martin* sailed as the *capitana* of the entire Armada. The Mediterranean ships that served in the Spanish Atlantic fleets came largely from Ragusa (Dubrovnic), whose seamen maintained strong ties with the King of Spain, but also from Genoa, Tuscany, Sicily, Naples and Venice. Thirty-three Ragusan ships took part in the Portuguese campaigns of 1580[26] and 1587 – twelve served in the Azores campaigns of 1582–3.[27] In the Armada there were

22. Duro, V, 1881, 441.
23. AGS GA 111, f.141.
24. AGS GA 111, f.188.
25. Labayru, 1900, 503.
26. AGS GA 106, f.85, see also f.93 and GA 95, ff.175 and 181.
27. Duro, 1886, 297 and 406; Thompson, 1976, 193.

two Venetian *naves*, at least one Sicilian, the galleon of the Grand Duke of Tuscany and seven other Mediterranean ships, at least some of which were Ragusan. The Tuscan galleon sailed with the Portuguese squadron, the rest with the Levant squadron.[28] The Armada did not put an end to the participation of Mediterranean ships in Spain's Atlantic forces. In March 1590, the Ragusans Pedro de Ivella and Estefano de Oliste contracted to serve Philip *en las armadas del Mar Oceano* with twelve new galleons constructed according to the 'quintessence of English, Basque and Ragusan galleon measurements'.[29] Only three of these galleons were Ragusan, the rest coming from the Kingdom of Naples. They ranged in size from 560 to 1,200 *toneles*, and do not appear to have entered service until 1594, when eight of them were 'dismissed as unsuitable for conditions in the Atlantic'.[30]

The participation of a relatively large number of Mediterranean ships over the last quarter of the century may have been due, in part, to the shortage of Basque ships. In 1582, the president and *consules* of the *consulado* of Seville proposed to Philip II that he allow up to ten *urcas esterlinas* to sail in the Indies fleets of 1583 and 1584 because 'the lack of Basque *naos* is notorious; so that even for your Majesty's service they cannot be found'.[31]

The shape and size of Spanish Armada ships:
naos and galleons
During the better part of the sixteenth century the overall proportions of most ships of the *naos* and *nave* type of more than 200 tons, from different parts of Europe, were based on the old shipwright's rule of thumb of 'one, two, three', where the keel and overall length were two and three times the beam respectively. Tome Cano, a pilot with some fifty-four years of sailing experience and author of another early treatise on shipbuilding (1611), stated that: 'all the shipwrights of Spain, Italy and other nations who build *naos*, have had the custom of giving them two and three *codos* of keel and overall length for each *codo* of beam; and for every three *codos* of beam, one of width in the floor of the hold; and a height [depth of hold] equal to three quarters of the beam'[32] (1 *codo*=57 cm). This rule was sometimes interpreted as: one (depth of hold), two (beam) and three (overall length).[33]

The Englishman William Borough, who between 1580 and 1598 was successively clerk of ships, surveyor of ships and comptroller for the English navy, in talking about the 'merchant ship for most profit' (keel/beam=2), stated that 'the mean and best proportion for shipping and merchandise,

likewise very serviceable for all purposes' was a keel/beam ratio of 2 to 2.25.[34] During the second half of the sixteenth century, however, there were a large number of Basque *naos* built with a keel/beam ratio of less than two.

Ships built along these lines were broad-beamed in relation to their overall length, in comparison with ships of later centuries but, generally speaking, they fulfilled their function as trading vessels well. Of course, some were better sailing ships than others due to a number of factors, including difference in the lines of entry and run of the hull and variation in the height of the sides above water.

In Spain, the Basque *nao* was considered the sturdiest and best-proportioned of vessels. By the mid-1500s, Spanish Basque shipwrights appear to have reached a consensus with regard to the most favourable proportions for the 'multipurpose' *nao* (beam=1; keel=1.9; length overall=3.1). These had two or three decks, depending on their size, as well as fore and stern castles, and carried three masts and a bowsprit.[35] In manuscript sources the terms *nao* and *galeon* are often used interchangeably to describe these ships, although it is clear that during the first half of the century the term *galeon* had a rather different connotation, being used to denote small vessels of ten or twenty tons.[36] During the second half of the sixteenth century the term came to be used for purpose-built fighting ships, even though in the majority of cases their hull shape differed little from that of the Basque *nao*.

Ship design, of course, was not static, and some experimentation took place to meet the demands of naval warfare. But, with the exception of twelve small galleons built from 1568–70, the changes were apparently not major. This is evident from a series of documents which have recently come to light on the building of the first Spanish galleons.

Avilés's twelve small galleons (1568–70), the galleons built by Barros in 1578 (two) and 1582–4 (nine) and the 'Twelve Apostles' (1589–91) were built either in Basque ports or in Guarnizo (Santander). Avilés's small, two-deck *galeoncetes* (of only 230 *toneles* each) were experimental in design; they were considerably longer in the keel and overall length in relation to the beam than other ships of similar size built during the same period in northern Spanish yards. Their overall proportions were: beam=1, keel=2.4, and overall length=3.5. However, according to the Basque shipwrights who built them, and to several experienced mariners who sailed in them, they left much to be desired. Amongst other things, they were considered too small for fighting ships and too narrow in the beam.

28. AGS GA 221, f.1 and GA 223, f.28 (also cited in Martin, 1977).
29. MN Madrid, Colección Fernández Navarrete, IX, doc. 27, f.309; Sanz Barutell, art. 5, no. 50 (6 March 1590).
30. MN Madrid, Sanz Barutell, art. 5, no. 53 (20 Nov. 1593); and Thompson, 1976, 193.
31. AGS GA 221, f.198.
32. Cano, 1964, 62.
33. Duro, V, 1881, 151.
34. Oppenheim, 1896, 126 cited in Glasgow, 1964, 179.
35. Barkham, 1985.
36. AHPGO, Partido de San Sebastian, leg. 327.

162

The three subsequent shipbuilding programmes undertaken by Philip II between 1578 and 1591 attempted to correct the flaws of Avilés's *galeoncetes* and develop a suitable warship. All of these ships were at least 50 per cent larger than Avilés's. They had three decks and were built along lines far closer to those of Basque *naos*, even though design features such as the height of decks and the beam varied (beam 1; keel 2/2.2; overall length=3.3/3.4). Uppermost in Barros's mind was to build large and strong fighting ships that could carry a great deal of sail, many guns and a large number of sailors and soldiers and allow the boarding of enemy ships from above. That these royal galleons were built relatively close to the 'one, two, three' principle, and to the Basque *nao*, is a clear indicator that in several quarters of the Spanish shipbuilding world, in which Barros's influence was considerable, these proportions were deemed satisfactory. It was not until the end of the century that experimentation in Spanish ship design quickened in pace and that the galleon shape gradually evolved through a series of important transformations.

Michael Barkham

163

8.1
Modern model of a Spanish galleon
Designed by David White; constructed by P. Wride; rigging designed by J. A. Lees, 1988

Scale: 1:96
National Maritime Museum

Spain did not possess a permanent force of sailing warships in the Atlantic before the 1570s. Twelve royal galleons built between 1568 and 1570 were deemed too small for fighting ships, and the three building programmes between 1578 and 1591 aimed to produce large ships that could carry a great deal of sail, many guns and would be able to overtop opponents. This model is not of a specific ship, but represents one of the new, large galleons of the Armada period.

8.2
Spanish votive ship model, mid 16th century

Wood and iron
1115×420×350
Museo Naval, Madrid

This sixteenth-century Spanish ship model represents a 'multi-purpose' *nao* of the type that sailed to the American colonies, on numerous European trade routes and also participated in royal fleets. It illustrates construction features of the period: the one-

storey sterncastle extending forward approximately to the main mast, a two-storey forecastle, wales (running the length of the ship) and vertical timbers reinforcing the hull and sides. The model was originally in the chapel of the Virgin of Consolation in Utrera, Seville. Votive ships were used to ask divine favour for a forthcoming voyage or to give thanks for deliverance from danger at sea.

8.3
Modern model of an English galleon
Designed by David White; constructed by P. Wride; rigging designed by J. A. Lees, 1988

Scale: 1:96
National Maritime Museum

This model shows the relatively low superstructure of an English warship of the Armada period. This form reduced wind resistance and made such vessels more manoeuvrable than their opponents, enabling the English to use stand-off gunnery tactics against the Spanish and to avoid the boarding actions that the Spanish sought. In 1588 a ship of this size would have carried some 300 mariners, 40 gunners and 150 soldiers.

8.4
Modern model of an English pinnace
Designed by David White; constructed by K. Thatcher; rigging designed by J. A. Lees, 1988

Scale: 1:96
National Maritime Museum

This model represents one of the low-built, lightly armed pinnaces used by the English navy in 1588 for scouting and communications work.

8.5
'Fragments of Ancient English Shipwrightry', *c*.1586
Matthew Baker (*c*.1530–1613) and others

Photographs of Pepysian Library MS 2820
Abell, 1948, 36–41; Glasgow, 1964, 183–5; Baynes and Pugh, 1981, 70–71, 74–5
By permission of the Master and Fellows of Magdalene College, Cambridge

This manuscript (named by Samuel Pepys) contains the earliest known English shipbuilding treatise, in the form of notes on ship design by the royal master-shipwright Matthew Baker. It is possible that they were intended for use in a book that was never published. Baker was deeply concerned with the application of mathematics and geometry to ship design. His skills in this field were highly regarded by contemporaries (even enemies); certain features of his writings suggest, however, he may to some extent have been putting a mathematical gloss on principles which had been established empirically. He none the less appears to have been an innovator in ship design (see above, pp. 152–3), and was certainly a skilful draughtsman.

8.6
Instrucion Nauthica, 1587
Diego García de Palacio (d.1595)

Pedro Orcharte, 1st ed., Mexico City
Printed book
200×150
Artiñano, 1920, 126; Guillén, 1944a and b; Bankston, 1986
British Library, London (C.31.e.38)

164 Born in Santander (northern Spain) in the first half of the sixteenth century, Palacio was already resident in the New World in 1573 when he was appointed as an *oidor* (judge) of the *audiencia* of Guatemala. As a result of Drake's raid on Nombre de Dios in the same year, he was entrusted with building two large galleons and later with pursuing the English corsair. In 1578 he moved to Mexico City, and in 1581 became both a doctor and the rector of Mexico University. In 1583 Palacio published his *Diálogos Militares*, a military compendium in the form of a dialogue between a Basque and a *Montañes* (native of Santander). He adopted this style for his second book, *Instrucion Nauthica*, which includes information on virtually every aspect of contemporary maritime technology: navigation, the tides, astronomy, chart-making, sea-warfare, the construction and fitting out of ships and the composition of ships' crews. As such it constitutes the first-known published treatise of its kind.

8.7
Drawing of the *Roberge* of M. de Monluc, 1565

MS
295×408
AGS E.145, f.221
Archivo General de Simancas, Valladolid (MPD XIX–87)

The *Roberge*, a ship of some 200 tons burden, was probably built in St Jean de Luz about 1565, apparently for Blaise de Monluc (*c*.1500–77), a *maréchal de France*. The ship was to have three masts, one topmast and was also to be powered by oars, with an armament of sixty guns (large and small). Her deck plan (orlop, main and a 'rope grating') was virtually the same as contemporary northern Spanish vessels of similar size, though she was considerably narrower than these (beam/keel 1:2.6). The plan appears to have come into Spanish hands by means of espionage.

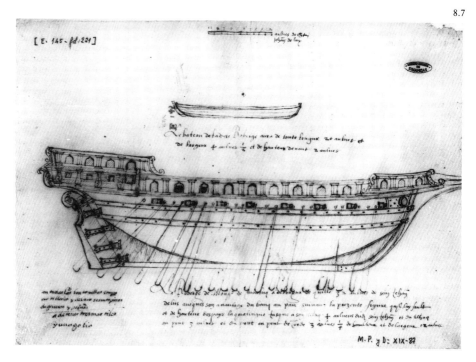

8.7

8.8
Cristóbal de Barros to Philip II, 21 March 1581

MS
310×215
Archivo General de Simancas, Valladolid (GA 111, f.166)

On 14 March Barros, the king's agent for shipping and shipbuilding on Spain's north coast, received a letter from Philip II instructing him to build eight galleons (later changed to nine) similar to those built for the Indies Guard by Pedro Menéndez de Avilés from 1568 to 1570. Barros's answer gives an insight into Spanish ship design immediately prior to the Armada. It contains not only the dimensions of the twelve small galleons built by Avilés and a list of their faults, but also Barros's opinion on how best to construct fighting ships, as well as modifications for the galleons he was to build. These ships, built from 1582 to 1584 in Guarnizo (Santander), were the nine galleons that sailed in the Castilian Squadron of the Armada.

8.9
Memorandum of Alonso de Leiva, Lisbon, 19–24 October 1587

MS (16ff.)
326×212
Archivo General de Simancas, Valladolid (GA 221, f.40)

Don Alonso de Leiva, one of the many royal officials in Lisbon charged with overseeing the fitting out of the Armada ships, compiled this summary of what the ships needed by way of rigging, anchor cables, sails and other gear. This detailed account is only one of a mass of similar reports, often sent to the king, which were drawn up well before the Armada sailed; it is representative of the administrative effort required and logistical problems posed by the gathering of a fleet of such size.

8.10
Account for building the Rye town pinnace, 1587–8

MS (10ff. with 1f. attached)
305×406
Dell, 1966, 1–3, 40–41
East Sussex Record Office (RYE 47/3/2)

This pinnace, a small vessel of some twenty-five tons, was built between October 1587 and May 1588 at a total cost of £53. She was intended for service with the fleet in the Channel, but seems to have been used solely for trade. As with most sea-going ships of the period, the pinnace was evidently carvel-built, her hull being fastened together with more than 2,400 trenails.

8.11
Account for fitting-out the *William* of Rye, 1588

MS (4ff.)
406×305
Dell, 1966, 39–41, 44–9; Mayhew, 1984, 119–20
East Sussex Record Office (RYE 72/1)

The *William* was a ship of sixty tons owned by a Captain Russell, a privateer and member of the refugee French Huguenot community in Rye. The town of Rye hired the ship from him for service in Seymour's squadron in the Channel in 1588, the cost of wages, stores and other items eventually amounting to £286. Repairs were made to the ship, and new equipment brought, including five compasses and three sand-glasses. Some effort was made to put the ship into a respectable state with paint, cloths for the tops and taffeta and silk to decorate the trumpets. Details of the *William*'s service are unclear, but two of her fifty-nine-man crew were injured.

8.12
Inventory of the Queen's ships, September–December 1588
John Austen and Richard Poulter

MS volume
330×245
Laughton, II, 1981, 241–54
Public Record Office, London (SP12/220)

This survey of the gear in the twenty-nine royal ships which returned to Chatham after the Armada campaign was concerned with finding out what would be needed to re-equip them. Each ship inventory was extremely detailed, listing items such as rigging, navigational instruments, anchors, cables and even the pots and pans of the cook-room. It shows that most of the equipment losses and damage were due to the wear-and-tear of being at sea, rather than combat with the Armada. Contemporary surveys of the ships' hulls confirm that the worst enemies of the queen's ships in 1588 were timber-rot and the weather, not the Spanish.

8.13
Adze blade from the Barents expedition, 1596

Iron
80×13
Veer, 1876; Braat, 1984
Rijksmuseum, Amsterdam (NM 7750)

The Dutch made three voyages into the icy seas north of Russia in 1594, 1595 and 1596–7, seeking a north-east passage to the riches of Asia. On the third voyage, the ship was caught in the ice off the island of Novaya Zemlya and the crew were forced to winter on land, living in a cabin made from parts of the ship and stocked with items from the wreck. The pilot of all three expeditions was Willem Barents, who died during the remarkable escape journey in two open boats. The survivors were eventually rescued by a Dutch ship trading to Russia. The camp was rediscovered in the last century and hundreds of well-preserved relics were taken back to Holland. Among these was the tool-kit of a shipwright, the only one known to survive from the period. Cat. nos. **8.13–18** are from the tool kit and, although presumably Dutch in origin, are little different from the tools that would have been used by English, Spanish or other European shipbuilders. The adze blade would originally have had a wooden handle; it was the archetypal wooden shipbuilder's tool, used for trimming timbers to the shapes required for frames, masts, yards and other parts of a ship.

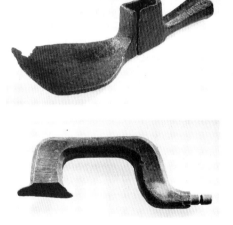

8.14
Hand-drill from the Barents expedition, 1596

Wood and iron
307×127×31
Veer, 1876; Braat, 1984
Rijksmuseum, Amsterdam (NM 7775–1)

This drill would have been used for making small nail-holes. The apparent modernity of its shape is explained by the fact that tools of this type reached their optimum form before the end of the sixteenth century.

8.15
Chisel blade from the Barents expedition, 1596

Wood and iron
194×28×15
Veer, 1876; Braat, 1984
Rijksmuseum, Amsterdam (NM 7666-1)

166

8.16
File blade from the Barents expedition, 1596

Iron
271×16×7
Veer, 1876; Braat, 1984
Rijksmuseum, Amsterdam (NM 7671-1)

This file would presumably once have had a wooden handle.

8.17
Caulking iron from the Barents expedition, 1596

Iron
155×41×37
Veer, 1876; Braat, 1984
Rijksmuseum, Amsterdam (NM 7772-1)

This tool would have been used with a large wooden caulking mallet (one of which was recovered from Novaya Zemlya) to force oakum (old, picked rope) between the plank seams of a ship. The oakum would be driven in very hard, and then covered with hot, melted pitch to make the seam watertight. The use of hot pitch could make caulking a somewhat hazardous operation.

8.18
Pair of compasses from the Barents expedition, 1596

Iron
200×16×20
Veer, 1976; Braat, 1984
Rijksmuseum, Amsterdam (NM 7673-1)

Iron compasses were used to mark off distances on timber or to scribe curves. A pair of large, mathematical compasses can be seen in the hands of the shipwright depicted in the English manuscript 'Fragments of Ancient English Shipwrightry' (see cat. no. 8.5).

8.19
Rigging block from the *Trinidad Valencera*

Wood and rope
230 lgth
Martin, 1979a, 32, fig. 19; Crédit Communal, 1985, 1.3
Ulster Museum, Belfast

Single block of a type common in the sixteenth century and later: it would have taken a rope of 15 mm diameter.

8.20
Euphroe or crowsfoot dead-eye from the *Trinidad Valencera*

Wood
205 lgth; 22 dpth
Crédit Communal, 1985, 1.4
Ulster Museum, Belfast

This item would probably have been used in the standing rigging. It is a pear-shaped flat piece of wood with five perforations along its median line, each 19 mm in diameter.

8.21
Heart from the rigging of the *Trinidad Valencera*

Wood
136×26
Crédit Communal, 1985, 1.5
Ulster Museum, Belfast

Pear-shaped block with a score 6 mm deep round the outside. Hearts were used, among other things, for helping to secure forestays.

8.22
Coak from the *Girona*

Bronze
80 wdth
Crédit Communal, 1985, 1.7a
Ulster Museum, Belfast

Square block with slightly tapering sides, and a central perforation 37 mm in diameter. Coaks were bearings set in the centre of a sheave to prevent its splitting and to reduce wear by the pin on which it turned. Their use seems to have become more widespread as the sixteenth century progressed, for the 1554 Padre Island wrecks appear to have only one coak apiece, each about 75 mm wide, probably for use in single heavy-duty blocks. More than forty coaks, however, have been retrieved from the wreck of the *Girona*.

8.23
Bronze pulley sheave from the *Gran Grifón*

Bronze
160 dia.; 36.5 wdth
Kemp, 1979, 778
Shetland Museum, Lerwick (G5/70)

Sheaves are the grooved wheels in a block, used on a ship to increase the efficiency of ropes in hauling up sails. They were usually made from bronze or a very hard wood such as *lignum vitae*, and this is the only known example from an Armada wreck.

8.24
Rigging shackle from the *Girona*

Iron
135×120
Ulster Museum, Belfast

This shackle was used to enclose a dead-eye in the standing rigging. It is a U-shaped piece of round-sectioned wrought iron, with a perforated lug at each end through which is passed a bolt or bar of cast iron, 25 mm in diameter and 170 mm long.

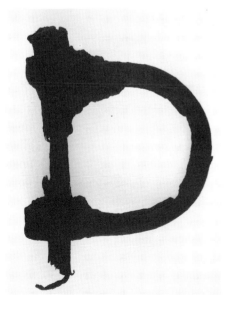

8.25
Shear hook from *Gran Grifón*

Iron
385×44×9
Manwaring and Perrin, II, 1921, 222–3;
Martin, 1975, 185
Shetland Museum, Lerwick (G79/70)

A curved iron blade, sharpened along the inside edge, and attached to the ship's yard-arm in order to tear down an enemy's rigging during grappling. Sir Henry Mainwaring described shear hooks as 'most unusefull and unnecessary things' because of the danger of breaking the yard-arm if the hook should lodge in the enemy's mast. The English fleet had ceased to use them by 1588.

8.26
Rope from the *Trinidad Valencera*

Hemp
180×30 dia.
Crédit Communal, 1985, 1.8
Ulster Museum, Belfast

Short piece of rope, laid right-handed, of three strands laid left-handed.

8.27
Anchor cable from the *Trinidad Valencera*

Hemp
2270×130 dia.
Martin, 1979a, 32
Ulster Museum, Belfast

Hempen cable composed of four strands, found wrapped round one of the anchors.

167

8.28
Rudder pintle from the *Gran Grifón*

Iron
482×400×210
Martin, 1975, 185
Shetland Museum, Lerwick (G84/70)

The pintle was a pin attached to the leading edge of the rudder and slotted into metal rings on the stern, allowing the rudder to be swung by means of the tiller. This method of attachment enabled the easy removal of the rudder for cleaning or repairs.

8.29
Fanal (lantern) used from *c.*1570 on *La Galera Capitana* of the Marquis of Santa Cruz

Wood, glass and brass
1870×700×700
La Marquesa de Santa Cruz

Fixed lanterns of this type largely denoted rank and also had some importance in station-keeping at night. They were of little use for signalling and for this purpose smaller lanterns were hoisted: the display of a lantern in a flagship's main-top might, for example, summon the captains to a council of war. The large decorative lanterns, meanwhile, also took on an important symbolic function on land: in peacetime Santa Cruz kept this lantern, an exceptional piece of craftsmanship, in his chapel beside examples he had captured from enemy commanders.

8.30
The *Ark Royal*, *c.*1588

Woodcut
512×740
Trustees of the British Museum, London (1874–8–8–1367)

The *Ark Royal* was built at Deptford in 1587 for Sir Walter Raleigh, but acquired before launching by the queen. She was used as Howard's flagship in 1588. The identification of this ship as the *Ark Royal* is based on a number of features: the flags and stern lantern indicate that the vessel is a flagship, and the arms of Howard are visible on the flag in the waist; the ship has four masts, as the *Ark Royal* had, and the fifty heavy guns on board roughly approximate to the size of the *Ark Royal*'s armament. The running rigging has been rather confusingly rendered, however, and as the *Ark Royal*'s only topmasts in 1588 were on the fore and main masts, the other top and topgallant masts seen here must have been added for effect.

8.31–8.35
The English warships *Tiger*, *Ark Royal*, *Griffin*, *Golden Lion* and *White Bear*
Claes Jansz. Visscher (1586–1652)
after ?Hendrick Cornelisz. Vroom
(1566–1640)

Engravings
133×187 each
Ottley, 1831; Waters, 1975; Howard, 1979,
55
National Maritime Museum

These engravings were made in the century following the Armada and are not accurate portraits. *White Bear* and *Golden Lion* resemble similar drawings said to be of Dutch ships and *Golden Lion*'s lateen mizzen and the dome-shaped structure attached to her quarter are doubtful. *Ark Royal*'s distinctive battlemented poop bulwarks are missing; the turrets are imaginary versions of her stern turrets and the rigging is a jumble. But her lowered forecastle, heavy shotted guns and four masts are shown, and these engravings do give some notion of the 'low-charged', seaworthy vessels designed for bombarding rather than boarding the enemy. *Griffin* was a merchant vessel appointed 'to serve westward under the charge of Sir Francis Drake', and *Tiger* was one of the ships fitted out and paid for by the City of London.

8.36
List of English ships that served against the Armada, 1588
MS (2ff.)
309×214
HMC, III, 1889, 340–41
*The Marquess of Salisbury, Hatfield House
(Cecil Papers 166/83)*

This lists 123 of the approximately 226 English ships mobilized for the Armada campaign. Included in the first thirty-nine vessels are all of the queen's ships and Howard's pinnace *Disdain*.

8.37
Declaration of James Nichol of Dundee, 7 February 1588
MS copy (3ff.)
312×214
*Archivo General de Simancas, Valladolid
(GA.220, f.161)*

Nichol was master of the ship *Red Lion*, one of four Scottish ships driven to take shelter in the Downs, off the English coast, where they were seized on the orders of the government. They were released after bribing an official with forty ducats and made for Andalusia. On arrival in San Lucar de Barrameda, Nichol told the Spanish that Drake was making ready to sail to Spain with about 100 ships, and Howard was preparing to resist Philip's invasion force of 450 ships with 200 well-manned vessels. Militia companies were training and soldiers, including Leicester, had recently come from the Netherlands. Nichol also claimed that the English were very fearful of the invasion, but they were accurately predicting that the Armada could not sail before the end of March.

8.38
La Felicissima Armada, 1588
Pedro de Paz Salas

Publ. Antonio Alvarez, 1st ed., 9 May,
Lisbon
Printed pamphlet
Annotations in French on cover; in Spanish,
French and English inside
461×435
AGS E.431 f.45; GA.221 f.158; GA.221
f.158 (May); GA.221 f.181 (July); Dyer,
1925, 419–24
British Library, London (192.f.17(1))

'The most happy fleet', or the 'Great fleet' was how the Armada of 1588 was described and there were three detailed accounts of it published in May 1588 – two in Lisbon and one in Madrid – based on the latest government figures. This copy was purchased by Jacques Boullain in Lisbon, but fell into Lord Burghley's hands soon after. He made some notes, mostly of nobles killed or ships lost. He also added the number of men and ships and underlined amounts of powder, as well as English, Irish and Scottish names he recognized. Such publications were rare but not unknown; often, unlike this one, they contained inflated figures, as their purpose was to overawe the enemy. A French edition appeared soon; an English translation of this was published in September 1588. The names of all the ships, their tonnages, guns,

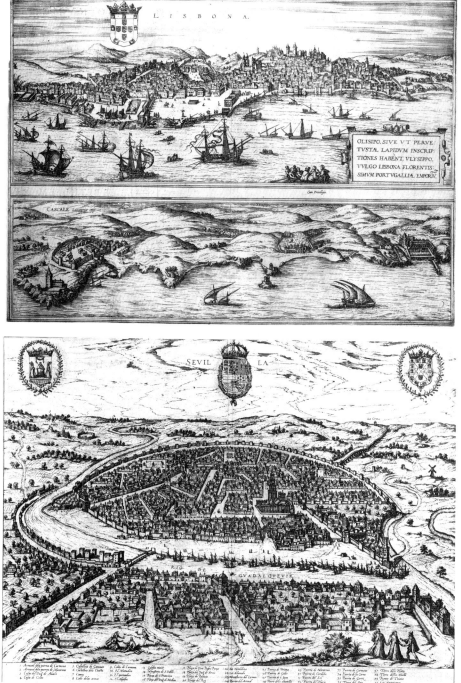

170

powder, numbers of men and some of the principal nobles are detailed here. This is the summary of the forces leaving Lisbon: One hundred and thirty-one ships, total 57,868 tons; 19,295 soldiers, 8,050 sailors; 2,431 pieces of artillery; 123,790 shot, 5,175 quintals of powder, 1,232 of lead, and 1,151 of cordage. The fleet was divided into ten squadrons: Portugal, Biscay, Castile, Andalusia, Guipuzcoa, Levant, Hulks, Pinnaces, Zabras, Galleys and Galleasses. The best warships, apart from the galleasses, were divided between the first six squadrons. The Madrid copy has some variants. By 28 May the fleet had increased to 141, with ten *falúas* not counted. A list of 15 July noted 131 ships ready to sail in La Coruña and a further eight missing: 7,050 sailors, and 17,097 regular soldiers. This later account does not mention the small craft, which were probably still with the fleet (Compare with the figures in Table 2, p. 31).

8.39
View of Lisbon and Cascaes, 1576
G. Braun and F. Hogenburg

Engraving
Inscribed *OLISIPO SIVE PERVETVSTA LAPIDVM INSCRIPTIONES HABENT, VLYSIPPO, VVLGO LISBONA FLORENTIS; SIMVM PORTVGALIAE EMPORIV̄*
470×340
National Maritime Museum (G33)

This view, from the great city atlas, *Civitates Orbis Terrarum*, illustrates the port from which the Armada sailed in May 1588.

8.40
View of Seville, c.1580

Line engraving
333×479
National Maritime Museum (80 G 33 R25)

Seville was the most important port in Castile, and in 1503 was chosen as the headquarters for the new Casa de la Contratación ('House of Trade'), the body set up to regulate and promote trade with the New World. All ships carrying bullion from the Indies had to unload at Seville, despite the difficulties of the journey from the sea up the winding and narrow river Guadalquivir.

Although the home ports of the great galleons in the Castilian Squadron of the Armada are not named, it is almost certain that many of them came from Seville.

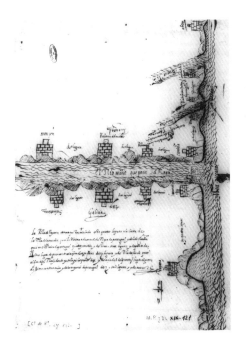

8.41
Sketch-map of the coast of Galicia and Portugal, 1574

Pen and ink
427×303
Teran, 1980, 511
*Archivo General de Simancas, Valladolid
(MPD XIX–121)*

A crude sketch showing the most important trading centres near Galicia – Ponte de Lima (sugar), Vila do Conde (cloth) and Porto, a major commercial mart in Portugal. The area on both sides of the border contributed victuals and other provisions for the Armada in 1588. Baiona and Vigo (due north but not on the map) were raided by the English fleet in 1585 and 1589.

8.42
Chart of San Sebastian, 1585
Richard Poulter (*fl.*1578–1605)

Vellum
Inscribed *The discripcions of Saint Sebastians in biskye June 1585*
205×300
British Library, London (MS Cott. Aug. I, i, f.14)

In 1585 Poulter paced out and sketched San Sebastian and its fortifications, and took its latitude. A former master in the Biscayan trade, Poulter turned increasingly to selling charts and navigational texts at St Katherine's Precinct, London. This chart, one of several acquired from him by Lord Burghley, actually illustrates the seizure of English ships by the Spanish. The harbour later serviced the Armada's Guipuzcoan Squadron.

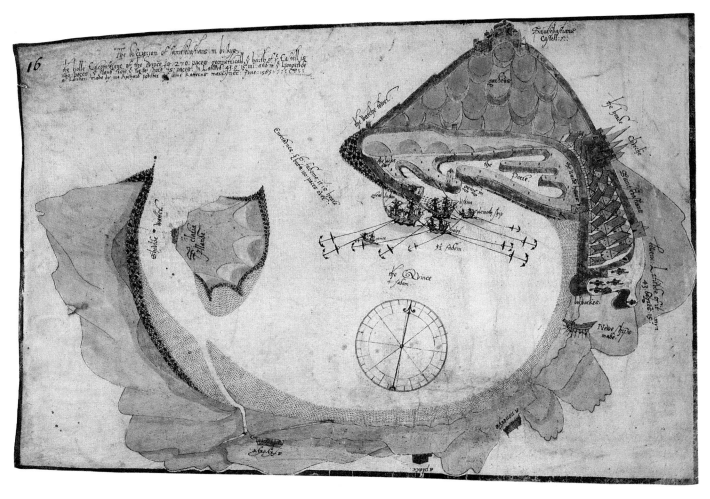

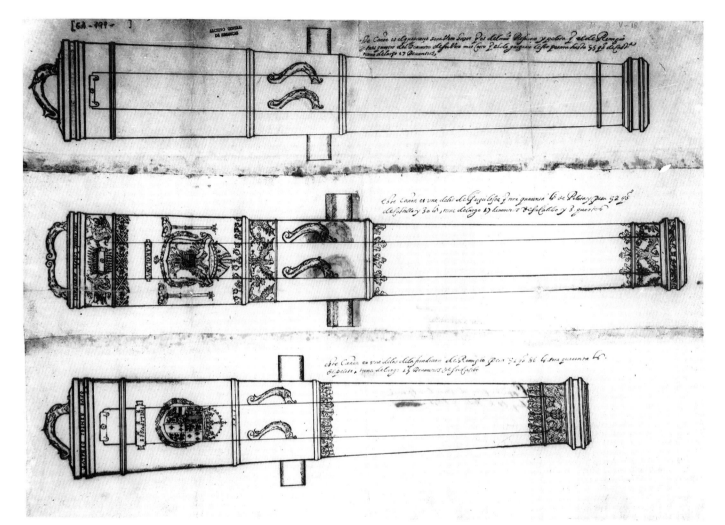

9.7 Three *cañones de batir*

9. Ordnance

(i) Armada Guns and Gunnery

According to the the muster held at Lisbon just before the fleet sailed, the Armada took with it a grand total of 2,431 pieces of artillery – 1,497 of bronze, and the remainder of iron. Until recently it was believed that the total Spanish armament was much heavier than that carried by the opposing English fleet,[1] but this was not the case. Instead of having a weight of armament one-third greater than the English, it now appears that the Spaniards had almost exactly one-third less.[2]

Another fallacy dating from the sixteenth century concerns the types of gun carried by the rival fleets. The Spaniards, it used to be believed, concentrated on 'cannon' types, which were short but strongly built, and threw a heavy shot over a relatively short distance. It was thought that the English went for 'culverin' types, which were much longer in relation to their bores, and threw a lighter shot over a greater range. In fact, far from increasing the range, lengthening the barrel beyond a certain point (about twenty-four times the diameter of the bore) actually reduces the muzzle velocity – and hence the range – of the piece. This could to some extent be compensated for by increasing the size of the powder charge, for long guns could withstand more pressure than short ones.[3] But, in practice, the question was an academic one: neither type of gun was likely to hit its target, or do much harm beyond about 200 yards, and effective damage could only be done when the adversaries were almost touching.

In any case, the Spaniards did not have a preponderance of heavy weapons. True, they did possess a number of full cannons – forty-pounders or thereabout – but these belonged to the siege-train destined for the campaign ashore, and attempts to use them afloat seem to have been largely unsuccessful. The English fleet did not carry many full culverins, although the records suggest that it did. To an Englishman of the time, any gun of around eighteen-pounder calibre would be called a culverin, even if it was (as most were) a relatively short piece of distinctively 'cannon' proportions. Full culverins were simply too long to use effectively at sea, and so they were shortened, while the name remained. The Spaniards reserved the term *culebrina* for true culverin types only, and called the cut-down versions *medios cañones*. Thus, on paper it appears that the Spaniards were going for 'heavy and short', while the English had opted for 'light and long', when in fact almost exactly the reverse is the case.

Artillery was perceived by the Spaniards as a supportive arm of their main offensive weapon – the soldiers on board. A broadside delivered just before clapping sides would cripple and confuse an enemy in the vital moments before the troops boarded. Boarding would itself be supported by a variety of close-range weapons: a fusillade of small-arms fire; stones and darts hurled from the fighting tops; shear hooks; firepots and trunks (torpedo-like fireworks mounted on the end of long poles) to set the ship ablaze and terrorize its defenders; and the quick-firing swivel guns, charged with flint or scrap iron.

These tactics conditioned the Spaniards' whole approach to sea gunnery. Before battle each gun would be prepared and run out by a crew of soldiers working under the direction of a gun captain. The soldiers would then disperse to their boarding stations, leaving the gun captain to discharge his piece on the command of the gunnery control officer allocated to his broadside. This would normally be done – as it was done in galley warfare – at 'clothes-burning' range. After discharge, the gun would remain lashed firm to the ship's side, for no arrangements were made to allow it to recoil inboard, and it could therefore be reloaded only with difficulty. Besides, by this time the boarding action should be well under way, and the crew no longer available.

But actions of this kind, especially if conducted against an adversary who possessed ships of superior sailing performance, require a measure of cooperation from the enemy. And, sensibly enough, the English denied the Spaniards that cooperation, preferring to fight a stand-off action in which they could exploit their advantages in manoeuvrability and firepower to the utmost. Without preparation or training, therefore, the Spaniards were forced to change their tactics and operating procedures and engage, for the first time in history, in a large-scale naval battle in which gunnery rather than boarding would be the decisive factor.

Their difficulties were greatly exacerbated by the design of the carriages upon which the Spanish guns were mounted. Because the need for rapid reloading during battle had not been envisaged, the Spaniards had eschewed the compact four-wheeled truck-carriage which had been in service aboard English ships for more than forty years and which, by 1588, had allowed the English to develop effective and speedy reloading drills.

Evidence of these unsuitable carriages has come to light both from the archives and from the wrecks. In Simancas a set of drawings shows late-sixteenth-century sea-carriages as utilitarian versions of the trailed land-carriage, fitted either with solid tripartite discs or simple cruciform wheels. A Venetian carriage recently discovered on the wreck of the *Trinidad Valencera* would, together with its gun,

1. Lewis, 1961.
2. Thompson, 1975.
3. Guilmartin, 1974, 277–83.

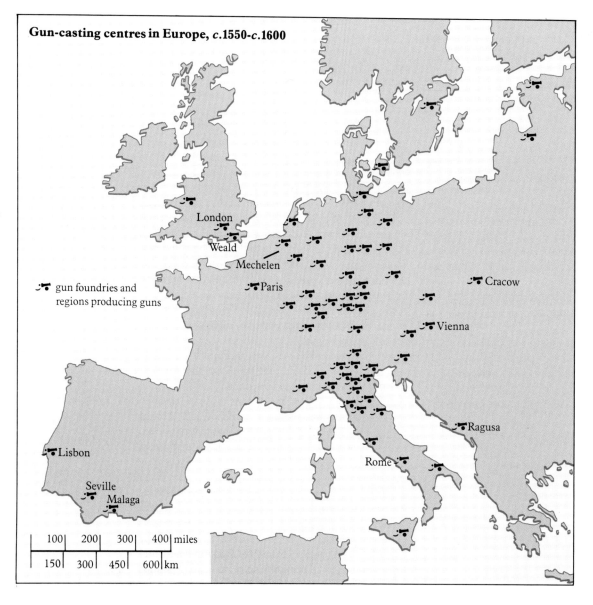

Gun-casting centres in Europe, c.1550-c.1600

gun foundries and
regions producing guns

London
Weald
Mechelen
Paris
Cracow
Vienna
Ragusa
Rome
Lisbon
Seville
Malaga

| 100| | 200| | 300| | 400| miles |
| 150| | 300| | 450| | 600| km |

174

have occupied more than twenty feet of deck space –
over half the maximum beam of the vessel. The
confusion of working such cumbersome guns without
proper drills and training, and in the heat of battle,
can only be imagined. A glimpse of the chaos which
must have pervaded the Armada's gun-decks is provided by the Dutch traveller, Van Linschoten, who in
1589 experienced a minor action with English
privateers while he was a passenger aboard the 1,600-
ton Portuguese carrack *Santa Cruz*. 'Whenever we
shot off a piece,' he wrote, 'we had at least an hour's
work to lade it in again, whereby we had so great a
noise and cry in the ship as if we had all been cast
away.' This largely explains the Spaniards' poor
gunnery performance in 1588.

Yet another adverse factor must be borne in
mind. In one sense the fleet was not a 'Spanish'
Armada at all, but one drawn from the length and
breadth of Europe. Its guns came from most of the
major foundries between the Baltic and the Adriatic.
Some were from England, Sweden, North Germany,
the Low Countries, France, Spain and Portugal.
Perhaps the majority came from the Italian states and
the republic of Ragusa on the eastern Adriatic. The
Trinidad Valencera even carried a huge Turkish
cañon, perhaps a trophy of Lepanto. The possible
variations in proportion, design and, most significantly, the bore of the guns were almost infinite. To
confuse matters still further each country – and
sometimes provinces within the same country – had

its own distinct system of weights and measures. Furthermore, gunnery instruments, as shown by those from the *Trinidad Valencera*, could be highly inaccurate.

At first, the English did not recognize their enemy's fundamental weakness. 'We never supposed,' wrote Lord Admiral Howard, 'that they could ever have found, gathered, and joined so great a force of puissant ships together, and so well appointed them with cannon, culverin, and other great pieces of brass ordnance . . .' Indeed, right up to the fireship attack at Calais, the English response was, in the words of an officer present, 'more coldly done than became the value of our nation and the credit of the English navy'. But then at Gravelines that all changed: the English came in close and hard, shooting fast and low into the Spanish hulls. What made them change their tactics?

I would suggest that the English had at last discovered how ineffectively the Spanish guns were being worked. Who first made this momentous discovery, and how, will probably never be known for sure. But it may well have been Drake who, at an early stage in the fighting, had captured Don Pedro de Valdés's flagship, *Nuestra Señora del Rosario*, one of the most heavily gunned ships in the Armada.[4]

Colin Martin

(ii) English Guns and Gunnery

At the time of the Armada, English naval guns and gunnery were thought to be, and probably were, the best in the world. This was a fairly recent development, beginning half a century earlier with Henry VIII's interest in developing a domestic supply of guns. The chief technical reasons for this success were the capability of the Wealden iron-founding industry and the development of the four-truck gun-carriage for use at sea.

Guns were cast from two types of metal, bronze (copper alloyed with tin or sometimes other metals – usually referred to as 'brass' at this time) and iron. Bronze gun-founding produced the best and most reliable guns, but was expensive – an expense usually reflected in the elaborate decoration of the weapons and the comparatively few bronze guns that could be afforded by even the most powerful states: too few to arm fully the large sailing ships that had become the chief fighting vessels. To fill the remaining gunports, governments were reduced to relying on a cheaper metal – iron. Originally such guns were made from wrought iron with bars, rings or sheets of the metal hammer-welded together. This was a more sophisticated method of construction than used to be

thought, as recent scientific investigation of surviving examples has shown. However, it was labour-intensive and required a high level of skill; not a process suited to producing the large number of guns required, nor giving the strength, and therefore the range and power that bronze guns possessed. Cast-iron guns were the obvious answer, but bronze was much easier to cast, without the flaws that were fatal to performance and, too often, to the gun crews. The problem of casting satisfactory large cast-iron guns seems to have been solved towards the end of Henry VIII's reign by a combination of imported foreign expertise and native iron founders. The mineralogical make-up of Wealden iron-ore seems to have been particularly suited to casting guns, and soon the area was producing guns not only for English use, but also (despite governmental prohibitions) for export. By the time of the Armada, wrought-iron guns were still in use, but thought of as outdated and were no longer being made.

The larger English guns fell into two main groups, short ones of comparatively short range and low power, usually intended to fire stone shot (by this time obsolescent), and longer ones which projected the denser and heavier iron shot. It is difficult to systematize the description of guns of this time when standardization was an unattainable ideal. The word 'bastard' was used to describe a gun which varied from the norm even more than usual, and it appears with monotonous frequency in lists. It would be many years before the logical system of describing guns by weight of shot fired and by length would be adopted. Contemporary English lists use type names taken mainly from falconry, whose exact meaning is not always clear. However, the largest guns were the 'cannon', which were normally of medium length and fired iron shot of roughly sixty to thirty pounds weight, the largest usually used at sea being the 'demi cannon'. The English favoured guns long in comparison to the diameter of their bore; the 'culverins' (about eighteen to ten pound shot), the 'demi-culverins' (nine pounds or thereabouts), and their smaller relatives – 'sakers' (six to five pounds), 'minions' (about four pounds), 'falcons' (three to two and a half pounds), 'falconets' (about one and a half pounds) and 'robinets' (under one pound). Even so, most English culverin-types had been shortened to a length – around twenty-five times their calibres – which not only made them more manageable aboard ship, but also (and unwittingly) brought them close to the proportions which gave maximum muzzle velocities. Guns which fired stone shot were usually referred to as 'perriers'. Small guns called 'port pieces' or 'murderers' were usually used to fire

175

4. Martin and Parker, 1988.

'haileshot' (spherical), 'diceshot' (square) or 'burreshot' (irregular) on the shotgun principle for anti-personnel work. These types of shot – usually in bags or cases – could also be fired from the larger guns which were used to fire projectiles of short range and little accuracy to destroy the enemy's rigging as well. These projectiles consisted of 'crossbar' or 'bar' shot (bars projecting out of a round shot) and 'cheyned shot' (two balls connected by a length of chain).

The gunpowder used was 'corned', that is, in very small lumps, which gave more even burning and imposed less stress on the barrel and was less likely to separate out into its constituents. It was still a very fast-burning explosive, which gave a fierce initial impulse and then died away to nothing. Too long a barrel therefore retarded, rather than increased, muzzle velocity, but longer barrels could withstand bigger charges in relation to their bores, and tended in any case to have stronger breeches. Guns were cast breech-down, so the greater the length, the greater the 'head' of molten metal, the denser and therefore stronger and freer from flaws the breech would be. Only port pieces and some other small guns retained breech-loading with separate 'chambers' (looking like beer tankards) wedged behind the barrel.

The chief difference in guns between the English and Spanish ships, apart from the fact that the former had proportionally more of the modern long-barrelled guns, was that the English used a form of gun-carriage far better adapted to shipboard. The true ship-carriage appears to be an English invention, apparently associated with the reign of Henry VIII, and was to become standard throughout the navies of Europe. Its basic constituents were a flat wooden bed with two axles and four small, solid wooden wheels ('trucks'). Two vertical 'cheeks' rose from the bed, upon which the gun rested on its 'trunnions' (axle-like projections from the sides), which were slightly forward from its point of balance. The breech rested on a wedge ('quoin') which could be moved in or out to depress or elevate the muzzle. This 'truck-carriage' was more compact and easier to move and manoeuvre in the crowded and difficult conditions of a ship's gun deck than the long-tailed, two-wheeled field-carriage and its derivatives, and therefore more suited to accurate firing and rapid reloading aboard a ship. The limited visual evidence available suggests that between the loss of the *Mary Rose* in 1545, and the Armada, English carriages became simpler and more standardized.

There are still misconceptions about how guns were used at this time. The late Professor Lewis wrote of 'ship-killing' guns. Although ships were very occasionally sunk by gunfire at this period, it is more realistic to describe the larger guns as 'ship smashing'. They were used to damage the hulls and armament of an enemy and knock out his crew, sails and rigging, depriving him of his motive and fighting power, to facilitate boarding and capture. The usual tactics in use at the time appear to have involved an advance on the enemy, firing bow guns, turning to present one broadside, and when this was fired, turning again to fire first the stern guns and finally the guns on the other side. Then the ship would draw off to reload. The rate of fire would be positively funereal by the standards of Nelson's navy for, at the time of the Armada, massed and rapid broadside gunfire was more than half a century in the future. Much more care was taken in aiming single guns and firing them separately. The gunner was of greater standing than later, and gun crews smaller, with more emphasis on marksmanship and care for individual shots. This was necessary partly because of the lack of standardization and precision in the manufacture of guns and ammunition than would be obtained later. Ships were armed with guns of all types, causing grave difficulties in ammunition supply. One of the main lessons of the Armada campaign for the English side was the need for greater reserves of ammunition. The Armada was chased up the North Sea by an English fleet left without powder and shot. Another lesson was that long-range, sporadic fire was not very effective, and that close-range and rapid fire were necessary for decisive results.[1]

David Lyon

176

1. Sources used for this essay include Lewis, 1961, Guilmartin, 1974, and IJNA, 1987. In addition, I have benefited from conversations with David Anderson, Ian Friel, Joe Guilmartin, Robert Hardy, Alexandra Hildred, Angus Konstam, Brian Lavery, Keith Muckelroy, Alan Pearsall, Bob Smith, Dr Smolarek, Charles Trollope, several members of the Institute of Nautical Archaeology at Texas A & M University and, above all, Colin Martin.

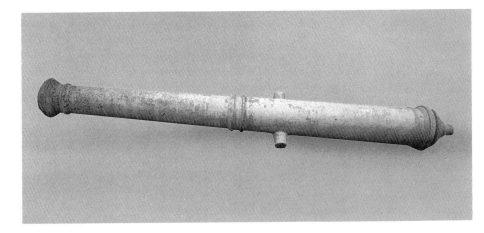

9.1
English cast-iron demi-culverin, 16th century

Cast iron
Inscribed *WP*
3,327 lgth; 108 cal.; *c.*2,036 kg
Royal Armouries, 1976, 62
The Royal Artillery Institution, Woolwich (III.6)

This long gun represents the favourite English type, the culverin. It bears the initials 'WP', which may stand for a certain William Pistor, who was granted a licence to export iron guns in 1579. It would have fired an iron ball weighing about nine pounds over a couple of hundred yards with reasonable accuracy, with a maximum 'random' range of a mile or so. This particular weapon (appropriately for a gun almost certainly cast in the Weald) was at Pevensey Castle in Sussex at the time of the Armada.

9.2
English bronze falcon, 1580
Henry Pitt (*fl.c.*1580–*c.*1615)

Bronze
Inscribed *ELIZABETH REGINA* (second reinforce); *HENRI PITT MADE ME 1580* (first reinforce); 5–2–3 (base ring, weight)
1778 lgth; 71 cal.; *c.*280 kg
Royal Armouries, 1976, 62
Trustees of the Royal Armouries, London (XIX.224)

The falcon was one of the smaller long-gun types, which would usually arm the upper-works of a large ship, though it might form the main armament of a smaller vessel such as a pinnace. This gun was cast by Henry Pitt, a royal gunfounder at the Tower of London. Most English bronze guns, then and later, were produced in or near London. Falcons fired cast-iron cannon balls of about

three pounds in weight. As a lighter weapon its effective range would be less than that of the culverins and demi-culverins that provided most of the heaviest fire from English ships at this time. It lacks the elaborate decoration of most larger bronze guns.

9.3
Long Venetian *sacre* from the *Trinidad Valencera*, second half of 16th century
Zuanne Alberghetti

Bronze
Inscribed *2959* (weight mark, probably in Venetian pounds); *ZA* (Zuanne Alberghetti)
3430 lgth; 95 cal.
Ulster Museum, Belfast

The founder's initials can be seen in relief towards the end of the chase. This gun must have been part of the ship's 'civilian' armament when she was impounded in Sicily by the King of Spain's officials in January 1587. The proportions of the piece – its length is nearly thirty-five times its bore – suggest that it may originally have been the centre-line gun aboard a galley.

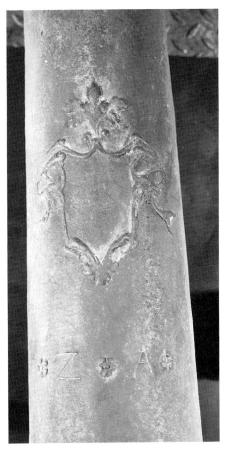

9.4
Swivel gun from the *Trinidad Valencera*

Bronze and wrought iron
1450 lgth; 90 cal.
Crédit Communal, 1985, 111
Ulster Museum, Belfast

9.4

This gun is probably of Venetian origin, and would have been called in Spanish a *falcón pedrero*. The piece is loaded and ready for action, with a two-pound stone shot in its barrel, a fine-grained powder charge in its removable breech-block and a small twist of hemp in the touch-hole to keep the priming dry. The wedge which locks the breech-block in place has a folded leather pad behind it to ensure a tight fit. Swivel guns were close-range, anti-personnel weapons, and were often loaded with scrap iron or fractured flint. They were used in attack for breaking up the troop concentrations on an enemy's deck, and when mounted on the superstructure fore and aft they could be used defensively to bring crossfire down on boarders crowded in the ship's own waist.

178

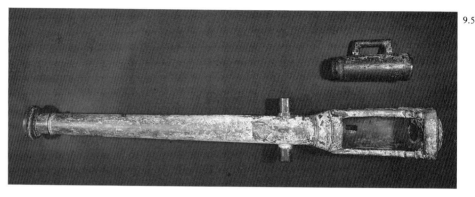

9.5

9.6

9.5
Swivel gun from the wreck of the *San Juan de Sicilia*

Bronze
Inscribed *1563* (on gun); monogram on chamber
1372 lgth; 50 cal. (approx.)
The Museum, Charterhouse

This gun, with its removable chamber or *mascolo*, was recovered in 1905 from Tobermory Bay. It fired an iron shot of about ten ounces. Such guns normally had two chambers and were, relatively speaking, quick-firing: a skilled gunner could probably reload one in about two minutes. The main hazard was blowback from the poorly sealed breech and, because much of the smoke came inboard, such guns were normally deployed on the open deck.

9.6
Broken muzzle-end of a *media culebrina* from the *Gran Grifón*

Bronze
650 lgth; 107 cal.
Shetland Museum, Lerwick (G2/70)

The muzzle-end is a relic of the hectic programme of gun-founding just before the Armada sailed, which perhaps explains its grotesquely off-centre bore. It is unlikely that the gun from which it came could ever have been fired.

9.7
Three *cañones de batir*, 1587

Pen and pencil drawing
442×565
Archivo General de Simancas, Valladolid
(MPD V–18)

This drawing was submitted by Captain-General of Artillery Juan de Acuña Vela to the king from Lisbon, 18 August 1587. It is of particular interest as an early example of technical illustration. From top to bottom: 1. *cañón* made by Remigy de Halut; 2. *cañón* by Gregorio Lefer; 3. *cañón* to serve as model for future production. By a fortunate coincidence the Remigy gun depicted – and identified by its precise weight mark – has been recently recovered from the wreck of the *Trinidad Valencera*. The Gregorio Lefer piece, cast at Augsburg in 1538 for the Emperor Charles V (his arms are depicted on it), also sailed with the Armada aboard Martín de Bertendona's Levantine flagship *Regazona*.

179

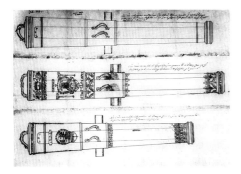

9.8
A gun mounted on a sea-carriage, 1594

Pen and pencil drawing
229×336
Archivo General de Simancas, Valladolid
(MPD XVIII–48)

A contemporary drawing of a Spanish sea-carriage with cruciform wheels, dated at Avila, 14 September 1594. This utility design bears strong similarities to the trailed field-carriage which (according to Sir Henry Mainwaring) the Spaniards also used aboard ship. It was ill-suited to use at sea, because the large-diameter wheels raised the line of recoil well above the deck, and limited the amount of muzzle which could project through the gun port. Its rearward-extending trail, moreover, projected awkwardly into the limited working-space behind the gun. The carriage for a large piece might reach the centre-line of the deck or even beyond, thereby encroaching upon the guns of the opposite broadside. These arrangements no doubt help to explain the confusion aboard the Spanish gun-decks during the Armada battles.

9.9–9.15
Armada shot

9.9 Iron shot from the *Girona* (70 cal.)

9.10 Iron shot from the *Girona* (130 cal.)

9.11 Iron shot for a swivel gun, from the *Trinidad Valencera* (75 cal.)

9.12 Iron shot from the *Trinidad Valencera* (155 cal.)

One of the most persistent myths about the Armada is that it ran out of ammunition; as these finds demonstrate, not all the ships did. Indeed some ships returned to Spain with the greater part of the round shot issued to them. This group shows iron shot of three pounds to thirty pounds (nominal weight), appropriate to guns ranging from *medio sacre* to *medio cañon* calibre. The stone shot was fired by various types of *pedreros*, light guns regarded as obsolescent by the English but much favoured by the Spaniards. The third type of shot was a wooden canister, called a 'lantern' because of its appearance, which contained iron nails or fractured flints.

9.13 Stone shot from the *Girona* (95 cal.)

9.14 Stone shot from the *Trinidad Valencera* (155 cal.)

9.16

Gunner's rule from the *Trinidad Valencera*

Boxwood
Inscribed with scales for shot calibre and weight
90 lgth
Crédit Communal, 1985, 114
Ulster Museum, Belfast

This device allowed a gunner to measure the bore of his piece and determine the weight of shot appropriate to it. On one side it is calibrated for iron shot, on the other for lead. Though simple enough in theory, many difficulties arose in practice: the calibrations were inconsistent and inaccurate.

9.15 Wood and iron canister shot from the *Trinidad Valencera* (90 cal.)

Crédit Communal, 1985, 114–15
Ulster Museum, Belfast

9.17
Copper powder scoop from the *Trinidad Valencera*

Copper
455 lgth
Crédit Communal, 1985, 113
Ulster Museum, Belfast

Mounted on the end of a long pole, and used either to ladle gunpowder directly into the barrel or to insert a previously filled linen cartridge. In either case, rotating the scoop through 180° dropped the charge in place so that the implement could be withdrawn.

181

9.18
Linstock head in the form of a dragon, from the *Trinidad Valencera*

Wood
90 lgth
Crédit Communal, 1985, 113
Ulster Museum, Belfast

Linstocks were used to hold the saltpetre-impregnated slow match used to touch off the guns. When found, a short length of fuse was still in place.

9.19
Linstock end, shaped as a clenched fist, from the *Trinidad Valencera*

Wood
450 lgth
Crédit Communal, 1985, 113
Ulster Museum, Belfast

This motif, and that of the dragon, are paralleled by finds from the *Mary Rose*, and they probably reflect a widespread gunners' tradition. This linstock has a hole at the heel for a short iron spike, which could be stuck in the ground or into the deck to keep the burning fuse out of harm's way.

9.20–9.22
Shot gauges from the *Trinidad Valencera*

Wood
120, 92 and 46 cal.
Crédit Communal, 1985, 114
Ulster Museum, Belfast

182

These were used in conjunction with the gunner's rule (cat. no. **9.16**) to size shot of different calibres and, since they were found in close proximity to it and to each other, are probably part of a single set.

9.23–9.24
Sponge heads from the *Trinidad Valencera*

Wood
400 lgth, 106 dia.; 264 lgth, 108 dia.
Ulster Museum, Belfast

These were encased in sheep- or goat-skin sheaths which, saturated with vinegar or urine, were used to swab out the guns after firing, to extinguish any trapped burning matter before the next charge was loaded.

9.25
Nine staves from a gunpowder barrel, *Trinidad Valencera*

Wood
605 lgth
Crédit Communal, 1985, 119
Ulster Museum, Belfast

When found, the charcoal residue of the powder still survived in excellent condition. Like all gunpowder barrels, no iron hoops were used for fear of causing sparks.

9.26
Practica Manual de Arteglieria . . ., 1586
Luigi Collado

1st ed., Venice
Printed book (92 pp.)
Inscribed *Thomas Digges June 1588*
230×117
British Library, London (C.54.k.2)

Collado was one of the few practising sixteenth-century artillerymen who wrote a treatise on gunnery. Most contemporary books on the subject were the work of theorists who had little real grasp of the problems involved. To Collado, the most serious obstacle to scientific gunnery was the lack of standardization. By way of illustration, he noted that over 200 different sizes of charging implements were needed to serve the guns stockpiled in the arsenal at Milan, whereas the system in his manual envisaged only eleven sizes. The problem created by unstandardized shot, he added, was just as serious. No doubt the Armada's gunners would have agreed with him.

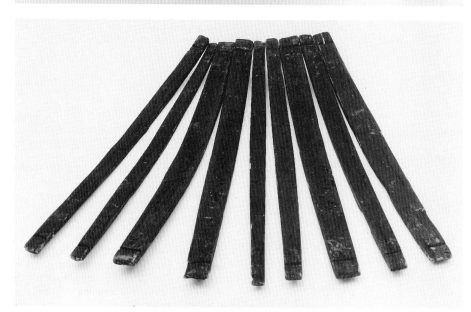

9.27

Letter from Don Juan de Acuña Vela to Philip II, 10 April 1588

MS
334×230
Archivo General de Simancas, Valladolid (GA 223, f.24)

The anxiety of Santa Cruz and other commanders to increase the firepower of the fleet forced Philip to purchase, commission and commandeer guns, especially cannons and culverins. Gun-foundries were hastily set up or enlarged. Many pieces of artillery were made in Lisbon during 1586–8 but, because time was so short and some of the cannon were intended for use on ship, Acuña agreed that these should be delivered 'without leaves and decorations, and only with a ribbon and fluted moulding added where absolutely necessary'. Nevertheless, Acuña believed that the artillery destined for the fortifications should be more attractive and decorated with the usual motifs, and he asked Philip to stipulate how these guns should be ornamented (see cat. no. **14.36**).

9.28

Inuentions or Deuises . . ., 1578
William Bourne (*fl.*1565–88)

Publ. Thomas Woodcocke, 1st ed., London
Printed book (99 pp.)
178×137
Taylor, 1970, 176, 323–4
British Library, London (C.71.cc.16)

William Bourne was a self-taught man who produced a series of handbooks on various practical subjects, writing in particular for seamen and gunners. His *Inuentions or Deuises . . .* is probably the first English printed work to discuss naval tactics. His eighth 'Deuise' describes how to use fireships against an enemy fleet in a harbour or river. He advises filling a number of 'bad or olde ships' with combustible materials, and sailing them down on the enemy when there is a favourable wind. The fireships were to be set alight when close to their objectives, their small crews escaping in boats. The enemy would have 'to let slip their Anckers' or be burned, and in the ensuing confusion an attack could be mounted. This is virtually a textbook description of the fireship attack at Calais ten years later. It is possible that this book, dedicated to Lord Howard of Effingham, gave the idea for this crucial attack.

9.29

The Arte of Shooting in Great Ordnance . . ., 1587
William Bourne (*fl.*1565–88)

Publ. T. Dawson for T. Woodcocke, 1st ed., London
173×136
Printed book (94 pp.)
Taylor, 1970, 176, 321, 323–4
British Library, London (C.122.b.6)

Bourne seems to have been a part-time gunner, serving either in the fort at Tilbury or that at Gravesend. He published a number of practical textbooks on subjects as diverse as naval and military tactics, navigation, surveying and ship design, as well as gunnery. *The Arte of Shooting* is the earliest known book by an Englishman on the subject of gunnery.

9.30

Survey of gun production in Kent, 1588–9

MS (4ff.)
Inscribed *Mr. Byngs certificat of the view of the Iron worcks in the weald of Kent*
290×203
Kennard, 1986
Staffordshire Record Office (D.593/S/4/28/3)

In 1588 the Weald of Kent and Sussex led the world in casting iron guns, for Wealden iron-ore was particularly suited to producing large, strong castings free from flaws. The forests of the Weald provided the necessary fuel (in the form of charcoal) and the many streams gave the power needed by the iron-works. This survey lists five Kentish gun-foundries in 1588: some idea of the scale of production is given by the fact that just over 250 sakers, minions and falcons are listed as either still at the ironworks or *en route* for delivery.

9.31

Drake's account for munitions supplied to six royal and thirty-two private ships under his command, 1587–8

MS (21ff.)
260×190
Laughton, I, 1981, 124–6
City of Plymouth Museums and Art Gallery (PCM 1971.4)

This account is of considerable importance, since detailed information on the arming of the English fleet in 1588 is not generally available. The material supplied included more than twenty-nine tons of powder, 5,220

9.31

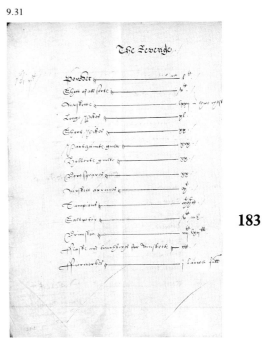

183

shot for guns, ranging from demi-cannon to falcons, 1,000 muskets and calivers (lighter muskets), 1,500 long and short pikes, 1,000 bills and even 200 bows with 600 sheaves of arrows. Besides these items there were 1,000 musket arrows, dice shot, match and other items. The apportionment of shot shows that the heaviest guns on seven of the private ships were demi-culverins, with sakers as the main armament on sixteen more and minions on six of the remainder. The larger guns, demi-cannon and culverins, were evidently confined to the queen's ships. Another interesting feature of the account is the number and variety of small arms supplied. Their selection may have been partly influenced by Drake's plan of March 1588 for a pre-emptive attack on the Armada before it sailed (he specifically requested the muskets and musket arrows), but it is also likely that the English were anticipating close-range fighting and boarding actions in the sea campaign.

10.6 Large bowl from the *Trinidad Valencera*

10.8 English plate from the *Trinidad Valencera*

(i) Life on Board Spanish Ships

While living-conditions on English ships may have been bad, how much worse they must have been on the Spanish ships: when the English fleet first put to sea, the Armada had been at sea for a week since it left La Coruña after an enforced stop, two months since it originally sailed from Lisbon. The Spanish ships were heavily laden with soldiers and invasion equipment, as well as supplies for a six-month campaign.

On paper, the Armada was well-provisioned: the statutory rations, with a daily established menu, were remarkably adequate. In theory each man was to receive 24 oz. of biscuit, 12 oz. of bacon, 18 oz. of tuna or sardine, 18 oz. of cheese, 4 oz. of rice, 9 oz. of beans or chickpeas, with over 2 pints of wine and an enormous allocation of 14 gallons of water per week. None the less, this was scarcely sufficient for the heavy labour required to work a ship: hoisting sails (the mainsail of a medium-sized Armada ship would have weighed over three tons), steering by means of a tiller or, even worse, rowing, as 300 men on each of the galleasses had to. Even more serious is the fact that there was no adequate provision against deficiency diseases, such as scurvy.

There survive in the Spanish archives detailed accounts of material and equipment actually loaded onto Armada ships: those for the *Trinidad Valencera*, for example, include details of a whole range of foodstuffs, such as 'Biscuit, 1,858 quintals and 61 pounds (weight of Castile); fresh mutton, 992 pounds (weight of Castile); rice, 96 quintals and 83 pounds (weight of Castile); octopus, 8 quintals (weight of Castile)'. Similar details are given for consignments of wine – often with information about the packaging: 'Wine of Candia, 696 *almudes* and four *canadas* (measure of Portugal) in twenty-three wooden butts and six quarters; wine, 8,894 *arrovas* (measure of Castile) in 326 pipes with 1,601 iron hoops.' In addition to the barrels of different sizes and types, other modes of packaging include hempen sacks and crates of Esparto grass, while some of the foodstuffs must have been in pottery containers like the olive-jars (one of which, from the *Trinidad*, contained lentils when recovered – see cat. no. **10.20**). In addition to the containers full of foodstuffs listed, there are others, presumably smaller, to which food and wine were transferred for distribution: for example, '669 wine-bottles', as well as scales and steelyards, with their weights, for weighing out dry measures, and measures of various sorts and sizes for liquids ('two large wooden buckets for measuring wine and nine smaller wooden buckets for measuring water'). Also listed, in addition to '256 pipes full of water and eight more', are '32 wooden barrels, each with four iron hoops, for water'. These water barrels led to trouble throughout the campaign, for many were of unseasoned wood, causing the water to become undrinkable.

Taking meals on a heavily laden Armada ship can hardly have been as idyllic as suggested by Diego García, where a benevolent steward set a table in the waist of the ship, from stern to bow, and weighed out the rations for groups of four men, although Medina Sidonia had found it necessary to order that the soldiers were not to 'go down and take or choose their rations by force', so that presumably some order was imposed. It is much more likely that the ordinary soldiers and sailors on board had their rations meted out, according to the regulations, into either their simple wooden bowls and platters, or their plates and bowls of standard-issue pottery, such as that included in Santa Cruz's proposals of March 1586, where a supply of some 100,000 pieces, consisting of plates, small bowls, pots and jugs was considered necessary, from potteries in Seville and Lisbon. Examples of these have been identified on the wrecks. Having received their due – and no more – they presumably consumed it where and when they could.

It is evident, however, that the officers and gentlemen did try to achieve a standard of elegance: the array of silver candlesticks, of fragments of decorated silver dishes and the silver forks, as well as a range of pewter – from the very best makers – adorned with their names or initials, suggests the maintenance of some sort of style. The existence of such a collection of candlesticks helps to explain why one of the special responsibilities of the boatswain was 'to kill the fire in the hearth with water, and all the candles, and inform himself if there is water in the pump'. To judge by the *Santa María de la Rosa* (a brand new ship, built at San Sebastian in 1587), the cooking was done on an open fire, on top of the ballast, fired at least in part with brushwood, without even the custom-built hearth of brick known from the *Mary Rose*. Possibly the explosion on the *San Salvador* in 1588 was set off by a much more mundane set of circumstances than suggested by the stories circulated.

Finding somewhere to sleep must have been one of the greatest difficulties encountered by the crews, faced with a simple choice of on the deck, if the weather was suitable (which it appears not often to have been in Armada year), or below decks, on the ballast. Since the ballast – apart from the accumulation of fetid water from the inevitable leaks – was the final resting place of every kind of waste product, human as well as, on some ships, animal, sleeping, eating or simply being there at all must have been an unpleasant experience. It is little wonder either that the more fastidious of the officers and gentlemen carried perfume flasks or that dysentery and other diseases generated by lack of sanitation were more or less endemic. Fine-toothed combs were necessary to attempt, at least, to combat the lice that were always present. A skeleton of a rat was recovered from the *Trinidad*.

It is perhaps surprising that the bulk of the textiles recovered from the wrecks have been woollen, when cotton might have been more readily expected, although the wearers must certainly have been glad of their woollen clothes in the cold weather of the Atlantic. Tantalizingly, the pieces of clothing recovered from the *Trinidad Valencera* are very fragmentary, although among them can be recognized parts of garments, such as yokes and pocket-flaps and a sock. Interestingly, much of the wool had been dyed with cochineal, which, of course, was yet another commodity imported from the Americas. While the survival of a multitude of gold buttons from the *Girona* is not surprising, the survival of a silk braid with silk-covered buttons from the *Trinidad* is more so. Both the *Girona* and *Trinidad* yielded parts of leather shoes, both uppers and soles. Whether the wearers of the leather shoes were the rich and noble, who presumably wore the silks and velvets, while the ordinary seamen and soldiers wore hempen sandals is unknown. Among the stores loaded onto the *Trinidad*, according to the accounts, were 2,000 pairs of hempen sandals, 401 pairs of shoes with soles of Spanish leather and 539 pairs of new leather shoes of two soles (this presumably means 'with a double thickness of leather' as, indeed, some of the soles recovered from the *Trinidad* have). Oddly enough, these items of footwear appear to be the only clothing listed in the manifest.

The Duke of Medina Sidonia had laid down strict rules for the moral welfare of the men under his command, expressly forbidding gambling and the presence of women on any of the ships under his command (though in fact an 'unofficial' ship sailed in the wake of the Armada and a German gunner on the *San Salvador* is reported to have brought his wife along with him). He had also ordered that every morning and evening the ships' boys would recite prayers at the foot of the mainmast. It would seem, from the lid of the altar-cruet found on the *Girona*, with its implication of the presence on board of a complete set of altar-plate necessary for the mass, that on some ships mass was said as well.

Though it may be difficult to imagine that there was either time, space or inclination for relaxation aboard, a stringed guitar-like instrument and a tambourine indicate that as well as the drums, fifes and trumpets (which were expected to play unceasingly during combat 'with the greatest arrogance, and as bravely as possible, because as well as enlivening their crew they are apt to frighten the enemy'), some of the crew found less martial music equally enlivening.

The Archaeology of the Armada
More than twenty ships of the Spanish Armada perished off the coast of Ireland. Of these, three have been located, identified and at least partly excavated. The first was the galleass *Girona*, of the Naples Squadron, sunk off Lacada Point, Co. Antrim. Found by Robert Sténuit, the Belgian nautical archaeologist, it produced a treasury of Renaissance jewellery and coinage, as well as guns, navigation equipment and vast quantities of lead. The *Santa María de la Rosa*, sunk in Blasket Sound, Co. Mayo, was found in 1968 by a team led by Sydney Wignall which included Colin Martin: this produced interesting information about ship construction and the packing of ballast, as well as lead and small arms, little of which has been preserved. The last to be located and excavated was the *Trinidad Valencera*, a converted Venetian merchant ship, wrecked in Kinnagoe Bay, Co. Donegal, found by the City of Derry Sub-Aqua Club and excavated by them under the direction of Colin Martin. It produced a whole range of material, including important pieces of ordnance, items of rigging, invasion equipment and material illustrating life on board at every level.

The wreck of the *Gran Grifón*, on Fair Isle, has also been located and excavated, again by a team led by Sydney Wignall and including Colin Martin: it produced very interesting information about the poor armament of the hulks.

Recently the three wrecks at Streedagh, Co. Sligo, have been located and identified – the *Labia*, the *Juliana* and the *Santa María de Visión*. Three guns have been raised from the *Juliana*, and her thirty-seven-foot rudder revealed.

Ireland's Armada legacy is enormous, a resource to be exploited with the utmost care and responsibility. The surviving material from the three excavated Irish wrecks is kept by the Ulster Museum, Belfast, the repository of some 95 per cent of all known objects surviving from Armada ships; objects from the *Gran Grifón* are kept by the Shetland Museum, Lerwick. For the first time this important material is exhibited within the context of a full visual survey of the background, cause, course and effect of the Armada campaign itself.

Laurence Flanagan

(ii) English Seafarers in 1588

A wide variety of trades and professions was represented in the English fleet in 1588. Besides the masters, pilots, mariners and boys there were gunners, soldiers, preachers, pursers, pressed landsmen and volunteer gentlemen. More than 16,000 men are known to have been employed for sea service in that year and, given the rapid turnover of crews caused by disease, the true figure was probably much higher. Mariners were the largest single group, but they may only just have been in the majority. In the thirty-four royal ships, only 58 per cent of total crews were seamen, the rest being mostly gunners and soldiers.[1] Even allowing for this, it is clear that more than half the English seafaring population of 17,000 or so was mobilized in the royal and private ships.[2]

England did not have a permanent body of naval officers and seamen in the late sixteenth century. Men were hired or pressed for service in the queen's ships as required, and usually discharged as soon as there was no immediate need for them. The great majority of English seamen passed their working lives in trading, privateering and piratical enterprises. The status of common mariners was very low, as shown by their rate of pay, which at 10 s. per month in the 1580s was less than that of an unskilled labourer. The work was hard and often dangerous, and there seem to have been few ordinary seamen over the age of forty. During the Armada campaign, the problem of low pay was exacerbated by the government's failure to pay wages regularly, causing discontent among the mariners and worry to the Lord Admiral (see cat. no. **11.10**). However, for all its drawbacks, life at sea did offer the chance of promotion to men of ability, and the pay and conditions of officers and masters were much better than those of the men.[3]

The food supplied to ships was almost entirely salted, to help preserve it, but even this did not stave off decay for very long, and food poisoning caused by rotten victuals seems to have been a major cause of death in the English fleet (see Introduction to Section 11). Most of the English ships were crowded with their wartime crews, making the spread of disease that much easier. For example, some 500 men were crammed into the royal warship *Elizabeth Jonas*, the hull of which measured only 142 feet (43.3 m) from stem to stern and 38 feet (11.6 m) across its beam.

Contracts for three English warships built in 1589 give some idea of what the interiors of fighting ships of the period were like. The vessels were similar in their general arrangements (two were in fact the same size as the *Revenge*), and in each the cook-room was in the hold with the victual stores, whilst the boatswain, purser and most of the other officers were quartered in cabins on the deck above this. 'Cabons' for the crew were to be put on the deck above this, wherever room could be found. The master and captain had rather better quarters, complete with windows, but some notion of the general conditions expected is contained in the specification for sealed planking in their cabins 'for avoydinge of myse and Ratts'.[4]

Given the nature of their lives and working conditions, it is perhaps remarkable that the English crews sailed and fought as well as they did.

Ian Friel

1. References to the crew sizes and tonnage of the English fleet are based on Laughton, II, 1981, 324–31.
2. Lloyd, 1968, 34.
3. See Scammell, 1970 and 1982, and Andrews, 1982.
4. PRO SP12/224, 46, 83 and 84.

187

10.1

Tableau of a Spanish ship at sea, 1588
Designed by David White and Martyn Bainbridge, 1988

1:4 scale
National Maritime Museum

The exhibition's third tableau presents a ship of the Armada as it might have been seen from the waist of an accompanying vessel, heading into the Channel at the end of July 1588. One can note characteristic features of a Spanish ship of the time, including the decoration (fairly restrained by comparison with that of English warships) and the clumsy, two-wheeled gun-carriages. The ship carries a lantern, signifying that it is the *capitana* (flagship) or *almiranta* (deputy commander's flagship) of a squadron. The design of the tableau was conceived through consulting a variety of visual and written sources for a number of Armada ship types.

10.2

English victuals

Modern reproduction
Laughton, I, 1981, 109–110
National Maritime Museum

The victuals provided for English mariners usually consisted of biscuit (hard, baked flour), beef, bacon, fish, cheese, butter, pease, beer and water. The meat and fish were generally salted, although fresh provisions of all kinds were provided on occasion. A note by Lord Burghley in 1588 envisaged restricting the consumption of beef to Sunday, Tuesday and Thursday, with bacon and pease eaten on Monday and fish on the other days. It is doubtful if this strict system was ever observed, but the amounts allotted per man per day were probably fairly realistic. There were two meals each day, and on a 'beef' day each man was to have a total of two pounds of salt beef, with one pound of biscuit and a gallon of beer. Rations were slightly better on a 'fish' day, because the quarter of fish was supplemented by the same amounts of beer and biscuit, and with 4 ounces of cheese and 2 ounces of butter as

188

well. The victuals were hardly sufficient for the heavy physical labour required to work a ship, but in terms of quantity may not have been worse than those eaten by farm labourers. What made sea victuals unhealthy was the salt in them and their long storage times, which encouraged decay. It is likely that more English mariners fell victim to their food than to the Spanish Armada.

10.3
Letter from Sir William Winter (d.1589) to the Lord Admiral, 21 October 1578

MS
300×203
HMC, II, 1888, 222; Oppenheim, 1896, 127–8
The Marquess of Salisbury, Hatfield House (Cecil MSS 161.90)

Winter proposed unsuccessfully that the cook-rooms of royal ships should be moved up from the hold to the orlop deck, and that the gravel ballast should be replaced with stone to allow easier examination of the frames and to let air circulate. The letter gives a glimpse of the unhealthy conditions in which food was cooked in most ships, the oven placed amid gravel made wet by beer leakages and water.

10.4
Spanish victuals

Modern reproduction

A ration-list issued to the master of the *zabra*, *Concepción*, at Lisbon on 21 April 1588 gives some idea of the food provided for the crews of Spanish ships. The basic daily ration consisted of one and a half (Castilian) pounds of biscuit or two pounds of fresh bread, with wine and water. On Mondays this was supplemented by six ounces of cheese and three ounces of beans or chickpeas, with bacon and rice on Sundays and Thursdays. Fish was provided on Tuesdays, Fridays and Saturdays, together with oil, and the fish was either tuna, salt cod or sardines (the Castilian and English pounds and ounces were roughly equivalent).

10.5
Spoiled victuals in the Armada: Bernabe de Pedroso to Philip II, Lisbon, 14 May 1588

MS
324×223
Archivo General de Simancas, Valladolid (GA.223, f.111)

Pedroso reports that they have thrown overboard many victuals because they had rotted. He blames the heat and the overcrowding in the ships, and warns Philip that they have already started eating provisions intended for the journey.

10.6
Large bowl from the *Trinidad Valencera*

Pewter
Inscribed with pewterer's touch-mark *IH*
353 dia.
Crédit Communal, 1985, 8.1
Ulster Museum, Belfast

The maker's mark on this bowl has not been identified.

10.7
Large dish from the *Trinidad Valencera*

Pewter
354 dia.
Crédit Communal, 1985, 8.3
Ulster Museum, Belfast

This dish has linear engraved decoration on the rim and engraved concentric circles in the centre.

10.7

10.10

10.9
Beaker from the *Trinidad Valencera*

Pewter
98 ht
Crédit Communal, 1985, 8.21a
Ulster Museum, Belfast

10.10
Goblet from the *Trinidad Valencera*

Pewter
133 ht
Crédit Communal, 1985, 8.22
Ulster Museum, Belfast

10.11
Jug from the *Trinidad Valencera*

Pewter
174 ht
Crédit Communal, 1985, 8.24
Ulster Museum, Belfast

Jug with a swan's-neck handle and a domed foot.

10.8
English plate from the *Trinidad Valencera*

Pewter
Inscribed with pewterer's touch-mark *E R*, and owner's initials *J Z*
257 dia.
Crédit Communal, 1985, 8.8
Ulster Museum, Belfast

A round pewter plate with circular decoration in the centre. It is stamped on both sides of the rim with a pewterer's touch-mark consisting of a crowned Tudor rose with the initials *E R*, for Edward Roe, Master of the London Company of Pewterers in 1582 and again in 1588. The initials *J Z* stamped on either side of the mark have been identified by Colin Martin as those of Juan Zapota, whose son, Sebastian, was on board the *Trinidad Valencera*.

10.12
Spoon from the *Trinidad Valencera*

Pewter
175 lgth
Crédit Communal, 1985, 8.27
Ulster Museum, Belfast

Pewter spoon with fiddle-shaped bowl and rat-tail handle.

10.13
Candle-holder from the *Trinidad Valencera*

Pewter
70 dia.
Crédit Communal, 1985, 8.28b
Ulster Museum, Belfast

Pewter candle-holder consisting of a short cylinder 33 mm in interior diameter.

10.14
Fork from the *Girona*

Silver
139 lgth
Crédit Communal, 1985, 8.36
Ulster Museum, Belfast

Two-pronged silver fork with baluster handle terminating in a horse's hoof, one of several from the *Girona*. Forks were generally the property of the rich.

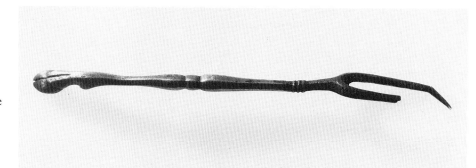

190

10.16
Brazil nut from the *Santa María de la Rosa*

52 lgth
Crédit Communal, 1985, 3.23
Ulster Museum, Belfast

This nut would have been imported from the New World.

10.15
Dish from the *Trinidad Valencera*

Copper
135 dia.
Crédit Communal, 1985, 8.45
Ulster Museum, Belfast

10.17
Bowl from the *Trinidad Valencera*

Wood
175 dia.
Crédit Communal, 1985, 8.47
Ulster Museum, Belfast

Small turned dish or bowl, probably used by common soldiers or sailors.

10.18
Spoon from the *Trinidad Valencera*

Wood
166 lgth
Crédit Communal, 1985, 8.48
Ulster Museum, Belfast

Wooden spoon decorated with three carved,
X-shaped motifs.

10.19
Chinese bowl from the *Trinidad Valencera*, possibly of the Wan Li dynasty

Porcelain
Inscribed with maker's mark on base
152 dia.
Crédit Communal, 1985, 8.52
Ulster Museum, Belfast

Straight-sided open bowl of pale blue
porcelain decorated outside with lively classical horses between three conventional, lifeless
birds. Inside, in the centre, is a quadriskele
motif, in dark blue. The Spanish Empire had
contacts with China through Portuguese
traders.

10.20
Olive-jar from the *Trinidad Valencera*

Unglazed, reddish, buff, coarse earthenware,
with a grey core
300 ht
Martin, 1979b, 279; Crédit Communal, 1985,
3.1
Ulster Museum, Belfast

This large globular container has a light
external slip and dark grey lining (probably a
resinous sealing compound). Despite the
name 'olive' jar, this specimen contained lentils when found.

10.21
Steelyard from the *Trinidad Valencera*

Bronze
520×10
Crédit Communal, 1985, 3.5; Flanagan, 1987
Ulster Museum, Belfast

Quadrangular bronze bar, beaten into a flat strip of metal, terminating in an elaborate fish-tail and used for weighing provisions and other items.

10.22
Steelyard weight from the *Trinidad Valencera*

Lead with sheet-bronze cladding
115 ht
Crédit Communal, 1985, 3.6; Flanagan, 1987
Ulster Museum, Belfast

This weight was originally covered in thin lead sheeting, decorated with rows of punch-marks and engraved lines, a portion of which survives.

10.23
Two nesting weights from the *Trinidad Valencera*

Bronze
Inscribed *N* on the interior of the base of the smaller weight
41 dia.; 24 dia.
Crédit Communal, 1985, 3.9
Ulster Museum, Belfast

Two small, circular hollow cups. The larger has a pair of parallel lines engraved on the inside just below the rim and a crudely executed cross on the bottom. The smaller has three lines engraved on the top of the rim and the mark 'N' on the inside of the base. They are probably from different sets.

10.24
Boatswain's pipe or call from the *Girona*

Silver
70 lgth
Crédit Communal, 1985, 1.12
Ulster Museum, Belfast

Three fragments of a boatswain's pipe comprising the chamber and two pieces of the tube. The tube is segmented and was joined to the chamber by a serpent-like creature. One of the duties of the boatswain was to stay by the pilot to transmit orders to the crew by means of his whistle.

10.25

Claw-hammer from the *Trinidad Valencera*

Wood and iron
220×50×50
Crédit Communal, 1985, 1.16
Ulster Museum, Belfast

Iron claw-hammer with a surviving portion of the haft. Such hammers were frequently carried on Spanish ships.

10.26

Bellows from the *Trinidad Valencera*

Wood
445 lgth
Crédit Communal, 1985, 1.18
Ulster Museum, Belfast

The front is decorated with concentric circles, and three iron nails survive where it was attached to the leather bag.

10.27

Whisk or brush from the *Trinidad Valencera*

Straw
345 lgth
Crédit Communal, 1985, 1.24
Ulster Museum, Belfast

This item consists of a bunch of straw tied at the middle, with a double-plaited straw forming a handle.

10.26

193

10.28–10.31
Buttons from the *Girona*

Gold
10.28 14 dia.
10.29 14 dia.
10.30 15 dia.
10.31 11 dia.
Crédit Communal, 1985, 7.1–4
Ulster Museum, Belfast

These four gold buttons are from different
sets and display a variety of motifs.

10.32
Bead from the *Trinidad Valencera*

Reddish-brown, blue and white glass
30 lgth
Crédit Communal, 1985, 7.6
Ulster Museum, Belfast

A large, crudely fashioned bead with a
biconical section. The decoration consists of
a median zigzag in blue glass, outlined in
white.

10.33
Buckle from the *Girona*

Copper
55 wdth
Crédit Communal, 1985, 7.10
Ulster Museum, Belfast

Bronze buckle with bicuspid bow and short,
triangular tongue.

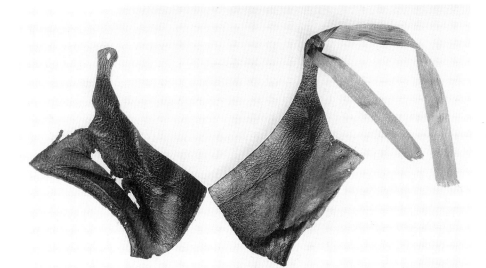

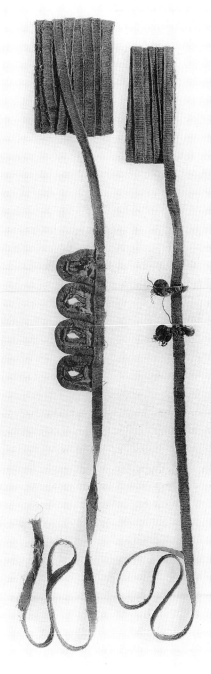

10.34
Shoe upper from the *Trinidad Valencera*

Leather and ribbon
115 lgth
Crédit Communal, 1985, 7.13
Ulster Museum, Belfast

Two side-pieces of the upper from a brown leather shoe, with two fastening strips and a piece of pink-brown ribbon.

10.35
Shoe sole from the *Trinidad Valencera*

Leather
258 lgth
Crédit Communal, 1985, 7.16
Ulster Museum, Belfast

Simple shoe sole in tanned leather, suitable for either a left or a right foot.

10.36
Tassel from the *Trinidad Valencera*

Silk
180 lgth
Crédit Communal, 1985, 7.26
Ulster Museum, Belfast

Tassel of golden-yellow silk, with a large knot from which is suspended a net. Such tassels were frequently worn by musketeers.

10.37
Braid from the *Trinidad Valencera*

Silk
9 wdth
Crédit Communal, 1985, 7.30a
Ulster Museum, Belfast

Bolt of gold braid, the end of which has four buttonholes of the same material, with handsome embroidered decoration.

196

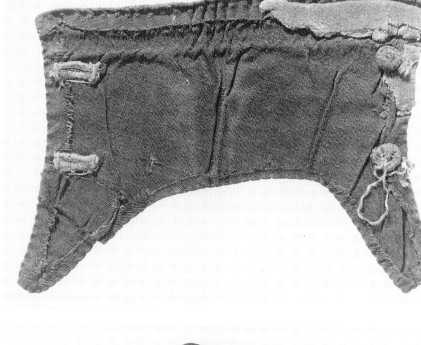

10.38
Collar from the *Trinidad Valencera*

Silk, velvet, wool and jute
500×58
Crédit Communal, 1985, 7.31
Ulster Museum, Belfast

Narrow collar in gold velvet, with a silk braid complete on only three sides; it is lined with wool and has traces of a jute interlining.

10.39
Legging or gaiter from the *Trinidad Valencera*

Silk and wool
190 lgth
Crédit Communal, 1985, 7.32
Ulster Museum, Belfast

In brown silk with a poplin finish, shaped rather like a crown, with traces of a woollen lining. There are two buttons covered in silk and two buttonholes.

10.40
Scent bottle and dropper from the *Girona*

Silver and crystal
48 ht (bottle); 35 lgth (dropper)
Sténuit, 1974, 185; Crédit Communal, 1985, 8.53
Ulster Museum, Belfast

Part of a small perfume flask or scent bottle, with a narrow knopped neck and flared collar. The dropper is a straight hexagonal rod of crystal, with a silver mounting at the end. The flask is one of many found on the site of the *Girona*.

10.41
Comb from the *Trinidad Valencera*

Wood
141 lgth
Crédit Communal, 1985, 8.54
Ulster Museum, Belfast

Double-sided comb, with sawn teeth in fine and coarse settings. The comb was probably used for removing the ubiquitous head-lice.

10.42
Tweezers from the *Girona*

Bronze
78×4
Crédit Communal, 1985, 8.55
Ulster Museum, Belfast

A simple strip of bronze or copper alloy bent back on itself, with a loop at the bend.

10.43
Pair of small wooden cups from the *Trinidad Valencera*

Wood
56 dia.
Crédit Communal, 1985, 8.56
Ulster Museum, Belfast

These turned wooden cups were thought to be gaming cups, but it seems more likely that they originally contained liners and served as salt-cellars.

10.44
Neck of a stringed instrument from the *Trinidad Valencera*

Wood
355×45×12
Crédit Communal, 1985, 8.57
Ulster Museum, Belfast

A straight piece of wood, with one end rounded. At the other end there is a small shoulder on one side where it would have joined the sounding-box. Eighteen small grooves have been cut across the neck, all except two containing bars of another kind of wood. There are impressions of strings on the bar nearest the end, but it is not possible to say how many strings were fitted.

10.45
Cage from the *Trinidad Valencera*

Wood
180 ht
Crédit Communal, 1985, 8.60
Ulster Museum, Belfast

These are parts of what appears to have been a small cage, perhaps used for a pet animal.

197

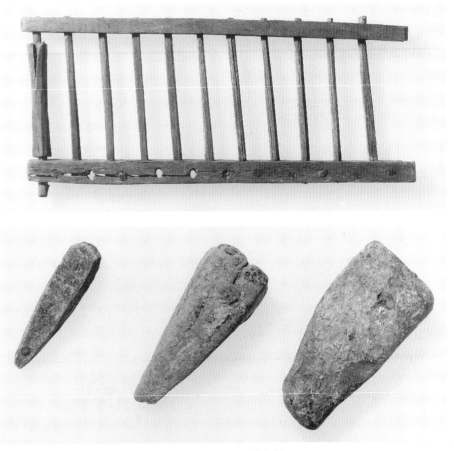

10.46
Fishing weights from the *Girona*

Lead
400, 240 and 50 g.
Crédit Communal, 1985, 8.61
Ulster Museum, Belfast

Catching fresh fish to supplement – or even replace – the food carried on board was a common practice on sixteenth-century ships.

10.47
Ear- and tooth-pick from the *Girona*

Gold
47 lgth
Sténuit, 1974, 190; Crédit Communal, 1985, 9.25
Ulster Museum, Belfast

A small gold object in the form of a dolphin: the flattened tail constitutes the ear-pick, the narrow pointed projection from the head, the toothpick. Such dual-purpose objects were quite common in the sixteenth century.

10.48
Four-*escudo* piece from the *Girona*

Gold
Inscribed (obv.) *PHILIPPVS DEI GRATIA*; (rev.) *REX HISPANIARVM* (clipping has removed some letters)
30 dia.
Castan and Cayon, 1978, type 77, no. 4417; Crédit Communal, 1985, 5.1
Ulster Museum, Belfast

Round, but clipped, four-*escudo* gold piece, minted at Seville; arms of Spain on obverse, *S* to left, *IIII* to right; cross with *fleurs-de-lys* on reverse. This coin and the four following cat. nos. represent the top wages paid to a seaman or soldier per month while serving on the Armada: that is, ten *escudos*.

10.49
Two-*escudo* piece from the *Girona*

Gold
Inscribed (obv.) *PHILIPPVS DEI GRATIA*; (rev.) *REX HISPANIARVM* (not wholly legible)
27 dia.
Castan and Cayon, 1978, type 72, no. 4379; Crédit Communal, 1985, 5.5
Ulster Museum, Belfast

Round, but slightly clipped, two-*escudo* gold piece, minted at Seville; arms of Spain on obverse, *S* to left, *II* to right; cross with *fleurs-de-lys* on reverse.

10.50
Two-*escudo* piece from the *Girona*

Gold
Inscribed (obv.) *PHILIPPVS DEI GRATIA* (practically all clipped off); (rev.) *REX HISPANIARVM* (badly clipped)
25 dia.
Castan and Cayon, 1978, type 72, no. 4375; Crédit Communal, 1985, 5.8
Ulster Museum, Belfast

Round, but clipped, two-*escudo* gold piece, minted at Granada; arms of Spain on obverse, *G* to left, *D & II* to right; cross with *fleurs-de-lys* on reverse.

10.51
One-*escudo* piece from the *Girona*

Gold
Inscribed (obv.) *JOANNA ET CAROLVS*; (rev.) *SICILIAE ET HISPANIARVM REGES*
23 dia.
Castan and Cayon, 1978, type 37, no. 2689; Crédit Communal, 1985, 5.15
Ulster Museum, Belfast

Round gold *escudo*, minted at Seville, with slight bent tear; arms of Spain on obverse, *S* to left; cross with *fleurs-de-lys* on reverse.

10.52
One-*escudo* piece from the *Girona*

Silver
Inscribed (obv.) *PHILIPP REX ARAGON VTRI SIC*; (rev.) *HILARITAS UNIVERSA*
39 dia.
Castan and Cayon, 1978, type 138, no. 5334; Crédit Communal, 1985, 5.30
Ulster Museum, Belfast

Large, round, silver *escudo*, minted at Naples, with a portrait of Philip facing to right on obverse; inscription in frame on reverse.

10.53
Account of clothing for soldiers in the Armada, 7 October 1587

MS
305×212
*Archivo General de Simancas, Valladolid
(GA.221, f.195)*

There were still no uniforms as such for soldiers or sailors. Clothing was most frequently provided by the captains or military entrepreneurs who took charge of the levies, or were contracted to supply and command a ship. In major or long campaigns, however, the crown had to make some provisions as well, particularly when men had to travel great distances (in this case from as far as the Azores and Netherlands) to their destination. This account gives details of 600 complete outfits being made in Seville for the soldiers under Alvaro Flores de Quiñones. It includes shirts, shoes, underpants, jerkins and hats. The price for each item is specified. Money would be deducted from the wages of the men to pay for this.

10.54
Jack of plate, English, *c.*1580

Canvas, iron
660 ht (approx.)
Dufty and Reid, 1968, pl. cxxiii
*Trustees of the Royal Armouries, London
(III.1277)*

A jack was a reinforced tunic for use in combat. This jack of peascod fashion, in the form of a sleeveless doublet contains small, overlapping, square, iron plates, sewn between two layers of canvas with crossbow twine. The collar and skirt are lined with mail. The jack of plate retained its popularity in England long after its use had ceased on the Continent, and became the characteristic defence for the humbler classes of the English infantry. They were also widely used for sea service in the Elizabethan period.

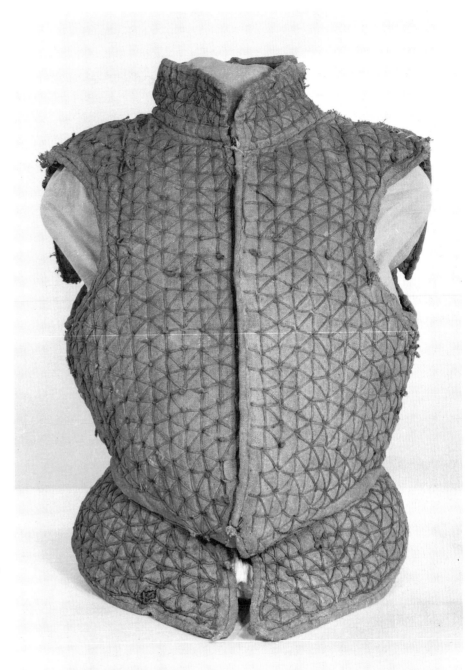

199

10.54

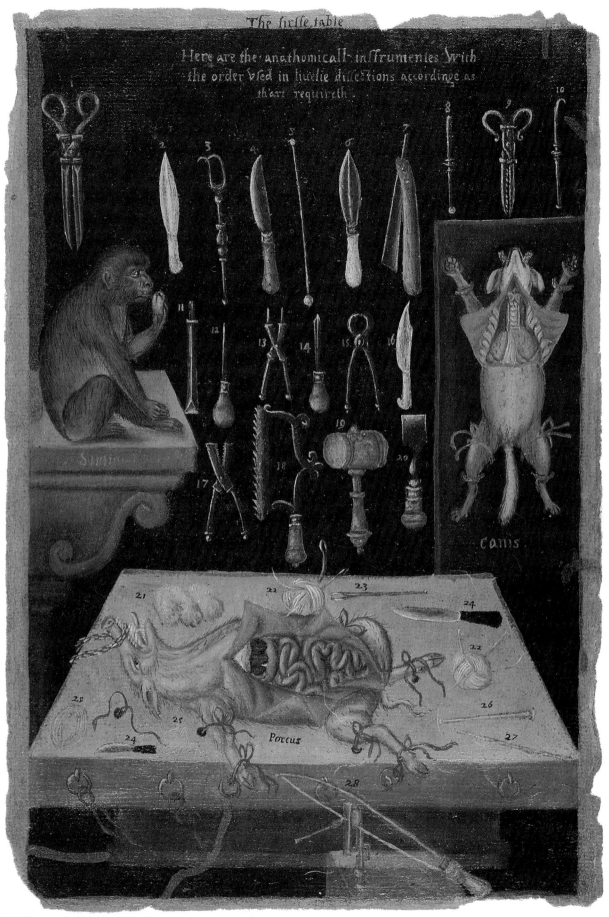

11.3 'Anatomical Tables', John Banester

(i) The English Fleet

The battle against the Armada seems to have been influenced as much by epidemics in both fleets as by the ships, guns and fighting qualities of the mariners. Illness, shortage of food, water and ammunition determined the strategy employed by the English to bring the battle to a successful conclusion.

The first hint of illness is contained in a letter from the Privy Council to the president of the 'College of the Doctors of Physic' on 6 April 1588, asking for 'lerned and skilfull physicions' to be sent to the fleet.[1] Four names were suggested, including that of Dr William Gilbert, who had contributed to the science of navigation through his work on magnetism. Two were eventually attached to the fleet, probably Drs Browne and Marbeck, but they left no record of the epidemic nor the remedies they employed.

William Clowes, the surgeon-general, who served in Howard's flagship, the *Ark Royal*, was an experienced naval and military surgeon who was then on the staff of St Bartholomew's Hospital, but had been recalled for the emergency. With his colleagues at Surgeons' Hall, he resolutely opposed the appointment of unqualified surgeons to the navy, though he often failed to prevent it. That very year, he published his *Prooved practise for all young Chirurgians*,[2] which provided sound practical advice on the management of injuries, including burns and gunshot wounds, illustrated from his own clinical records. Like his fellow Tudor surgeons, he successfully operated upon wounds of the head, chest and abdomen, and aimed to attain healing without infection. Amputations were carried out after the limb had been anaesthetized by means of a tight tourniquet, with the loss of only four ounces of blood. A shrewd observer, he recognized that scurvy and beriberi were caused by deficiencies in the seaman's diet and identified fresh foods which would aid their cure.

It would never have occurred to the Privy Council to consult the surgeon-general about the epidemic, for sea diseases were the province of the physician, and physicians, not surgeons, were needed in the English fleet. English casualties from Spanish gunfire were insignificant, and not more than a hundred men were injured.

The English had no hospital ships and no hospitals for seamen. During a battle, casualties were brought down to the hold and laid on mattresses among other sick sailors and there surgeons, with varying degrees of competence, operated upon them. On return to port, local arrangements were made for the care of the sick in taverns, private houses or even farm outbuildings.

When Howard joined Drake at Plymouth in June 1588, he was impressed by the quality of the sailors whom he described as 'the gallantest company . . . ever seen in England'.[3] They included the healthy and experienced mariners of privately owned ships, fitted-out and victualled by the coastal towns, but he makes no reference to the recent epidemic in his own ships, victualled irregularly and for short periods by naval contractors. He twice reduced the ration to make his provisions last longer. While at sea in June, the epidemic broke out afresh and, when he returned on 22 July, it was to seek more men for, as he explained to Burghley, 'we have cast many overboard and a number in great extremity which we have discharged'.[4] In the absence of any clinical description or, at this stage, reference to spoiled provisions, the most likely cause of this illness was typhus fever, spread by the infected clothing of pressed men in the unhygienic conditions of hot, ill-ventilated ships battened down against the high seas of that gale-ridden summer. Howard seems to have thought so, because he considered the infection contagious and had already commented upon the state of the men's clothing.[5] When the epidemic recurred with increased virulence after the battle, he attributed it to being so long at sea with 'so little shift of apparel' and pleaded for £1,000-worth of doublets, shirts, hose and shoes.[6]

Shortage of food and increasing sickness were two of the factors which caused Howard to send fireships among the Armada anchored in Calais Roads in order to drive the Spanish to sea and force a decisive action. Sir Thomas Heneage reported that Howard himself was reduced to living on beans, and some men had even drunk their own urine.[7] It may only have been hearsay, but Howard wrote to Burghley on 20 August that 'sickness and mortality begins wonderfully to grow amongst us' and men were dying in the streets of Margate. The *Elizabeth Jonas* had been the worst affected and had lost 200 of her 500 seamen during the first three weeks after her arrival in Plymouth. Howard had ordered her men ashore and repeatedly fumigated the ship, but to no avail. Tall, healthy men had been found to man her afresh, but the infection increased and men died faster than ever.[8] On 1 September, he informed the queen that many of her ships were now infected, men sickened one day and died the next.[9] He had been compelled to divide the fleet into two parts and send as many men as possible ashore in the hope that fresh food would cure them. During the epidemic, countless numbers of men died and the ships were frequently remanned, but no estimate of the total mortality is possible. On 20 August, Howard was

1. APC, 24.5, 28 March 1588 (os).
2. See cat. no. **11.2**.
3. Howard to Burghley, 6 June 1588, PRO SP12/210, 35.
4. Howard to Walsingham, 23 July 1588, PRO SP12/212, 42.
5. Howard to Burghley, 25 February 1588, PRO SP12/208, 70.
6. Howard to Burghley, 20 August 1588, PRO SP12/214, 66.
7. Sir Thomas Heneage to Walsingham, 19 August 1588, PRO SP12/214, 53.
8. Howard to Burghley, 20 August 1588, PRO SP12/214, 66.
9. Howard to Queen Elizabeth, 1 September 1588, PRO SP12/215, 40.

complaining that sick men were discharged ashore without pay, without nursing care and without food, and pleaded for money to relieve them. He personally commandeered barns and outhouses for their shelter and provided for many of them out of his own pocket.[10]

The West Country ships under Drake appear to have remained reasonably healthy, and Lord Henry Seymour considered the sickness in the Narrow Seas fleet to be caused by nothing more serious than 'cold nights and cold mornings'.[11] The epidemic, therefore, appears to have been confined largely to Howard's division, which never seems to have recovered from its earlier typhus fever. The new symptoms, however, were far more alarming, for men sickened and died immediately on coming on board. The short incubation period, profound prostration and early death suggest a toxic form of food poisoning. It could have been due to inadequately salted and hastily prepared victuals which decomposed in the heat of the hold where they were stored, or to contamination during the preparation of meals, for the ships had not been cleaned for weeks. Drake had a reputation for clean ships and his division escaped; so apparently did that of Seymour. Howard, a perceptive observer, blamed the sour beer and accused the brewer. A memorandum to the Admiralty during the early Stuart period reveals how unscrupulous brewers used broom instead of hops and ashes instead of malt, with salt water to improve the flavour. At first it tasted good, but within a month 'was worse than stinking water'.[12] That was how Howard described it and it may also account for the thirst the men experienced. Perhaps the brewer, unable to meet the insatiable demands of the fleet, had used contaminated ingredients which spread disease and death among the victors.

Sir James Watt

(ii) The Spanish Fleet

Long years of war in the Netherlands and Mediterranean had taught Philip II the wisdom of making adequate medical arrangements for his troops.[1] Consequently, there was nothing unusual in the fact that the Marquis of Santa Cruz specified what hospital facilities were required in his proposal for the campaign in 1586. He requested a medical corps of fifty-five, headed by five physicians and five surgeons, which was also to include four barbers, two apothecaries and various ancillary staff.[2] Reality fell far short of this ideal. There seem to have been few physicians available in Lisbon, although a field-hospital was fully operational when, in November

1587, a mysterious epidemic spread among the troops arriving from Naples and the Netherlands. By the end of the month there were 1,000 men in hospital; another 400 sick were forced to remain on board their vessels owing to lack of facilities. The government was frightened that the soldiers would desert if allowed ashore, but they finally decided to quarter them around Cascaes, having concluded that losses would be higher through disease and death than desertion.[3] In early December, 854 men were reported unfit for service (out of a total of 11,616), showing that the epidemic had abated, but was not yet over.[4]

As a result of these misfortunes, more experienced medical staff were recruited, some were even sent from court. These physicians and doctors had served in the wars of the Netherlands, Portugal and the Azores.[5] On 30 March 1588 there were thirty-five people serving in the hospital; by 15 July, ninety-three officials are listed.[6] Earlier, in June, the hulk carrying most of the medical facilities was blown off course in the gales that scattered the fleet off La Coruña. Soon after, it sank in Santander, but men and supplies were rescued.[7] Meanwhile, Medina Sidonia scoured the Galician towns and countryside for medicines and shelter, to treat the 500 men who fell sick soon after arriving at La Coruña. He was adamant that seasickness and rotten food had caused this new epidemic. After the long, hot period at sea in overcrowded, filthy vessels, many provisions were putrid and the water was well-nigh undrinkable, and in short supply.[8] The duke prohibited the eating of fresh fish, but secured supplies of fresh meat and water. Doubtless this helped to keep mortality rates very low. The medical staff and provisions soon rejoined the fleet, travelling on three French pinnaces. The bulk of the hospital and medical stores were transferred to the hulk *San Pedro el Mayor*; the rest may have remained in one of the pinnaces.[9]

This was not the only medical assistance available to the troops. The Spanish and Italian infantry and the artillery corps had two or three physicians and surgeons of their own, and other corps are likely to have made similar independent provisions. Moreover, a number of monks with the fleet had medical skills. When the Armada sailed out of La Coruña, only 250 men were left behind sick, none seriously. Given the many delays and tribulations already endured, this is remarkable.[10]

The strict discipline maintained by the fleet on its way up the Channel ensured that casualties were dealt with up to the final battle of Gravelines. Nevertheless, the drawbacks of having the bulk of the medical services in one ship were to be proved once

10. Howard to Burghley, 20 August 1588, PRO SP12/214, 66. (See cat. no. **15.15**.)
11. Seymour to Walsingham, 29 August 1588, PRO SP12/215, 34.
12. Treatise of Nathaniel Knott, PRO SP12/279, 106.

1. Parker, 1972, 167–9.
2. Gracia Rivas, 1983, 64–5.
3. AGS E.429 f.34, Santa Cruz to Philip II, Lisbon, 29 November 1587.
4. AGS GA.221 f.44.
5. AGS GA.234 ff.34–6, *consulta* of the council of war, 26 January 1588; Gracia Rivas, 1983.
6. AGS GA.221 ff.113–14 (March), GA.221 f.181 (July).
7. See cat. no. **11.11**; AGS GA.225 f.87, f.101, f.39; GA.221 f.44.
8. AGS GA.225 f.39, letter to Philip, 11 July.
9. AGS GA.225 f.75; GA.225 f.40.
10. Ibid.

again when ill winds scattered the fleet in August. Many of those injured in the final clashes with the English were left to nurse their wounds and burns with inadequate support. At the end of October, the *San Pedro el Mayor* foundered off Salcombe with its sad cargo of medicines and men, 'so greatly diseased', that the survivors were quarantined in isolated barns and outbuildings to prevent contagion.[11] During the arduous journey home, when they needed it most, few enjoyed the benefits of Philip's careful medical provisions.

M. J. Rodríguez-Salgado

11. APC 24, 373. I am grateful to Sir James Watt for providing this information. See also Laughton, II, 1981, 289–91 and 371–5.

11.1
Certaine workes of Chirurgurie . . ., 1563
Thomas Gale (1507–87)

Publ. Rowland Hall, London
Printed book
150×110
Keevil, 1957, 128–31; Watt, 1983, 7
Wellcome Institute for the History of Medicine, London

Gale was a leading English barber-surgeon and a fierce opponent of quacks, whom he had encountered during service with the English and Spanish armies in the 1540s and 1550s. The 'wound man' shown in the centre of the book illustrates the great variety of wounds that the sixteenth-century military surgeon might have to deal with. The original of this illustration came from a book on military surgery written in 1517 by Hans von Gersdorff.

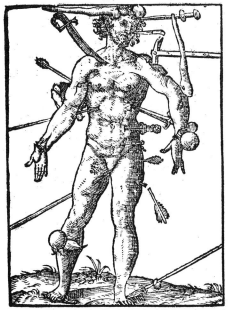

11.2
A prooved practise for all young Chirurgians . . ., 1588
William Clowes (1544–1604)

Publ. Thomas Orwyn for Thomas Cadman, London
Printed book
190×143
Keevil, 1957, 129–37; Watt, 1983, 3, 5–7
Wellcome Institute for the History of Medicine, London

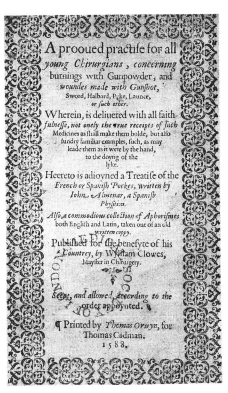

Clowes's work was the first English textbook on sea-surgery, the result of a close study of contemporary surgical thought and several years' service, first as a military surgeon and later in the royal fleet. Like Gale, Clowes was passionately concerned to raise the status of the surgeon and criticized the quacks who gave surgery a bad name. *A prooved practise*

. . . is illustrated with examples from his own experience, which show a concern to minimize the blood-loss and trauma suffered by the patient. Although Clowes was the leading surgeon of his day, his views were unfortunately not very influential. They had little effect on either the practices or the prevalence of the 'sory Surgeons' found in many ships.

203

11.3
'Anatomical Tables', 1581
John Banester (1540–1610)

Oil on paper
305×210
Keevil, 1957, 65–6, 92, 136–7; Watt, 1983, 12, 15
Librarian of Glasgow University Library (MS Hunter 364, Table I)

Banester was a surgeon of wide experience who served in a number of military campaigns and was chief surgeon in the

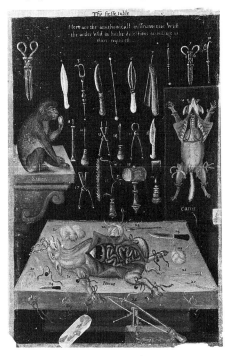

unsuccessful East Indies voyage of 1582–3. His writings were not as popular with students as those of Clowes, but his 'Anatomical Tables' offer vivid illustrations of Elizabethan surgical knowledge and practice. This table depicts vivisection, but also shows the instruments commonly used by Tudor barber-surgeons, including a saw, mallet, chisel, folding knife, pincers and other items.

11.4
Cleaver from an English hunting trousse, *c*.1560–80

Steel, brass and mahogany
230×50×10
Watt, 1983, 11–12
Science Museum, London

11.5
Saw from an English hunting trousse, *c*.1560–80

Steel, brass and mahogany
375×60×18
Watt, 1983, 11–12
Science Museum, London

Although cat. nos. **11.4** and **11.5** are from a set of hunting instruments, they give some idea of the finest Tudor surgical instruments. Items such as these would have been reserved for use at the court or in aristocratic households: the instruments carried by surgeons in the fleet would have been much plainer, with simple wooden handles, such as those found on the *Mary Rose*.

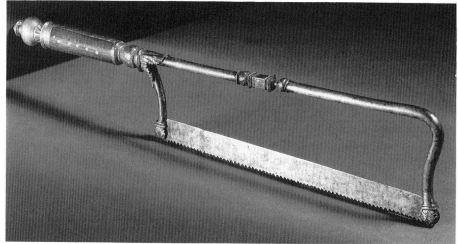

11.6
Surgical instrument case

Reproduction
185×60
Watt, 1983, 5
Master and Wardens of the Worshipful Company of Barbers, London

This item is a replica of a case presented to the Company of Barbers by Henry VIII, in thanks for their help in establishing a naval medical service. The selection of surgeons for the navy was to remain a responsibility of the company for several centuries.

11.7
Pestle from the *Trinidad Valencera*

Bronze
214 lgth
Crédit Communal, 1985, 3.10
Ulster Museum, Belfast

11.8
Mortar from the *Trinidad Valencera*

Bronze
94 ht
Crédit Communal, 1985, 3.11
Ulster Museum, Belfast

Heavy cast-bronze mortar. One side has been slightly crushed, which has resulted in some cracking of the metal. Mortars and pestles were used by apothecaries for grinding up the ingredients for drugs.

11.9
Delft apothecary's jar, late 16th century

Tin-glazed earthenware
59 ht
Museum of London (A 4457)

This jar is typical of the containers used by apothecaries for the storage of ointments or drugs.

11.10
Letter from Lord Howard to the Privy Council, 1 September 1588

MS
310×210
Laughton, II, 1981, 139–42
Public Record Office, London (SP12/215, 41)

Howard's letter graphically illustrates the havoc wrought by disease in his part of the English fleet. He states that 'the fleete is greavously infected', with new men joining ships and dying the next day, and some vessels so weakly manned that they cannot weigh anchor. He suggests splitting the fleet into two parts, one at Margate or Gore-End, and the other in the Downs, the sick men being put ashore and supplied with fresh victuals. Howard notes that the men are very discontented at not receiving their full pay, and requests that they be paid up to 25 August (OS). He was worried that the Armada would return and the English fleet would be insufficiently manned. He also felt the pity and injustice of men who had fought well not receiving their rightful pay and dying for want of fresh food.

205

11.11
Letter of Pedro de Igualdo on the fate of the hospital ship, Laredo, 11 July 1588

MS
293×210
Archivo General de Simancas, Valladolid (GA.225, f.103)

The hulk named *Casa de Paz Grande* (*the Large House of Peace*) carried most of the hospital facilities. It was struck by the storm which scattered the fleet off La Coruña on the night of 19 June and later foundered, but staff and stores were saved. Igualdo reports the seizure of three Breton pinnaces to which the medicines and hospital were transferred. It proved impossible to load into them the large wheels of siege-gun-carriages which the hulk had also been carrying.

12.3 *The Mariners Mirrour*, Lucas Jansz. Waghenaer. Frontispiece by Theodor de Bry

12. Navigation

At the time of the Armada the Spanish and Portuguese were still the acknowledged leaders in the skills of oceanic navigation. Although individual French and English navigators equalled them in skill, and were soon to overtake them in enterprise and invention, the two nations which had been first in the field mustered by far the largest body of trained pilots available amongst the maritime nations. For it was the ability to establish a ship's position out of sight of land, developed by them in the previous century, which had enabled first the Portuguese and then the Spanish to chart and exploit the greater part of the habitable globe and to bring home the wealth which made an enterprise such as the Armada possible.

The techniques of navigation had changed little in the intervening years, and the ordered daily routine found necessary for the safe conduct of a ship was familiar to seamen of all nationalities. This routine centred around the noon sight of the sun taken when it was at its highest, with the ship bearing due south. Its angular height above the horizon, observed with a sea-astrolabe or cross staff, when combined with mathematical tables of the sun's declination for that day in the year, gave the navigator his latitude. Simultaneously, he was provided with a check on the accuracy of the steering compass and the precise moment to turn the glass and start the account for the next twenty-four hours. Should the sun be obscured by cloud, he could try for a direct observation of his latitude at dusk by an angular height of the Pole Star, provided he was in the northern hemisphere.

Latitude alone, however, did not provide him with a precise position. To do this he needed to know his longitude, but it was to be a further two centuries before a method would be evolved to achieve this. The best he could do was to keep an accurate 'account' of the ship's movements throughout the twenty-four hours. Ship's time was kept by one or more half-hour glasses. As they were turned, the striking of a bell was a reassurance that the watch was awake and the routine in place. Each hour the mean course steered and the estimated distance run was carefully recorded on a traverse board. At noon the following day the navigator would assemble this information and combine it with his observation for latitude into a most likely position. This he would mark, or 'prick', onto his chart.

If the sun could not be sighted, the estimated or 'dead reckoning' position had to be extended a further twenty-four hours, and if several days passed without a sight, it would become rapidly less reliable. Thus in northern, cloudy latitudes, navigation was more an art than a science. When ships sailed in company it was common practice for the admiral to assemble all the pilots of the fleet to compare their estimated positions and to reach a consensus. This was no easy task, as these often differed wildly.

However, the route of the Armada as planned was to be a straightforward coasting voyage as practised by numerous small trading vessels equipped with nothing more complicated than a simple compass, a sounding lead and perhaps a pilot book as an *aide-mémoire*. Medina Sidonia had some pilots familiar with the route to the Baltic through the English Channel who could fulfil the requirement for a good coaster laid down by William Bourne in 1574: 'to know every place by the sight thereof'. Expectation of a coastal voyage did not mean that the pilots of the Armada ships would have left their instruments behind, for these were their personal property, at once their pride and mark of their profession. They would have carried them at all times and, in the event, they were to make full use of them.

As the Armada sailed northward out of the North Sea, Medina Sidonia ordered a route home which took them on a wide sweep into the Atlantic, well away from the coast of Ireland which he regarded – rightly, it transpired – as very dangerous. Isolated from the principal European trade routes and dangerously exposed to Atlantic gales, the west coast of Ireland was little known to pilots and poorly charted. Those ships of the Armada which closed the shore did so because they were desperate for water, provisions or repair, and their loss could not be laid at the door of inadequate navigation. The fact that over two-thirds returned safely to their home ports with no landfalls between the Shetlands and Finisterre and through some of the worst autumn gales on record, is a resounding tribute to the navigating skills of their pilots.

Christopher Terrell

12.1
Pocket tidal almanac, *c.*1546
Guillaume Brouscon

MS and woodcut on vellum
108×87×14
Taylor, 1971, 170; Howse, 1980
National Maritime Museum (NVT 40)

This pocket-sized tidal almanac, devised by a
Breton seaman and once owned by Samuel
Pepys, has been described as the most
remarkable gift of north-west Europe to navigation. By the ingenious use of colours and
symbols Brouscon made it usable by seamen
of all nationalities, literate or not. It provided
the means of finding the time of high water
over much of the coast of northern Europe,
together with a perpetual lunar calendar and
much other useful navigational information,
all in an easily portable form.

12.2
Dutch volume of sailing directions, 1579

MS in 18th-century calf binding with pen
and colour wash (47ff.)
249×207
Destombes, 1968; Skelton and Summerson,
1971, 69
*The Marquess of Salisbury, Hatfield House
(CPM Supp. 17)*

A manuscript book of sailing directions,
comprising both pilotage notes and charts,
compiled by an unknown Dutch seafarer and
covering the coasts of Europe from Holland
to Lisbon. As well as twelve charts, which
are some of the earliest to include depth
soundings, it contains notes on the best
routes and distances between ports, a table of
tidal differences and other useful navigational
information. This rare survival contains the
sort of information a well-organized coasting
master would collect for his own use and
pass on to his successors. It forms a link
between the simple pilotage notebook of the
Middle Ages and the much more elaborate
and comprehensive sea-atlases printed by
Waghenaer and later Dutch publishers. It is
probable that Waghenaer compiled his great
work from information culled from many
private volumes such as these.

208

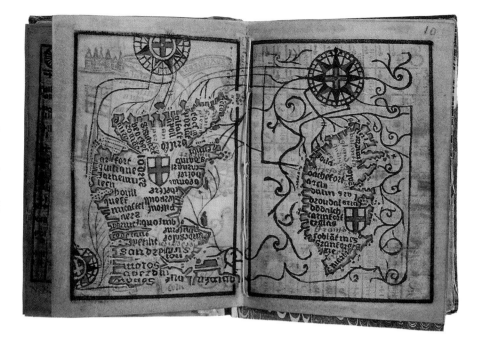

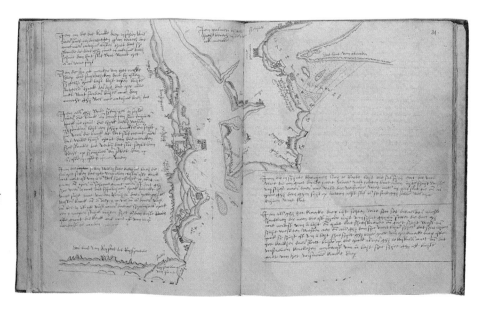

12.3
The Mariners Mirrour, 1588
Lucas Jansz. Waghenaer (1533–1606)
Frontispiece by Theodor de Bry

Publ. Anthony Ashley, London
Printed book (116 pp.)
400×295; scale 1:240,000
Taylor, 1971, 210
National Maritime Museum (D8264)

In 1584 Lucas Jansz. Waghenaer, a Dutch
master-pilot of Enkhuisen in Holland,
published a work which was to have a profound effect on the practice of navigation by
all nations. Called the *Spieghel der Zeevaerdt*
('The Mariner's Mirror') it brought together
in one volume charts, sailing directions,
coastal views and navigational tables,
previously only available separately. The
forty-four coastal charts, engraved by J. van
Doetecum at a standard scale of 1:240,000,
contained more detailed information than had
ever previously been available and covered
the entire coast of Europe from the Straits of
Gibraltar to the North Cape.

This new concept, the first comprehensive printed sea-atlas, set a fashion which was
followed by all the maritime nations for the
next three centuries. The *Spieghel* itself was
translated into several languages and ran to
many editions, and was soon followed by
similar productions from the printing houses
of Amsterdam based on the same principles.
In England its influence was such that thereafter all sea-atlases became known by seamen
as 'waggoners'.

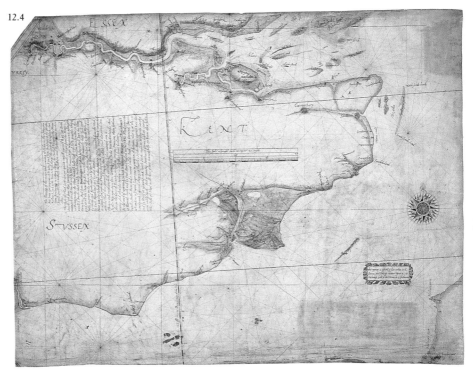

In 1585 the Privy Council of England
were persuaded by Lord Howard of
Effingham, the Lord Admiral of England, to
have the charts re-engraved and published in
English for the benefit of their country's seamen. The clerk to the council, Sir Anthony
Ashley, was instructed to supervise the under-
taking and the work was published as *The
Mariners Mirrour* in October 1588, shortly
after the end of the Armada campaign.

12.4
Chart of Kent and Sussex Coasts, 1596
William Borough (1537–99)

Pen and watercolour on vellum
485×645; scale approx. 1:200,000
Robinson, 1962, 31 and Pl.11; Skelton, 1957
*British Library, London (MS Cott.
Aug.I,i,f.17)*

This chart, notable for its detailed tidal description of the coast from Goring to
Woolwich, was commissioned in November
1596 in response to a Spanish threat. Its
emphasis on the Ryrap Shoal, the River
Rother and Romney Marshes, indicates concern that navigational factors like tides
favoured a landing in the area. William
Borough utilized earlier Thames charts by
Robert Norman, Philip Symondson and
Richard Poulter, Robert Norman's rutter
Safeguard of Sailers (1584) and his own
sketch survey of 1588 in preparing this chart.

12.5
Breve compendio de la sphera y de la arte de navegar . . ., 1551
Martín Cortes

Publ. Antonio Alvarez, Seville
Printed book (197 pp.)
340×235
Waters, 1958, 39–71, 348; Haring, 1964,
311; Baldwin, 1980, 118–53, 530–39
National Maritime Museum (E5140)

209

By 1545, Martín Cortes had established his reputation as a teacher of navigation and had already written this navigation manual, dedicated to Emperor Charles V. It was soon adopted as a concise standard textbook by the navigation school of the Casa de la Contratación in Seville. Encapsulating the whole technology of celestial navigation, instrument manufacture and the making and use of charts, this manual was an immensely important compendium which significantly widened adoption of celestial navigation techniques.

210

12.6
The Arte of Navigation . . ., 1561
Martín Cortes; trans. Richard Eden
(1521–76)

Publ. Richard Jugge, London
Printed book (168 pp.)
180×140
Waters, 1958, 100–113, 130, 148–51, 215–16, 315–19; Baldwin, 1980, 143, 152–3, 230–41, 530–39
National Maritime Museum (E5214)

In 1558 Philip II allowed the English navigator Stephen Borough (1525–84) to visit the navigation school of the Casa de Contratación in Seville. Borough returned with a copy of Cortes's manual and persuaded four London merchants to fund an English translation to teach English sailors celestial navigation. Richard Eden was chosen for the work. He had acted as interpreter in the Prince of

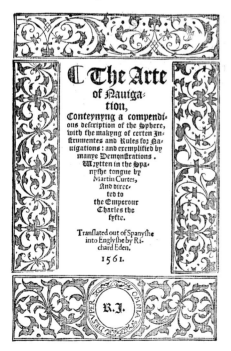

Spain's treasury from 1553–5, and translated the books of Sebastian Munster (1553), Peter Martyr d'Anghiera (1555), and edited Oviedo's account as an Atlantic rutter in 1555. Borough and Eden hoped to encourage English trans-oceanic enterprise by making the techniques of celestial navigation available in England. There were nine subsequent editions of this work, published between 1572 and 1630, attesting to its popularity.

12.7
Compendio del Arte de Navegar . . ., 1588
Rodrigo Zamorano

Publ. Ioan de Leon, Seville
Printed book
Marked on title page with two official stamps of the pilot-major and the cosmographer-major
193×135
Haring, 1964, 313; Baldwin, 1980, 143, 194; Destombes, 1987, 317
British Library, London (1397.b.1)

Zamorano, a mathematician, became in turn king's reader in navigation and cosmography, then cosmographer-major and pilot-major, although the two posts were formally merged from 1596 to 1612. Unlike Rafael Pardo de Figueroa and Juan de Moya, who tried unsuccessfully to better Cortes's manual, Zamorano's work was clearer and more concise. Adopted as the standard teaching-text at Seville from 1582, it was later translated into Dutch and English. Edward Wright added a translation of Zamorano's text on the making and use of the plane chart and tables of leagues to each degree of latitude to his revised *Certaine Errors of Navigation* in 1610.

12.8
A Regiment for the Sea . . ., c.1576
William Bourne (fl.1565–88)

Publ. T. Dawson and T. Gardyner, 1st ed., London
Printed book (128 pp.)
185×135
Waters, 1958, 15; Taylor, 1963, 201–206
National Maritime Museum (D1161)

This was the first English-produced textbook on navigation. While owing much to earlier Spanish examples it contains a great deal of original material, for example the first description of the log and line for measuring speed, an English invention. It dispenses sound advice for masters and pilots on navigation matters and on the conduct of ships

and their crews in general. The book attests to the rising confidence of the English in maritime affairs.

12.9
Universal planispheric astrolabe, 1588

Brass-gilt
Inscribed *Factum Heidelbergae MDLXXXVIII*
250 dia.
National Maritime Museum (A50)

The planispheric astrolabe, a model of the spherical heavens reproduced on a flat surface, was probably a Greek invention of about the second century B C. It can be used to solve problems of time-finding and position-fixing and for simple observations, but travellers had to carry different plates to be used in varying latitudes. The universal astrolabe was developed in the sixteenth and seventeenth centuries in the west to overcome this problem. This example, made in Augsburg in 1588, is a kind of universal astrolabe known as the Gemma Frisius type. The mariner's astrolabe was a simpler version of the planispheric astrolabe.

12.10
Astronomical compendium, 1569
Humphrey Cole (1530?–91)

Brass-gilt
Inscribed *Humfray Colle made this diall anno 1569*
63.5×55.9
National Maritime Museum (D318)

A knowledge of astronomy is needed for navigation on land and sea, and for time-telling. In the sixteenth century the astronomical theory for solving such problems was known, but the technology was not available in practice. Men like Humphrey Cole, Augustine Ryther and Christopher Schissler were the forerunners of the seventeenth-century expansion in the art of scientific instrumentation. This brass-gilt compendium by Cole incorporates a number of astronomical instruments into one small case. It includes a nocturnal and lunar and solar dials for time-telling, a compass, a table of cities with their latitudes and information for determining high water. The compendium folds flat when not in use. Cole is regarded as the finest Elizabethan instrument-maker; a wide range of his instruments still exists. Although this compendium was once reputed to have belonged to Sir Francis Drake, the supporting evidence is inconclusive.

12.11
Sundial, 1582
Christopher Schissler (1531–1608)

Brass-gilt
Inscribed *CHRISTOPHORVS SCHISSLER IVNIOR FACIEBAT AVGVSTA ANNO 1582*
76.2×76.2
National Maritime Museum (D29)

Christopher Schissler, who worked in Augsburg, was one of the leading instrument-makers in Europe. This adjustable horizontal dial of 1582 is one of many remaining examples of his work.

12.13
Astrolabe from the *Girona*

Bronze
189 dia.
Sténuit, 1974, 185; Crédit Communal, 1985,
6.2
Ulster Museum, Belfast

Circle of bronze with the base of a suspension-loop at the top, it is divided in four by bars meeting at the centre to form a perforated boss where the alidade would have been mounted. At the bottom of the hoop a semicircular piece of bronze serves as a weight. The calibrations round the circumference do not survive.

12.12
Sundial, 1588
Augustine Ryther (*fl.*1576–95)

Brass with silvered scales
Inscribed *A. Ryther ★ Fecit ★ 1588 ★;*
WILLIAM PAWLEY OWETH THIS
SAME IN ANNO DOMINI 1588
55 dia.
Science Museum, London (1985–2021)

The dial by Ryther and the central instrument in the Cole compendium are both universal equinoctial dials. They are 'universal' because the sundial can be adjusted to tell the time from different locations, and 'equinoctial' because the hour ring is always set in the plane of the equator. The bar across the centre of the hour ring houses the gnomon, which casts the shadow and indicates the time. Ryther was the source of the instrument-making trade in the Grocers' Company, to which mathematical-instrument-makers could belong. Only one other instrument by him has survived. Like many of the early makers, Ryther combined the skills of the instrument-maker's craft with the engraver's art. Among his engravings were maps for Saxton's atlas and the Armada plates drawn by Robert Adams.

12.14
Mariner's astrolabe

Brass
178 dia.
Lecky, 1874, 120; Gunther, 1932, 318;
Baldwin, 1980, 63–4, 527; Stimson, 1983
National Maritime Museum (NA/A55)

Found on Valencia Island in 1845, this
unfinished astrolabe is presumed to come
from one of the Armada ships wrecked in
Blasket Sound in mid-September 1588. It
had never been officially approved, because
its degree scale was not fully engraved. Its
size, weight and style suggest manufacture in
Lisbon, before over-hasty or illicit issue to
the Armada gathering there. Mariner's astrolabes were in use between *c.*1500 and *c.*1700,
and were a means of determining latitude by
measuring the height of the sun.

214

12.15
Magnetic compass, *c.*1580
?Italian maker

Ivory case and vellum card
114 dia.
Hitchins and May, 1952
National Maritime Museum (NA/C82)

References to the use of magnetized needles
for directing a ship's sailing occur from the
twelfth century onwards. Compasses soon
became indispensable for ships making long
voyages out of sight of land, and by the fifteenth century they had become essential
ships' stores. Early survivors are rare, the
earliest being three steering compasses
recently recovered from the *Mary Rose*, sunk
in 1545. This beautifully made example was
too fine to have served as a ship's compass
and was most likely the personal property of
a nobleman or wealthy ship master.

12.16
Mariner's compass from the *Trinidad Valencera*

Wood and steel
104 dia.
Crédit Communal, 1985, 6.1
Ulster Museum, Belfast

Turned wooden circular base of a compass, with stepped edge and slightly dished upper surface. A small steel pin, now bent, rises from a small circular platform in the centre. The card would have been balanced on this.

12.17
Lodestone, *c.*1570

Magnetized oxide of iron with engraved brass decoration
58×64×46
Hitchins and May, 1952
National Maritime Museum (NA/M.8/37-31C)

A lodestone ('lead' stone) was a piece of naturally magnetic oxide of iron used by navigators to stroke or 're-touch' the needle of their compass in order to restore its magnetism. They were usually elaborately decorated to emphasize their importance.

12.18
Pair of compasses from the Barents expedition, 1596

Brass
80×13
Waters, 1958
Rijksmuseum, Amsterdam (NM 7750)

These compasses (or dividers) were designed to be used with one hand. They were indispensable for taking off and laying off courses, bearings and distances on a chart.

12.19
Navigational dividers from the *Trinidad Valencera*

Bronze
120 lgth
Crédit Communal, 1985, 6.4
Ulster Museum, Belfast

These dividers consist of two similar tapering straight legs terminating in points, the tops in the form of 'G's, held together by a bronze rivet. The upper portions of the legs are decorated with pairs of 'M's. The dividers still function perfectly.

215

12.18

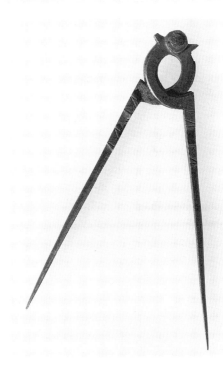

12.19

12.20
Hand-lead from the Barents expedition, 1596

Lead
280×38
Rijksmuseum, Amsterdam (NM 7819)

The lead on its line has been used to find the depth of water since antiquity. A recess in its base could be armed (filled) with tallow, so that a sample of the seabed could be brought up. Together they enabled an experienced pilot to estimate the ship's position.

12.21
Sounding lead from the *Trinidad Valencera*

Lead
189 lgth
Sténuit, 1974, 185; Crédit Communal, 1985, 6.9
Ulster Museum, Belfast

Long, conical piece of lead, tapering almost to a point, through which is a small circular hole to take the line; there is a circular depression in the base to take wax for sampling the seabed.

12.22
?English sand-glass, 17th century

Wood and glass
356 ht
Waters, 1958, 35–6, 137–8
National Maritime Museum (38–1671c/H29)

This ship's sand-glass has six wooden uprights and holes in the base for a rope becket (to help secure the piece). It would have been used for measuring the passage of an hour. Sand-glasses were invaluable for monitoring time on board ship, and helped to keep a check on a vessel's progress.

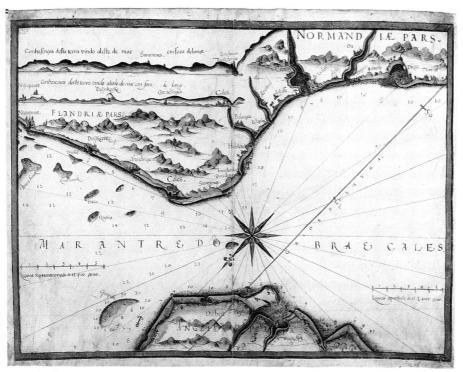

12.23

Chart of Dover Strait, *c.*1587–8
Luis Teixeira (*fl.*1564–*c.*1613)

Watercolour on vellum
Inscribed *MAR ANTRE; DOBRA; CALES*
518×406; scale 1:400,000
National Maritime Museum (G218:6721)

As this chart closely resembles one in Lucas
Waghenaer's *Spieghel der Zeevaerdt*, published in 1584, it is thought to be a copy
made by Luis Teixeira in Lisbon for the
Armada. As such it would partly fulfil
Philip's promise of April 1588 to provide
Medina Sidonia's fleet with detailed coastal
descriptions, charts and expert pilots from
Oquendo's fleet. This chart covers the planned areas of Spanish combined operations in
which Medina Sidonia was to secure safe
passage for Parma's army from Flanders to
England. It shows Nieuport and Dunkirk,
where Parma intended to embark, despite
their offshore sandbanks and currents, and
east Kent, where they hoped to land.

12.24

**Derrotero de las Costas de Bretaña,
Normandia, Picardia hasta Flandes,
y de la de Inglaterra, Manga de
Bristol y Sant Iorge, y parte de la
Costa de Irlanda, 30 March 1588**
Antonio Alvarez, 1588 ed., Lisbon

Printed pamphlet
320×215
Herrera Oria, 1929, 156–80
*Archivo General de Simancas, Valladolid
(E.431, f.17)*

This rutter, prepared for issue to the Armada
in 1588 by a Calabrian, was printed by
Antonio Alvarez, who had made his reputation publishing navigational works since
1545. It advises how best to sail to the Channel ports of England, France and Flanders as
far as Blanckenburg and Nieuport, and
around the Irish Sea, without describing the
hazardous northern and western coasts of
Scotland and Ireland. Itself a translation of a
text used for regular commercial navigation,
it advises where to obtain pilots, and what
courses to steer between coastal features, also
describing tidal patterns and locations where
easy anchoring was possible near beaches and
sand dunes. Manuscript notes in Philip II's
hand show he personally checked distances
given in the rutter against two charts and
Ortelius's atlas, discerning thereby various
discrepancies.

12.25

**Notes by Philip II on the rutter for
the Armada**
Philip II (1527–98)

MS
310×205
*Archivo General de Simancas, Valladolid
(E.431, f.15)*

Philip was very concerned to test the
accuracy of the rutter supplied for the
Armada (see cat. no. **12.24**). He ordered his
secretary to bring him a copy of 'el teatro',
the atlas by Abraham Ortelius entitled
Theatrum Orbis Terrarum. He tested the rutter's descriptions of the coast around Brest
and Ushant against Ortelius's depiction of
the same area, and finally compared the distances given. He also found a discrepancy
between the chart and the rutter of some ten
to fifteen leagues for the distances given
between the Isle of Wight and Dunkirk.

217

13.2 Don Alvaro de Bazán, 1st Marquis of Santa Cruz (1526–88),
Spanish School

**13.19 Charles Howard, Lord Effingham and Earl of Nottingham
(1536–1624),** Daniel Mytens

13. Commanders

(i) Spanish Commanders

The king was the pinnacle of a complex and often overlapping structure of command that organized and guided the Armada of 1588. Philip personally attended to the detailed business of fitting out the fleet, and determined its strategy. He believed that a sovereign must concern himself with all affairs of state. Major decisions were made with advice, but without paying undue attention to any one interest. The Duke of Parma and the Marquis of Santa Cruz were the most influential advisers on strategy in 1588, but experts such as Don Juan de Acuña Vela, captain-general of the artillery, had considerable influence and latitude in their fields. Orders and decisions were processed by the councils and state secretaries at court, who also advised on the selection of officers. The most important were the Council of War, the Council of State, and the financial departments, the *Contadurías*. The Council of War had been reformed and expanded in 1586 and was staffed largely by military experts. Officials throughout the empire played their part: the viceroys and general commanders of areas supplying men and materials, and especially the cardinal-archduke, Albert, who governed Portugal.[1]

Once the fleet sailed, it was under the command of the Duke of Medina Sidonia, captain-general of the fleet and army of the Ocean Sea. He was an experienced administrator, with ample practice of fitting out fleets for the New World and defending southern Spain against corsair and pirate raids. His high rank, matched only by Parma, and his considerable wealth recommended him to the king after the Marquis of Santa Cruz died in February 1588. He was efficient, affable and modest. Conscious of his own shortcomings, Medina Sidonia wisely relied on the many experienced seamen and military commanders at hand to make important decisions.[2] His second-in-command was one such person: Juan Martínez de Recalde, also captain-general of the Biscayan Squadron. There were eight other squadron commanders: General Diego Flores de Valdés (Castilian), Don Pedro de Valdés (Andalusian), General Miguel de Oquendo (Guipuzcoan), *cabo* (corporal or chief of a squadron) Martín de Bertendona (Levantine), *cabo* Juan Gómez de Medina (hulks), *cabo* Don Antonio Hurtado de Mendoza (the rest of the hulks and pinnaces), Don Hugo de Moncada (in charge of the Neapolitan galleasses), Don Diego de Medrano (in charge of the four Portuguese galleys). They had particular responsibility for each section of the fleet.

On each ship there were various sources of authority. The soldiers were under their own commanders. There were five *tercios* represented, each

Command structure of the Armada

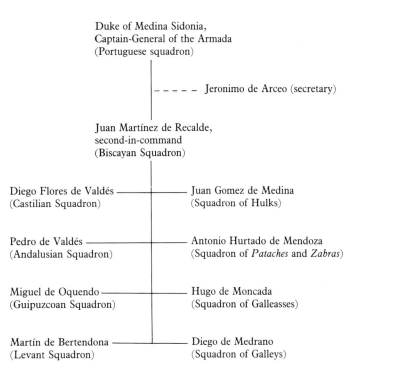

Duke of Medina Sidonia, Captain-General of the Armada (Portuguese squadron)

— — — — Jeronimo de Arceo (secretary)

Juan Martínez de Recalde, second-in-command (Biscayan Squadron)

Diego Flores de Valdés (Castilian Squadron) —————— Juan Gomez de Medina (Squadron of Hulks)

Pedro de Valdés (Andalusian Squadron) —————— Antonio Hurtado de Mendoza (Squadron of *Pataches* and *Zabras*)

Miguel de Oquendo (Guipuzcoan Squadron) —————— Hugo de Moncada (Squadron of Galleasses)

Martín de Bertendona (Levant Squadron) —————— Diego de Medrano (Squadron of Galleys)

with a *maestre de campo* – commander of a large regiment, often 2,000 to 3,000 men – or substitute, and some twenty-five captains under each, who commanded a company within the *tercio*. But there were also 'loose companies', taken from various fortifications or areas, each with their commanders. These and the *tercios* added up to about 176 companies. The largest military units, such as the *tercio* of Sicily, had their own officials, but most of the forces relied on the royal officials for pay, provisions, medical facilities and scribners. Don Lópe Manrique was *veedor general* (general inspector of the forces); Bernabe de Pedroso was the *proveedor* (purveyor or commissary general); Juan de Huerta, was the *pagador* (paymaster); and there were various *contadores* (auditors).[3]

Other groups within the fleet had subsidiary command structures, notably the artillery, headed by Alonso de Cespedes, *teniente general* (lieutenant-general) of artillery; and the hospital, commanded by the general administrator, Don Martín de Alarcón. More problematic were the groups outside the regular army and bureaucratic structures – the *aventureros* and *entretenidos*, whose high rank and considerable military experience created a potential conflict with commanders of regular troops, and the likelihood of insubordination. The king feared only

1. Thompson, 1976, esp. Chapters 2, 7.
2. Thompson, 1969; Mattingly, 1983, esp. 192–6.
3. AGS E.431 f.45; GA.221 f.158; GA.221 f.181.

220

the conflict between Medina Sidonia and Parma. He gave Santa Cruz and his successor command of the fleet until it joined Parma; subsequently, the two generals were to decide strategy jointly, and Parma would be sole commander of the invasion forces once on land. Santa Cruz almost resigned when he realized that the campaign in effect had joint command. Parma wanted full control too, but he was given control of the land forces only, which were structured as their military counterparts in the fleet. The king ordered them to obey or resign.[4] Since Parma was the most experienced soldier and held higher rank, and since the fleet had to be given a full command, Philip could see no other option. Nevertheless, he remained uneasy, conscious that division among the chief commanders might seriously impair the campaign.

M. J. Rodríguez-Salgado

back to guard the coast whilst the Armada was chased northwards, Seymour complained to Walsingham that Howard was jealously trying to deprive him of further honour in the campaign.

Like many commanders of the time, Howard used the council of war as a means of achieving some form of consensus among the leading officers of the fleet. The perilous decision to pursue the Armada north was taken at such a council, and a memorandum to this effect was signed by all present. Although Howard had high social rank and, theoretically, absolute powers of command, he wisely heeded good advice when it was offered, and managed to hold together the largest English fleet seen for decades.

Ian Friel

4. AGS E.165 f.29, E.594 f.2 in particular.

(ii) English Commanders

The command structure of the English fleet was rather fluid, and entirely dependent on what the commander-in-chief, Howard, lord high admiral of England, thought was appropriate at the time. His first vice-admiral was Lord Henry Seymour, in command of the force in the Narrow Seas guarding against an invasion attempt by Parma. When Sir Francis Drake was sent to Plymouth with a group of ships in May 1588, he did not have a formal rank, but was made a vice-admiral at the time Howard joined him there in June. Additional commanders were appointed after the battle off the Isle of Wight, when Howard split his fleet into four squadrons, one commanded by himself, the second by Drake, the third by John Hawkins and the fourth by Martin Frobisher. The knighting of the last two a couple of days later, whilst clearly a reward, may also have been intended to raise their social status to a level regarded as more appropriate for such commands.

The lord admiral could exercise little tactical control of his forces once battle was joined, because systems of signalling were almost non-existent. He could summon his chief officers to a conference on his flagship by putting out a 'flag of council', or he could order his fleet to follow his stern lantern at night, but once ships had sailed off on an operation, there was not much he could do to change their orders. Added to this were the problems of having senior commanders who were aggressive individualists of varying social degrees with a strong financial interest in the disposition of prizes. Frobisher accused Drake of trying to cheat others of prize money, and threatened his life; when Howard sensibly ordered Seymour

Command structure of the English fleet

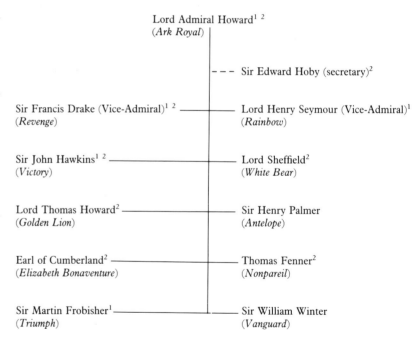

Note: Those listed above were members of the English fleet's Council of War.
Sir Roger Williams, the military commander, was appointed to the Council of War in June 1588, but soon returned to service on land.

1. squadron commander
2. present at the council of war on 10 August 1588

of Lepanto (see cat. no. **2.32**). Santa Cruz
was admiral of the Spanish forces engaged in
the conquest of Portugal and the Azores
(1580–83), winning the battle of São Miguel
in 1582 against a French force, and complet-
ing the campaign with the capture of
Terceira in the following year. He was
appointed captain-general of the Ocean Sea
in 1584, and was a strong proponent of an
expedition against England. Philip told him
to draw up an estimate for this: his initial

221

13.1
**The 'Burgundy Cross' armour of
Philip II**, 1551
Wolfgang Groschedel of Landshut
(d.1562)

Steel, with etched and gilded decoration;
velvet and leather backing on shield; steel,
wood and silk in saddle
suit: 1780 ht; shield: 550 dia.; saddle:
500×580×550; shaffron: 350×235×160
Valencia de Don Juan, 1898, 86–9;
Reitzenstein, 1954, 151
*Patrimonio Nacional. Real Armería de Madrid
(A263, A265, A269, A270)*

This field armour for man and horse, made
for Philip II, is decorated with etched and
gilt bands of which the central motif is the St
Andrew's cross of Burgundy, from which the
harness derives its name. The complete
armour includes spare shaffrons (headpieces
for the horse), a parade shield and elements
of a child's armour, as well as plates etched
with several different types of decoration

from which the patron was asked to select.
The Burgundian emblems allude to the
Order of the Golden Fleece. Groschedel, the
maker, is first recorded as one of the
'Almain' (German) armourers of Henry VIII
at Greenwich, and later produced many
important armours both for Philip II and the
Imperial court at Vienna.

13.2
**Don Alvaro de Bazán, 1st Marquis
of Santa Cruz (1526–88)**, ?c.1585–90
Spanish School

Oil on canvas
1246×900
Tenison, IV, 1933, II, 5, 5
La Marquesa de Santa Cruz

Don Alvaro de Bazán was the son of one of
Charles V's galley commanders, and gained
much early experience of seafaring and naval
command. He was put in charge of the
Neapolitan galley squadron by Philip II in
1568, and played a crucial part in the victory

plan called for a force of about 800 ships and
94,000 men, but by 1588 this had been
brought down to a more realistic level. He
organized the Armada which sailed in 1588,
although not without conflict between him
and Philip over finance and other matters.
His death in February 1588 was a great blow
to the Armada plans. This is the only known
early portrait of him (though the inscription
at the bottom is not contemporary) and may
have been painted shortly after the beginning
of the Portuguese campaign, or when he was
appointed captain-general. He is depicted in
full armour, holding a commander's baton.

13.3
**Don Alvaro de Bazán, 1st Marquis
of Santa Cruz (1526–88)**

Engraving
152×124
National Maritime Museum (P.70)

13.4

Don Alonso Pérez de Guzmán el Bueno, 7th Duke of Medina Sidonia (1550–1619)

Photograph of original portrait in possession of La Duquesa de Medina Sidonia
Inscribed *EL EXCELENTISS Sr DVQVE DE MEDINA CIDONIA D ALONSO PERES D G (VZM) AN EL BVENO E . . . NDA OR OESTES TVARIO*

Medina Sidonia was a member of one of the wealthiest and most powerful families in Spain. He was widely respected and known for his magnanimity and honesty. Contemporaries were not surprised when he was appointed to command the fleet, in succession to Santa Cruz.

Medina Sidonia maintained a formidable discipline in the Armada, concentrating on the prime objective, to link up with Parma, until circumstances made this impossible. His personal courage was considerable, and his flagship *San Martín* was often in the thick of the fighting. The failure of the Armada made him unpopular in Spain, but Philip II did not hold him to blame, and he went on to hold other high naval and military commands. Cat. no. **13.4** is a reproduction of the only known portrait of him, painted after 1610. He is shown wearing the insignia of the Order of the Golden Fleece.

13.5

Copy of the appointment of the Duke of Medina Sidonia as General of the Fleet and Army of the Ocean Sea, 21 March 1588

MS (4ff.)
312×212
AGS GA.221 f.158; Thompson, 1969, 197–216
Archivo General de Simancas, Valladolid (GA.222, f.13)

Medina Sidonia was appointed to command the Armada on 14 February. This and his captaincy of the coast of Andalusia brought him 1,000 *escudos* per month. There were many reasons for his appointment. He had considerable experience of fitting out New World fleets and their convoys, he had organized the military forces of Andalusia and had been involved in the preparations for the Armada since 1586. He also played a key role in the defence of Cadiz against the English in 1587. He was the first grandee of Spain; this ensured that he would be obeyed by the many high-status participants in the Armada. Additionally, he was the richest man in Castile and lent some 20,000 *escudos* for the campaign.

13.6

Cross of a Knight of Santiago de Compostela, from the *Girona*

Gold and enamel
44 lgth
Crédit Communal, 1985, 9.4
Ulster Museum, Belfast

This cross is in the form of the lily-sword of St James, patron of the Order of Santiago de Compostela. The owner was Don Alonso de Leiva, a former captain-general of the galleys of Naples and captain-general of the Milanese infantry and one of the leading commanders of the Armada, who drowned in the wreck of the *Girona*.

13.7

Salamander pendant from the *Girona*

Gold with rubies
42 lgth
Sténuit, 1974, 183; Crédit Communal, 1985, 9.1
Ulster Museum, Belfast

A gold pendant in the form of a salamander, with four legs, two wings and a curved tail. The surface detail is minutely delineated and the creature wears a gold collar. Its back is embellished with table-cut rubies, set in the

form of a cross, but only three of the original nine survive. On the underside of each wing is a little ring for attaching a chain, of which one link is left. The fitting from which it hung, now separated from the main body, was small and almost triangular, with a single ruby. From the base of the triangle hang small chains with alternate circular links of fine gold wire. It is possible that the pendant represents *Draco volans*, a flying lizard known from the East Indies and the Philippines. Renaissance jewellers frequently depicted exotic creatures with deliberate ambiguity. The gold of the pendant may be of either Old or New World origin and the rubies are most likely to have come from Burma. As a piece of considerable contemporary value, it is likely to have belonged to one of the *Girona*'s highest-ranking officers.

222

13.8
Cross of a Knight of the Hospital of St John of Jerusalem, from the *Girona*

Gold and enamel
60 lgth
Sténuit, 1974, 202; Crédit Communal, 1985, 9.2
Ulster Museum, Belfast

The surface of this 'Maltese' cross is keyed for enamel, and some traces of white enamel survive. The suspension-loop at the top of the cross is in the form of a double coil of gold wire, rather like a modern key-ring. Between the arms of the cross are small motifs similar to *fleur-de-lys* which Robert Sténuit suggests were a symbol of the Spinola family, and that the cross therefore belonged to Fabricio Spinola, captain of the *Girona*, but a similar motif commonly appears on other crosses of the order.

13.9
Cross of a Knight of the Order of Alcantara, from the *Girona*

Gold
28 lgth
Sténuit, 1974, 212; Crédit Communal, 1985, 9.3
Ulster Museum, Belfast

A small, oval, gold receptacle, one side consisting of a flat plate with a narrow pelletted rim and an engraving of a long-haired, bearded saint with a stylized pear tree and a waterfall, symbolic of St Julian, the patron saint of the Order of Alcantara. This side forms the lid of the little receptacle which may originally have contained a relic. The

body consists of an openwork cross fleury, each terminal ending in a *fleur-de-lys*. No traces of enamel survive. The owner of the cross has not been identified.

13.10
Chain from the *Girona*

Gold
1220 lgth
Sténuit, 1974, pl. 33; Crédit Communal, 1985, 9.5
Ulster Museum, Belfast

A plain, heavy gold chain consisting of 136 separate oval links, each some 13 mm long and made of gold wire about 2 mm thick. The joints are not soldered, and some are slightly open. Two complete chains like this were recovered from the *Girona* site, as well as portions and stray links of others. They were common symbols of wealth and status and had a practical function as well: the links could readily be detached to pay for goods or services.

13.11
Ring from the *Girona*

Gold
Inscribed *MADAME DE CHAMPAGNEY MDXXIIII*
27 dia.
Sténuit, 1974, 196–201; Crédit Communal, 1985, 9.12
Ulster Museum, Belfast

Heavy gold ring with a slightly crushed rectangular bezel, from which the stone is missing. The significance of the inscription was revealed by Robert Sténuit: the ring was an heirloom of the Perrenot family, made in 1524 to commemorate the birth of Jerome, son of Nicole Bonvalot, lady of the manor of Champagney, and Nicholas Perrenot. Their grandson, Jean-Tomas, was with Don Alonso de Leiva in the *Girona* and perished with him.

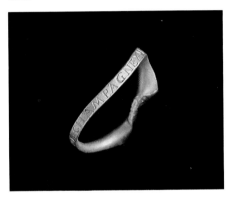

223

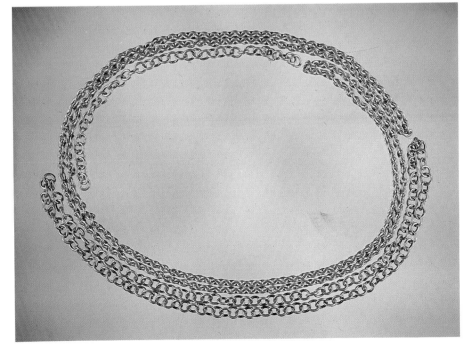

13.12
Ring from the *Girona*

Gold with diamonds
25 dia.
Sténuit, 1974; Crédit Communal, 1985, 9.14
Ulster Museum, Belfast

Gold ring with crushed bezel of four settings, one of which still contains a fragment of diamond; on each of the shoulders are three settings in line, one retaining a diamond. The diamonds may have come from India.

13.13
Cameo from the *Girona*

Gold with lapis lazuli and pearls
41 dia.
Sténuit, 1974, 193; Crédit Communal, 1985, 9.24
Ulster Museum, Belfast

This is one of a series of eleven (out of a presumed original twelve) gold frames, six of which retain lapis lazuli cameos. The top of each frame consists of a grotesque mask, supported by scrolls; on each shoulder is a small setting filled with green enamel. Originally each frame probably had four matched pearls, perforated and strung on a fine gold wire. The cameos themselves are backed by oval plates of gold sheet, held in place by triangular gold teeth, bent alternatively. There is no agreement as to whether the emperors depicted are Roman or Byzantine. The pearls could have come from the extensive pearl-fisheries in the Red Sea and Persian Gulf, or from the New World, where

pearls had been fished before the Spanish conquest. The lapis lazuli, on the other hand, almost certainly came from Afghanistan, where the deposits on the Kokcha River had been worked since prehistoric times.

13.14
Filigree from the *Girona*

Gold
20 dia.
Crédit Communal, 1985, 9.26
Ulster Museum, Belfast

A scalloped circle consisting of twelve separate segments of fine filigree work in twisted wire, stemming from a central circular opening. When found, the object was badly crushed.

13.15
Ring from the *Girona*

Gold
Inscribed *NO TENGO MAS QUE DARTE* (I have nothing more to give thee)
21 dia.
Sténuit, 1974; Crédit Communal, 1985, 9.11
Ulster Museum, Belfast

One terminal of the ring is in the form of a hand holding a heart, the other a buckle (it has been suggested that this represents the unfastened buckle of a chastity-belt). The ring was probably closed originally. It may have been the farewell present from a lady to her departing lover and is one of the most poignant and personal artefacts recovered from the Armada wreck, reminding us of the innumerable personal tragedies involved.

13.16–13.17
Plates from the *Santa María de la Rosa*

Pewter
Inscribed *MATUTE*
202 dia. each
Martin, 1975, 113; Crédit Communal, 1985, 8.9
Ulster Museum, Belfast

These two small plates proved that the wreck discovered in Blasket Sound, Co. Kerry, in 1968 was the *Santa María de la Rosa*, serving with the Guipuzcoan Squadron of the Armada and commanded by Martín de Villafranca, her civilian owner. Among the officers of the 225 soldiers embarked on her was Francisco Ruiz Matute, captain of infantry in the Sicilian *tercio* of Don Diego de Pimentel.

13.19
Charles Howard, Lord Effingham and Earl of Nottingham (1536–1624), *c.*1620
Daniel Mytens (1590–1648)

Oil on canvas
Inscribed *Carolus Baro Howard de Effingham Comes / Nottingham. Lummies Angliae Admirallus / ductor classium (anno) 1588 obyt anno 1624*
2515×1447
Millar, 1960, 7
National Maritime Museum (BHC2786)

This portrait of the lord high admiral was originally in the collection of Charles I and was presented to Greenwich Hospital in 1825 by George IV. Painted shortly after the sitter had retired from active service in 1618 (with the inscription presumably added after his death), it is a fine example of the style of formal full-length portraiture for which Mytens, a Netherlandish artist working in England, became renowned. Howard is portrayed wearing Garter robes and a gold embroidered skull-cap; beyond is represented the admiral's flagship in action, perhaps during the Armada campaign on which his fame largely rested. He had been appointed lord high admiral in 1585, and in December 1587 was designated 'lieutenant-general and commander-in-chief of the navy prepared to the seas against Spain'. The picture has been enlarged on the top and right-hand sides; this was probably undertaken later in the seventeenth century.

13.18
Fragment of the *San Mateo* pennant, 1588

Painted linen
3900×2940
Calvo Pérez and González, 1983, 81
Stedelijk Museum De Lakenhal, Leiden (3186)

The remaining part of a pennant, originally about twelve metres long. The complete flag was painted with a crucifixion and the text *EXURGE CHRISTE ET JUDICA CAUSAM TUAM* (Arise O Christ and judge thy cause) and the royal arms of Spain or Portugal. The *San Mateo* was crippled in battle by the ships of Lord Henry Seymour and Sir William Winter, captured by the Dutch on 9 August and towed into Flushing. She sank shortly afterwards, having been stripped of her ordnance and looted. The vice-admiral of Holland, Pieter van der Does, who led the Dutch attack, took the pennant home to Leiden, where it hung in the Pieterschurch for nearly 300 years.

226

13.20
Cast of the seal of Lord Howard of Effingham, 1585–1619

Resin
Inscribed *SIGIL D'CAROLI HOWARD BARON DE EFFINGHAM (PRAECL)ARI OR(DINIS GA)RTER (II.MIL)ITIS.MAG(NI) ADMIRALLI ANGLIAE.ET.CET: AO 1585*
122 dia.
Brindley, 1938, 29
National Maritime Museum

This depicts an Elizabethan two-decker with the shield of arms of Howard encircled by the Garter on the mainsail.

13.21
Sir Francis Drake (*c*.1540–96)
?Marcus Gheeraerts the Younger (1561–1635)

Oil on panel
Inscribed *SIC PARVIS MAGNA*, with arms of Drake; dated 1591
1168×915
Strong, 1963b, 154; Strong, I, 1969a, 71
National Maritime Museum (BHC2662)

The best-remembered of all English seafarers is portrayed here with an array of accessories denoting his contemporary fame and achievements: the sword refers to his service to his country, the globe to his circumnavigation of the world (1577–80) and the 'Drake pendant' and coat of arms reveal his prominent social and economic status. From relatively humble beginnings, and early experience at sea with John Lovell and John Hawkins (his cousin), Drake pursued an outstandingly successful career as a privateer. His voyage around the world, underwritten by the queen and involving a series of highly profitable raids on Spanish ships and ports, netted £160,000 for

the treasury, a healthy additional percentage for himself and a knighthood. His privateering venture to the West Indies (1585–6) was followed by his daring raid on Cadiz (see cat. no. **5.19**) in 1587; he captured the silver ship, the *San Felipe*, on his way home. In the Armada campaign Drake was a vice-admiral with his own force of thirty-nine ships. Subsequently, his joint leadership of the disastrous Portuguese expedition in 1589 brought him a court-martial and temporary disfavour until 1594. Another version of this portrait, formerly at Buckland Abbey, dates from that year. It has been suggested that the picture exhibited here may be an early copy of the 1594 work and not by Gheeraerts himself, but its given date (1591), inscription and handling seem quite consistent with the artist's own hand, and the possibility that it is in fact an earlier version by Gheeraerts cannot be discounted. By repute, it was formerly in the collection of a now-extinct branch of the Drake family.

13.22
Sir Francis Drake (*c*.1540–96)
Nicholas Hilliard (1547–1619) or studio

Miniature
Inscribed *AEtatis Suae 42, Ano Dni: 1581*
28 dia.
Auerbach, 1961, 44
National Portrait Gallery (4851)

A version of the larger oval portrait in the Kunsthistorisches Museum in Vienna. It was painted some years before the Armada campaign had helped to confirm Drake's status as a contemporary hero.

13.23
Replica of Drake's side drum
James Manning, *c*.1950

620×620
City of Plymouth Museums and Art Gallery (AR 1987.2)

The original drum (now at Buckland Abbey) may have accompanied Drake on his last voyage; probably English made, it is an early example of a type well known in the late sixteenth and early seventeenth centuries. The legend that the drum might be used to summon Drake in time of danger has not been traced before 1895.

227

13.24

228

13.24
Lord Henry Seymour (b.1540), Admiral of the Narrow Seas, 1588
Circle of Federico Zucchero
(1540/1–1609)

Oil on panel
690×630
*The Collection at Parham Park, West Sussex
(206)*

Lord Henry Seymour was appointed admiral of the Narrow Seas in 1588. His flagship was the *Rainbow*, one of the latest of the new low-built warships. A man of considerable sea experience, his principal job was to protect the coast and English shipping against raids by the Spanish forces in the Netherlands. Seymour's force joined the main fleet on its arrival on 6 August, but three days later, after the action at Gravelines, he was ordered back to patrol the straits in case Parma seized the opportunity to cross the Channel with his invading force.

13.25
Sir John Hawkins (1532–95), 1581
English school, 16th century

Oil on panel
Inscribed *AETATIS SVAE 44   ANN°.
DÑI. 1581   Sr JOHN HAWKINS*
620×520
Oppenheim, 1896, 397; Williamson, 1969, viii; Waters, 1975, 4, 9; Pollitt, 1980, 76; Quinn and Ryan, 1983, 28, 66
National Maritime Museum (BHC2755)

Sir John Hawkins was a key figure in the Elizabethan navy. He became treasurer of the navy in 1578, improving efficiency and making economies. He may also have contributed to improvements in English ship design. During the Armada campaign he commanded the *Victory*. His honesty as an administrator has been questioned, but he was effective, methodical, cautious, yet aggressive – a 'rough masterful man'. The sash around the sitter's neck has a signet of office.

13.26
Sir Richard Hawkins (1562–1622),
c.1590
English school, 16th century

Oil on panel
Inscribed *VNDIS. ARVNDO VIRES.
REPARAT./COEDENS. Q̄. FOVETVR/
FVNDITVS.AT. RVPES. E/
SCOPVLOSA. RVIT*
599×394
Hawkins, 1622, xxi; Hawkins, 1888, 137;
Laughton, I, 1981, 16
National Maritime Museum (BHC4186)

This portrait is thought to be the only surviving likeness of Sir Richard, son of Sir John Hawkins. He was the commander of the *Swallow* during the Armada campaign, a ship appointed to his father's squadron. Later he captained the *Dainty* on Sir John's expedition to the Azores in 1590, and subsequently embarked on an ambitious voyage against the world-wide interests of the Spanish Empire. His published account of his early career is an important source for naval history. The precise meaning of the picture's background vignette and inscription (The reed recovers strength amidst the waves, and by yielding grows strong; but the rugged cliff perishes utterly) is unclear – although of apparent general relevance to a naval commander.

13.27
Sir Martin Frobisher (*c*.1537–94), 1577

Cornelius Ketel (1548–1616)

Oil on canvas
Inscribed *A⁰ DNI 1577 / AETATIS SVAE / CK. F* (plus a later inscription)
2100×990
Cust, 1912, 88–94; Poole, I, 1912, 20;
Strong, I, 1969a, 154; Waterhouse, 1978, 25
The Curators of the Bodleian Library, Oxford

This striking portrait was painted on Frobisher's return in 1577 from the second of his three Arctic voyages; it is one of a series commissioned by the Cathay Company. Full-length portraits were still rare in English painting during the 1570s, though they became increasingly popular thereafter. Frobisher is portrayed here wearing a sailor's cord round his neck, with attached whistle (later known as a boatswain's call), used for conveying orders at sea. He holds a wheel-lock pistol.

Frobisher was vice-admiral during Drake's expedition of 1585–6 and took a prominent part in the Armada campaign as captain of the *Triumph*. He was knighted by the lord admiral on board the flagship.

13.29
Charles Blount, Earl of Devonshire (1563–1606)
Nicholas Hilliard (1547–1619)

Miniature
Inscribed *Amor Amoris Premium. Ano Dni 1587*
51×38
Auerbach, 1961, 71
Lent privately

One of the queen's favourites, Blount served in the Netherlands, the Armada campaign and Brittany. This is one of Hilliard's finest portraits, notable for the fine rendering of armour and lace.

231

13.28
George Clifford, 3rd Earl of Cumberland (1558–1605), *c.*1590
Nicholas Hilliard (1547–1619)

Watercolour on vellum
255×180
Strong, 1977, 152
National Maritime Museum (10.1605)

Cumberland commanded the *Elizabeth Bonaventure* against the Armada. After the action off Gravelines, he brought news of the victory to the camp at Tilbury. He was a courtier, gambler and privateer, as well as a mathematician and a navigator. He lost his inherited wealth financing his many eventful but unprofitable expeditions against the bullion fleet. Hilliard's famous miniature portrays him as Queen's Champion and Knight of Pendragon Castle at the Accession Day tournament in 1590.

14.1 The English and Spanish fleets engaged, English school, 16th century

14. The Battle at Sea

September 1587 to 30 July 1588

Philip II issued detailed orders for the invasion of England to the Marquis of Santa Cruz and the Duke of Parma in September 1587. He hoped that the fleet would sail that October, but delays kept it at Lisbon into the New Year, and the preparations suffered a heavy blow when Santa Cruz died on 9 February. Medina Sidonia was appointed to succeed him.

The Duke of Medina Sidonia's counterpart, Lord Howard of Effingham, had been put in command of the queen's 'whole fleet and army at sea . . . fitted forth against the Spaniards and their allies', at the end of 1587. The English fleet was disposed in two groups by early June: a force of about ninety ships under Howard and Drake at Plymouth, and Seymour's thirty or so ships stationed in the Downs. The vessels at Plymouth were to intercept the Armada or, as Drake and Howard proposed, to attack it on the Spanish coast, whilst the ships in the Narrow Seas were to prevent an invasion attempt by Parma from the Low Countries.

In the meantime, preparations for the Armada continued. The fleet moved down the Tagus from Lisbon to Belem on 9 May, but strong winds prevented it from sailing until 30 May (see cat. no. **14.45**). Adverse winds likewise made the journey up the coast very slow: concern over depleted victuals and necessary repairs led to a decision to put into La Coruña on 19 June. That night a storm scattered the fleet, and a month was to pass before the Armada was revictualled and repaired, and the missing ships returned. Some of the Spanish vessels had got as far as the Scilly Islands and the Cornish coast. At the end of June, Howard began to receive ominous reports from English ships of encounters with hostile ships bearing red crosses on their sails.

But soon there was news that the Armada was in a bad way, dispersed in the northern Spanish ports, and it was decided to make an attack, with the aim of destroying the Spanish fleet. The English fleet left Plymouth on 18 July, but a south-west wind prevented it from reaching Spain, and the force was back in port on 22 July. Howard and his commanders knew that a south-west wind could bring the Armada, and so the English ships were revictualled, awaiting word from the scout vessels that Howard had left out in the Channel. That same day, a fleet of 138 ships, with over 24,000 men, sailed out from La Coruña.

The Armada's passage to the Channel was marred by a mixture of calm and bad weather. A gale dispersed some ships on 27 July, and the four galleys, together with the *capitana* of the Biscayan squadron, the *Santa Ana*, were forced to make for the French coast. The galley flagship was wrecked and none of

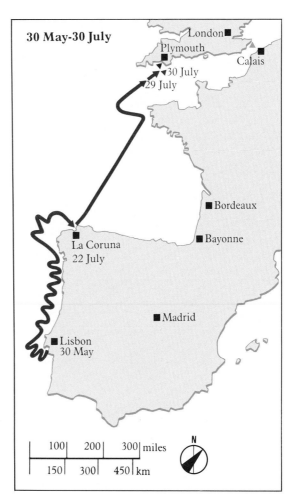

the other vessels took any further part in the campaign.

The Armada was rejoined by the rest of the missing ships off the Lizard, which was sighted at 4 p.m. on 29 July. The Spanish were in their turn spotted by one of Howard's scouts, the *Golden Hind*, which returned to Plymouth with the news. By dint of skilled seamanship, Howard, Drake and their captains were able to warp fifty-four ships out of harbour. That is, the ships' boats were used to take their anchors forward, drop them, and the vessels pulled forward on the anchor cables. Tidal conditions would not have made this possible until after 9 p.m., but by 3 p.m. the following afternoon Howard's force had reached the Eddystone Rock and was in sight of the Armada.

That Saturday, 30 July, with beacons flaring on the Cornish coast, the Armada was put in battle order. The Levant Squadron and the galleasses of Hugo de Moncada were placed in the vanguard, with Medina Sidonia commanding the main body, the

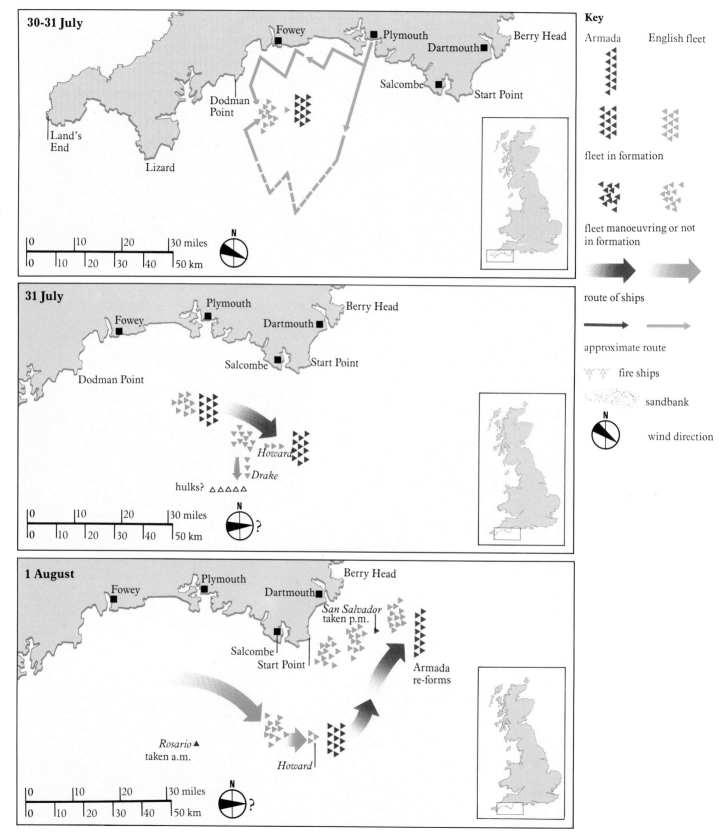

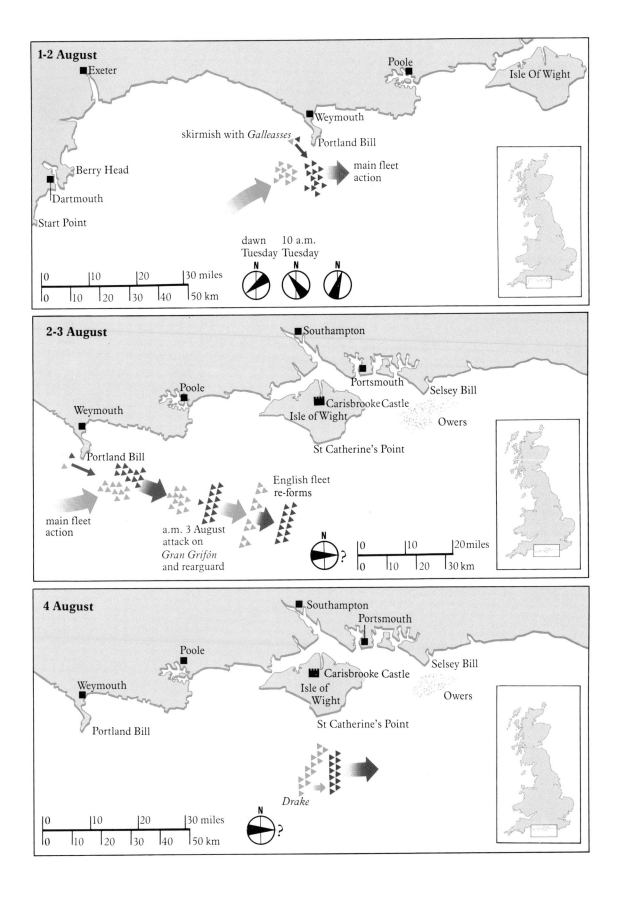

1-2 August

Exeter
Poole
Isle Of Wight
Weymouth
skirmish with *Galleasses*
Portland Bill
main fleet action
Berry Head
Dartmouth
Start Point

dawn Tuesday
10 a.m. Tuesday

0   10   20   30 miles
0   10   20   30   40   50 km

2-3 August

Southampton
Portsmouth
Selsey Bill
Carisbrooke Castle
Isle of Wight
Owers
Poole
Weymouth
St Catherine's Point
Portland Bill
English fleet re-forms
main fleet action
a.m. 3 August attack on *Gran Grifón* and rearguard

0   10   20 miles
0   10   20   30 km

4 August

Southampton
Portsmouth
Carisbrooke Castle
Selsey Bill
Poole
Isle of Wight
Owers
Weymouth
St Catherine's Point
Portland Bill
Drake

0   10   20   30 miles
0   10   20   30   40   50 km

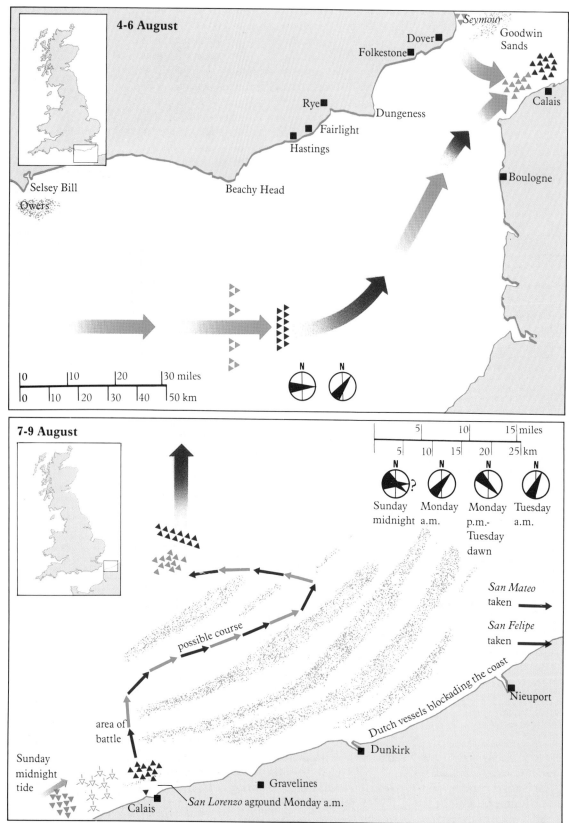

4-6 August

Seymour

Dover

Folkestone

Goodwin
Sands

Calais

Rye

Dungeness

Fairlight

Hastings

Beachy Head

Boulogne

Selsey Bill

Owers

| 0 | | 10 | | 20 | | 30 miles |
| 0 | 10 | 20 | 30 | 40 | | 50 km |

N   N

7-9 August

| | | 5 | | 10 | | 15 | miles |
| | 5 | 10 | 15 | 20 | 25 | km |

N   N   N   N

?

Sunday
midnight

Monday
a.m.

Monday
p.m.-
Tuesday
dawn

Tuesday
a.m.

San Mateo
taken

San Felipe
taken

possible course

Dutch vessels blockading the coast

Nieuport

area of
battle

Dunkirk

Sunday
midnight
tide

Gravelines

San Lorenzo aground Monday a.m.

Calais

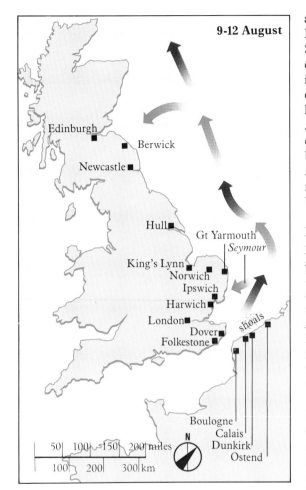

9-12 August

Edinburgh
Berwick
Newcastle
Hull
Gt Yarmouth
Seymour
King's Lynn
Norwich
Ipswich
Harwich
London
Dover
Folkestone
shoals
Boulogne
Calais
Dunkirk
Ostend

50 100 150 200 miles
100 200 300 km
N

Andalusian Squadron (under Don Pedro de Valdés) and the Guipuzcoan Squadron (under Don Miguel de Oquendo) being disposed on either wing. The hulks were put in the centre and a rearguard was established under the command of Juan Martínez de Recalde. Drizzle and mist made it impossible for the Spanish to count the number of English ships, but for the moment the west-south-westerly wind still kept them to windward of their opponents.

Around midnight a scouting *zabra* returned to Medina Sidonia with four captured Falmouth fishermen and the first direct intelligence of the English fleet. He learnt that his adversaries were commanded by Howard and Drake.

Sunday, 31 July

Wind and weather: wind begins to change about 2 a.m., and is west-north-west by early morning; wind and sea rise during the day, and the sea becomes rough.

The change in the wind enabled Howard's and Drake's ships to get the weather gage of the Armada

and come in astern of it. However, a further eleven English ships had been late getting out of Plymouth Sound, and it is possible that the first shots of the campaign were exchanged as these vessels tacked inshore of the Spanish. According to Howard, the opening shot was fired by his pinnace *Disdain*, at what he thought was the enemy flagship (in fact it was Alonso de Leiva's *Rata Encoronada*). This ceremonial gesture of defiance does not seem to have been noticed by the Spanish, but about this time Medina Sidonia hoisted the royal banner on the mainmast of his flagship *San Martín*, to signify that battle had begun.

The skirmish off Plymouth lasted about four hours. Howard's *Ark Royal* attacked the *Rata*, but pulled back when other Spanish ships came to her aid. Drake (*Revenge*), Hawkins (*Victory*) and Frobisher (*Triumph*) assailed the rearguard, but the Armada continued its advance. The only ship which stayed to fight them was Recalde's *San Juan de Portugal*, which withstood their attack for over an hour, losing some men and suffering damage to her foremast. The English withdrew when the *Gran Grin*, the galleon *San Juan* and the *San Mateo* sailed up to support her. Fighting stopped at about 1 p.m.

Medina Sidonia was now convinced that the English did not want to fight boarding actions, but only to hamper their progress, and so he ordered the Armada to advance. The battle was inconclusive, but it left both sides with strong impressions of the qualities of their enemies. The Spanish found the English ships heavily armed, swift and highly manoeuvrable: they were 'so well handled that they did what they wanted with them'. The English were impressed by the size and firepower of the Spanish ships, and the determination of their crews. Drake sent a warning letter to Seymour, in which he remarked: 'we perceive they are determined to sell their lives with blows' (see cat. no. **14.46**).

Accidents befell two of the Armada ships later in the day. About 5 p.m., Valdés's flagship, *Nuestra Señora del Rosario*, collided with the *Santa Catalina*: as a result, she lost her bowsprit and the foremast later fell against the main yard. Attempts to put a tow-line aboard her were thwarted by the rising seas, and Medina Sidonia's chief adviser, Don Diego Flores de Valdés, urged that the fleet should continue on its way. Vessels could be left behind to either tow the *Rosario* or to take off her men and money if she got into serious difficulties (see cat. no. **15.5**).

As it got dark and the weather worsened, the *Rosario* became separated from her supporting ships. The *Margaret and John* of London, a ship in Howard's force, seems to have found her about this

237

time. The officers of the English ship later claimed that the *Rosario* was showing no lights and gave little sign of life or fight. They left her at midnight, fearing punishment for deserting the fleet, but put in a claim for this rich prize to Howard the following morning. They must have been dismayed to learn that in the interim she had been taken by Drake.

The second accident occurred shortly after the first, when a barrel of gunpowder exploded on the Guipuzcoan ship *San Salvador*, blowing up her decks and stern and wrecking the steering gear. The resulting fire was eventually brought under control, and the ship was taken into the fleet for the night by two galleasses.

After the morning's skirmish, Howard had decided to refrain from further fighting until he had been joined by the forty or so ships still left in Plymouth. Drake was appointed to track the Armada through the night, his stern lantern acting as a marker to the rest of the English fleet. However, he broke off the pursuit to investigate some hulks sighted to the south, or so he claimed. His real reason was almost certainly a desire to make the *Rosario* his prize, which he did the next day. It was left to the *Ark Royal*, with the *Bear* and *Mary Rose* astern, to follow the Armada closely through the night. The remainder of the English fleet, uncertain of who to follow, hung back.

Monday, 1 August
Wind and weather: apparently a continuing west wind, perhaps light to moderate; weather becomes calm at night.

By dawn the Armada was off Berry Head, with the English fleet far behind. Howard was forced to wait for his ships to rejoin him: Drake had done so by the evening, but some ships did not appear until the following day. An urgent message was sent to Portsmouth for all of the ships in that port to join Howard without delay.

That morning Medina Sidonia completed reforming the Armada's defensive order, creating a formation that to the English resembled a crescent. Alonso de Leiva and forty-three of the best ships, including three galleasses, the galleons *San Mateo*, *San Luis*, *Florencia* and *Santiago*, passed from the van to the rear (the right wing), ready to confront the enemy. Medina Sidonia took direct charge of the rest of the fleet, now called the vanguard. Apart from councils of war, the main method of transmitting orders around the fleet was by means of sergeants-major in swift pinnaces. These men, supported by soldiers and even a hangman, took written orders to captains which informed them they would be hanged if their ships left their stations.

Valdés's *Rosario* surrendered to Drake in the morning. Although in chaotic order, the ship was not seriously damaged and this rich prize, still containing the royal money-chest, capitulated without a shot. The second prize taken that day was the crippled *San Salvador*, abandoned after her surviving crew and some of the stores had been taken off. She was in far worse condition than the *Rosario*, and filled with the stench of burned corpses. These two were the only ships to be captured by the English, and both were taken into port, the *Rosario* to Dartmouth and the *San Salvador* to Weymouth.

Medina Sidonia sent an ensign, Juan Gil, to Parma with news of their situation and an urgent request for pilots to take the Armada up the Channel and guide them along the Flemish coast, if the wind drove them in that direction. He estimated that the English fleet was already more than one hundred strong.

Tuesday, 2 August
Wind and weather: light north-east to easterly wind springs up at dawn, later veering to south-east and then south-south-west, the change to a southerly direction occurring about 10 a.m.

At dawn the Armada was to the north of the English, near Portland Bill, and had the weather gage. Both fleets turned east, the English vainly attempting to get to windward and the Spanish heading inshore to maintain their advantage. The English manoeuvres apparently caused Medina Sidonia to decide on an attack, for the Armada now came to leeward, offering battle (although the Spanish may have been forced south by the strong Portland Race). Bertendona, in the *Regazona*, attacked the *Ark Royal* and tried to board her, but the *Ark* went to leeward and out to sea. The *Ark*, with the *Nonpareil*, *Elizabeth Jonas* and *Victory*, then faced the *Regazona*, which was now supported by the *San Mateo*, *Rata Encoronada* and *San Juan de Sicilia*, but the Spanish fell astern of the *Nonpareil*, which was the sternmost English ship.

In the meantime, another battle had developed in the lee of Portland Bill. The *Triumph*, with the *Merchant Royal*, *Centurion*, *Margaret and John*, *Mary Rose* and *Golden Lion*, had got too far to leeward and were separated from the main fleet. The galleasses attacked them and 'assaulted them sharply' for about an hour and a half. When the wind veered south, Howard was able to send help to the *Triumph* and the other ships. The *Ark* joined in, but so also did Medina Sidonia's *San Martín* and half a dozen or more other Spanish ships, including the *Trinidad Valencera*. The *San Martín* was actually isolated and attacked for more than an hour by the *Ark* and other English vessels before she received any help. Medina Sidonia made an attempt to board, which Howard avoided and answered with close-range shot. The English ships were able to turn faster than the Spanish vessels and had a much higher rate of fire, but despite the expenditure of a great deal of shot, they caused little real damage to the enemy. As the shifting of the wind to south-south-west eventually gave the English the weather gage, the Spanish broke off the fight and re-formed.

The high rate of fire was costly for both sides. Howard sent orders to the coast for powder and shot to be taken out of the two prizes and quickly brought to the fleet. That same day Seymour, anchored off Dover, received Drake's warning letter and passed it on to the Privy Council with a request for fresh supplies of powder, shot and victuals for his force, mentioning that he had requested reinforcements from the fleets of Holland and Zeeland. He believed, as did some other English commanders, that the Armada's objective was the Isle of Wight.

Wednesday, 3 August
Wind and weather: calm, with some light wind.

This day the fleets were off the Isle of Wight. Medina Sidonia divided the forty-three ships of the rearguard between Recalde and Leiva. In the morning the English attacked the hulk *Gran Grifón*, which was straggling behind, causing considerable damage. English sources do not mention the action, which lasted about two hours, but the English vessels appear to have been led by the *Revenge*. The *Gran Grifón* was defended by the Spanish rearguard and eventually towed back into the formation. The English finally broke off the action when the main enemy force threatened to become involved.

Small ships and pinnaces were sent from the English fleet to the shore to get more munitions. A council of war was held by Howard, and it was decided to divide the fleet into four squadrons, under the Lord Admiral, Drake, Hawkins and Frobisher. The inspiration for this change probably came from the superb organizational discipline displayed by the enemy, and it was aimed at making the English fleet more manageable. In the afternoon Howard ordered that six merchant ships from each squadron were to make simultaneous attacks on the Armada that night, to keep the Spanish awake, but the weather was so calm that nothing could be done.

Thursday, 4 August
Wind and weather: calm, with light winds, probably from the west.

Stragglers from the Armada again tempted the English to attack. Hawkins used boats to tow his squadron towards the isolated ships, the hulk *Santa Ana* and the Portuguese galleon *San Luis*, but the boats were beaten off by musket shot. Three galleasses, followed by the *Rata* and the *San Juan de Sicilia*, came to help the stragglers, whilst the *Ark* and *Golden Lion* were towed into battle against the galleasses by their own longboats. Howard thought that he had inflicted a shattering defeat on the galleasses in the action that followed, neutralizing them as fighting units, but the damage caused seems to have been superficial.

Meanwhile, as the wind rose slightly, Frobisher's squadron went into action against the *San Martín*, which had again become isolated. The heavy guns of the English seriously damaged the Spanish flagship, twice holing her below the water-line, but other Spanish ships arrived to shield her before any further harm could be done. All of the English ships bar Frobisher's *Triumph* escaped to leeward. The Spanish thought that he had a damaged rudder, but it is possible he was trying to use his knowledge of the tidal race to either trap the Spanish galleasses or, more likely, to flee from them. The Spanish attempted to board him, but the wind got up and he sailed off. The two fastest galleons in the Armada were sent in pursuit, but even they were too slow to catch the *Triumph*.

As this action was in progress, Drake was active on the seaward wing of the Armada, trying to force the Spanish ships northwards so that the tide would carry them on to the Owers, where many would have been lost. However, by this time Medina Sidonia, seeing the danger and deciding that it was useless trying to force the English to come to close quarters, gave the signal to disengage and re-form.

Like the previous encounters, this battle was not decisive, and its only serious effect was to make both fleets use up large amounts of ammunition. Medina Sidonia sent to Parma for fresh supplies, whilst Howard decided not to risk further action until he had been joined by Seymour's squadron.

Friday, 5 August
Wind and weather: wind drops before dawn, and it is not until sunset that a light wind springs up, probably from the west.

Neither fleet made much progress this day. Medina Sidonia sent another messenger to Parma, repeating his request for pilots and ammunition, and

239

also asking for forty to fifty *filibotes* or other small, light craft. His plan was to use these vessels to close with the English and engage them long enough to allow the large ships of the Armada to come up (see cat. no. **14.47**). Then boarding – and victory – would be possible. He also hoped that Parma was ready to sail from Dunkirk, but suspected that he was not.

Howard's main activity was to knight a number of men, including Hawkins and Frobisher, as a reward for their services.

As the sun set, a light wind sprang up, and the Armada made for Calais, followed by the English.

Saturday, 6 August
Wind and weather: south-westerly wind, heavy showers and poor visibility.

The two fleets were very close, but avoided conflict and there were no stragglers. The Armada sighted the French coast, near Boulogne, at 10 a.m. and continued towards Calais, anchoring there at 7 p.m. Medina Sidonia called a council of war to discuss what to do next. The pilots were adamant that if they continued to advance it was likely that the winds would carry them up into the North Sea. It would be difficult to beat back and join Parma once they were on this course. The Calais anchorage was dangerous and exposed, but Medina Sidonia decided to wait there for Parma, who should have been ready to sail from Dunkirk. Captain Pedro de Heredia was sent to M. Gourdan, the governor of Calais, to assure him that the intentions of the Spanish were friendly. Meanwhile, the duke's own secretary, Jeronimo de Arceo, was sent to Parma, repeating the urgent request for small craft.

The English fleet anchored about the same time as the Armada, off Calais Cliffs. It was joined a while later by Seymour's squadron, bringing the total number of English ships to about 140. It is a measure of how important Howard considered the danger from the Armada that he should have called Seymour from his duties patrolling against a crossing by Parma. Unbeknownst to the English, Justin of Nassau had left Flushing with a large number of rebel ships, and was preventing Parma from leaving the canals.

Howard sent for Sir William Winter, who was commanding the *Vanguard* in Seymour's squadron, to discuss the best way to deal with the Armada. By his own account, Winter suggested an attack with fireships. Howard was much taken with this, and said that it would be put in hand at a council of war (see cat. no. **14.48**).

Sunday, 7 August
Wind and weather: calm until 5 a.m., wind freshening with showers, probably from the south-west or south-south-west, perhaps later veering to the west and north-west.

Medina Sidonia received some bad news: Parma was still at Bruges, and had not started to embark men or munitions. This was followed by a despondent note from Arceo which said that Parma would not be able to sail for another fortnight. Medina Sidonia decided to stay put, sending Don Jorge Manrique to Parma that evening with a message to make all haste.

During the day, the purveyor-general, Bernabe de Pedroso, and the paymaster, Juan de Huerta, were sent to buy cheese, vegetables and medicines in Calais, and there they witnessed the fireship attack.

The fireship attack had been agreed upon at a council of war on the *Ark Royal* early that morning, and Sir Henry Palmer was sent to Dover to get suitable vessels and flammable materials. It was soon realized that he would not be able to return that night and, accordingly, eight privately owned ships already in the fleet were chosen for the attack. These vessels ranged from ninety to 200 tons, and were made ready for midnight, with their guns loaded and ready to go off as they bore down on the Spanish. The ships were to be set on fire after they had left the fleet, and then abandoned by their crews. However, it seems that at least two were lit before they were properly under way, for the Spanish saw two fires in the English fleet and so gained some advance warning.

The fireships had the wind with them, together with the North Sea current and the flood-tide, the tidal streams amounting to about three knots. The Spanish, fearing that these were floating bombs, sent out boats to deflect them, and at least two seem to have been successfully grappled and towed away. The others continued their progress towards the closely anchored Armada, but Medina Sidonia had time to send trusted men round the fleet, ordering it to sail out of danger and then resume battle positions in the same area as soon as possible. It is commonly asserted that the Spanish panicked and fled, but this is not borne out by the Spanish accounts, or the fact that this complicated and dangerous night-time manoeuvre resulted in only one collision, in which the galleass flagship *San Lorenzo* broke its rudder and made for Calais. The rest of the fleet was driven towards Dunkirk.

The fireship attack was the single most effective tactical device used by the English. It drove the Armada from its only anchorage, temporarily dispersed it and caused it to lose many irreplaceable anchors and cables. The fleet was not otherwise damaged by the action, but as the pilots had predicted, it was never able to return to Calais. The fighting now began to move northwards, away from the possibility of a link-up with Parma.

Monday, 8 August

Wind and weather: English reports of the wind in the morning being from the south-south-west; eventually freshens from the north-west; by nightfall the sea was very rough, with a west-north-westerly wind.

At dawn, Medina Sidonia found himself with only a few ships close by – Oquendo in the *San Marcos*, Recalde in the *San Juan Bautista*, and the *San Mateo* a little further off. The English fleet moved in for the attack, and Medina Sidonia fired his guns to call the Armada to battle, but they were too far off to obey immediately. The battle began between 7 and 9 a.m., with at first a mere five Spanish ships facing the English force. The fighting in this encounter, now known as the battle of Gravelines, lasted until late afternoon or early evening, the longest and bloodiest action of the campaign.

The galleass *San Lorenzo* had, in the meantime, grounded on a sandbank just off Calais, and it is a mark of the fear that these vessels inspired in the English that Howard decided to give this his immediate personal attention, sending the other squadrons after the main Spanish fleet. The shoals prevented the English warships from coming in close, so a boarding action was begun using ships' boats. Fierce fighting ensued for some time, but eventually the commander of the galleass squadron, Don Hugo de Moncada, was shot through the head by a musket and killed. At this most of the defenders fled to the shore, leaving the English to pillage the galleass. M. Gourdan, the governor of Calais, allowed the pillage to continue, despite the entreaties of Bernabe de Pedroso, who was still on land. However, he did allow Pedroso to collect the 150 or so soldiers who had escaped from the galleass, and drove the English off with cannon shot to prevent them from taking away the galleass and its ordnance. The galleass was then looted by the French, but eventually handed back to the Spanish, who recovered more than fifty guns from her (of which thirty-six were on carriages), together with food, ammunition and other stores. The survivors and stores were sent to join Parma, but the galleass, stuck fast on the sand, was left to rot.

It is very difficult to follow the course of the battle of Gravelines in detail, because the surviving accounts are fragmentary and it is unlikely that even the participants had a very clear idea of what was happening. Howard had been due to 'give the first

charge' on the enemy, and Drake the second, but Howard's preoccupation with the galleass meant that the honour fell to Drake. His first target was the flagship *San Martín*.

By his own account, Medina Sidonia decided to face the English with his meagre force because he was afraid that, unless he did so, the rest of the Armada would be driven on to the dangerous sandbanks off nearby Dunkirk. He aimed to sacrifice his own ship and the few galleons at hand in order to save the main fleet. The *San Martín* withstood several hours of close-range fighting: Drake's *Revenge* opened fire at arquebus range, and was followed in by the *Triumph*, *Victory* and other ships. One of the officers in the *San Martín* reckoned that the ship was hit more than 200 times by cannon shot, and sustained considerable damage to both the hull and rigging. Other Spanish ships sailed in to join the fight, and somehow the Armada was able to regain its defensive formation. According to Sir William Winter, 'they went into a proportion of a half moon', with sixteen vessels in each wing, and the flagship and main fleet in the centre. The galleass, the Portuguese 'armados . . . and other good ships' were disposed in the wings.

The English, as ever, avoided being boarded by the Spanish, but came in very close to use their heavy guns and small arms to best effect. Sir William Winter, in the *Vanguard*, attacked the right wing of the Armada, firing at no more that 120 paces, and was followed by other English ships. He said that the ships in the wing tried to retreat into the centre, four of them colliding in the process. One managed to escape, but the others were then lost to view.

No casualty figures are known, but it is likely that the slaughter on the Spanish side was considerable, both from cannon and musket fire. By the closing stages of the battle, some of the Armada's first-line fighting ships were so low on cannon shot that they could only reply to English attacks with small-arms fire. The Portuguese galleons *San Luis*, *San Felipe* and *San Mateo* were unfit for further service, and the latter two failed to keep up with the fleet. They were driven inshore and taken by the Dutch, as was a pinnace called the *San Antonio*. One other known loss was the Biscayan ship *Maria Juan*, which foundered in heavy seas with the loss of most of her crew. In the confused conditions that prevailed, other ships may also have sunk: the English claimed to have sunk three and driven others ashore.

After the fleets had disengaged, Medina Sidonia decided to fight once again. His overriding concern was still to meet with Parma, and he knew that the price of maintaining his position off the

Flemish coast would be a further encounter with the English. However, the English were very low on ammunition (Winter, for example, reckoned to have fired 500 demi-cannon, culverin and demi-culverin shot that day), and not able to fight. By the evening, a hard north-westerly wind was blowing the Armada towards the land, and Medina Sidonia's pilots told him that the only way to save the fleet from the shoals was to head up into the North Sea. They passed between Dover and Calais but even so Medina Sidonia held back, still hoping for contact with Parma.

The English reviewed the events of the day with some satisfaction, although their crews and munitions were close to exhaustion. The Armada appeared to have sustained considerable damage, and was in danger of wreck on the shoals. Yet, they maintained their order and still seemed, as Howard put it 'wonderful great and strong'.

Tuesday, 9 August

Wind and weather: strong north-westerly wind until dawn, then abating; wind changes to the south-west and then to a strong south-south-westerly.

Through the night and early morning, the Armada was driven closer to the sandbanks. The English were very close behind the rearguard, consisting of the *San Martín*, five other ships and the three galleasses. Medina Sidonia ordered the fleet into line as he turned with the rearguard, proposing to fight the English. He sent out pilots to order the ships to keep close to the wind because of the danger of the shoals, but this same danger kept the English back, and they did not fight. Wind and tide were taking the Armada inexorably towards the sandbanks.

Disaster seemed inevitable for the Spanish when, with the lead lines registering a mere six and a half fathoms of water, the wind changed to west-south-west, pushing the Armada away from the shore. Medina Sidonia held a council of war which determined that they would return to Calais if the weather allowed, but recognized that on their present course northwards they would have to go around Scotland and Ireland in order to reach La Coruña. Medina Sidonia ordered a redistribution of bread and water, and noted that they were short of all other victuals and munitions. Ahead lay a journey of 750 leagues through rough and unknown waters, in battered ships.

Howard also held a council of war, which also came to a perilous decision: to pursue the enemy as far north as the Firth of Forth, despite their own 'extreme scarcity' of victuals and ammunition. The danger was increased by the necessity of sending Seymour's squadron back to the Narrow Seas to guard against the possibility of a crossing by Parma.

Wednesday, 10 August

Wind and weather: strong south-westerly winds and heavy seas, with the wind abating in the evening.

The pursuit continued. As the wind lessened the English gained rapidly on the Armada. Medina Sidonia expected a fight and signalled to his ships to heave to and wait for the rearguard, which consisted of a few ships under Recalde. This deterred the English, who shortened sail: lacking ammunition they were only able, as Howard termed it, to put 'a brag countenance' on their pursuit.

Thursday, 11 August

Wind and weather: strong south-westerly wind.

Medina Sidonia ordered the execution of Don Cristóbal de Avila, captain of the hulk *Santa Barbara*, and some other captains were sentenced to the galleys on charges of cowardice or disobedience.

The English again closed with the Armada, and the rearguard hove to and waited for them: as before, there was no battle.

Friday, 12 August

Wind and weather: south to south-westerly wind.

The fleets came close at dawn, and the Armada was reported to be in good order, but still no fighting took place. At about 56°N, the English broke off and made for the Firth of Forth, hoping to get fresh supplies of victuals and ammunition. Howard sent some pinnaces after the Armada to ensure that they continued northwards, and the English fleet headed for home. Over the next few days the ships put into Great Yarmouth, Harwich and the Downs. Although no one could yet be wholly certain of it, the Armada campaign was over.

M. J. Rodríguez-Salgado and Ian Friel

A note on sources
Primary: AGS E.165, f.280; E.431, f.47; E.594, ff.114–18, 121–2, 131, 171, 177, 182; GA.221, f.190; GA.225, f.39; GA.226, ff.8, 14, 16, 104; GA.227, ff.45, 47, 157; GA.244, f.256; GA.246, ff.156, 160, 295.
Secondary: CSPD, 1581–90; Duro, I and II, 1884–5; Herrera Oria, 1946; Waters, 1975; Douglas, Lamb and Loader, 1978; Douglas and Loader, 1979; Laughton, I and II, 1981; Mattingly, 1983. In addition, various Admiralty pilot books, tide tables and charts have been consulted for the Channel and North Sea areas.

14.1
The English and Spanish fleets engaged, 1588
English school, 16th century

Oil on panel
1118×1435
National Maritime Museum (BHC0262)

Possibly conceived as a design for a tapestry, the picture is datable to the years immediately following the event. No other contemporary image of the Armada conveys a comparable sense of the drama and colour occasioned by the confrontation between two powerful European navies. If the action depicted was meant to represent any one part of the campaign, then it must be the battle of Gravelines, the only point at which large numbers of ships from both sides were engaged in sustained conflict. However, the emblematic foreground arrangement of a Spanish galleass flanked by two English warships suggests that the picture was intended primarily as a symbol of the Armada campaign as a whole. But it is a symbol edged with satire. Aboard the galleass is a jester in company with a number of figures (many portrayed as sinister zealots) led by a preaching monk, rendering her a 'ship of fools'; she flies the papal banner. Heightening the effect of this quietly humorous anti-Catholic invective is a representation of a distraught Spaniard (perhaps meant for Philip II or Medina Sidonia) in a boat near the stern of the galleass; elsewhere, monks disappear beneath the waves as the battle rages.

The ships, particularly those in the foreground, are painted with care and some evident accuracy of detail, even if it is hard to identify them with certainty. The four-master on the right bearing the royal standard seems to represent the *Ark Royal*, and the ship on the left may be meant for the *Revenge*. The galleass may be associated with Medina Sidonia, although his flagship, the *San Martín*, was in fact a galleon; like many English observers the artist was evidently

impressed by the few galleasses in the Spanish fleet. Generally the proportions of the hulls, masts and yards are credible for warships of the period. A variety of ship types can be seen in the background, including galleons of both countries and a sprit-rigged ship, possibly of Dutch origin.

14.2–14.11
The Armada charts from *Expeditionis Hispanorum in Angliam vera descriptio Anno Do:MDLXXXVIII*, 1590
Augustine Ryther (*fl.*1576–95), after Robert Adams (1540–95)

Engravings with contemporary colouring
381×508 each
Hind, I, 1952, 24–5, 138–49
National Maritime Museum

The Armada charts accompanied a brief history of the campaign written by the Florentine Petruccio Ubaldini. This account was in its turn based on Howard's own record of the battle, so the plates are a visual record of the 'official' story. This set of plates is from the first state of the engravings: in the second state, a number of brief explanatory remarks were added. The Armada plates later formed the basis of the designs made by Vroom for tapestries ordered by Lord Howard (see cat. nos. **14.12–14.21**).

243

14.2
1: The Spanish fleet off the coast of Cornwall (29 July)

This plate represents the Armada sighting the Lizard: a Spanish *zabra* can be seen capturing the Falmouth fishing-boat off Dodman Point, and the track of the *Golden Hind* is shown, going into Plymouth with her warning message (see above, pp. 233, 237).

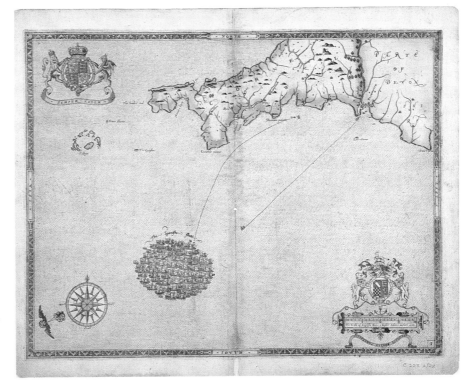

14.3

2: The Spanish and English fleets near Plymouth (30–31 July)

The English fleet is shown coming out of Plymouth, the main body crossing ahead of the Armada, getting to windward and coming in from behind. Inshore, the track of the ships that left after Howard is visible, tacking along the coast. The action is shown up to 9 a.m. on 31 July, when Howard's pinnace *Disdain* allegedly delivered the opening shot. The Armada appears in full crescent formation, with galleasses on the wings, but this formation was not complete until 1 August (see above, p. 237).

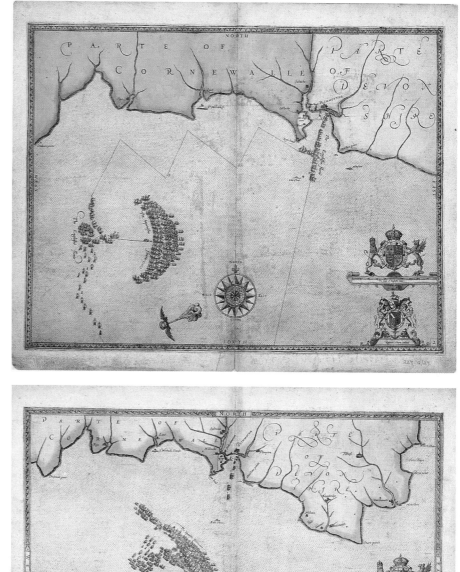

14.4

3: The English engage the Spanish fleet near Plymouth (31 July)

The skirmish off Plymouth is shown on the left, with the English attacking the Spanish rearguard. To the right is the pursuit by the English, with further ships issuing out of Plymouth to the north. The four ships leaving the English formation to the south are led by the *Revenge* and are seen making for the small group of ships shown in the lower part of the picture. These are the hulks which Drake alleged he went to investigate, disobeying Howard's order to stay close to the Armada through the night.

244

14.5

4: The English pursue the Spanish fleet east of Plymouth
(31 July–1 August)

Here the Armada is pursued through the night at culverin range by Howard in the *Ark Royal*, with the *Bear* and *Mary Rose* (four ships are shown, apparently in error). The rest of the English fleet, lacking Drake's light to follow, hangs a long way back. To the south can be seen Drake's capture of the *Rosario* on the morning of 1 August.

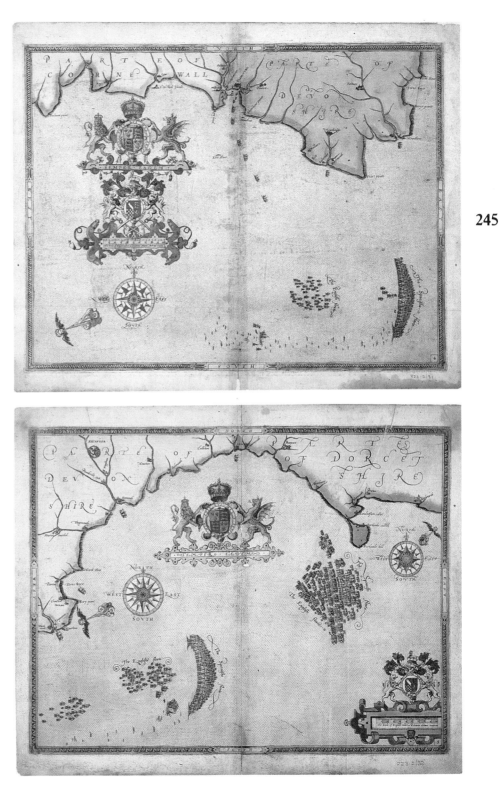

245

14.6

5: The fleets off Berry Head and the engagement near Portland Bill
(1–2 August)

The scene on the left shows the English in chase, some ships taking possession of the *San Salvador* (which blew up on 31 July). To the right is the battle off Portland Bill, with the *Triumph* and other ships in action with the galleasses to the north and the main battle taking place to the south.

14.7

6: Engagement of the fleets between Portland Bill and the Isle of Wight
(2–3 August)

This plate illustrates the continuation of the battle off Portland Bill, and then takes the story forward to 3 August, when the English fleet was re-formed into four squadrons.

14.8

7: The battle off the Isle of Wight
(4 August)

The plate shows some of the English ships being towed towards the Armada by boats, a tactic made necessary by the light wind. Some of the Spanish vessels on the south wing of the Armada, where Drake attacked, have turned to face the English.

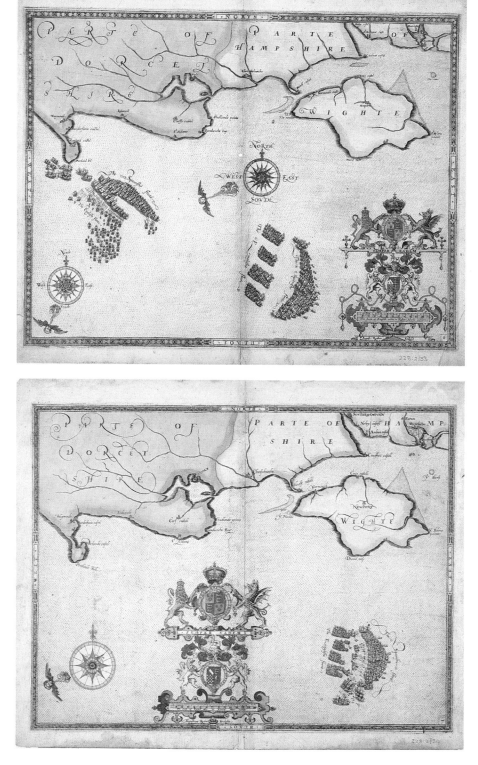

14.9

8: The voyage to Calais (4–6 August)

The voyage to Calais was relatively uneventful: Medina Sidonia was determined to reach Parma as soon as possible, and Howard did not want to risk further action until he had been joined by Seymour. As in some of the other plates, ships can be seen leaving the English coast, evidently heading for the fray: the participation of these 'voluntary ships' in the campaign was clearly regarded as worthy of note. To the north-west, in the Narrow Seas, Seymour's squadron can be seen leaving the Downs to join Howard's force off Calais Cliffs.

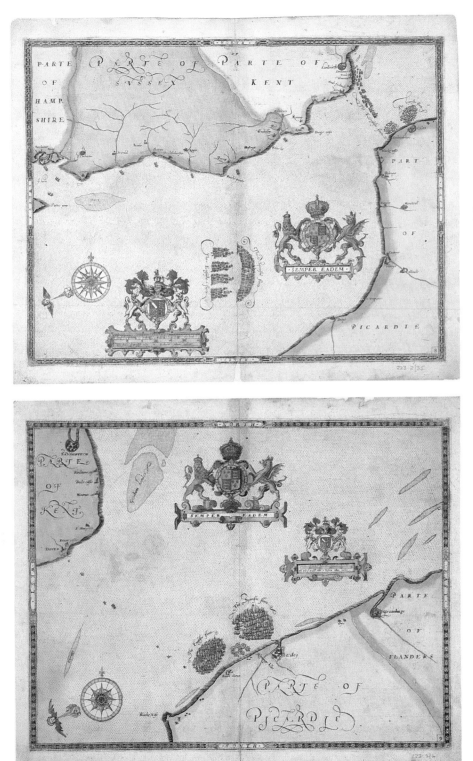

14.10

9: The fireship attack (7 August)

The midnight attack with eight fireships served to disperse the Armada temporarily, and caused the Spanish fleet to lose many irreplaceable anchors and cables. It was the single most successful attack by the English.

14.11
10: The battle off Gravelines
(8 August)

This plate shows a number of the events of 8
August. Off Calais, the boats of Howard's
squadron can be seen attacking the galleass
San Lorenzo, stranded after the fireship
attack. In their turn, the English are being
fired on by the guns of Calais castle, which
eventually drove them off. To the north the
main battle is under way, with a great deal of
firing in progress, at least one Spanish ship
sinking and three others heading towards the
dangerous Flemish sandbanks. However, the
Armada has regrouped, and despite its stragglers, is proceeding up into the North Sea in
a disciplined formation.

14.12–14.21
The Pine engravings of the House of
Lords Armada Tapestries
Engraved and published by John Pine
(1690–1756), London, 1739

Inscribed with the names of English
commanders in borders
380×660 each
Pine, 1739; Yates Thomson, 1919; Russell,
1983, 121–37
National Maritime Museum

Lord Howard of Effingham commissioned
the weaver Francis Spierincx of Brussels to
make a series of large tapestries telling the
story of the Armada campaign. Spierincx
hired Vroom to make the designs for them,
which he did on the basis of a set of the
charts by Adams. The tapestries were
delivered to Howard in 1595, and later sold
by him to James I. They were installed in
the House of Lords in 1650, but all but one
were destroyed in the fire of 1834. The only
tapestry to escape had been stolen before the
fire; its whereabouts today is unknown.

Vroom was able to transform Adams's
rather schematic scenes into a series of
panoramic views of the campaign, giving a
vivid impression of movement and action.
However, in the Pine series Vroom's original
work is seen through two filters: the work of
the tapestry weaver and that of the engraver.
The general style of the ships depicted is not
greatly different from that found in other
tapestries designed by Vroom, but some
details of the ships, such as rig, superstructures and decoration recall eighteenth-century
ships rather than those of Vroom's time.

248

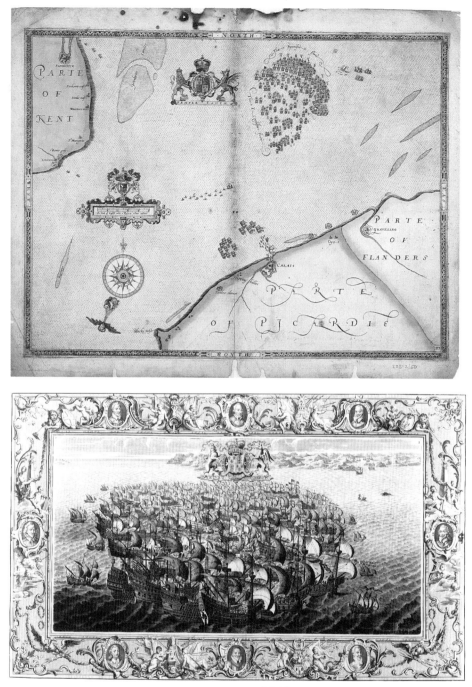

14.12
1: The Spanish fleet off the coast of
Cornwall (29 July)

14.13
2: The Spanish and English fleets near Plymouth (30–31 July)

14.14
3: The English engage the Spanish fleet near Plymouth (31 July)

The hulks which Drake claimed to have left his station to investigate are shown here in the foreground; they appear to be Dutch, for one is flying the flag of Amsterdam.

14.15
4: The English pursue the Spanish fleet east of Plymouth
(31 July–1 August)

Drake's capture of the *Rosario* is shown in the lower left-hand corner, and is depicted as a desperate boarding action: in reality, the ship surrendered to Drake without firing a shot.

14.16
5: The English and Spanish fleets off Berry Head, and the engagement near Portland Bill (1–2 August)

250

14.17
6: Engagement of the English and Spanish fleets between Portland Bill and the Isle of Wight (2–3 August)

14.18
7: The battle off the Isle of Wight (4 August)

14.19
8: The voyage to Calais (4–6 August)

14.20
9: The fireship attack (7 August)

14.21
10: The battle off Gravelines
(8 August)

14.22–14.26
The Armada's progress from Plymouth to Gravelines, before 1615
Claes Jansz. Visscher (1587–1652), possibly after Hendrick C. Vroom (1566–1640)

Engravings
134×128 each
Ottley, 1831
National Maritime Museum (70 I 1588)

14.22
Inscribed *PLIMMOVTH*. The first of the five engravings (which were published along with cat. nos. **8.31–35**, and may have been engraved after Vroom's early designs for the Armada tapestries) appears to describe the action of 31 July, although in this skirmish the Spanish were attacked from the rear, rather than the front as shown here.

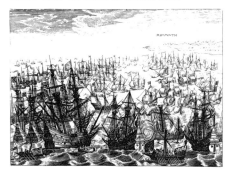

14.23
Inscribed *POORTLANT*. This shows the battle off Portland; the representation of the English coast is highly inaccurate.

14.24
A generalized view of the chase up the Channel

14.25
Inscribed *DVNNE.NOSE*. This was the sixteenth-century name for St Catherine's Point on the Isle of Wight, and it is clear that the engraving was meant to represent the battle near there.

14.26
Inscribed *DOEVER*; *CALIS*; *S.AND* (St Andrew, on topsail of Spanish ship). This engraving conflates the events of 7–8 August (the fireship attack and the battle of Gravelines), but appears to show the action moving south instead of north.

14.27
The launch of the English fireships against the Armada at Calais, 7 August 1588
Netherlandish school, 16th century

Oil on canvas
990×1730
National Maritime Museum (BHC0263)

This painting has been formerly associated with the work of Aert Antonisz. (*fl.*1579–1620) and Hendrick Vroom (1566–1640) although neither attribution can be substantiated. The artist was none the less a skilful marine painter; with the exception of the ungainly foreshortening of the two ships in the left foreground, and the choice of a daytime rather than night-time setting, the representation of one of the best-known incidents in the Armada campaign is convincing. There is a particularly interesting emphasis on the exchange of musket fire between rival ships. The principal action in the foreground concerns a Spanish galleon, left, engaged with an English galleon; another Spanish galleon lies just to the right.

14.28
The seventh day of the battle of the Armada, *c.*1600
Hendrick C. Vroom (1566–1640)

Oil on canvas
Inscribed *VROOm, 160. .*
1528×914
Mander, 1604, fol. 287a–b; Bol, 1973, 12–13; Russell, 1983, 146–9
Tiroler Landesmuseum Ferdinandeum, Innsbruck (1668)

According to Carel van Mander, Hendrick Vroom 'painted a large canvas of the seventh day of the battle of the English against the Spanish fleet. This painting showed a marvellous wealth of details and was seen with surprise and warm approval by His Excellency Count Maurits and the Admiral Justinus.' It is thought that the picture mentioned is the one exhibited here. Vroom presents a composite picture of significant incidents that marked the 'seventh day'. The fireships are seen in the middle distance, with the Spanish ships making their escape northwards. Tiny city profiles along the far horizon accurately illustrate the coastline from Dunkirk to Ostend. The engagement of Spanish and English ships in the foreground seems to represent the Battle off Gravelines. The *Ark Royal* lies astern of the *San Martín* which is on the left. The English ship on the right exchanging fire with the *San Martín* may be the *Revenge*.

14.29

The Armada in the Strait of Dover
Flemish school, *c*.1600–10

Gouache on vellum
Inscribed *ARMÉE NAVALE
D'ESPAIGNE / SURNOMÉE
INVINCIBLE VAINCUE / PAR LES
ANGLOIS LE 22 JUILLET 1588* and
bearing the royal arms and initials (*IR*) of
James I of England
133×318
National Maritime Museum (PR 82–17)

This rare miniature combines various images
of the campaign. In the right distance appear
the beacons on the English coast, which is
defended by an army bearing the personal
standard of Elizabeth I. Offshore lies the
English fleet with the *Ark Royal* flying the
royal standard in the middle distance. The
English fireship attack of 7–8 August appears
in the centre. (The inscribed O S date refers
to the battle off Portland.) To the left, small
Dutch craft attack a Spanish ship. Two ships
were lost to the Zeelanders in this way and
the prominence of the incident here suggests
the picture may have been intended as a
Dutch diplomatic gift to James I. There are
similarities with cat. nos. **14.30** and **14.31**,
suggesting common sources.

14.30

The Armada in the Strait of Dover,
c.1600–10
Netherlandish School, 17th century

Engraving
775×1000
Nederlands Scheepvaart Museum, Amsterdam

This elaborate and large print shares the
common sources of cat. nos. **14.29** and
14.31. The fireship attack in the centre
divides the opposing forces of Spanish vessels
to the left from the English on the right. The
Armada beacons and a fanciful representation
of Dover are visible on the English coast but
on the far left the artist appears to be showing a view of the Dutch banks and coastline.
The *Ark Royal* is clearly shown centre right,
flying the royal standard and flags with Lord
Howard's motto. An English army appears
improbably in the bottom right with a
Spanish ship flying the arms of Spain and the
Spanish Netherlands to its left. This is
attacked by a Dutch vessel apparently flying
the cross-key flag of Leiden. To left and
right of the Latin description of events are
shown the arms of England and the Dutch
provinces in revolt against Spain. The winds
are shown raining down death in the form of
skulls, bones and pierced hearts on the
Armada and victors' crowns on the English.

14.31
The Armada in the Strait of Dover, *c*.1602
Netherlandish School, 17th century

Engraving
383×510
Groot and Vorstman, 1980, 10, 12
Nederlands Scheepvaart Museum, Amsterdam

The Latin title describes this as 'The
celebrated Spanish fleet which in the famous
year 1588 came and perished between France
and England.' Calais and the Spaniards lie to
the left, Dover and the English to the right
with the fireship attack in the centre. The
Ark Royal lies in the middle distance to the
right of the fireships, flying the royal
standard and a banner with the motto of
Lord Howard: *Desir n'a repos* (Desire has no
repose). The English ship in the foreground
flies the same banner, and the Spanish flagship, bottom left, flies the ragged cross flag
of the Spanish Netherlands.

14.32
Map of Plymouth and
Plymouth Sound, 1601–1602
Federigo Gianibelli (b.*c*.1530)

Pen and wash
425×460
British Library, London (MS Cott. Aug., I, i, 40)

Federigo Gianibelli, Italian military engineer,
prepared defences on the Thames against the
Armada. His map of Plymouth accompanied
his report of 1601–1602 on the fortifications
begun after the Armada. The meticulous
detail of the fortifications contrasts with
rough representations of the surrounding
country. Rame Head and Penlee Point are
visible, as are ships and beacons. Plymouth
was the temporary base for the ships of
Howard and Drake in 1588 and it was off
Plymouth Sound that the Armada and the
English forces first met in battle.

14.32

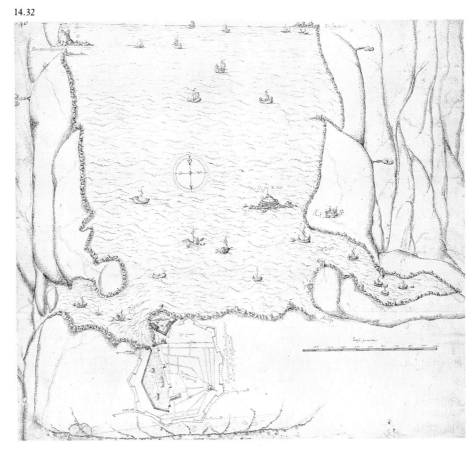

255

14.33
Elizabethan chart of the Isle of
Portland and Weymouth Bay,
c.1590–1600

Coloured chart on vellum
435×320
British Museum, I, 1844, 70; Oppenheim,
1908, 206; Colvin *et al*., 1982, 469
British Library, London (MS Cott. Aug., I, i, 32)

This chart marks the 'Portland Race', the
strong tidal race off the Isle which the
English used to help them bear down on the
windward wing of the Armada, when wind
and tide conditions changed during the battle
off Portland. It depicts a small gun-platform
(*Smal Platforme*) at Weymouth/Melcombe
which was not built until 1587–8, with the
aim of defending Weymouth Road. It did not
receive any guns in 1588, however, the
government perhaps regarding the forts at
Portland and Sandsfoot (on which £611 had
been spent in repairs and other work, 1584–
6) as adequate for local defence. The style of
the royal warships anchored off Portland
Castle suggests that the chart cannot be
much later than *c*.1600.

14.34

Chart of the Medway and the mouth of the Thames, *c.*1580

Pen, pencil and colour wash
427×576
Skelton and Summerson, 1971, no. 43.
*The Marquess of Salisbury, Hatfield House
(CPM II/47)*

This chart, probably compiled for Lord
Burghley from sketches by local pilots,
depicts coastal and river defences including
Upnor Castle (1567) and Sheerness Fort
(*c.*1574). The pencilled additions show beacons and a projected boom across the Medway, which was actually put in place in 1585.
Eighteen ships are shown at anchor between
Upnor Castle and Rochester Bridge.

14.35

'Thamesis Descriptio', 1588
Robert Adams (1540–95)

Coloured map on vellum
Inscribed *The Names of the principall places;
The Pricked Line sheweth her Maties progresse*

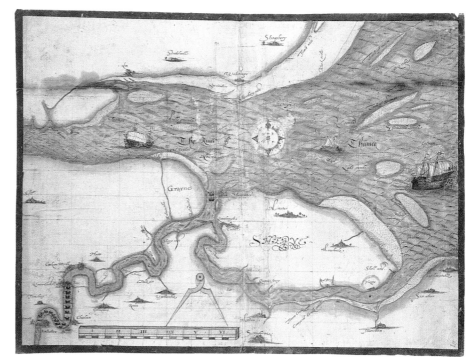

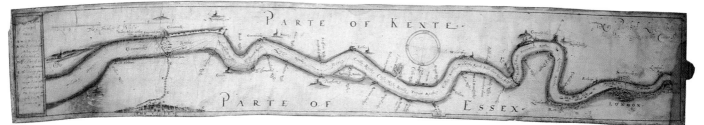

to the Campe; Rober: Adams authore 1588
115×705; scale: 1:63,360
Hind, I, 1952, 145
British Library, London (Add. MS 44839)

This plan shows existing and proposed
defences on the Thames between Westminster and Tilbury in 1588. The lines radiating
across the river represent the fields of fire of
cannon that might be sighted on the banks.
A boom defence is shown between Gravesend
and Tilbury, and the *Pricked Line* shows the
route of Elizabeth's progress to Leicester's
camp at West Tilbury. Elizabeth's visit to
Tilbury and her review of the troops there on
18–19 August are among the best-known episodes of the Armada campaign. Her famous
speech to the troops was aimed at showing
her as the beloved monarch of her people,
fearlessly leading them in war for God and
country. Delivered at the right psychological
moment, it was rapturously received.

14.36

Bronze *medio sacre* from the *Gran Grifón*

Bronze
2430 lgth; 74 cal.; 450 kg
Shetland Museum, Lerwick (G47/70)

This piece weighs some 1,000 pounds and
fired a three-pound shot. It lacks the
mandatory royal arms: regulations demanded
Philip's full titles and escutcheon on guns
weighing 2,000 pounds or more, and just his
name and crown if the weight was less.
However, Philip waived these regulations to
speed up production in the crash programme
of gun-founding just before the Armada
sailed. Production pressures also took their
toll on quality, and many corners were cut –
resulting in a number of horrifying accidents
at the Lisbon foundry, when inadequately
baked moulds burst or when guns failed their
proofing tests (see cat. no. **9.27**).

14.37

Spanish matchlock musket for shipboard use, 16th century

Iron and wood
Inscribed *G* and *S* in a medallion
2030 lgth (barrel 1570); 27 cal.
Museo del Ejército, Madrid (1.932)

This heavy muzzle-loading musket is equipped with a peg which would have fitted into
a hole in the rail of a ship, allowing the gun
to supplement the vessel's firepower. The
weapon might also have been used in defending fortifications. It has an incised stock and
an iron ramrod. Spanish naval tactics made
such close-range weapons very important.

14.38
Spanish matchlock musket, 15th to 16th centuries

Wood and iron
1300 lgth (barrel 930); 11.5 cal.
Museo Arqueológico Nacional, 1980
Museo Arqueológico Nacional, Madrid (51.987)

This simple matchlock musket is typical of Spanish and other European military firearms of the period. It has a trefoil mark on the barrel. Muskets formed part of the armament of virtually every ship of the time.

14.39
Ceramic fire grenade from the *Trinidad Valencera*

Semi-glazed earthenware
111 lgth
Crédit Communal, 1985, 135
Ulster Museum, Belfast

An *alcancía*, or ceramic fire grenade was filled with a mixture of gunpowder, spirits and resin. It could be thrown, with lighted fuses tied round it, onto an enemy's deck, where it would burst and scatter its fiercely burning, napalm-like contents.

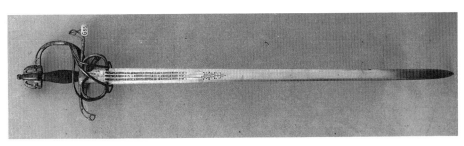

257

14.40
Spanish sword, late 16th century
Sebastian Hernández of Toledo (blade)

Steel
Inscribed *DE SEBASTIAN HERNANDEZ TOLEDANO*
1060×225 lgth (blade 910×40)
Valencia de Don Juan, 1898, 227; Norman, 1980, 55
Patrimonio Nacional. Real Armería de Madrid (G.55)

The blade and hilt of this sword are believed to be contemporary, and the hilt is apparently Spanish work, although some similar examples from other countries are known.

14.41
Five impacted musket balls from the *Gran Grifón*

Lead
19.05 dia.
Martin, 1972, 65–6
Shetland Museum, Lerwick (G54/70)

14.42
Five impacted arquebus balls from the *Gran Grifón*

Lead
12.7 dia.
Martin, 1972, 65–6
Shetland Museum, Lerwick (G55/70)

These musket and arquebus balls are presumably of English origin, and bear out the accounts of close-range firing.

14.43
Nine impacted musket balls from the *Girona*

Lead
11.32 g. av. wt.
Crédit Communal, 1985, 4.9
Ulster Museum, Belfast

The participation of galleasses in most of the actions of the campaign is borne out by these expended musket balls, presumably of English origin.

14.44

'Rules of conduct for the Armada', 21 May 1588

Printed pamphlet (4 pp.) publ. ?Lisbon
Inscribed with signatures of Medina Sidonia
and his secretary
311×212
Public Record Office, London (SP 12/210, 12)

This pamphlet, at once a statement of
principle and detailed instruction for the
comportment of the fleet, was published on
the orders of the Duke of Medina Sidonia. A
signed copy was handed to all the ships, and
this one probably came from one of those
taken by the English. It was to be publicly
read in all vessels twice a week from 21 May.
Medina Sidonia started with a reminder that
the expedition was intended to serve God and
restore Catholicism. He then outlined strict
rules of personal conduct based on Philip's
own instructions to him. There was to be no
swearing, gaming, duels, quarrels; no prostitutes or other women on board. All men
were to go to confession before boarding and
prayers were to be said every day. On a technical level, a system of communications was
outlined, using mainly shots (from heavy or
light guns), but also flags and, at night,
lights. Distress calls, the sighting of land or
enemy sail and the fleet's formation are dealt
with, but they would have been supplemented by messages sent in light pinnaces. Pass-
words, salutes and meeting-places where the
fleet should gather if scattered were also
outlined, and even the sailors' quarters, the
method of distributing rations and where to
keep wet cloths to put out fires. The prohibitions were accompanied by details of the
punishments for transgressions, ranging from
deprivation of the wine ration to execution
and loss of all possessions.

14.45

Letter from the Duke of Medina Sidonia to Philip II, Cascaes, 29 May 1588

MS (2ff.; autograph)
332×220
*Archivo General de Simancas, Valladolid
(GA.223, f.74)*

Medina Sidonia had reported on the previous
day that the ships had started to leave
Lisbon. Now 'God and his blessed Mother
willed that the morning should be good and
the wind, although not very fresh, sufficient
to enable the rest of the fleet to go, with the
help of the galleys.' Only two galleons
remained in Lisbon so they anchored off
Cascaes to await them. 'When the time

19

DON ALONSO
PEREZ DE GVZMAN EL
BVENO DVQVE DE LA CIVDAD DE MEDINA
Sidonia, Conde de Niebla, Marques de Caçaça en Africa ; Señor de la Ciudad
de Sant Lucar, Capitan General del Mar Oceano, y de la Costa del An-
daluzia, y desta Real Armada y Exercito de su Magestad, y Cavalle-
ro de la Insigne Orden del Tuson, &c.

LO QVE ORDENO Y MANDO QVE
hagan y cumplan los Generales, Maestros de Campo, Capita-
nes, y Officiales de Infanteria, y de Mar, Pilotos, Maestres, Sol-
dados , Marineros , y Officiales , y qualquier otra gente de
guerra y mar que viniere en esta dicha Armada todo el tiempo
que durare esta Iornada, es lo siguiente:

PRIMERAMENTE Y ante todas cosas han de entender todos los su
sodichos dende el mayor hasta el menor, que el principal fundamento con
que su Magestad se ha mouido a hazer y emprender esta Iornada ha sido y es a
fin de seruir a Dios nuestro Señor, y reduzir a su Yglesia y Gremio muchos
Pueblos y Almas , que oprimidos por los Ereges enemigos de nuestra Sancta
Fee Catholica, los tienen sugetos a sus setas y desuenturas: y para que todos va
yan puestos los ojos a este blanco, como estamos obligados, encargo y ruego mu
cho, den orden a sus inferiores y toda la gente de sus cargos , que entren en las
naos confessados y comulgados, con tan gran contricion de sus peccados , como yo espero que lo haran todos, para que mediante esta preuencion, y el ze-
lo con que vamos de hazer a Dios tan gran seruicio, nos guie y encamine como mas se sirua, que es lo que particular y principalmente se pretende.
¶ Ansimismo les encargo y mando, tengan particular cuydado que ningun sol
dado marinero, ni otra persona que sirua y ande en esta Armada , no blasfeme,
ni reniegue de nuestro Señor Dios, ni de nuestra Señora, ni de los Sanctos, sope-
na que sea por ello asperamente corregido y muy bien castigado como nos paresciere , y para otros juramentos menos graues los superiores en las proprias
naos procuraran reparar todo lo que pudieren, castigandolos con quitalles la ra-
cion del vino, o con otra pena como les paresciere , y porque las mayores oca-
siones suelen susceder del juego, procurareys escusarlo, y menos los prohibidos, y
que ningunos jueguen de noche por ningun caso.

¶ Y Por

comes I will spread my sails and follow my
course. I hope God will grant me good
weather and Your Majesty the success in this
expedition which You desire and all of us
pray for. The men are in high spirits . . .
they cannot contain their pleasure, and I con-
fess to your Majesty that I share that joy
more than anyone.' He believed the good
conditions of their departure augured well,
but notified the king that he was short of victuals which must be sent after them.

14.46
Letter from Drake to Seymour, 31 July 1588

MS (autograph signature and postscript)
Inscribed with endorsement addressing the letter to Seymour or, in his absence, Sir William Winter
310×210
Laughton, I, 1981, 289–90
Public Record Office, London (SP12/212, 82)

Drake wrote this letter on the *Revenge*, off Start Point, the evening after the first contact between the English and Spanish fleets. Its purpose was to alert Seymour to the fact that the Armada was off the coast and to convey Howard's order that he was to make his ships ready to attack the Spanish when they entered the Narrow Seas. Drake mentions the action off Plymouth and the evident determination of the enemy: 'as we perceive they are determined to sell their lives with blows'. However, he was able to pass on the heartening message that although the Armada had more than a hundred ships, Drake thought 'not half of them men-of-war'. This dramatic letter, written on Howard's orders, was conveyed up the Channel in the thirty-ton caravel attached to Drake's force.

14.47
Copy of a letter from Medina Sidonia to Parma, 5 August 1588

MS (2ff.)
311×195
Archivo General de Simancas, Valladolid (E.594, f.117)

By the time he was six leagues off Beachy Head, Medina Sidonia was extremely anxious to know if Parma was ready to sail. This letter was one of several sent to Parma as the Armada advanced up the Channel. Copies were sent to Philip from the Netherlands in mid-August. Medina Sidonia urgently requested information, pilots and, especially, ammunition and gunpowder. Above all, he wished to promote a new strategy designed to enable the cumbersome Armada vessels to board the fast English ships. It required forty to fifty flyboats (small, fast craft) to be sent from the Netherlands. The bearer, the pilot Domingo de Ochoa, was to explain the plan fully to Parma (see pp. 239–40).

14.46

259

14.48
Letter from Sir William Winter to Walsingham, 10 August 1588

MS (autograph signature)
310×210
Laughton, II, 1981, 7–14
Public Record Office, London (SP12/214, 7)

Winter commanded the *Vanguard* in Seymour's force guarding the Narrow Seas. His letter describes events from 6–10 August, including the fireship attack, the assault on the galleass, the battle of Gravelines and the decision to chase the Armada to the north. Winter claims that he suggested the idea of the fireship attack to Howard, 'and his Lordship did like very well of it', although this tactical device was not a novel one. The fireship attack was the single most effective action by the English fleet: for the loss of eight ships the Armada was dispersed, the possibility of it joining Parma's forces was lost and the Spanish ships were deprived of cables and anchors they could ill afford to lose. Along with the rest of Seymour's force, Winter was sent back to Harwich to guard the coast against any possible crossing by Parma, whilst the main body of the English fleet pursued the Armada northwards.

14.49
Letter from Howard to Walsingham, 8 August 1588

MS (autograph signature and first postscript)
303×205
Laughton, I, 1981, 340–41
Public Record Office, London (SP12/213, 64)

Lord Charles Howard's letter was sent in reply to one from Walsingham, asking for a list of powder and shot required. Much of the letter is concerned with the attack on the galleass *San Lorenzo*. The vessel was captured and stripped by the English but seized by the governor of Calais. Howard asks Walsingham to write to the governor requesting either the return of this formidable ship, or that it should not be given back to the Spanish. Howard's summing-up of the campaign to this point, 'we pluck their feathers by little and little', was a realistic assessment on the basis of the information available to him.

14.50
Letter from Parma to Philip II, 10 August 1588

MS
305×212
Archivo General de Simancas, Valladolid (E.594, f.125)

Parma had just heard news of the fireship attack and northward voyage of the Armada when he wrote this. He realized that the expedition was over and was anxious to prove his loyalty to the king. He repeatedly stated that he was ready to sail, but had been prevented from doing so by contrary winds and the knowledge that there were enemy ships nearby. He reminded Philip of his concern that the Armada had no friendly port to shelter in while waiting, and chastised Medina Sidonia for thinking that he could provide him with small flyboats to fight the English at such short notice (see cat. no. **14.47**). By way of comfort he reminded Philip that such events were God's work and God would give him the means to remedy the situation.

14.51
Account by Pedro Coco Calderón, 1588

MS (autograph)
326×222
Archivo General de Simancas, Valladolid (GA.221, f.190)

This is one of the most detailed accounts of the Armada campaign for the period from 20 July to the return of Coco Calderón's ship, the hulk *San Salvador*, to Santander on 23 September. As the king's accountant on the expedition, Coco Calderón was well informed; additionally, he gives more details than any others on the fate of many nobles. The *San Salvador* was directly involved in the battle on 8 August. Surrounded by a large number of English ships, the hulk was severely damaged. Coco Calderón claims to have warned Medina Sidonia on 24 August that the fleet should pull further out because they were too close to the coast of Ireland. Violent storms and heavy seas separated his ship from the fleet for most of their return journey, but whenever they encountered other ships they shared their food with them.

261

14.52
Sir Francis Drake's personal accounts, 1587–8
Jonas Bodenham

MS (4ff.)
Annotations by Lord Burghley (1528–98)
and by a modern hand
285×208
Eliott-Drake, 1911, 93
*City of Plymouth Museums and Art Gallery
(PCM 1971.5)*

These accounts give Drake's total expenses
for wages and other items between December
1587 and September 1588 as just over
£4,751. There are payments to a wide range
of trades and professions in the English fleet,
including mariners, ship-masters, soldiers,
surgeons and gentlemen. More than twenty-
five journeys are recorded between Drake
and government officials in London taking
letters, prisoners and messages. Drake also
claimed expenses for his custody of Don
Pedro de Valdés, and for the loss of his ship
the *Thomas*, burned as a fireship at Calais.
The amount of notation in Burghley's hand
suggests that Drake's claims were closely
scrutinized.

14.53
The Spanish Armada, *c*.1590
English school, 16th century

Oil on canvas
1219×2845
Busby, 1948
*The property of the Society of Apothecaries,
London*

Painted in celebration of the defeat of the
Armada, this picture provides a loose summary of several aspects of the event, rather
than attempting a literal representation of
fact. It amalgamates a number of locations
and occurrences into one imaginative scene:
Elizabeth's address to her troops at Tilbury
is portrayed on the left; the action offshore
refers to several phases in the battle; and the
English coastline is represented with beacons,
but given an exotic Mediterranean flavour
(characteristic of earlier sixteenth-century
Flemish painting). The galleon on the right
flying the royal standard seems intended for
the *Ark Royal*, but the Spanish ships to her
left are not identifiable. The absence of
certain necessary spars, rigging and sails suggests that the artist was not a marine painter
by training. A traditional attribution to
Nicholas Hilliard – on the basis of a report
that an Armada subject by Hilliard had been
in Charles I's collection – is intriguing if
none the less improbable.

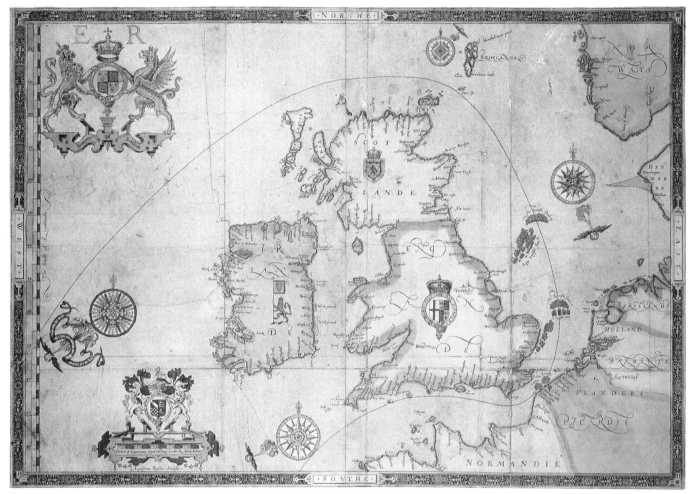

15.1 Chart showing the track of the Armada, Augustine Ryther after Robert Adams

15. 'The Terrible Journey'

On 12 August Medina Sidonia issued new orders to the fleet to sail north, around the Shetlands, then to the west and then to make for La Coruña.

The Armada's homeward journey is a tale of a disaster. The first blow to the demoralized Spaniards came the very next day, when the daily rations were reduced to a meagre half pound of biscuit, half a pint of wine and a single pint of water. To save water – most of which was fouling in the barrels – the horses and mules were to be thrown overboard. The farther north they sailed, the colder it got: 1588 seems to have been as bad for temperatures as it was for storms. One hapless participant complained: 'in latitude 62° it is not warm', which seems a masterly understatement, for shortly they encountered freezing fog, making it difficult to maintain contact. On 3 September the duke reported to the king that since the 21st there had been four nights of storms, and seventeen ships had disappeared.

Three of the missing ships were hulks, the *Barca de Amburg*, the *Gran Grifón* and the *Castillo Negro*; with them was a large Venetian merchant ship, the *Trinidad Valencera*. On 1 September the *Barca* could no longer be kept afloat – she was taking water quicker than her pumps could handle. Her company of 250 were taken aboard the *Gran Grifón* and the *Trinidad Valencera*. Almost immediately she went down, somewhere off the north coast of Ireland. A few days later the other three ships lost contact. The *Castillo Negro* disappeared. The *Trinidad Valencera* was caught in a bad storm on the night of 12 September, during which she sustained so much damage that her pumps could not cope, and had no option but to run for land. At Kinnagoe Bay at the eastern tip of Malin Head she grounded on a reef. The *Gran Grifón* fared little better – she ploughed on, on a south-westerly course into the Atlantic, until caught in a severe storm on 7 September. She was driven backwards and forwards for several days 'while the wind was so strong and the sea so wild that the men were all exhausted and unable to keep down the water that leaked through our gaping seams'. Eventually, on 27 September, she fetched up on Fair Isle.

Other Armada ships were faring little better. In Co. Sligo, a violent storm on 20 September drove three great Armada ships onto the shelving strand at Streedagh, pounding and tearing them to pieces. The three ships were the *Juliana*, *Labia* and the *Santa María de Visión*. Nearly 1,000 perished, but there was one notable survivor, Captain Francisco Cuellar, who reached Flanders and wrote an account of his ordeal.

All along the west coast of Ireland similar tragedies were taking place: in the mouth of the river Shannon seven ships sought refuge and fresh water, but were refused permission to send landing parties ashore and were forced to put to sea again, despite the raging storm. At Galway the entire crew of the *Falcón Blanco Mediano*, with the exception of her captain, were summarily executed, in accordance with the directive issued from Dublin Castle by the lord deputy 'to apprehend and execute all Spaniards found there, of what quality soever'.

Down in the south-west, at Blasket Sound, Co. Kerry, a stark drama was taking place. The first to enter the small anchorage was Juan Martínez de Recalde in the *San Juan de Portugal*. He was followed by the *San Juan Bautista*. Then, on 21 September, the *Santa María de la Rosa* entered, clearly in distress – her sails were in tatters except for her foresail. As she came in she fired one shot, then another. She cast her sole remaining anchor and seemed to ride peacefully enough until, at two o'clock, without further warning, she sank with all on board, 'a most extraordinary and terrifying thing'. Shortly afterwards another *San Juan Bautista* entered the anchorage, in bad shape, with her mainmast gone, so it was decided to evacuate her crew and then scuttle her.

The *Rata Encoronada*, commanded by the redoubtable Don Alonso de Leiva entered Blacksod Bay, Co. Mayo on 17 September and ran aground. Leiva successfully disembarked all his crew, occupied a small castle at Doona and fired his ship so that no useful spoils would accrue to the enemy. When he heard that another Armada ship, the *Duquesa Santa Ana* was nearby, he re-embarked his men and set sail again. Unfortunately, he suffered his second wreck at Loughros More, in Co. Donegal. Again he disembarked his men, and again occupied an abandoned fort, on an island in Kiltoorish Lake. There he learned that the *Girona*, a galleass of the Naples Squadron, was in Killybegs, some twenty miles away across the mountains. He went there, organized repairs to the *Girona* and set off once again. The *Girona* was now carrying some 1,300 men, from four Armada ships. He set sail for south-west Scotland, from which he hoped to get his men safely to mainland Europe. Unfortunately, the *Girona* struck the jagged spear of Lacada Point in Co. Antrim and was wrecked on 26 October. The Irish coast had claimed its last victim.

Many Armada ships did reach safety in northern Spanish ports, but the human cost of the expedition was appalling. Perhaps 11,000 of those in the Armada may have perished.

Laurence Flanagan

264

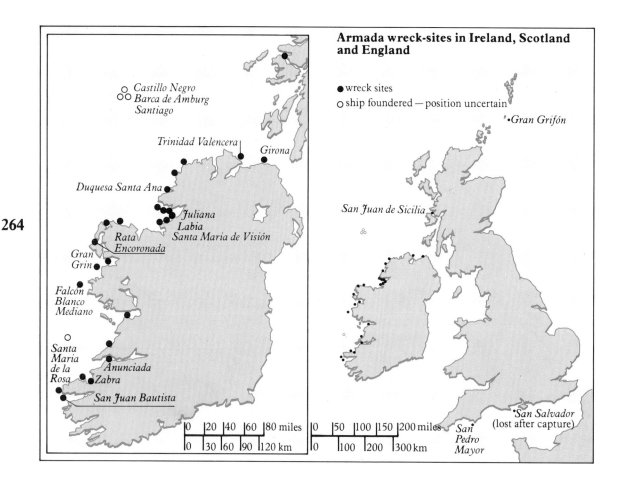

Armada wreck-sites in Ireland, Scotland and England

● wreck sites
○ ship foundered — position uncertain

Castillo Negro
Barca de Amburg
Santiago

Trinidad Valencera

Girona

Duquesa Santa Ana

Juliana
Labia
Santa Maria de Visión

Rata
Encoronada

Gran
Grin

Falcón
Blanco
Mediano

Santa
Maria
de la
Rosa

Anunciada
Zabra

San Juan Bautista

Gran Grifón

San Juan de Sicilia

San Salvador
(lost after capture)

San
Pedro
Mayor

0 | 20 | 40 | 60 | 80 miles
0 | 30 | 60 | 90 | 120 km

0 | 50 | 100 | 150 | 200 miles
0 | 100 | 200 | 300 km

15.1
Chart showing the track of the Armada, 1590
Augustine Ryther after Robert Adams (1540–95)

Engraving with contemporary colouring
795×545; scale 1:3,500,000
Ubaldini, 1590, 25; Hind, I, 1952, 138–49
National Maritime Museum (G218:1/8)

Fleeing from Gravelines, Medina Sidonia ordered the Armada home northwards via Scotland and the west coast of Ireland. The English fleet followed to the Firth of Forth, and two ships shadowed them past the Orkneys. Many of the ships were unable to follow their admiral's safe course and foundered, as shown, on the west coasts of Scotland and Ireland in mid-September. This chart is from *Expeditionis Hispanorum in Angliam vera descriptio*.

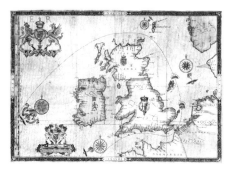

15.2
Account of ships lost in Ireland, sent by Don Beltrán de Salto to Philip II, 10 April 1589

MS (82ff.)
346×218
AGS GA.244, f.256, E.596, f.20, GA.247, f.1; Hardy, 1966; Sténuit, 1974; Martin, 1975
Archivo General de Simancas, Valladolid (GA.247, f.2)

Don Beltrán de Salto had been on the *Barca de Amburg* and transferred to the *Trinidad Valencera*. He took advantage of Elizabeth's limited general pardon (along with some seventy to eighty survivors) to give himself up. He gave the following details from captivity:

1. The *Rata Encoronada*: men saved and ship burnt in Blacksod Bay, Co. Mayo.
2. The hulk *Duquesa Santa Ana*, with men from the *Rata*, sunk in Loughros Mor

Bay, Co. Donegal, the men saved.

3. The galleass *Girona* took these and other survivors, but was wrecked on Lacada Point, Co. Antrim. All but six men drowned.
4. The hulk *Falcón Blanco Mediano*. All survivors executed.
5. The hulk *Barca de Amburg* lost at sea, men transferred to nos. 6 and 7.
6. The *Trinidad Valencera* wrecked at Kinnagoe Bay, Co. Donegal.
7. The *Gran Grin* lost in Galway; other accounts say Clare Island, Co. Mayo. The survivors, estimated here at 500, were all executed.
8. The *San Nicolás Prodaneli* thought lost in Galway and all executed.
9. The Santa *María de Visión* also lost.
10 and 11. The *Labia* and *Juliana* here reported as lost together, probably off Co. Donegal with about a hundred survivors.
12. The *Ciervo Volante*, a hulk, here said to be commanded by Don Luís de Córdoba, one of the few survivors.
13. The *Gran Grifón*, which foundered off Fair Isle.

15.3

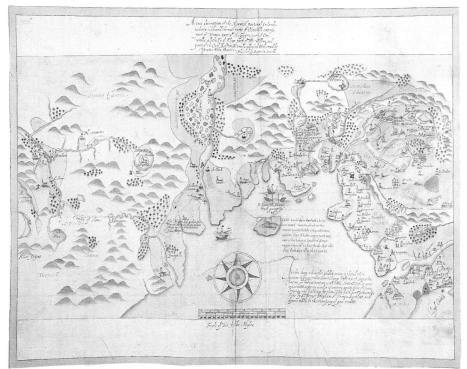

15.3

15.3
Map of Donegal Bay, *c*.1603
John Baxter and Baptista Boazio
(*fl.*1583–1606)

Pen and watercolour
Inscribed *A true discription of the Norwest partes of Irelande, wherin is shewed the west part of O'Donnell's contrye, part of Tirones part of Mr. Guyres part of Orowickes, all of the Co. of Sligo, Part of Mr. Willms and part of the Co. Roscommon; truly collected and observed by Captayne John Baxter. Finished by Baptista Boazio*
550×420; scale 1:125,000
Taylor, 1970, 167; Martin, 1975, 27, 91
National Maritime Museum (MS 53/073 P/49)

Boazio worked as a 'pacer' on surveys of Ireland commissioned by Burghley, Sidney and Hatton (1583–92) before establishing his reputation for watercolour finishes. This map shows the sites of three unnamed Armada wrecks.

15.4
Examination of Don Pedro de Valdés, 14 August 1588

MS
288×198
Laughton, II, 1981, 27–9; Mattingly, 1983, 244–6
Public Record Office, London (SP12/214,22)

Don Pedro de Valdés, commander of the Andalusian Squadron, was an experienced and independent-minded seaman. His ship *Nuestra Señora del Rosario* suffered the loss of bowsprit and foremast in collision with the *Santa Catalina* after the action off Plymouth, and had been abandoned by Medina Sidonia on advice from Don Pedro's cousin and enemy Diego Flores de Valdés. Don Pedro inexplicably surrendered to Drake without a fight and without having attempted to repair his ship, and was sent to London where he was treated courteously in the household of Drake's kinsman, Richard Drake, pending his ransom. He later returned to Spain in unimpaired health. His examination, in contrast to the deposition of the Dutch sailors (cat. no. **15.6**) is informed and generally accurate. His interrogation, recorded here in Spanish, put Philip's intention to conquer England beyond doubt and reinforced fears of the strength of the invasion force.

15.5
Letter from Don Pedro de Valdés to Philip II, 'Exer', 18 January 1589

MS (2ff.; autograph)
294×204
AGS GA.244, f.256; E.165, f.247; Laughton, II, 1981, 133–6, 215–17, 374–5, 384; Mattingly, 1983, 258–61, 368–9
Archivo General de Simancas, Valladolid (GA.244, f.256)

Don Pedro de Valdés claimed that he had been abandoned by Medina Sidonia, here presented as incompetent and malicious. He omits to say that the duke had tried to help him. A bitter controversy arose over this incident and Diego Flores de Valdés, who advised Medina Sidonia to leave the *Rosario* because the English were closing in, was imprisoned on his return. Several people testified that this act lowered morale in the Armada, but Philip was not entirely convinced. Pedro de Valdés left England three years later, having paid Drake a large ransom of £3,000. He was not given a naval command again.

265

266

15.7

15.6
Depositions of two Dutch sailors who served in the Armada, 11 August 1588

MS (10ff.) in French
320×215
Laughton, II, 1981, 77–8; HMC, III, 1889, 343–6
The Marquess of Salisbury, Hatfield House (Cecil Papers 17/23)

The depositions of Jan Henricx and Jacob Cornelis, both from Broek in Holland, who served in a Spanish ship, contain a mixture of exaggerated hearsay and personal observation. They said that there were about 130 ships; that except for the galleys, few had cannons; that there were 10,000 seasoned soldiers; and that the rest of the men were vinegrowers, shepherds and the like. The English were better sailors, they claimed, and easily took and kept the weather gage, firing three shots for every one of the Spanish. They assured their captors that if the fleet returned to Spain without conquering England they would be hanged. The two sailors said that they had deserted from their ship when it was off the coast of the Low Countries, escaping in the boat tied to her stern.

15.7
Sir Richard Bingham (1528–99), 1564
English school, 16th century

Oil on panel
Inscribed *A.D.1564./AETATIS 36/SIR RICH.D/BYNGHAM*
584×495
Falls, 1950, 154–67; Strong, I, 1969a, 22
National Portrait Gallery (3793)

Bingham, of whom this is the earliest-known portrait, had a varied career fighting in English, Spanish, Venetian and Dutch service. He was appointed governor of Connaught in 1584 and two years later suppressed a rising in his province with great ruthlessness. Conflict with the lord deputy, Perrott, and charges of corruption, led to his temporary transfer to the English forces in the Low Countries. He was reinstated as governor in 1588, and with the new lord deputy, Fitzwilliam, was responsible for much of the killing of Armada survivors. His actions were harsh even by the standards of the time, and motivated by the fear that the Spanish might be able to overwhelm the weak English forces stationed in Ireland.

15.8
Letter from Sir Richard Bingham to the Queen, 23 December 1588

MS (autograph)
290×215
Laughton, II, 1981, 299–301
Public Record Office, London (SP63/139, 2)

Sir Richard Bingham's letter summarizes his activities in dealing with the Spanish survivors. There were some twelve to fifteen Armada wrecks in his province of Connaught. Virtually all the survivors were 'put to the sword', apart from fifty or so gentlemen and officers whom Bingham spared until given a definite order from the lord deputy to kill them. He attaches a list of some of their names (see cat. no. **15.9**), and notes that he has only kept alive one Don Luís de Córdoba and his nephew until the queen's pleasure is known. Bingham clearly felt that he had done his duty and proudly reported his actions.

15.9
List of executed Armada survivors, December 1588

MS
310×128
Laughton, II, 1981, 301–303
Public Record Office, London (SP63/139, 2, I)

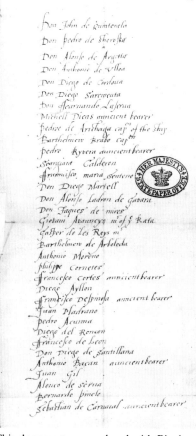

This document was enclosed with Bingham's letter to the queen of 23 December (see cat. no. **15.8**). It names thirty-three gentlemen and officers out of fifty from the Armada who had been taken prisoner by Bingham and later executed on the orders of the lord deputy. Their names include Pedro de Arechaga, captain of the hulk *Falcón Blanco Mayor*, Gaspar de los Reyes, master of *Gran Grin* and Juan Gil, who had been an ensign on Medina Sidonia's flagship. Although this poignant list has annotations in English, the names do not appear to have been written in an English hand, making it possible that the writer was himself one of those killed.

15.10
Letter from Medina Sidonia to Philip II, 23 September 1588

MS (2ff.; autograph)
305×212
AGS GA.227, f.45
Archivo General de Simancas, Valladolid (E.594, f.171)

In this brief note, Medina Sidonia announces his safe arrival in Santander and accredits Don Francisco de Bobadilla to speak to the king at length. The duke was very ill and begged licence to go home. Until he received it, he had to help set up a makeshift organization to deal with the sick, refit the vessels returning, as well as quarter the troops and prevent desertion. Philip allowed him to go home without having to go to court first, and Medina Sidonia set out in October. The king did not blame him for the failure of the Armada and he remained in royal service.

15.11
Account of Marcos de Aramburu, 19 October 1588

MS (4ff.)
310×230
Archivo General de Simancas, Valladolid (GA.227, f.157)

Aramburu was the commander of the *San Juan Bautista* (Castilian Squadron). His diary, from 25 August to 14 October when he entered Santander, is full of technical information and details of the voyage home. The horror of the countless storms and high seas is not lessened by his curt style. The ship was alone much of the time, and almost wrecked on several occasions. They encountered Recalde on 15 September and sheltered with him and other ships in Blasket Sound. They witnessed the sudden sinking of the *Santa María de la Rosa* and took on board the men from another ship, the *San Juan Bautista*, which was scuttled there.

15.12
Petition of Pedro de Idiáquez to Philip II, 13 December 1588

MS
305×210
AGS GA.242, ff.31–2
Archivo General de Simancas, Valladolid (GA.242, f.30)

Pedro de Idiáquez joined the Armada as a gentleman-adventurer, paying his own costs and those of his two servants. He was posted to Recalde's galleon *San Juan*, the vice-

admiral of the fleet, which was involved in all the skirmishes with the English. On Monday, 8 August, while engaged in fierce combat with the English fleet, he was hit by English fire. His left index-finger was blown off and three fingers were severely injured, so that he could no longer use that hand. He asked Philip to consider his good service, the large sum he had spent in royal service and his wound, and grant him favours as befitted his rank and service. This is typical of the many petitions sent to the king after the Armada.

15.13
Letter from Juan Gómez de Medina to Philip II, 3 March 1589

MS (2ff.; autograph)
302×212
AGS GA.246, ff.155, 159, 160, 161
Archivo General de Simancas, Valladolid (GA.246, f.295)

Gómez de Medina commanded the flagship of the hulks, the *Gran Grifón*, which was badly damaged in the fighting. It was sinking when they sighted Fair Isle, but they managed to disembark before the ship went down. Between 300 and 350 men, some saved from the *Barca de Amburg*, sheltered in 'seventeen huts of these savages'. The officers went to Shetland and hired two ships; by the time they returned, only 250 men were alive; the rest had died of starvation and cold. James VI received them well and refused to hand them over to the English. He allowed them to arrange transport but insisted that Gómez de Medina should stay as hostage to a Scottish merchant whose son had been imprisoned by the Inquisition in Seville. He eventually returned with thirty officers and monks in early March 1589.

15.14
Petition of Doña María de la Cueva to Philip II, 19 December 1588

MS
306×212
Rivas, 1983, 82–3
Archivo General de Simancas, Valladolid (GA.242, f.22)

Dr Diego de Santander was one of the five royal physicians in the Armada. He had been with Don Alonso de Leiva, who thought highly of his skills as a doctor and mathematician. It is likely that he drowned in one of Leiva's three shipwrecks, but his death was not known when this petition was presented on 19 December 1588. His wife and daughter, who were in straitened circumstances, begged the king to pay them his salary. A note on the left shows that it was discussed on 21 December and merely set aside 'with others of the same status'. In a similar case, Philip agreed to pay the family of Dr Rubio, who was on the *San Marcos*, from the time of the fleet's departure until the ship was lost.

15.15
Letter from Howard to Burghley, 20 August 1588

MS (autograph)
Laughton, II, 1981, 96–7
342×240
Public Record Office, London (SP12/214, 66)

15.16
The Chatham chest, 1625

Wrought iron
1060×630×590
Oppenheim, 1896, 245–7
National Maritime Museum

This chest has an elaborate lock mechanism operating eight bolts inside the lid. Although such coffers are sometimes called 'Armada chests', the term has no historic significance and they were simply the strong-boxes of the sixteenth and seventeenth centuries. This particular chest was ordered in 1625 to hold the funds of the 'Chest at Chatham', established in 1590 by the treasurer of the navy, Sir John Hawkins, and others, to provide pensions for disabled seamen. The fund was established as a result of the privations suffered by English seamen in the wake of the Armada campaign. All seamen were required to contribute sixpence a month to the fund from their wages. In an attempt to prevent misuse of funds, five officers held the separate keys to the padlocks securing the hasps and the main keyhole concealed in the centre of the lid.

Lord Charles Howard (1536–1624) paints a stark picture of the suffering caused by sickness among the men under his command, both before and after the Armada campaign. Disease had killed 200 of the 500 crew of the *Elizabeth Jonas* at Plymouth, and despite extensive efforts to fumigate the vessel with fires of wet broom, the infection had broken out again with renewed force. Sick men put ashore were simply dying in the streets of Margate, and Howard, moved by pity for their plight, had attempted to find lodgings for them, but could only get the use of farm outbuildings. He asks Burghley for a large supply of hose, doublets, shirts and shoes to clothe his ill-clad men, money to discharge the sick and new mariners to take their places.

16.1 Elizabeth I: the 'Armada' portrait, English school, 16th century

16. After the Armada

'I do warrant you all the world never saw such a force as theirs was.' Howard's comment after the defeat of the Armada conveys the awe that it had inspired, and belies the bragging of the Protestant propaganda which flooded Europe after the event. Philip II's reputation was dented by the defeat, but contemporaries were more impressed by the size and strength of the fleet he had sent against England. His failure did not lead them to belittle his power, rather to regard him with new respect and fear.

English opinion was divided on the best means to follow up the victory. When Elizabeth was certain that the Armada had rounded Scotland, she ordered her fleet to sail at once and intercept the treasure fleets from the New World. Howard and the other commanders were unenthusiastic. The fleet needed urgent repairs, and demobilization of the sick and famished troops was essential. The commanders were more receptive to an attack against Spanish stragglers and survivors, which would require fewer forces; they agreed to this in September 1588. From the start, however, this operation was linked to an attack against Portugal. In part this was because the survivors were expected to return to Lisbon, but Elizabeth also wished to use the Portuguese pretender, Dom Antonio, who had promised financial and commercial aid if she supported his bid for the throne. In addition, she hoped that the plan would appeal to foreign powers, especially to the Dutch and the Moroccan sultan.[1]

According to Burghley, the queen's aims late in 1588 were, first, to destroy Philip's fleet in its ports; second, to take Lisbon; and third, to seize the Azores, whence the English could disrupt New World trade. This programme would shatter the power of the Spanish monarchy, starting with the Northern fleet, continuing with the separation of key areas of the empire (Portugal and the Netherlands), and ending with the elimination of that life-line of bullion from the New World.

Although much was at stake, Elizabeth was unwilling to fund the campaign. Expenditure during 1588 had been two and a half times the average, and she was eager to reduce costs. It was decided that the queen would put up a third of the estimated cost (£20,000), the rest to be raised by public subscription. Drake and Norris combined their financial and military resources and were accepted to lead the expedition. Naturally, the attacks on Lisbon and the Azores were now given greater prominence. English investors were willing to fund privateering ventures that promised immediate or future returns, but they had little interest in destroying the battered survivors of the Armada campaign. Most of the money was raised and more soldiers than needed, but Elizabeth in the end had to contribute twice as much as she intended. Securing foreign aid proved more difficult. The Moroccan support never materialized, and although the Dutch at first agreed to provide troops, transports, powder and other provisions to a maximum value of £10,000, relations between the allies became so poor in the course of 1589 that little was given. Dutch involvement was largely involuntary, as sixty of their ships were taken in England and used to transport troops and victuals. Despite Elizabeth's call for urgent action, the English fleet was not ready to sail until April.

Philip's initial reaction to the defeat of the Armada had been to prepare another fleet. He believed that without another show of force his open enemies would take heart and others might be tempted to join the affray if they thought him seriously weakened. The king ordered the unfortunate survivors, however ill or destitute, to remain where they landed on pain of imprisonment, notwithstanding the lack of facilities in the northern ports. Twelve new galleons were commissioned,[2] and artillery was urgently ordered from Milan: 100 large bronze pieces were already on their way by early December 1588.[3] One of the chief impediments to rearmament was finance. The Castilians had responded with great generosity to the disaster, granting additional taxation, but more was needed. Philip approached the pope, but he refused to pay the promised one million ducats aid for the 1588 attack or to contribute to the new invasion until the Spanish soldiers set foot in England.[4]

From January to April 1589 Philip received accurate reports of the English strategy, but varying assessments of the strength of the fleet. Most accounts put the number of ships at 150–80 and the troops at 18,000 to 20,000, and all spoke of Portuguese conspiracies and the support of North African states.[5] Reluctantly, Philip abandoned hopes of retaliation and accepted the need to concentrate on defence. By March he despaired of his own strength and asked Parma to organize a diversion, an amphibious operation against the Isle of Wight or another suitable target in England to deflect the attack. Parma was ill and unwilling to comply. In May he announced that the army was mutinous, and there were not enough boats to transport the men.[6] As in England in 1588, the Iberian states responded to invasion with a combination of regular garrisons and the ill-trained local militias who provided little resistance to the regular enemy forces. Unlike England, Spain had no powerful navy for defence: the refitted fleet was not ready to sail until July.

1. Wernham, 1984, esp. chapters 1–6 for a most detailed account of English policies after the Armada; also Read, 1960.
2. AGS GA.245, f.11; GA.228 f.134, and pp. 158 and 160.
3. AGS GA.228 f.46.
4. AGS E.952 ff.10–11.
5. AGS E.596 f.18, f.73; GA.246 f.61, f.62.
6. AGS E.596 f.62.

272

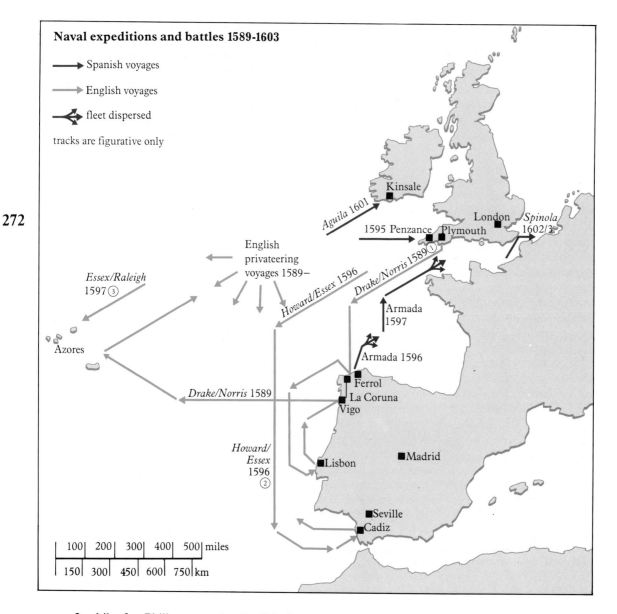

Naval expeditions and battles 1589-1603

→ Spanish voyages

→ English voyages

→← fleet dispersed

tracks are figurative only

Kinsale

Aguila 1601

London

1595 Penzance Plymouth *Spinola 1602/3*

English privateering voyages 1589–

Essex/Raleigh 1597 ③

Howard/Essex 1596 *Drake/Norris 1589* ①

Armada 1597

Armada 1596

Azores

Drake/Norris 1589

Ferrol
La Coruna
Vigo

Howard/Essex 1596 ②

■Madrid

■Lisbon

■Seville
Cadiz

| 100| 200| 300| 400| 500| miles |
| 150| 300| 450| 600| 750| km |

Luckily for Philip, once the English fleet sailed on 18 April 1589, Elizabeth had little authority over it. She was adamant that the destruction of the Armada was the first priority of the expedition, but Drake and Norris would not risk their ships on a difficult crossing to the Biscayan ports where the Armada survivors had taken refuge (San Sebastian, Santander). Instead they attacked La Coruña, sacking and burning its environs.[7] Having failed to take the port, they proceeded to Lisbon where they burnt some ships and took others – sixty German hulks which had to be returned afterwards for fear of reprisals. The Portuguese did not rise against Philip, although the soldiers he maintained fled before the English. Without local or Muslim help, the English

were unable to advance in the peninsula, so they made for the Azores, stopping briefly to sack Vigo. But this time not even Drake managed to find rich prizes, and they missed the New World fleets. 'They went to places more for profit than for service,' was Elizabeth's dour comment. She was right, of course, but then as investors they felt justified in following what promised most profit.

As many as 11,000 men lost their lives in the campaign, and the state of the ships on their return was lamentable.[8] Consequently, her order for the fleet to put again to sea in July 1589 to destroy the Armada survivors and seize the New World bullion was once more contravened. Although none of her aims was achieved, this and other naval operations in

7. Accounts of the campaign, BN Madrid Mss 1750 ff.241–7v; Mss 1761, esp. f.426, ff.427–34, ff.414–414v, 415.

8. Wernham, 1984, 127.

1589 – one under Grenville, another under the Earl of Cumberland, sent to raid the Azores, and the Channel guard – had raised England's reputation and forced Philip to change his strategy.[9]

The score was even by the autumn of 1589 and all seemed set for an escalation of the Anglo-Spanish conflict, yet this did not happen. The unofficial war certainly showed great vigour – there were between 100 and 200 English privateering expeditions against the Spanish Monarchy each year after the Armada.[10] They contrast with the scant success or impact of the official expeditions of Howard and Grenville in 1590, and Borough and Frobisher in 1591. The Spaniards landed by mistake at Mousehole in 1595 and set fire to Penzance, prompting an official retaliation, led by Drake, against the Canary Islands. The war rekindled in 1596 when Philip prepared a large fleet against Ireland, but it was driven back by storms. Elizabeth sent her ships to intercept the fleet and disrupt the preparations; this expedition ended with the spectacular sack of Cadiz by Essex and Howard. The following year Philip retaliated with another large invasion force, once again driven back by violent storms. At the time England was utterly unprepared to meet the crisis: its fleet was away chasing that evergreen mirage of the bullion ships. Storms disposed of all major Armadas sent from Spain until the peace of 1604.

Perhaps if either side had met with greater success, there would have been further large-scale actions. But England and the Spanish monarchy were forced to increase expenditure on defence. This was due to the invasion threats and the intensification of the rebellions in Ireland and the Netherlands, where Philip and Elizabeth played analogous roles. More importantly, both were diverted by the wars in France.

The murder of the Duke and Cardinal of Guise in December 1588 deprived the Catholic League of its leaders and Philip of his allies. It also offered Elizabeth a chance to renew her alliance with the king of France and strengthen the cause of the French Protestants. Philip and Parma suspected that Henri III would turn his forces against the Netherlands if he gained control of his troubled kingdom, particularly if he were in league with England.[11] The assassination of Henri III in July 1589 made war between royalists and leaguers inevitable. Elizabeth supported the Protestant Henri IV while Philip backed the Catholic candidate, Charles, Cardinal of Bourbon. Later he advanced the claims of his own daughter to the French throne. By the autumn of 1589 Philip and Elizabeth were openly committed to the struggle in France, which deflected much of their energies until 1598, when Henri IV and Philip II made peace. Elizabeth's main concern was to prevent Philip from gaining a Channel port, and Philip felt his empire would collapse if a Protestant allied to England secured the French crown. The Anglo-Spanish war continued therefore, but it was no longer primarily a naval conflict. In effect, it was fought mostly in the battlefields of Brittany, Normandy, the Netherlands and Ireland.

In military and political terms the Armada was of limited significance. It did not radically alter the policies of either state or cause serious damage to their interests. Nevertheless, the campaign assumed extraordinary significance in England and the Netherlands. It boosted the morale of both states and heightened the conviction that God favoured their cause. A large number of pamphlets, counters and medals were produced immediately after the event, praising the English and Dutch actions and, above all, God's help. But the bulk of the images and propaganda was produced in the wave of anti-Catholic hysteria that swept through seventeenth-century England.

It was after this that the Armada became an enduring symbol of England's salvation, frequently associated in the popular mind with the Gunpowder Plot. Subsequently, English and other Protestant historians gave great prominence to the event and the Spanish themselves came to reflect upon it, starting from the premise that it was a major defeat. In this, as in many aspects of the Hispanic 'Black Legend', they absorbed rather than challenged the image created by their opponents. The myths surrounding the battle, so often presented as a stark conflict of good and evil, heroes and villains, endure to this day.

M. J. Rodríguez-Salgado

9. Accounts of Cumberland's voyage: Oppenheim, I, 1902, 226ff; Hakluyt, VII, 1904, 1–38.
10. Andrews, 1964.
11. AGS E.596, f.3, for example.

273

16.1

Elizabeth I: the 'Armada' portrait
English school, 16th century

Oil on panel
1130×1280
Strong, 1987, 131–3
William Tyrwhitt-Drake, Esq.

In its complete form – an unusual horizontal format – the 'Armada' portrait exists in two versions, one of which, now at Woburn Abbey, has been attributed to George Gower. The prime version, which seems to have been owned originally by Sir Francis Drake, is exhibited here. Though it is by an as-yet unidentified painter, it is amongst the most powerful of contemporary eulogies to the queen and her posited status. The defeat of the Armada is represented in the top left by a group of English ships looking out towards the distant crescent of the Spanish fleet, approached by fireships, and in the top right by the wrecking of the enemy forces off a rocky coastline. In between these episodes denoting the start and finish of a successful campaign sits its architect, the queen, resting her hand on a globe to signify her new international might. At her shoulder an imperial crown stands not just as a prize to which she claims a moral right (see cat. no. **3.22**) but one now within her possession. After the Armada, Elizabeth was, according to this as well as a wide range of other imagery in several media, the 'great Empresse of the world'.

16.2

Order of the Queen's victory procession to St Paul's, 24 November 1588 (os)
Sir William Segar (d.1633)

MS (2ff.)
290×188
Public Record Office, London (SP12/218, 38)

This list shows the elaborate ordering of Elizabeth's procession along the Strand from Somerset House to St Paul's (see cat. no. **16.3**) and depicts the ceremonial sword borne before her.

16.3

A songe made by her Majestie and songe before her at her cominge from White Hall to Powles throughe Fleete streete in Anno domini 1588: a poem on the Armada victory, said to have been composed by Queen Elizabeth I, 1588

MS
294×198
Waters, 1975, 100–102
National Maritime Museum (SNG/4)

A great thanksgiving ceremony was held in St Paul's Cathedral in November 1588, and this song was probably sung before the queen. Protestants were eager to emphasize divine intervention and the song specifically refers to the nature of the defeat:

> he made the wynds and waters rise
> To scatter all myne enemyes

16.3

This Josephes Lorde and Israells god
the fyry piller and dayes clowde
That saved his saincts from wicked men
And drenshet the honor of the prowde
And hathe preservud in tender love
The spirit of his Turtle dove

16.4
A Joyfull new Ballad declaring the happy obtaining of the great Galeazzo . . ., 1588
Thomas Deloney (?1543–?1607)

Broadsheet
452×348
Maltby, 1971, 82
British Library, London (C.18.e.2(62))

Broadsheets were traditionally used for proclamations, official notices and ballads. Printed in 'English' or 'black-letter' type, the ballads were known as 'black-letter ballads' and extensively used for political and religious purposes. Thomas Deloney, 'the balleting silkweaver of Norwich', wrote ballads notable for their vigorous rhythm and metrical virtuosity. This one celebrates the capture of the *Nuestra Señora del Rosario*, commanded by Don Pedro de Valdés.

16.5
A packe of Spanyshe lyes . . ., 1588

Publ. Christopher Barker, London
Pamphlet
189×265
Mattingly, 1983, 306; Maltby, 1971, 82
British Library, London (292.f.24(1))

Rumour in Europe was rife after the Armada sailed north and the English abandoned pursuit. Mendoza even reported a Spanish victory to Philip. The Privy Council arranged for a reply to this and other inaccurate and false reports: *A packe of Spanyshe lyes* was printed in two columns, the Spanish claims paragraph by paragraph on one side of the page and, over against them, a detailed and scornful refutation, usually several times as long. The pamphlet was translated into every major language in Europe.

16.6
Certain Advertisements out of Ireland . . ., 1588

Publ. I. Vautrollier for Richard Field, London
Printed book
185×135
Maltby, 1971, 81
British Library, London (292.e.9(1))

This book was published in the autumn of 1588, and was the first printed account of the disasters that befell the Spanish ships on the Irish coast. It also formed part of the English propaganda effort aimed at showing that the Armada had ended in catastrophic failure.

16.7
The Copie of a Letter sent out of England to Don Bernadin Mendoza Ambassadour in France for the King . . ., 1588
William Cecil, Lord Burghley (1528–98)

Publ. I. Vautrollier for Richard Field, 1st ed., London
Printed book (44 pp.)
182×140
Maltby, 1971, 77, 79, 80, 148 n.3
National Maritime Museum (E4066)

This 'letter', allegedly by a Catholic missionary called Richard Field (executed for treason in 1588), was in fact a propaganda piece written by Burghley and subsequently translated into a number of other languages. The pamphlet was aimed at countering stories of the Armada's success put out by Mendoza, and was also intended to show that the Armada had been utterly defeated by a united and powerful England, with the Catholic cause there in ruins (see cat. nos. **16.8–16.10**).

16.8
La Copie d'une Lettre . . ., 1588
William Cecil, Lord Burghley (1528–98)

1st ed., London
Printed book
188×125
CSPS, 1587–1603, 484
National Maritime Museum (E2866)

This French translation of Burghley's propaganda piece was available by the middle of November 1588, and many copies were said to have been sent to France.

275

16.9
Essempio d'una Lettera . . ., 1588
William Cecil, Lord Burghley (1528–98)

Publ. Arrigo del Bosco, 1st ed., Leiden
Printed book
155×105
British Library, London (C.55.b.14)

The English printer John Wolfe was granted permission by Walsingham to publish an Italian translation of *The Copie of a Letter . . .* and received a licence on 1 November 1588. This edition, published in the Netherlands, was presumably copied from Wolfe's publication.

16.10
Copije van eenen Brief . . ., 1588
William Cecil, Lord Burghley (1528–98)

Publ. Cornelis Claeszoon, 1st ed., Amsterdam
Printed book
300×200
British Library, London (1197.d.35(2))

This Dutch translation of *The Copie of a Letter . . .* appeared in October 1588.

16.11
Gewisse und warhafftige Zeittung von der Engelendischen und Spanischen Armada, 1588

Printed book, s.1.
200×160
British Library, London (G.6149)

This is one of a number of works in German which were in circulation shortly after the end of the Armada campaign, giving 'certain and true news' of the events. This particular book celebrates the English victory.

16.12
Dutch medal, 1588

Silver
Inscribed (obv.) *FLAVIT* [JEHOVAH] (in Hebrew) *ET.DISSIPATI.SVNT.1588* (He blew and they were scattered);
(rev.) *ALLIDOR.NON.LAEDOR.* (I am assailed not injured)
51 dia.
Hawkins *et al.*, 1885, 145; Milford Haven, 1919, 5
National Maritime Museum (A6)

The failure of the Spanish invasion was regarded by the Dutch to be as much their victory as that of the English. These medals

are some of the many produced in the rebel provinces to celebrate the event. On the obverse, the Spanish fleet is scattered and wrecked, and above in the clouds the name of Jehovah is inscribed in Hebrew. On the reverse a church on a rock is portrayed amid tempestuous waves, symbolizing the threat to the Protestant religion, with a crowned shield below bearing the arms of Prince Maurits. The medal was struck at Middelburg, probably on his orders.

16.13
Dutch medal, 1588

Silver
Inscribed (obv.) *DURUM.EST.CONTRA. STIMVLOS.CALCITARE.* (It is hard to kick against the spikes – Acts 9:5); *O.COECAS.HOMINVM.MENTES.O. PECTORA.COECA.* (Oh, the blind minds, the blind hearts of men); (rev.) *TV.DEVS. MAGNVS.ET.MAGNA.FACIS.TV. SOLVS.DEVS.* (Thou, God, art great and doest wondrous things; thou art God alone – Psalms 86:10); *VENI.VIDE.VIVE. 1588* (come, see, live)
51 dia.
Hawkins *et al.*, 1885, 144–5; Milford Haven, 1919, 4–5
National Maritime Museum (A5)

On the obverse, the pope, kings, bishops and others are shown seated in council, with bandaged eyes, the floor covered with spikes. This satirizes the unsuccessful confederation of the pope, the emperor, Philip II, the Duke of Guise and other princes against Elizabeth. The reverse shows the Spanish fleet driven against rocks and ascribes its destruction to the direct intervention of heaven.

16.14
Dutch counter, 1588

Silver
Inscribed (obv.) *VENIT.IVIT.FVIT.1588* (It came, it went, it was no more); *CLASSIS.HISP.* (The Spanish fleet); (rev.) *SOLI.DEO.GLORIA.* (To God alone the glory)
33 dia.
Hawkins *et al.*, 1885, 146; Milford Haven, 1919, 6
National Maritime Museum (B8)

A counter struck in Middelburg, whose castle symbol is shown on both sides. On the obverse two ships in battle are shown; on the reverse, the crowned shield of Zeeland.

16.15
Dutch counter, 1588

Silver
Inscribed (obv.) *HOMO.PROPONIT.
DEVS. DISPONIT.* (Man proposes, God
disposes) *1588*; (rev.) *HISPANI.FUGIVT.
ET.PEREVT.NEMINE.SEQVETE.* (The
Spaniards flee and perish, no one pursuing)
30 dia.
Hawkins *et al.*, 1885, 147; Milford Haven,
1919, 7
National Maritime Museum (B10)

On the obverse, a man, a woman and two
children kneel in prayer. Above, rays proceed from a cloud. The whole scene
represents general gratitude for divine
deliverance. On the reverse a Spanish ship is
portrayed breaking in two.

277

16.16
Dutch counter, 1589

Silver
Inscribed (obv.) *NON.NOBIS.DOMINE.
NON.NOBIS.1589* (Not unto us, O Lord,
not unto us); (rev.) *SED.NOMINI.TVO.
DA.GLORIAM.* (But unto thy name give
the praise – Psalms 115:1)
33 dia.
Hawkins *et al.*, 1885, 153; Milford Haven,
1919, 10
National Maritime Museum (B11)

On the obverse is shown the shield of Zeeland, crowned. On the reverse is a Spanish
ship pursued by two English ships.

16.17
Dutch counter, 1589

Silver
Inscribed (obv.) *TANDEM.BONA.CAVSA.
TRIVMPHAT.1589* (At length the good
cause triumphs) *ONSE VADER IN DEN
HEMEL UWEN NAEM WERD GEHEY.*;
(rev.) *SI.NON.VIRIBUS.AT.CAVSA.
POTIORES.* (If not in strength, yet in our
cause more powerful); (insc.) *BELV
NECESS* (Necessary war)
29 dia.
Hawkins *et al.*, 1885, 153; Milford Haven,
1919, 10
National Maritime Museum (B12)

On the obverse, Queen Elizabeth is seated in
a triumphal car, holding a palm branch and
an open prayer book, inscribed with the first
line of the Lord's Prayer in Dutch. On the
reverse a tree is shown containing a nest of
fledglings, defending themselves against a
bird of prey.

16.18
The Armada fireback, 1588

Cast iron
Inscribed *1588/IFC*
870×1040×38
Campbell, 1985, 42
*The Board of Trustees of the Victoria & Albert
Museum, London (M.77–1957)*

This item was probably made in Sussex, and
has been called the Armada fireback because
of its date, even though one of similar design
bearing the initials 'IFC' and dated 1582 is in
existence. A number of domestic artefacts
were produced in celebration of the 1588
campaign.

16.19
Advice of the Council of War to
Philip II, regarding further attacks
against England, 17 December 1588

MS
Inscribed with monograms of five members
of the Council of War; marginal notes by
Philip II
304×214
*Archivo General de Simancas, Valladolid
(GA.235, f.213)*

The Council of War approved recent proposals to prepare a fleet for another invasion
of England. Defensive war was the only
alternative, and they believed this to be both
more expensive and politically dangerous, as
Philip's enemies would be encouraged to
attack him. The councillors trusted that the

Spanish realms would respond generously to the crisis if Philip acted firmly and promptly. They reminded the king that he had to seek more artillery and victuals urgently, and to speed up the construction of new galleons. They also advised him to seize all suitable ships to join the remnants of the Armada. Philip replied (in the margin of the document), thanking the councillors and assuring them that he was eager to organize the force, and the matter was already in hand. He urged them to expedite all business relating to the fleet, and if they needed to recruit foreign soldiers and sailors, to do so immediately.

278

Als achtzig nun die faarzal war,
Don Erften tag Augufti zwar,
Henricus Valoifus fkat
Brugert fchwur Paris die Stat,
Ein Predger Mönch Jacob Clemment
Gehn Pont Sanct Clou Kompt, und furwmi,

Wie er heimliche fachen hätt
An Konigliche Maierftet.
Der Procurator Generael
Left in zum König in den Saal
An ftat des letzten brieffs Clemment
Ein Meffer aufs dem Ermel brengt,

Vndt fticht dem König in fin bauch,
Vnder den Naabel, beim fchlauch.
Als nun der König hefftig rieff,
Trabanten vnd viel volcks zulieff,
Clemment balt thodt gestochen wardt,
Doch danck er got auff feiner fardt.

Das er ein fo genedig endt
Bekommen het fo gar befkendt
Sein Ieder Corper wardt durch Schloff
Gefchleifft gespant an vier Roff,
Zerfprengt in vier ftuck zuhandt,
Vndt endtlich gar zu puluer brandt.

Si ubi Gallorum Fama est incognita Regis,
Eumtum vita confule, doctus eris.

16.20
Sketch survey of La Coruña and Rias de Batanzos, Ares and Ferrol, 1589

MS
280×385
Woodcocke, 1589; Corbett, II, 1898, 330–42; Martin, 1975, 38; Usherwood, 1978, 87–93
British Library, London (MS Cott. Aug. I, ii, f.12)

La Coruña, called here *citie of the Groyne*, was a major port and had served as a storm refuge for the Armada in June 1588. In 1589 the Drake–Norris expedition set out with thirty ships and 15,000 troops to destroy such ships as had returned to Spain and Portugal from September 1588 onwards. This map, prepared for the expedition, shows that landing was envisaged on the sandy Ensenada del Orzán, flanking the groyne that sheltered the Armada's anchorage. The famous Roman lighthouse of La Coruña is shown.

16.21
The assassination of Henri III in 1589

Engraving
Inscribed *Si ubi Gallorum Fama est incognita Regis/Eumtum vitae consule, doctus eris.*
215×255
Trustees of the British Museum, London (48-9-11-5hh)

Although Henri III never renounced Catholicism, his murder of the Guise brothers and determination to be succeeded by the Huguenot leader, Henri of Navarre, led to his repudiation by extreme Catholics as an ungodly tyrant. This print shows the monk Jacques Clément receiving the blessing of the Church for the assassination with a knife thrust into the king's stomach. There are also vignettes from Clément's execution, when he was drawn and quartered. The murder unleashed new wars between Catholics and Protestants, royalists and extremists in France and led to the immediate involvement of Philip and Elizabeth.

16.22
The Duke of Parma on his deathbed, 1592

Netherlandish school, 16th century

Oil on canvas
280×390
Oudenaarde, 1983, 90–91
Stedelijk Museum, Oudenaarde (S36)

Parma wears the insignia of the Golden Fleece, and a monk's habit – the latter common funeral wear amongst Catholic aristocracy. He suffered some loss of favour after the Armada disaster, but Philip did not blame him directly and he kept his post. He led the king's forces in the wars in France after 1589, but disobeyed orders to invade in 1591. The king recalled him, but he died before his replacement arrived.

16.23
The last fight of the *Revenge*, August 1591
Designed by Hendrick C. Vroom

Wool and silk tapestry
Inscribed *ANNO 1598*
3187×3350
Clowes *et al.*, 1897, 494–7; Hakluyt, VII, 1904, 38–53; Ysselsteyn, 1936, 246; National Maritime Museum, 1937, 16
N. C. Worms, Esq.

In 1591 Lord Thomas Howard and seven vessels lay in wait off the Azores for the Spanish treasure fleet. Instead, they encountered an overwhelming force of Indian Guard galleons. Howard ordered anchors to be weighed and sailed before the wind out of the Spaniards' reach. Only Sir Richard Grenville, vice-admiral and commander of the *Revenge*, ignored the order and fought vigorously against the Spaniards. After inflicting heavy losses, the *Revenge* surrendered. The battle, in which Grenville was fatally wounded, became one of the most celebrated legends of English naval history. The tapestry shows the *Revenge* with her foremast shot away, surrounded by four Spanish ships. To her starboard are two flagships, probably the *San Felipe* and to the left the *San Paulo*, flying the flag of Bazán, the Spanish commander. The rest of the Spanish fleet is seen approaching from the left, while the English ships are retreating on the right. The island of Pico appears on the horizon. The composition is consistent with that of the Armada and Middelburg tapestries designed by Hendrick Vroom. The weaver may have been de Maecht in Middelburg, or Spierincx in Brussels, for whom Vroom worked.

16.24
The attack on Cadiz, 31 June 1596, 1615
Attributed to Jan Theodor de Bry (1561–1623)

Engraving
275×350
Corbett, 1902; Usherwood, 1983
National Maritime Museum (70 H 1596a)

The great Anglo-Dutch expedition against Cadiz was commanded by Lord Howard and the Earl of Essex. The town was captured and looted with comparative ease, but Medina Sidonia ordered the Spanish fleet, bound for the Indies and trapped by the attackers, to be burnt with all its treasure. The print shows the English fleet breaking through the line of ships that the Spanish were using to defend the inner harbour.

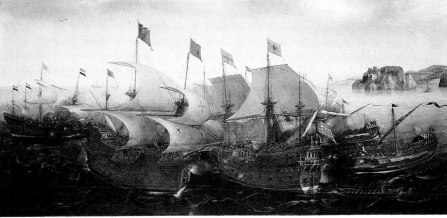

16.25
A sea action, possibly the Battle of Cadiz, 1596
Hendrick C. Vroom (1566–1640)

Oil on canvas
Inscribed *H VROOM* (not contemporary)
1020×2150
Clowes *et al.*, 1897, 508–16; Russell, 1983, 154, App. V.
Lent privately

The picture and its companion (which portrays ships in a sea storm) have been traditionally identified as depicting the action and aftermath of the Armada, but this cannot be certainly substantiated. It seems more likely that the subject of cat. no. **16.25** is the battle of Cadiz, a clash between Spanish ships and a combined Anglo-Dutch fleet of 150 vessels (commanded by Howard) in 1596. The latter had been sent to Cadiz to undertake a pre-emptive strike against a Spanish fleet which, it was feared, was preparing once again to invade England. On 20 June they arrived off Cadiz and the next day entered the harbour, overwhelming the Spanish ships and capturing the city. The painting seems to show an imaginary encounter on the open sea near Port San Felipe (right) involving the flagships of the three fleets. In the left foreground appears to be the Spanish *San Felipe*, and behind her the Dutch four-master *Neptunus*. The English vessel flying the flag of St George seems intended for Effingham's flagship the *Merhonor*. Spanish galleys lie to the right.

280

16.26
Queen Elizabeth, 1596
Attributed to Crispin de Passe
(*c*.1565–1637)

Publ. John Wootneel
Engraving
Inscribed with title in Latin, and four Latin elegiac couplets in two columns; below is the imprint *In honorem serenissimae suae Maiestatis hanc effigiem fieri curabat Ioannes Wootnelius belga Anno 1596*
353×259
Hind, I, 1952, 285; O'Donoghue, II, 1910, 153
National Maritime Museum

The queen stands between two columns upon which are two forms of a phoenix device and in the background is a representation of England. Wootneel, bookseller and printseller from the Netherlands, worked in England from 1592–*c*.1614, and was probably de Passe's agent in London (there is no record of

the latter visiting England). On this basis, as well as for stylistic reasons, Hind attributes this unsigned plate to de Passe.

16.27
The Heneage Jewel, *c*.1600

Enamelled gold, set with diamonds and rubies
Inside a miniature portrait of Elizabeth I by Nicholas Hilliard (1547–1619)
Inscribed (obv.) *Elizabetha D.G. Ang. Fra. et Hib. Regina*; (rev.) *Saevas tranquilla per undas* (Peaceful on violent waves); miniature: *Ano 1580*
71×52×11
V & A, 1980, 60
The Board of Trustees of the Victoria & Albert Museum, London (M81-1935)

This locket, traditionally known as the Armada Jewel, was said to have been given by Elizabeth on the defeat of the Armada to Sir Thomas Heneage (1556–95), Vice-Chamberlain of the Royal Household and Privy Counsellor. But the jewel is evidently of a slightly later date and the inscription *Ano 1580* is not contemporary. The open strapwork frame of the jewel is of gold, enamelled in colour and set with diamonds and rubies. On the obverse is a gold relief profile bust of Elizabeth. The reverse of the locket opens to reveal a painted miniature by Nicholas Hilliard of the queen in a costume from the very end of the reign. The enamelled back cover depicts on the exterior the Ark, symbol of the Church, riding a stormy sea. This Ark device had previously appeared on medals commemorating the defeat of the Armada. Enamelled on the inside of the back cover is a red Tudor rose with a Latin verse.

16.28
'Minerva' medal, 1602

Gold
Inscribed (obv.) *CADET.A.LATERE.TVO. Mᵉ.ET.X.Mᵃ. A.DEXTRIS.TVIS.ELIZ. REGINA.a.w.* (A thousand shall fall beside thee and ten thousand at thy right hand, O Elizabeth, Queen – Psalms 91:7); (rev.) *CASTIS. DIADEMA.PERENNE.* (For the chaste, an eternal crown); *MINERVA 1602*
40.5 dia.
Hawkins *et al.*, 1885, 181–2
National Maritime Museum (L5)

On the obverse is a half-length figure of Elizabeth I. On the reverse she is depicted as Minerva, the goddess of wisdom, trampling underfoot a dragon and a snail, representing her enemies. Her right hand points to a heavenly crown, her future reward.

16.29

***The proceeding at Queene Elizabeth's
funerall, from Whitehall to the
Cathedral church at Westminster on
Thursday the xxviijth of Aprill. 1603***
Augustine Vincent (*c.*1581–1626)

Ink and colour on paper
216×130
Godfrey *et al.*, 1963, 233–5; Campbell and
Steer, 1988, 376–87
*College of Arms, London (Vincent Collection,
MS 151)*

Elizabeth I died in 1603. This manuscript
forms pages 522–35 of Vincent's *Precedents* (a
monumental compilation, now bound in two
volumes, concerning the ordering of public
ceremonies) giving the order and composition
of the queen's funeral cortège, with illustrations of the standards, banners, horses
covered with black cloth, the coat of the
royal arms and other items borne in the procession. There is also a picture of the queen's
hearse (the canopy over her coffin during the
funeral) and an engraving of her tomb.
Vincent was a scholar and antiquary who
became Rose Rouge Pursuivant of the College of Arms in 1616 and ended his career as
Windsor Herald, attaining this post in 1624.

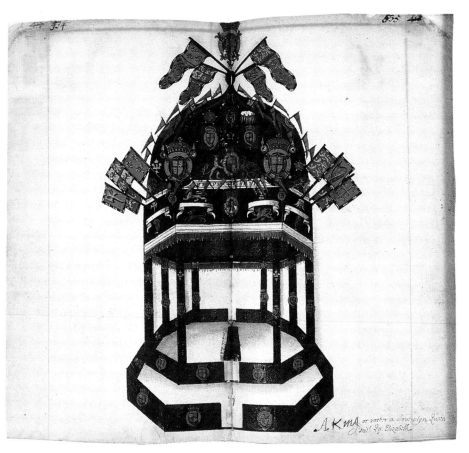

281

16.30
**An allegory of the defeat of the
Spanish Armada as St George and
the Dragon,** *c.*1610
Robert Stephenson

Oil on panel
1525×2045
Lent privately

The famous crescent-like formation of the
Armada is shown as a dragon, over which
England (represented by the troops on the
coast in the bottom right) triumphs under
the flag of St George. Burning ships –
perhaps meant for the English fireships – lie
in the centre of the dragon's arc, and Spanish
ships are wrecked off Scotland and Ireland to
the top right and left. The inscription's
reference to 'Great Britain' and the lack of
any representation of Queen Elizabeth
together suggest that this naïvely painted and
important allegorical picture dates from the
reign of James I rather than the period of the
event itself. It is conceivable that Robert
Stephenson was a parishioner of the Lincoln-
shire church from which the painting
originates.

16.31
The defeat of the Armada:
Elizabeth I at Tilbury
English school, 17th century

Oil on panel
2185×1585
Parish Church of St Faith, Gaywood

One of a pair of paintings from St Faith's; the second portrays the discovery of the Gunpowder Plot. They were bequeathed to the church by Thomas Hares (1572–1634), rector of the parish for thirty-six years, who may have commissioned them. The theme of both is the sovereign's gratitude to God for delivering the nation from Catholic assault: at the top of the Armada panel Elizabeth is shown at prayer, declaring: *Blessed be the great God of my salvation.* This picture also proclaims and praises Elizabeth's own role, through her special relationship with God, in the successful defence of her country and its religion. She is depicted on her famous visit to Tilbury (whose fort lies to the upper left), while in the background Spanish ships burn fiercely, as if directed from above by the queen as God's agent. Below, a lengthy paraphrase of Elizabeth's speech to her troops is flanked by two cherubs, that on the right bearing an olive branch to denote peace maintained. The names of the principal protagonists (including *Papa* and *Draco*) are inscribed on the frame. Both pictures were heavily restored in 1905, and there is evidence of more recent overpainting in some areas, but they stand as important examples of early-seventeenth-century anti-Catholic propaganda.

16.32
Embroidered cushion-cover depicting the Armada and the Gunpowder Plot, *c.*1630–50

Tent-stitch in silk thread on linen canvas
520×650
National Museums and Galleries on Merseyside, Lady Lever Art Gallery (LL.5292)

The illustration of historical or political events was extremely rare in English seventeenth-century embroidery. This piece was based on an engraving designed by the Ipswich Puritan preacher Samuel Ward (1577–1640) and printed at Amsterdam in 1621. The Spanish ambassador in London protested that the print was an insult to his royal master, and Ward was temporarily imprisoned.

16.32

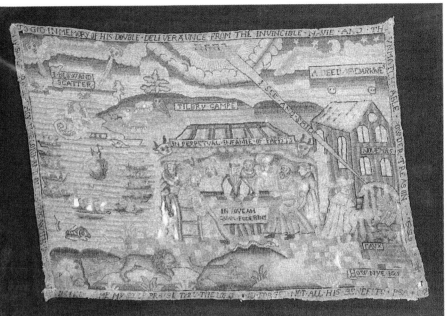

283

16.33
Dutch rummer glass commemorating the Armada, 1626

Glass
Inscribed with designs after Hogenburg
235 ht; 104 dia.
Stedelijk Museum De Lakenhal, Leiden (3356)

The psychological impact of the defeat of the Armada in England and the United Provinces outweighed its military significance. This drinking glass links the Battle of Gravelines with another famous Protestant victory, the relief of Leiden in 1574. The Dutch war against Spain was renewed in 1621 and ended in 1648.

16.34
Playing cards, *c.*1675–1700

Engravings
88×53 each
National Maritime Museum

These cards are selected from a set printed long after the Armada, and demonstrate the persistently strong anti-Catholic feelings in seventeenth-century England. The first card shows torture instruments, a contemporary myth embodied in the Tower of London's so-called 'Spanish Armoury'. Others represent priests as knaves, inviting comparison with the 'Popish Plot' playing cards of the same era.

Severall strange Weapons taken from the Spaniard which were provid'd to destroy y'English

More then halfe y Spanish Fleet Taken and Sunck

Queene Eliz: Riding in Triumph through London in a Chariot drawn by two Horses and all y Companies attending her w'th their Baners

16.35
The Somerset House Conference, 1604

Juan Pantoja de la Cruz (1551–1608)

Oil on canvas
Inscribed with names of participants and *Juan Pantoxa de la X*
2045×2700
Strong, I, 1969a, 351–3
National Maritime Museum (BHC2787)

The peace negotiations between England and Spain, initiated by James I and Philip III, took place at Somerset House on the Strand from May to August 1604. This painting is one of two versions (the other at the National Portrait Gallery) which commemorate the signing of the treaty on 28 August. The commissioners are shown seated in strict order of precedence, with the most important placed next to the window. On the right, the English delegation: Thomas Sackville, Earl of Dorset; Charles Howard, Earl of Nottingham; Charles Blount, Earl of Devonshire; Henry Howard, Earl of Northampton; Robert Cecil, Earl of Salisbury. On the left is the Spanish and Flemish delegation: Juan de Velasco, Duke of Frias, Constable of Castile; Juan de Tassis, Count of Villa Mediana; Alessandro Robido, Senator of Milan; Charles de Ligne, Count of Aremberg; Jean Richardot, president of the Privy Council; Louis Vereyken, principal secretary. Considerable pains were taken to prepare the house for the conference, and this painting shows the richness of furnishings. Fine tapestries have been hung on the walls, the long table is covered with a splendid, small-pattern 'Holbein' rug from Anatolia, possibly one of Henry VIII's collection of over 400. Each of the delegates is seated in a sumptuously decorated 'X'-frame chair of state which denotes his exalted status. Despite the grandeur of the furniture, rushes are strewn on the floor. Both versions are apparently signed by Juan Pantoja de la Cruz, that at the National Portrait Gallery being dated 1594. Strong suggests that the inscriptions in both cases are early additions, and that the paintings may be the work of another artist, possibly Flemish.

16.36
Ratification by Philip III of the 1604 peace treaty, 15 June 1605

Illuminated bound volume with wax seal,
seal tag and silken seal bag (4 pp.)
350×230
Public Record Office, London (E30/1705)

This was the formal ratification of the peace
treaty between England and Spain, finally
negotiated in London in 1604 (see cat. no.
16.35). It is illustrated with a miniature
portrait of Philip III and may have been the
work of a Flemish artist. A similar ratification was sent from England to Spain.

The treaty brought to an end nearly
twenty years of war. Negotiations centred
around the issues of trade, religious toleration for Catholics in England and English
support to the Dutch rebels. England
secured the freedom to trade with Spanish
possessions in Europe, and Spain secured a
ban on English privateering exploits against
Spanish interests, although aside from
terminating the state of war the terms of the
treaty had little practical or long-term effect
on the issues they addressed.

Bibliography

Unless otherwise specified, the place of publication of works in English is London.

Abell, W., 1948. *The Shipwright's Trade*, Cambridge.

Adams, S., 1984. 'Eliza Enthroned? The Court and its politics', in Haigh, 1984.

Ainaud de Lasarte, J., 1952. *Ceramica y Vidrio. Ars Hispanie X*, Madrid.

Albèri, E. (ed.), 1851. *Relazioni degli Ambasciatori Veneti al Senato*, Ser. I, Vol. 5, Florence.

Alvarez de Teran, M. C., 1980. *Archivo General de Simancas. Catálogo XXIX. Mapas, Planas y Dibujos*, I, Valladolid.

Anderson, R. C., 1960. 'The Mary Gonson', *MM* 46, 199–204.

Anderson, R. C., 1957. 'A List of the Royal Navy in 1590–1591', *MM* 48, 322–3.

Anderson, R. C., 1974. *List of English Men-of-War, 1509–1649*, Greenwich.

Andrews, K. R., 1964. *Elizabethan Privateering*, Cambridge.

Andrews, K. R., 1982. 'The Elizabethan Seaman', *MM* 68, 245–62.

Andrews, K. R., 1984. *Trade, Plunder and Settlement. Maritime Enterprise and the Genesis of the British Empire 1480–1630*, Cambridge.

Armand, A., 1883. *Les Medailleurs Italiens des XV et XVI Siècles*, Paris.

Arnold, J.B. and Weddle, R. S., 1978. *Nautical Archaeology of Padre Island. Spanish Shipwrecks of 1554*, New York.

Artiñano y Galcadano, G. de, 1920. *La Arquitectura Naval Española en Madera*, Madrid.

Auerbach, E., 1961. *Nicholas Hilliard*.

Auerbach, G. and Adams, C. K., 1972. *Paintings and Sculpture at Hatfield House*.

Baldwin, R. C. D., 1980. 'The international interchange of navigational information between the maritime communities of Iberia, Asia and North Western Europe, 1500–1620', M. Litt. thesis, University of Durham.

Bankston, J. (trans. and ed.), 1986. *Nautical Instruction*, by Diego García de Palacio (1587), Bisbee, Arizona.

Barkham, M., 1985. 'Sixteenth-century Spanish Basque ships and shipbuilding: the multipurpose nao', in Cederlund, 1985, 113–35.

Baynes, K. and Pugh, F., 1981. *The Art of the Engineer*, Guildford.

Beeching, J., 1982. *The Galleys at Lepanto*.

Blair, C., 1958. *European Armour, c.1066–c.1700*.

Blair, C. (ed.), 1983. *Pollard's History of Firearms*, Feltham.

Bol, J. L., 1973. *Die Hollandische Marinemalerei des 17. Jahrhunderts*, Brunswick.

Boon, K. G., I and II, 1978. *Netherlandish Drawings of the Fifteenth and Sixteenth Centuries in the Rijksmuseum*, 2 Vols, The Hague.

Borg, A., 1976. 'The Spanish Armoury in the Tower', *Archaeologia*, CV, 1976, 332–52.

Borrett, S. E., 1984. 'The Drake Colours', *Military Modelling*, April, 288.

Boynton, L., 1971. *The Elizabethan Militia, 1558–1638*, Newton Abbot.

Braat, J., 1984. 'Dutch activities in the North and Arctic during the sixteenth and seventeenth centuries', *Arctic*, 37.4.

Bradford, E., 1961. *The Great Siege*.

Braudel, F., I and II, 1972. *The Mediterranean and the Mediterranean World in the Age of Philip II*, 2 Vols.

Brindley, H. H., 1938. *Catalogue of the Seal Room, National Maritime Museum*, Greenwich.

British Library, 1977. *Sir Francis Drake. An Exhibition to Commemorate Francis Drake's Voyage around the World 1577–80*.

British Museum, I, 1844. *Catalogue of the Manuscript Maps, Charts and Plans and of the Topographical Drawings in the British Museum*, Vol. I.

British Museum, I, 1870. *Catalogue of the Prints and Drawings in the British Museum. Division I. Personal and Political Satires*, Vol. I – 1320–1689.

British Museum, 1979. *Medallic Illustrations of the History of Britain and Ireland*, Lawrence, Mass.

Bromley, J. S., and Kossmann, E. H. (eds), 1975. *Britain and the Netherlands*, V, The Hague.

Buchanan, G. (ed. W. A. Gatherer), 1958. *The Tyrannous Reign of Mary Stuart*.

Busby, E., 1948. Letter to *Country Life*, XIII, 476.

Buttin, C., 1914. 'L'armoure et le chanfrein de Philippe II', *La Revue de L'Art Ancien et Moderne*, 183–98.

Calvo Pérez, J. L. and González, L. G., 1983, *Banderas de Espana*, Madrid.

Campbell, M., 1985. *Decorative Ironwork*.

Campbell, L., and Steer, F., 1988. *Catalogue of the Manuscripts in the College of Arms*, I.

Cano, T., 1964. *Arte para fabricar y aparejar naos (1611)*, Instituto de Estudios Canarios, La Laguna, Tenerife.

Castan, C. and Cayon, J. R., 1978. *Las Monedas Españolas desde Don Pelayo a Juan Carlos I, años 718 a 1979*, Madrid.

Caw, J. L., 1904. 'The portraits of the Cecils', in *Historical Monographs, William Cecil, Lord Burghley*.

Caw, J. L., 1936. *Catalogue of Pictures at Pollok House*, Glasgow.

Cederlund, C. O. (ed.), 1985. *Postmedieval Boat and Ship Archaeology*, B.A.R. International Series 256, Oxford.

Chaunu, P. and H., I–XI, 1955–9. *Seville et l'Atlantique, 1504–1650*, 11 Vols, Paris.

Chudoba, B., 1952. *Spain and the Empire, 1519–1643*, Chicago.

Clarke, J., 1981. 'The Buildings and Patronage of Robert Dudley, Earl of Leicester', MA thesis, Courtauld Institute of Art.

Clowes, W. S. L. *et. al.* (eds.), 1897. *The Royal Navy. A History. I.*

Codoin, 1–112, 1842–96. *Colección de Documentos Ineditos para la Historia de España*, Madrid.

Coligny, 1974. *Actes du Colloque l'Admiral Coligny et son Temps*, Paris.

Colliard, L., 1963. 'Tableaux representant des bals a la cour des Valois', *Gazette des Beaux-Arts*, 147–56.

Colvin, H. M., Summerson, J., Hale, J. R. and Merriman, M., 1982. *The History of the King's Works. Vol. IV 1485–1660 (Part II)*.

Conselho da Europa, 1983. *Os Descobrimentos Portugueses e a Europa do Renascimento. Tomo: 'O Homen e A Homa São Um Só'*, Lisbon.

Constant, J.-M., 1984. *Les Guises*, Paris.

Corbett, J., I and II, 1898. *Drake and the Tudor Navy*, 2 Vols.

Corbett, J. (ed.), 1902. 'Relation of the voyage to Cadiz, 1596', *Naval Miscellany I*, NRS 20, 25–92.

Cortesão, A. and Texeira de Mota, A. (eds), I–V 1960. *Portugalia Monumenta Cartographica*, Lisbon.

Crédit Communal, 1985. *Trésors de l'Armada*, Brussels.

Cruikshank, C. G., 1966. *Elizabeth's Army*, Cambridge.

Cust, L., 1912. 'The painter HE ('Hans Eworth')', *Walpole Society*, 2, 1–44.

Danvila, A., 1954. *Felipe II y el Rey Don Sebastian de Portugal*, Madrid.

Danvila, A., 1956. *Felipe II y la sucesión de Portugal*, Madrid.

Davis, R., 1972. *The Rise of the English Shipping Industry in the Seventeenth and Eighteenth Centuries*, Newton Abbot.

Dell, R. F. (ed.), 1966. *Rye Shipping Records 1566–1590*, Sussex Record Society, Lewes.

Destombes, M., 1968. 'Les plus anciens sondages portés sur les cartes nautiques aux XVIe et XVIIe siècles', *Bulletin de l'Institut Océanographique*, Numero Spécial 2, Monaco.

Destombes, M., 1987. 'Une astrolabe nautique de Seville, 1563', in Schilder *et al.*, 1987, 289–324.

Díaz-Plaja, S., 1958. *La Historia de España en sus Documentos. El Siglo XVI*, Madrid.

Dimier, L., 1904. *French Painting in the XVI Century*.

Dolley, M., 1967. 'The historical background to the 1580 map of Smerwick', *MM* 53, 74–5.

Dominguez Ortíz, A. and Vincent, B., 1978. *Historia de los Moriscos*, Madrid.

Douglas, K. S. and Lamb, H. H., 1979. *Weather Observations and a Tentative Meteorological Analysis of the Period May to July 1588*, Climatic Research Unit Report 6A, University of East Anglia, Norwich.

Douglas, K. S., Lamb, H. H. and Loader, C., 1978. *A Meteorological Study of July to October 1588: the Spanish Armada Storms*, Climatic Research Unit Report 6, University of East Anglia, Norwich.

Dufty, A. R. and Reid, W., 1968. *European Armour in the Tower of London*.

Dunlop, I., 1962. *Palaces and Progresses of Elizabeth I*.

Dunlop, R., 1905. '16th century maps of Ireland', *English Historical Review*, XX.

Duro, C. Fernández, I–VI, 1876–91. *Disquisiciones Nauticas*, 6 Vols, Madrid.

Duro, C. Fernández, I and II, 1884–5. *La Armada Invencible*, 2 Vols, Madrid.

Duro, C. Fernández, 1886. *La Conquista de los Azores (1583)*, Madrid.

Dutuit, E. 1885. *Manuel de l'Amateur des Estampes*, Vol. III, Paris and London.

Dyer, F. E., 1925. 'Burghley's notes on the Spanish Armada', *MM* 11, 419–24.

Eliott-Drake, Lady E. F., 1911. *The Family and Heirs of Sir Francis Drake*, Vol. I.

Elliott, J. H., 1967. *Imperial Spain 1469–1716*.

Escalante de Mendoza, J., 1575. *Itinerario de navegación de los mares y tierras occidentales*, in Duro, V, 1890, 413–515.

Evans, R. J. W., 1973. *Rudolf II and his World*, Oxford.

Falls, C., 1950. *Elizabeth's Irish Wars*.

Fernández Alvarez, M., 1951. *Tres Embajadores de Felipe II en Inglaterra*, Madrid.

Fernández Duro, see Duro, C. Fernández.

Flanagan, L. N. W., 1987. 'Steelyards and steelyard weights', *IJNA*, 16.

Fonseca, B. da 1978. *Dom Sebastião antes e depois de Alcácer-Quibir*, 2 Vols, Lisbon.

Forrer, L., I–VIII, 1904–30. *Biographical Dictionary of Medallists, etc.*, 8 Vols.

Frothingham, A. W., 1936. *Catalogue of Hispano-Mooresque Pottery in the Collection of the Hispanic Society of America*, New York.

Fuente, V. de la, 1868. *Obras escogidas del Padre Pedro de Rivadaneira*, Madrid.

Fyers, E. W. H., 1925. 'The story of the machine vessels', *MM* 11, 50–90.

Gachard, L. (ed.), 1884. *Lettres de Philippe II à ses filles Isabelle et Catherine, écrites pendant son voyage en Portugal (1581–1583)*, Paris.

Glasgow, T., 1964. 'The shape of ships that defeated the Spanish Armada', *MM* 50, 177–87.

Glasgow, T., 1966. 'English ships pictured on the Smerwick Map, 1580. Background, authentication and evaluation', *MM* 52, 157–62.

Gómez-Centurion, Jiminéz, C., 1986. 'Las relaciones Hispano-Hanseaticas durante el reinado de Felipe II', *Revista de Historia Naval*, 15, 65–83.

Godfrey, W. H., *et al.*, 1963. *The College of Arms*, Survey of London Committee, 16.

Goggin, J. M., 1960. *The Spanish Olive Jar, an Introductory Study*, Yale University Publication on Anthropology, 62.

Gosse, P., 1930. *Sir John Hawkins*.

Gracia Rivas, M., 1983. 'El personal sanitario que participó en la Jornada de Inglaterra. Nuevas aportaciones', *Revista de Historia Naval*, I, no. 2, 63–90.

Groot, I. de and Vorstman, R. 1980. *Maritime Prints by the Dutch Masters*.

Grosz, A. and Thomas, B., 1936. *Katalog der Waffensammlung in der Neuen Burg Kunsthistorisches Museum*, Vienna.

Guillén, J. F. (ed.), 1944a. *Diálogos Militares (1583)*, by Diego García de Palacio, Ediciones Cultura Hispánica VI, Madrid.

Guillén, J. F. (ed.), 1944b. *Instrución Náuthica (1587)*, by Diego García de Palacio, Ediciones Cultura Hispánica VIII, Madrid.

Guilmartin, J. F., 1974. *Gunpowder and Galleys: Changing Technology and Mediterranean Warfare at Sea in the Sixteenth Century*, Cambridge.

Gunther, R. T., 1932. *The Astrolabes of the World*, Vol. II, Oxford.

HMC, II and III, 1888–9. *Calendar of the Salisbury Manuscripts*.

Haigh, C. (ed.), 1984. *The Reign of Elizabeth I*.

Hakluyt, R., I–XII, 1903–1905. *The Prinicipal Navigations, Voyages, Traffiques and Discoveries of the English Nation*, 12 Vols, Glasgow.

Hale, J. R., 1983. *Renaissance War Studies*.

Halls, Z., 1970. *Men's Costume, 1580–1750*.

Halpin, A., 1986. Note in *Proceedings of the Royal Irish Academy* 86, 5.

Hardy, E., 1966. *Survivors of the Armada*.

Haring, C. H., 1964. *Trade and Navigation between Spain and the Indies in the Time of the Hapsburgs*, Gloucester, Mass.

Hawkins, E., Franks, A. W. and Grueber, H. A. (eds), 1885. *Medallic Illustrations of the History of Great Britain and Ireland to the Death of George III*, Vol. I, London.

Hawkins, M. W. S., 1888. *Plymouth Armada Heroes*, Plymouth.

Hawkins, R., 1622. *Observations, Etc.*

Hayward, J., 1959. 'English firearms of the 16th century', *Journal of the Arms and Armour Society*, III, 117–41.

Herrera Oria, E. (ed.), 1929. *La Armada Invencible. Documentos procedentes de Archivo General de Simancas (1587–1589)*, Archivo Histórico Español II, Valladolid.

Herrera Oria, E. (ed.), 1930. *Colección de Documentos Inéditos para la Historia de España y de sus Indias*, Tomo II, Academia de Estudíos Histórico Sociales de Valladolid, Madrid.

Herrera Oria, E., 1946. *Felipe II y el Marques de Santa Cruz en la Empresa de Inglaterra*, Madrid.

Hess, A. C., 1968. 'The Moriscos, an Ottoman Fifth Column in sixteenth century Spain', *American Historical Review*, 74, 1–25.

Hess, A. C., 1978. *The Forgotten Frontier: A History of the Sixteenth Century Ibero-African Frontier*, Chicago.

Hickson, M., 1892. 'Lord Grey of Wilton at Smerwick in 1580', *The Antiquary*, XXV, 259–65.

Hind, A. M., I, 1952. *Engraving in England in the Sixteenth and Seventeenth Centuries. Part I. The Tudor Period*, Cambridge.

Hind, A. M., II, 1955. Ibid., *Part II. The Reign of James I*, Cambridge.

Hitchins, H. L. and May, W. E., 1952. *From Lodestone to Gyro Compass*.

Hobson, R. L., 1903. *Catalogue of English Pottery in the British Museum*.

Hollstein, F. W. H., 1980. (Comp. G. S. Keyes, ed. K. G. Boon) *Hollstein's Dutch and Flemish Etchings, Engravings and Woodcuts ca.1450–1700*, Vol. XXIII, Amsterdam.

Howard, F., 1979. *Sailing Ships of War 1400–1860*.

Howse, H. D. (ed.), 1980. *Sir Francis Drake's Nautical Almanac, 1546*, Nottingham.

IJNA, 1987. 'Proceedings of the 1986 "Guns at Sea" symposium', *IJNA*, 16.

Ilchester, Earl of, 1921. 'Queen Elizabeth's visit to Blackfriars, June 16, 1600', *Walpole Society*, IX, 1–19.

Jacques, D., 1822. *A Visit to Goodwood*.

Jensen, D. L., 1964. *Diplomacy and Dogmatism. Bernadino de Mendoza and the French Catholic League*, Cambridge, Mass.

Jones, F., 1878. *The Life of Sir Martin Frobisher*.

Jones, F. M., 1954–6. 'The plan of the Golden Fort at Smerwick, 1580', *Irish Sword*, II, 41–2.

Keevil, J. J., 1957. *Medicine and the Navy. I. 1200–1649*.

Kemp, P. (ed.), 1979. *The Oxford Companion to Ships and the Sea*, Oxford.

Kennard, A. N., 1986. *Gunfounding and Gunfounders*.

Kenyon, W. A., 1975. *Tokens of Possession: the Northern Voyages of Martin Frobisher*, Toronto.

Keyes, G. S., 1980. See Hollstein, 1980

Kublen, G. and Soria, M., 1959. *Art and Architecture in Spain and Portugal, and their American Dominions 1500–1800*.

Labayru y Goioechea, E. J., de 1900. *Historia General del Señorío de Bizcaya*, IV, Bilbao.

Lagomarsino, P. D., 1973. 'Court Factions and the Formulation of Spanish Policy toward the Netherlands, 1559–1567', Ph.D. thesis, University of Cambridge.

Laughton, J. K. (ed.), I and II, 1981. *State Papers relating to the Defeat of the Spanish Armada*, 2 Vols, NRS 1 and 2 (reprint of 1895 edn).

Lebel, G., 1948. 'British-French artistic relations in the 16th century', *Gazette des Beaux-Arts*, XXXII, 278ff.

Lecky, R. J., 1874. *Monthly Notices of the Royal Astronomical Society of London*, 34, 120.

Lewis, M., 1961. *Armada Guns*.

Lewis, M., 1966. *The Spanish Armada*.

Lewis, M., 1969. *The Hawkins Dynasty: Three Generations of a Tudor Family*.

Lloyd, C. C., 1968. *The British Seaman*.

Loades, D. M., 1979. *The Reign of Mary Tudor*.

Loades, D. M., 1986. *The Tudor Court*.

Loon, G. van, I–V, 1732–5. *Histoire Medallique des XVII Provinces des Pays-Bas*, The Hague.

Louveiro, F. S., 1978. *D. Sebastião antes e depois de Alcácer-Quibir*, Lisbon.

Love, R. W. (ed.), 1980. *Changing Interpretations and New Sources in Naval History*, Annapolis.

MacCaffrey, W. T., 1981. *Queen Elizabeth and the Making of Policy 1572–1588*, Princeton.

McFee, W., 1928. *Sir Martin Frobisher*.

McGurk, J. J. N., 1970. 'Armada preparations in Kent and arrangements made after the defeat (1587–1589)', *Archaeologia Cantiana*, LXXXV, 71–93.

Mackie, J. D., 1978. *History of Scotland*.

Maltby, W. S., 1971. *The Black Legend in England*, Durham, NC.

Maltby, W. S., 1983. *Alba: A Biography of Fernándo Alvarez de Toledo, third Duke of Alba 1507–1582*.

Mander, C. van, 1604. *Het Schilder-Boeck*, Haarlem.

Manwaring, G. E. and Perrin, W. G. (eds), 1921. *The Life and Works of Sir Henry Mainwaring*, NRS, 56.

Martin, C. J. M., 1972. '*El Gran Grifón*, An Armada wreck on Fair Isle', *IJNA*, 1, 59–71.

Martin, C. J. M., 1975. *Full Fathom Five*.

Martin, C. J. M., 1977. 'Spánish Armada tonnages', *MM* 63, 365–7.

Martin, C. J. M., 1979a. '*La Trinidad Valencera*: an Armada invasion transport lost off Donegal', *IJNA*, 8, 13–38.

Martin, C. J. M., 1979b. 'Spanish Armada pottery', *IJNA*, 8, 271–302.

Martin, C. J. M. and Parker, G., 1988. *The Spanish Armada*.

Martínez-Hidalgo, J. M., 1971. *Lepanto. Exposicion Conmemorativa del IV Centenario de la Batalla*, Barcelona. Martínez Sierra, G., *c.* 1921. *Juan Pantoja de la Cruz*, Madrid, s.d.

Martínez-Sierra, G., *c.*1921. *Juan Pantoja de la Cruz*, Madrid, s.d.

Mattingly, G., 1983. *The Defeat of the Spanish Armada*.

Maura Gamazo, G., 1957. *El Designio de Felipe II y el Episodio de la Armada Invencible*, Madrid.

Mayhew, G. J., 1984. 'Rye and the defence of the Narrow Seas: a 16th century town at war', *Sussex Archaeological Collections*, 122, 107–126.

Middeldorf, U., 1975. 'On some portrait busts attributed to Leone Leoni', *Burlington Magazine*, February, 84.

Migeon, G., 1904. *Catalogue des Bronzes et Cuivres au Musée du Louvre*, Paris.

Milford Haven, Admiral the Marquess of, 1919. *British Naval Medals*.

Milford Haven, Admiral the Marquess of, 1921. *Naval Medals of . . . France, the Netherlands, Spain and Portugal*, I.

Millar, O. (ed.), 1960. 'Abraham Van der Doort's catalogue of the collections of Charles I', *Walpole Society*, XXXVIII, 1–228.

Millar, O., I and II, 1963. *The Tudor, Stuart and Early Georgian Pictures in the Collection of H.M. the Queen*, 2 Vols.

Mollat, du Jourdin, M., *et al.*, 1984. *Sea Charts of the Early Explorers*, New York.

Motley, J. L., I–III, 1884. *The Rise of the Dutch Republic*, 3 Vols.

Muñoz, A., 1887. *Sumaria y verdadera relación del buen viaje que el Principe Don Felipe hizo en Inglaterra*, Sociedad de Bibliófilos Españoles 15, Madrid.

Murdoch, J., *et al.*, 1981. *The English Miniature*, Newhaven and London.

Musée Carnavalet, 1979. 'Paris au XVIe Siècle et sous le Règne d'Henri IV: Salles permanentes du Musee Carnavalet', *Bulletin du Musée Carnavalet*, I–II.

Musée de L'Art Wallon, 1966. *Lambert Lombard et Son Temps*, Liège.

Museo Arqueológico Nacional, 1980. *Catálogo de los Armas de Fuego*, Madrid.

Museum of London, 1985. *The Quiet Conquest. The Huguenots, 1685 to 1985*.

National Maritime Museum, 1937. *Catalogue*.

Neale, J. E., 1930. 'Elizabeth and the Netherlands', *English Historical Review* 45, 373–96.

Nichols, J., 1823, I–III. *The Progresses and Public Processions of Queen Elizabeth*, 3 Vols.

Norman, A. V. B., 1980. *The Rapier and Small Sword, 1460–1820*.

Norman, A. V. B., and Wilson, G., 1982. *Treasures of the Tower of London*, University of East Anglia, Norwich.

Oastler, C. L., 1975. *John Day, Elizabethan Printer*, Oxford Bibliographical Society, Bodleian Library, Oxford.

O'Donnell y Duque de Estrada, H., 1986a. 'El contingente de Infantería Española para la Empresa de Inglaterra de 1588', *Revista de Historia Naval*, IV, no. 13, 37–50.

O'Donnell y Duque de Estrada, H., 1986b. 'La Infantería Italiana para la Empresa de Inglaterra', *Revista de Historia Naval*, IV, no. 15, 5–18.

O'Donoghue, F. M., 1894. *Portraits of Elizabeth*.

O'Donoghue, F. M., I–VI, 1908–25. *Catalogue of Engraved British Portraits preserved in the Department of Prints and Drawings in the British Museum*.

Olds, D. L., 1976. *Texas Legacy from the Gulf*, Texas Memorial Museum, Miscellaneous Paper no. 5.

Oliva, J. de Y. and López-Chaves Sánchez, L. 1965. *Catálogo de los Reales de Ocho Españoles*. Madrid.

O'Neil, B. H. St J., 1940. 'The fortification of Weybourne Hope, 1588', *Norfolk Archaeology*, XXVII, Part 2, 250–62.

O'Neil, B. H. St J., 1960. *Castles and Cannon. A Study of Artillery Fortification in England*.

Oppenheim, M. M., 1896. *A History of the Administration of the Royal Navy, 1509–1660*.

Oppenheim, M. M. (ed.), I and II, 1902. *The Naval Tracts of Sir William Monson*, NRS 22 and 23.

Oppenheim, M. M., 1908. 'Maritime History' in Page, 1908.

Osten Sacken, C. von der, 1984. *El Escorial, Estudio Iconológico*, Bilbao.

Ottley, W. Y., 1831. *Notices of Engravers*.

Oudenaarde, 1983. *Stedelijk Museum Oudenaarde, Deel 1 Schilderijen*, Oudenaarde.

Page, W. (ed.), 1908. *Victoria County History of Dorset*, II.

Parker, G., 1972. *The Army of Flanders and the Spanish Road 1567–1659*, Cambridge.

Parker, G., 1976. 'If the Armada had landed', *History*, LXI, 358–68.

Parker, G., 1977. *The Dutch Revolt*.

Parry, J. H., 1966. *The Spanish Seaborne Empire*.

Patrimonio Nacional, 1986. *V Centenario del Monasterio de El Escorial. Las Casas Reales*, Madrid.

Perrin, W. G. (ed.), 1918. *The Autobiography of Phineas Pett*, NRS 51.

Pierson, P., 1975. *Philip II of Spain*.

Pine, J., 1739. *The Tapestry Hangings of the House of Lords: representing the several Engagements between the English and Spanish Fleets in the ever memorable Year 1588*.

Plon, E., 1887. *Leone Leoni et Pompeo Leoni*, Paris.

Pollard, A. F., 1964. *An English Garner. Tudor Tracts 1532–1588*, New York.

Pollitt, R., 1974. 'Bureaucracy and the Armada: the administrator's battle', *MM*, 60, 119–32.

Pollitt, R., 1980. 'Rationality and expedience in the growth of Elizabethan naval administration', in Love, 1980, 68–79.

Poole, R., L. I–IV, 1912. *Catalogue of Oxford Portraits*, 4 Vols.

Powell, P. W., 1971. *The Tree of Hate*, New York.

Prado, 1985. *Catálogo de las Pinturas*, Museo del Prado, Madrid.

Public Record Office, 1967. *Maps and Plans in the Public Record Office. Vol. I. British Isles, c. 1410–1860*.

Quinn, D. B. (ed.), 1955. *The Roanoke Voyages 1584–1590*, Hakluyt Society, Second Series, 104 and 105, London.

Quinn, D. B., 1974. *England and the Discovery of America*.

Quinn, D. B., 1985. *Set Fair for Roanoke*, Chapel Hill, NC.

Quinn, D. B. and Ryan, A. N., 1983. *England's Sea Empire, 1550–1642*.

Rackham, B., 1939. 'Early Tudor Pottery', *Transactions of the English Ceramic Circle*, 2, no. 6, 15–25.

Ranke, L. von, 1908. *The History of the Popes* (ed. G. R. Dennis), III.

Read, C., 1925. *Mr Secretary Walsingham and the Policy of Queen Elizabeth*, III.

Read, C., 1960. *Lord Burghley and Queen Elizabeth*.

Read, H. and Tonnochy, A. B, 1928. *Catalogue of the Silver Plate, Mediaeval and Later, Bequeathed to the British Museum by Sir Augustus Wollaston Franks*.

Redlich, F., 1964. *The German Military Enterpriser and His Work Force. A Study in European Economic and Social History*, 2 Vols, Wiesbaden.

Reitzenstein, A. von, 1954. 'Die Landsuter Plattner Wolfgang und Franz Groschedel', *Münchner Jahrbuch der bildenden Kunst*, Third Series, V.

Rijksmuseum, 1976. *All the Paintings of the Rijksmuseum in Amsterdam*, Amsterdam.

Rijksmuseum, 1984. *Willem van Oranje. Om vrijheid van geweten*, Amsterdam.

Robinson, A. H. W., 1962. *Marine Cartography in Britain: A History of the Sea Chart to 1855*, Leicester.

Rodríguez-Salgado, M. J., 1988. *The Changing Face of Empire: Charles V, Philip II and Habsburg Authority, 1551–9*, Cambridge.

Rodríguez-Salgado, M. J. and Adams, S., 1985. 'The Count of Feria's dispatch to Philip II of 14 November 1558', *Camden Miscellany*, XXVIII, Fourth Series, 29, 302–44.

Rowse, A. L., 1947. *Tudor Cornwall. Portrait of a Community*.

Royal Academy, 1983. *The Genius of Venice*.

Royal Armouries, 1976. *The Armouries of the Tower of London. I. Ordnance*.

Russell, C., 1971. *The Crisis of Parliaments. English History 1509–1660*.

Russell, M., 1983. *Visions of the Sea. Hendrick C. Vroom and the Origins of Dutch Marine Painting*, Leiden.

SNPG, 1975. *Painting in Scotland 1570–1640*, Edinburgh.

SNPG, 1987. *The Queen's Image* (H. Smailes and D. Thomson, eds), Edinburgh.

Salisbury, W., 1966. 'The ships', *MM*, 52, 163–5.

Scammell, G. V., 1970. 'Manning the English merchant service in the sixteenth century', *MM*, 56, 131–45.

Scammell, G. V., 1982. 'European seamanship in the great age of discovery', *MM*, 68, 357–76.

Scharf, G., 1890. *A Descriptive and Historical Catalogue of the Pictures at Woburn Abbey*, Privately printed.

Schilder, G., *et al.* (eds) 1987. M. Destombes. *Contributions selectionées a l'Histoire de la Cartographie et des Instruments Scientifiques*, Paris.

Schott, H., 1986. *A Catalogue of Keyboard Instruments in the Victoria and Albert Museum*.

Seaby, W. A., 1966. 'A pair of pre-Plantation spurs', *Ulster Journal of Archaeology*, 29, 112, pl. XVIIa.

Shaaber, M. A., 1929. *Some Forerunners of the Newspaper in England, 1476–1622*, Philadelphia and London.

Skelton, R. A., 1957. 'Two English maps of the sixteenth century', *British Museum Quarterly*, XXI.

Skelton, R. A. and Summerson, J., 1971. *A Description of the Maps and Architectural Drawings in the Collection made by William Cecil, First Baron Burghley, now at Hatfield House*, Roxburghe Club.

Starkey, D. (ed.), 1987. *The English Court from the Wars of the Roses to the Civil War*.

Stedelijk Museum, 1984. *Prins Willem van Oranje*, Stedelijk Museum het Prinsenhof Delft, Delft.

Stefansson, V., 1938. *The Three Voyages of Martin Frobisher*, 2 Vols.

Sténuit, R., 1974. *Treasures of the Armada*.

Stimson, A., 1983. 'The Mariner's Astrolabe. A survey of 48 surviving examples', *IV Reuniao Internacional de Historia da Nautica e da Hidrografia*, Sagres/Lagos, 1983, n.p.

Stone, G. C., 1961. *A Glossary of the Construction, Decoration and Use of Arms and Armor*, New York.

Stone, L., 1964. *The Crisis of the Aristocracy, 1558–1640*, Oxford.

Strada, R. P. Famianus, 1635. *De Bello Belgicae . . . 1550–1590*, 2 Vols, Antwerp.

Strong, R., 1963a. *Portraits of Queen Elizabeth I*, Oxford.

Strong, R., 1963b. 'Elizabethan Painting: an approach through inscriptions – III. Marcus Gheeraerts the Younger', *Burlington Magazine*, CV, April, 149–58.

Strong, R., I and II, 1969a. *Catalogue of Tudor and Jacobean Portraits in the National Portrait Gallery*, 2 Vols.

Strong, R., 1969b. *The English Icon*, London and New York.

Strong, R., 1977. *The Cult of Elizabeth: Elizabethan Portraiture and Pageantry*.

Strong, R., 1983. *Artists of the Tudor Court*.

Strong, R., 1987. *Gloriana: The Portraits of Queen Elizabeth I*.

Suárez Fernández, L., 1966. *Política Internacional de Isabel la Católica*, Valladolid.

Suárez Fernández, L. and Fernández Alvarez, Fernández M., 1969. *Historia de España. La España de los Reyes Católicos*, Vol. II, Madrid.

Sutherland, N. M., 1973. *The Massacre of St Bartholemew and the European Conflict, 1559–1572*.

Tait, H., 1968. *Masterpieces of Glass*. British Museum.

Tait, H., 1979. *The Golden Age of Venetian Glass*.

Taylor, E. G. R. (ed.), 1959. *The Troublesome Voyage of Captain Edward Fenton 1582–3*, Hakluyt Society, Second Series, 113, Cambridge.

Taylor, E. G. R. (ed.), 1963. *A Regiment for the Sea and other Writings on Navigation*, Hakluyt Society, Second Series, 121, Cambridge.

Taylor, E. G. R., 1970. *The Mathematical Practitioners of Tudor and Stuart England, 1485–1714*, Cambridge.

Taylor, E. G. R., 1971. *The Haven-Finding Art*.

Taylor, R., 1967. 'Architecture and magic. Considerations on the idea of the Escorial', in *Essays on the History of Architecture presented to Rudolph Wittkower*, I.

Tenison, E. M., I–XIV, 1933–61. *Elizabethan England*, 14 Vols and portfolio, Leamington Spa.

Thompson, I. A. A., 1969. 'The appointment of the Duke of Medina Sidonia to the command of the Spanish Armada', *The Historical Journal*, XII, 197–216.

Thompson, I. A. A., 1975. 'Spanish Armada guns', *MM*, 61, 355–71.

Thompson, I. A. A., 1976. *War and Government in Habsburg Spain 1560–1620*.

Thornton, P. K., 1968. *Musical Instruments as Works of Art*.

Tonnochy, A. B., 1952. *Catalogue of Seal-Dies in the British Museum*.

Tower of London, 1960. *Exhibition of Spanish Royal Armour in H.M. Tower of London*.

Twemlow, J. A. (ed.), 1935, 244–5. *Liverpool Town Books*, II, Liverpool.

Ubaldini, P., 1590. *A Discourse concerninge the Spanishe fleete invadinge England in the yeere 1588*.

Ulloa, M., 1977. *La Hacienda Real de Castilla en el Reinado de Felipe II*, Madrid.

Usherwood, S., 1978. *The Great Enterprise*.

Usherwood, S. and J., 1983. *The Counter-Armada, 1596. The Journall of the Mary Rose*.

V & A, 1966. *Victoria and Albert Museum, Department of Prints and Drawings and Department of Paintings: Accessions*, Vol. II, Edgar Seligman Gift.

V & A, 1980. *Princely Magnificence. Court Jewels of the Renaissance 1500–1630*, Victoria and Albert Museum.

Valencia de Don Juan, El Conde de, 1898. *Catálogo Histórico-Descriptivo de la Real Armería*.

Veer, G. de, 1876. *The Three Voyages of William Barents to the Arctic Regions*, Hakluyt Society, First Series, 54.

Wagenhaer, 1984. *Lucas Jansz. Wagenhaer van Enckhuisen*, Enkhuizen.

Washington, 1985. *The Treasure Houses of Britain: Five Hundred Years of Private Patronage and Art Collecting*, National Gallery of Art, Washington.

Waterhouse, E., 1978. *Painting in Britain, 1530 to 1790*.

Waters, D. W., 1958. *The Art of Navigation in England in Elizabethan and Early Stuart Times.*

Waters, D. W. (ed.), 1970. *An Inventory of the Navigation and Astronomy Collections in the National Maritime Museum, Greenwich*, I Greenwich.

Waters, D. W., 1975. *The Elizabethan Navy and the Armada of Spain*, NMM, Maritime Monograph no. 17, Greenwich.

Watt, J., 1983. 'Surgeons of the Mary Rose: the practice of surgery in Tudor England', *MM*, 69, 3–18.

Webb, H. J., 1965. *Elizabethan Military Science. The Books and the Practice*, Madison, Milwaukee and London.

Wernham, R. B., 1966. *Before the Armada: the Growth of English Foreign Policy 1485–1588.*

Wernham, R. B., 1984. *After the Armada. Elizabethan England and the Struggle for Western Europe, 1588–1595*, Oxford.

Wernham, R. B., 1988. *The Expedition of Sir John Norris and Sir Francis Drake to Spain and Portugal, 1589*, NRS.

Williamson, J. A., 1927. *Sir John Hawkins: the Time and the Man*, Oxford.

Williamson, J. A., 1969. *Hawkins of Plymouth.*

Wilson, C., 1970. *Queen Elizabeth and the Revolt of the Netherlands*, Berkeley.

Wilson, G. M., 1984. 'Notes of some early Basket-Hilted Swords', *Journal of the Arms and Armour Society*, XII.

Wilson, T., 1986. *Flags at Sea.*

Woltjer, J. J., 1975. 'Dutch privileges, real and imaginary', in Bromley and Kossmann, 1975.

Wood, A. A., 1813. *Athenae Oxonienses*, I.

Woodcocke, T., 1589. *Ephemeris expeditionis Norreysii & Draki in Lusitaniam.*

Woodroffe, T., 1958. *The Enterprise of England.*

Wright, L. B. and Fowler, G. W., 1968. *English Colonization of North America.*

Wright, P., 1987. 'A change in direction. The ramifications of a female household, 1558–1603', in Starkey, 1987.

Wyon, A. B. and A., 1887. *Great Seals of England from the Earliest Period to the Present Time.*

Yahya, D., 1981. *Morocco in the Sixteenth Century: Problems and Patterns in African Foreign Policy*, Harlow.

Yates, F. A., 1977. *Astraea. The Imperial Theme in the Sixteenth Century.*

Yates Thompson, H., 1919. *Lord Howard of Effingham and the Spanish Armada*, Roxburghe Club.

Ysselsteyn, G. T. van, 1936. *Geschiedenis der Tapijtweverijen in de Noordelijke Nederlanden*, I.

Zarco Cuevas, J. (ed.), 1917. *Documentos para la historia del monasterio de San Lorenzo el Real de El Escorial*, Madrid.

290

Index

294